THE GUARDIAN'S BRIDE

Highland Secrets, Book 3

Susan King

ARE YOU SIGNED UP FOR DRAGONBLADE'S BLOG?

You'll get the latest news and information on exclusive giveaways, exclusive excerpts, coming releases, sales, free books, cover reveals and more.

Check out our complete list of authors, too!

No spam, no junk. That's a promise!

Sign Up Here

www.dragonbladepublishing.com

Dearest Reader;

Thank you for your support of a small press. At Dragonblade Publishing, we strive to bring you the highest quality Historical Romance from some of the best authors in the business. Without your support, there is no 'us', so we sincerely hope you adore these stories and find some new favorite authors along the way.

Happy Reading!

CEO, Dragonblade Publishing

Additional Dragonblade books by Author Susan King

Highland Secrets Series
The Scottish Bride (Book 1)
The Forest Bride (Book 2)
The Guardian's Bride (Book 3)

Celtic Hearts Series
The Hawk Laird (Book 1)
The Falcon Laird (Book 2)
The Swan Laird (Book 3)

Three lasses, three ladies, three brides all
Born and flowering in Kincraig's hall
One shall loose an arrow in the heart of greenside
One shall heal a king and woe betide
And one shall be the harper's bride . . .

—Prophecy of the Keiths of Kincraig

PROLOGUE

Scotland, Lanarkshire
Spring, 1297

WITH A GLANCE toward Kincraig Castle, all gray stone against a blue sky, stark and massive on its promontory, Lady Rowena Keith turned and ran into the forest, certain no one would miss her for a little while. Her father was meeting with a council of knights and barons that included her great-grandfather and her older brother; and her sisters were with their tutor, a local priest. Rowena hurried to see her own tutor, Dame Una Keith, her aunt, whose cottage was just inside of the forest on Kincraig land. For several years, Rowena had studied herbal medicine with her, and now, just past her seventeenth birthday, she was Una's apprentice.

Yet her dream of dedicating herself to healing work might be short-lived. Her father was about to fix her betrothal to a fine young knight, although he was Sir Robert Keith's second choice for his oldest daughter. She scarcely remembered the betrothal that had been canceled when she was quite small. Once married, she would leave Kincraig and life would change unforeseeably.

But she loved the healing arts and meant to devote herself to them no matter where life took her. For now, she would learn all she could while she had the chance.

Along the way, she gathered plants useful in healing, plucking up ferns, berries, leaves, and stems, fallen nuts, and more.

Stooping to pick clusters of violets, green ferns, and wild garlic that grew beside a small rushing burn, she added those too, eager to learn anything Una could teach her about healing properties and ways to prepare plants by drying, simmering, crushing, making salves and potions and more. Violets could help lung ailments; ferns were useful for treating burns, coughs, and painful joints. And garlic, like nettle and yarrow, was excellent for wounds and ailments.

Glimpsing the cottage in a grove of trees, she paused to gather a few pretty stones from the clear water of the burn, adding those to her basket. Una had begun to teach her about charm stones in healing too, how to cleanse them in sun, smoke, and running water, how various crystals could help illness, how chants could enhance that power.

"Rowena!"

She turned to see Una at the door. A handsome woman, strong and fierce, raven-haired like Rowena, with white strands mixed in now, Una Keith was reclusive, unmarried, and content with the healing work. Her cottage was filled with fragrant herbs and plants, crammed with pots, bottles, and books. Rowena waved.

"We have a guest!" Una called.

An elderly man stepped out then. Surprised, delighted to see her great-grandfather—she had thought he was in the morning meeting at Kincraig—Rowena ran. Sir Thomas Learmont, called Thomas the Rhymer, waved. Tall, thin, shoulders bent, long beard silvery, he leaned on a walking stick and came toward her while Una ducked back into the house.

"Grandda!" She took his arm to help him sit on a broad fallen log at the edge of Una's grove. "I thought you were with Papa and his guests."

"I left early, wanting to see my niece Una today. They will still be arguing the fate of Scotland when I return."

Elderly yet lively, Thomas had come to Kincraig to visit his Keith kinfolk and to meet with Sir Robert and others to discuss the heated conflict between Scotland and England. King Edward was determined to bring Scotland under his rule by hammering his way through the land; concern was growing among the Scottish nobility.

The troubles had not yet touched the peaceful glen that cradled Kincraig Castle. Today, the sun was bright, the spring breeze fresh and cool, and Rowena was glad to have some time with her remarkable great-grandfather, a musician and soothsayer faery-blessed with prophecy, so they said.

"Now, lass," he said, "Una says thou art a fine student who learns quickly and will soon be a healing woman to rival her." He had an archaic way of speaking, perhaps his age or even his years spent in the faery realm. Though he spoke little of those years, he claimed it was true.

"I love the healing work, though I may never have Una's knowledge," she said.

"Thou art a healer, even when marriage and family come to thee someday. Sir Robert is arranging betrothals for thee and thy sisters as well."

She nodded. "Papa waited until I was old enough to marry this time."

"Ah, it comes back to me now. The first time, that lad's guardian did not agree with the match. But be of good cheer. Thou will find thy match, and then find it again, a bride and herb-wife too."

She frowned, confused. Though the Rhymer's prophecies were sought and treasured, and even King Edward wanted his future foretold, sometimes Thomas spoke in ways she did not quite understand.

"Find my match, and find it again? What do you mean, sir?"

"All will come clear someday. Tell me about healing. What is most essential?"

She tilted her head, considering, for he did not need a recitation of plants and their uses. "One needs knowledge and skill, the ability to identify plants and such, and know how to use them.

That is only part of it," she said. "A healer also needs compassion, patience, and kindness. Even a smile can encourage healing, Una says."

His blue eyes twinkled. "True. Now, what is stronger than any remedy?"

She hesitated. "I am learning about plants and stones, and I know there is much I do not know. I am not sure what is strongest among those remedies."

"Not among the elements. This," he said, lifting a long finger up to the heavens. "Time is a great healer. But naught is stronger than Death when that time comes."

"I see." She felt the truth of it sink into her being.

"A healer uses wisdom, knowledge, skill, and kindness. There is magic in healing too, for we cannot always understand how it comes about."

"Una says there is magic in stones and chants too."

"Sometimes." He smiled. "The work is challenging and humbling. But thou art suited to it and will do well. I say it so."

"Thank you, sir." She felt humbled to have his company and would treasure the small prophecy he had just granted her.

He watched the swaying treetops, his eyes a keen, sparkling blue despite age. "I am thinking it is time," he said.

"Time, sir?"

"I am old, near a hundred! I have gifts for thee and thy siblings before I go."

"Grandda," she protested, not sure if he meant his current visit—or death.

"This is for thee." He held out a hand. Something sparkled between his fingers. "Una has been its keeper, but we agree it is time to pass it along." He opened his fingers to reveal a glimmering crystal.

"How beautiful!" She stared. The clear crystalline stone was smaller than a plum, round and smooth, caged in a setting of silver bands. It winked and sparkled as if it had an inner light.

"The Queen of Elfland gave this to me."

"This one, truly? Aunt Una sometimes dips this stone in water and says chants over it. She has never told me much about it, though."

"It was not time yet. Here." He placed it in her cupped hands. "Long ago, a beautiful lady with golden hair and eyes like stars owned this. She had a laugh like bells and a wicked cruelty to her, but a gentle gift for healing. She charmed this stone herself, which makes it something special."

Light played inside the bright, clear stone. "I want to know more about charm stones."

"The ancients called them *krystallos*, others *querertz*. Quartz, we say, or crystals. There are various colors, but this one has a rare clear purity. Thee will learn more. Listen now." He laid a hand over hers as she held the crystal. A sense of something magical, mystical, filled her. The stone seemed to grow warm in their hands. "This crystal can help the gravest injuries and illnesses. Use it sparingly, and always remember Death may win."

"Aye." The stone glinted between their layered hands, old and young.

"Thou art its guardian now. One day, this wee stone could save Scotland. Keep it secret. Keep it safe. Use it wisely."

Though she did not quite understand, she knew this was a great responsibility. "I will keep care of it always. I promise."

"Good." He released her hands. "Wrap it in silk. Now walk with me back to the castle. I am hungry. I wonder if the cook would make some fresh hot bannocks even though it is past breakfast."

She put a hand under his bony elbow to help him stand. "I am sure she will. Thank you for this, Grandda." The stone gleamed in her hand. "Guardian of the stone. I like that. It is an honor."

"It is. There is another, but that one has a different purpose."

"Another stone or another guardian?"

"As thee guards this, another will guard thee. The man with the crown knows."

"The king?" He loved a riddle, especially if he was the only one who understood it. But he only smiled as they walked.

He did not answer. "Will there be rowanberry jam? I like jam on bannocks."

"I think we have some, Grandda."

Guardian stone. She loved the stone and the privilege the Rhymer had granted her. The crystal was warm and vibrant in her hand as she dropped it in her linen bag.

CHAPTER ONE

Scone, Scotland
March, 1306

S TANDING IN THE cold rain and a bitter March wind, Sir Aedan MacDuff, knight, interim clan chief, Guardian of the Realm of Scotland, and laird of Castle Black in Fife, watched a solemn ceremony on the hill at Scone Abbey. He rolled his shoulders to ease stiffness, having ridden hard through the night to escort his niece here in time for this. Pride erased fatigue as he witnessed Lady Isabella MacDuff of Buchan—his late brother's daughter and wife of an English sympathizer—step forward to crown a Scottish king.

His heart filled with affection and admiration. Only nineteen, Isabella had shown courage and determination in stealing her husband's horses to ride hellbent for Scone with her uncle. Despite hours over rough roads, she never complained, aware of her duty as a MacDuff and as the absent earl's sister: she carried the ancient blood-right of crowning Scottish kings. Sharing that blood, Aedan felt a fierce duty as a protective uncle and a warrior ready to defend his king.

Isabella, a delicate blonde, lifted the crown of hammered gold high; the circlet with three plain trefoils symbolized trinity, sovereignty, and heaven's guidance. She set it on the head of Robert Bruce, Earl of Carrick, a silent declaration that he was true King of Scots. Her simple action made it so.

Encircled by lords, knights, earls, and bishops, Robert Bruce sat on a plain stone bench rather than the revered Stone of Destiny upon which Scottish kings had been crowned for generations; the English king had confiscated the ancient stone along with the Scottish regalia and chests of documents, all carted down to London in a show of tyranny.

In one hand, Bruce gripped a sword topped with a gleaming stone. Aedan had brought the old blade that day to replace another stolen by English soldiers. Behind the new king, the rescued banner of Scotland, red lion and lilies on yellow cloth, flapped in a brisk wind.

The bishop set a slim golden circlet on the head of Lady Elizabeth de Burgh, Robert's young wife and now queen consort. She leaned toward her husband.

"Sir, we are like a king and queen of the May," she murmured.

Close enough to hear, Aedan understood her wry remark. Robert Bruce was now King of Scots—not Scotland, not the land, but of the people. Gradually word would spread to the Scots that finally they had a warrior-king to fight for them against King Edward, who continued to ravage the land, pushing for surrender.

Scotland was in the soup, Aedan thought, with loyalties divided among Scotsmen, but Aedan knew his heart. He respected the bold courage and recklessness of their new leader, even though days ago, Bruce had slain his rival claimant to the throne, Sir John Comyn, in a church. That impulsive action had thrown the gauntlet full in the face of King Edward.

Beside Aedan, Sir Brian Lauder, his foster brother and close longtime friend, spoke low. "Well done for Scotland. But there may be terrible consequences. I only hope we are prepared to meet them."

"We will do what we must," Aedan murmured. He knew this day would ignite King Edward's wrath.

"Whatever Bruce needs," Brian replied. "Although you carry

much on your shoulders already, with your nephew the earl, and your uncle both hostage in England. Fife is depending on you now."

"*Ach,* I am a big lad. I can carry more." As the ceremony concluded, Aedan cheered with the rest as the bishop presented the new king and queen.

But he felt dread mingle with triumph. He had sacrificed much, setting aside his needs for the sake of Fife and Scotland, and he did not regret taking on those responsibilities. Had King Edward never set a greedy eye on Scotland, Aedan might still be just a laird, knight, and husband, guarding only his family and his estate. His wife might yet be alive, his wee son a brother to siblings by now.

He had set aside dreams, storing grief and wishes on a shelf in his heart, and put a lock on that heart. He summoned smiles he did not always feel, and made himself move on. He was a guardian in many ways now, and a lonely man. So be it.

"With luck," Brian said, "this day will turn the tide for Scotland."

"With luck." Aedan felt as if they all hurtled forward on the tails of one man's courage. May that passion fire the spirit they needed, he thought.

Later, as others greeted the new monarch and he stood by, he saw Lady Isabella coming toward him. "Uncle!" She kissed his cheek. "Thank you."

"Anything for you, love," he said lightly, and meant it deeply.

AFTER SUPPER, WHILE guests found beds in tents or on pallets on the ground, Aedan stood by a blazing fire, pensive, hoping Isabella would agree to return to Castle Black with him for safety. He doubted her Comyn husband, with his English ties, would welcome her now.

Hearing his name, he turned. "Sire!" He bowed his head as Robert Bruce approached.

Strong, muscular, large-boned, Bruce had the intense gaze

and truculent look of a man who would never give up. With a plaid cloak tossed over his shoulders against the chill, he wore no crown on his thick dark hair. A warrior and leader to his bones, he was not pretentious about it.

"Aedan! Thank you for bringing Isabella. I could not be a true king without her hand on the crown. The Scots need to know this was done properly by tradition."

"My niece was determined to be here. I could not let her risk her neck riding in the dark and the rain." Aedan gave a wry smile.

"I am indebted to you for it, and for bringing the sword as well."

"It was at Castle Black, part of our clan legacy. They say it once belonged to King Macbeth of ancient days, if not to kings before him. I thought you should have it."

Bruce nodded. "I am glad to have the old sword and the new crown too. The bishop is anxious that the new regalia be stored elsewhere since the English stole the originals and could do it again. But I cannot take them with me. I am a renegade king, and so I need a trustworthy man to watch over these things."

"Sire?"

"I want you to take the regalia and put it somewhere safe."

"I am humbled, but—"

"I trust only a few. In the morning, take the regalia with you. Find a place for it."

"As you wish."

"Also, Lady Isabella can hardly return to her husband after this deed. The Comyns hate my very existence and King Edward will judge her actions as treasonous. My wife wants Isabella to stay with her and my daughter and sisters. Soon I will send them to Norway until it is safe to bring them home."

"I will tell her, Sire."

"Aye. When we meet again, I will have other tasks for you if you are willing."

"Always willing, Sire." He bowed his head.

DAYS LATER, IN Fife, he hid the regalia away in a cave by the sea and told no one. He gave orders to his men to guard Castle Black, leaving it in the keeping of Sir Michael Balfour, his cousin and seneschal. Then, he kissed his sister and aunt farewell and held his little son tight. Draping his plaid and sheathing his sword, he walked down to the beach beyond the castle, past the caves where doves cooed, to wait for a boat sent for him by a renegade king.

He felt alone, even with companions in the cause. Solitude was his fate now, so it seemed. Once peace returned to Scotland, he would revive the dreams he had set aside. Until then, he would favor secrecy and stealth with a smile, for life had taught him that a smile could hide more secrets than a scowl.

CHAPTER TWO

Holyoak Abbey, Scotland
February, 1307

SHE WAS NOT certain he would live. Rowena Keith leaned forward to set another cool wet cloth on the man's fevered brow and touched his bare shoulder and chest. The skin felt hot and dry. Soon she must change the poultices on his wounds, although Holyoak's abbot was adamant that a monk be present due to the location of the gash on the man's thigh. Such caution seemed unnecessary; she was familiar with the male physique, having tended to many wounded men over several years of war and strife. Besides, she was a widow, even if her marriage had been very brief.

But this patient was restless and brawny, and she might need help given his strength and size. In candlelight, she examined the lesser gashes on his face and forearm, and then heard voices murmuring outside. Brother Gideon and his twin, Sir Gilchrist Seton, must have come out of midnight prayers. If they came by the infirmary to inquire about the man who had collapsed at the abbey gates days ago, she would enlist their help to hold him down while she applied fresh poultices.

She sighed, patting the man's broad shoulder. He was asleep at last and she did not want to disturb his rest. Yesterday he had thrashed and muttered about swords and gold and kings in Gaelic and English, and had fought efforts to treat him. Only when

Brother Gideon arrived to subdue him—all but sitting on him—could she treat his wounds.

Tilting her head, she studied him. Under the swelling and bruises distorting his face, he was handsome, despite the hedge of his brown beard and the long, unruly chestnut curls she had rinsed in lavender water that morning. She saw strength and elegance in the high cheekbones, squared jaw, and long arched nose where a bump indicated a previous break. His lips were cracked but full beneath the overgrown mustache; his closed eyes were long-lidded and thickly lashed under straight dark brows.

She wondered what color his eyes were, what he was called, if he had family. And she hoped she could do enough to save his life. An almost desperate feeling went through her with that desire; she reminded herself to be a more neutral caretaker.

Drawing back the woolen blanket, she took a quick breath at the sight of his robust nearly nude body. He was solidly beautiful in shadows and candlelight, chest rising and falling, gleaming muscle dusted with bronze and golden hair. His left arm, closest to her, was taut with strength, bent and bandaged across his torso. His long fingers were nimble, almost graceful, slightly calloused. No doubt, he was a warrior, judging by his fitness and the pattern of his wounds. A big warrior, too—the narrow bed barely held him, wide shoulders touching the sides, feet dangling off the end of the cot, toes covered in the clean knitted socks the monks had provided.

Carefully she peeled away the wrapping on his forearm to look at the long cut that angled from elbow nearly to wrist. Days ago when she had arrived, his condition had alarmed her. She did all she could to treat the cuts and gashes, some minor and some serious. Cleansing and dressing the wounds in wine and honey, she had applied poultices and ointments in blends of garlic, nettle, yarrow, onion, honey, and more, and had reopened his half-healed wounds to clean and stitch them neatly with silk thread.

The monks said the man had been in a battle on a sea loch between Bruce's forces and English, a rousing defeat for the

Scots. The big warrior had a wild look; Rowena could imagine him roaring, brandishing a sword, giving no quarter. Though she had only heard him mumble, even so his voice had power.

The wound on his forearm looked less angry than before. Pleased, she replaced the bandaging and drew up the covers. Brushing back messy tendrils of hair from his brow, she studied the stitched cut along his left cheek that glistened with ointment. His facial cuts would not scar badly. But the most serious wound on his leg already had stirred a fever that could be beyond curatives.

She glanced down the length of the infirmary room, a plain wooden building dim in the light of candles and braziers. Several patients lay in two long rows, but the man she tended had a bed apart from the rest, earning privacy as the most serious case. In the few days she had been here, she had spent time with each patient—a fever, old age, a broken leg, apoplexy, two men with wounds gained in a skirmish. The infirmarian and his assistants did good work and did not need her help there.

But the infirmarian had despaired of the brawny warrior's fevered condition and sent word to Kincraig for Rowena to come quickly. She often helped at Holyoak's small hospital and was skilled in treating wounds after years of seeing men hurt in battle or skirmishes. After Aunt Una's death three years ago, Rowena had continued her legacy as a capable healer, so she set out immediately when Brother Gideon and his twin, Sir Gilchrist Seton, arrived as her escort. Her young husband, Sir John Sinclair, had died in an English attack, and she'd had no chance to help him; now she did what she could to help other Scots soldiers.

The door to the ward opened and Gideon and Gilchrist came toward her. Seeing the twins together, she smiled. Both were tall, blond, and identically handsome, though one was a tonsured monk and the other a knight in chainmail and English surcoat, though he was a Scot who balanced duties to two kings, preferring Bruce over the other. "My lady," Brother Gideon murmured. "How is he?"

"Resting, but the fever has not abated. I hope what I have done will be enough."

"Will the leg need amputating?" Gilchrist asked.

"I pray not. The abbot would need to send for a physician or a blacksmith-surgeon, as I could not do that without help. The next few days will tell."

"The abbot, our reverend uncle, says you may stay in the guest house as long as you like," Gideon said.

"Thank you. You mentioned this man's name earlier," she said. "I was so busy at the time that I did not hear what was said." His needs mattered more to her than his name, but she was curious.

"MacDuff. Apparently, he was wounded in the fray at Loch Ryan. One of the monks recognized him as Sir Aedan MacDuff, a knight of Fife," Gilchrist said.

"Clan MacDuff is significant," she said. "Close to the Crown of Scotland since ancient times, I believe." She touched MacDuff's cheek and his bare shoulder. Hot and dry. That worried her. His name tapped a childhood memory, some link with her father. She could not place it.

"Aye, by ancient tradition, the MacDuffs have the sole right to crown Scottish kings," Gideon replied. "If he is one of that kinship, he could be a significant man."

"Edward of England would do away with the crowning right in Scotland if he could," Sir Gilchrist said. "One way would be to eliminate the MacDuffs. The current earl is young, and lives in England as Edward's ward, for the boy's mother is Edward's niece. That lad may never leave England, though he is one of the seven primary Scottish earls. His sister is Lady Isabella of Buchan."

Rowena looked up. "The brave young countess who crowned Robert Bruce secretly? My brother mentioned it. But she was captured last autumn with Bruce's queen and other kinswomen. A terrible situation."

"Horrible," Gilchrist agreed. "King Edward has accused Lady

Isabella of treason for the act of crowning Bruce, and had her placed in an iron cage displayed at Berwick Castle as a cruel warning to Scots. If this man is kin to the earl and his sister, he might also be under threat from Edward."

"He will need to stay here a while yet, so will be safe," Rowena said. "His fever needs watching and his wounds are concerning. I do not know—if he will ever leave."

As she spoke, she drew the blankets down to reveal his bare torso and the braies he wore, a simple linen undergarment. As she examined his thigh wound, the Seton brothers did not comment on propriety but continued to murmur between them.

His legs were long, keenly shaped, and powerfully muscled. The gash on the left leg angled downward between hip and knee, sparing his groin. Above the flimsy covering of the braies, his abdomen was taut; bronze and golden hair arrowed beneath the waist cord of the undergarment. He need not worry about his manhood if he recovered from his wounds, she thought, for the mound under the cloth appeared as virile as any part of him.

She glanced away, feeling a hot blush. As many males as she had seen in her healing work, this man had a curious effect on her, bringing flashes of unwarranted thoughts and sensations in her body. She blew out a breath as a quick yearning swept through her, just loneliness. She knew the feeling.

"There are no streaks in the skin," she told the Setons. "That is in his favor."

Then, with Gideon's assistance, she cleaned the wounds anew, rinsing them in wine and honey and dousing them with strong spirit—*uisge beatha* made by the monks. The man nearly bolted from the bed. Grateful that his reflexes were so keen, she was equally glad to have help calming him. Then she slathered the stitching with the ointment she had prepared from honey, garlic, willow, and other herbs, and applied fresh poultices. "He will rest now," Gideon said when the man subsided and seemed to doze. "You should too, Lady Rowena. You have hardly left his side."

"I am fine. I will sit with him tonight until I know he is improving. You and Gilchrist should go to your beds too. Thank you for your help, truly."

Sir Gilchrist nodded reluctantly and Brother Gideon promised to return to relieve her soon. She waved them away, smiling to hide her weariness. Turning to her patient, she sat quietly, but after a while began to feel sleepy in the silence. Propping her arm on the table by the bed, she rested her head.

Then she jarred awake, uncertain how long she had dozed. Aedan MacDuff growled a few blurred Gaelic words in his sleep. In flickering candlelight, she touched his flushed cheeks. His fever was high again. Dipping a cloth in cool water, she wiped his brow.

"What brought you here, so wounded and ill?" she murmured, frowning in concern. She knew the attack on Bruce's ships two weeks past had been a disaster, with two of Bruce's own brothers captured and executed already. Somehow this MacDuff had traveled across Scotland, severely wounded. Likely he was trying to get home to Fife. No wonder he was fevered and ill by the time he collapsed at Holyoak's gates.

She bathed his forehead, drops sliding down his hot cheek. Earlier she had dosed him with an infusion of poppy and clove. She was exceedingly careful with doses of the potion called the "Great Rest," a treatment for pain. It could bring sleep or silently kill.

Two jugs of water sat on a small table beside her. She dipped a cloth in one and drizzled water between his lips. He needed fluids, yet was too weak to sit up to drink. If he did not improve, she feared she lacked the skill to save him. Worried, frustrated, she pushed back tendrils of her dark hair slipping out of the braid beneath her widow's veil. The loneliness sliced through her again, sharp and hurting.

Perhaps she kept thinking of John Sinclair tonight because she wanted to save this wounded Scot. The weeks she had had with John four, nearly five, years ago had been sweet. Then he had left for knight's duty—and never came back. A month later, the child she had started was gone too. She breathed against the pain, shook her head.

Of all the wounded men she had helped since John's death, this MacDuff brought back the yearning for a husband, a child, the life she had wanted. The pain was not sharp, but a deep pull, as if her spirit stretched for what she could neither reach nor see.

Stop, she told herself. Think. What else could she do for Sir Aedan MacDuff?

There was one remedy that she rarely resorted to trying. Touching the embroidered pouch looped to her belt, she felt the weight of the Rhymer's stone there. Had the time come to use it? Thomas had said it could save a life.

MacDuff snored, a reassuring sound. Weary, Rowena set her elbow on the bed, chin in hand, arm resting on his solid, too-warm chest. She thought about all the ways to treat wounds she had learned from Una. She had tried everything she knew.

She slipped her hand into the drawstring pouch and felt the round shape of the crystal charm stone her great-grandfather had given her. Something told her it was needed now. Perhaps it was her fatigue and frustration insisting on it.

Pondering, she was startled by his sudden grip on her wrist, his hand hot.

"Lass," he said hoarsely. "I need you."

"Sir, be easy. All is well. I am here."

"All is not very well. If I die, neither you nor I will be pleased." A tiny smile moved his lips. He let go of her.

"You will not die. I will not let you." She said it fiercely, felt it in her core, her soul. Something tugged deep in her chest. She would not give up on this man.

"I am cold." His hands shook. "Sweetling. I am in your debt."

The February chill drifted through the room; she felt it too. But braziers about the room radiated cozy heat, one of them nearby. Yet MacDuff was chilled and trembling with fever.

She fetched her cloak from a hook on the wall and returned

to spread it over him. The dark blue wool, lined in a plaid of dark green and black, would provide extra warmth. Pulling it high on his chest, she smoothed his thick, messy hair, scented with lavender and garlic and man. His hand found hers, gripped it, gentle now.

"The world is spinning. Or am I?" His eyes rolled back, but he rallied.

Wiping the wet cloth over his brow, she felt sure what she must do. Setting the cloth aside, she reached into her pouch to remove the stone wrapped in white silk. The round crystal had beautiful cloudlike strands floating inside that winked in the candlelight. She dropped it into the unused jug of water.

Listening to his ragged breathing, feeling the heat of his skin, she waited. Then she extracted the charm stone, dried it in the silk, and poured some of the water from the jug into a wooden cup.

"Drink this."

"No wine," he protested hoarsely.

"Water," she said, and supported his shoulders as he lifted his head. He sipped, losing some of the liquid into his beard. As she drizzled water between his lips, he sucked it, took some from her fingers, then sank back in exhaustion, eyes closed.

The charm stone grew warm, cupped in her hand. She held it up to the candlelight. It sparkled inside, bright and alive somehow. Rotating the gleaming sphere in her hand, she drew a breath, another, readying herself.

Then she touched the stone gently to Sir Aedan's brow and held it there. A tiny golden glow bloomed in the heart of the crystal. She trailed it down to touch his lips. His breathing slowed, calmed.

Tracing the stone along, she touched the stone to the hollow of his throat next, and moved it to his breastbone. The crystal was nearly hot in her hand, as if it absorbed the fever and radiated some power.

When she had first used the stone, Aunt Una and Grandda Thomas taught her to dip the faery crystal in water to impart its healing power into water that could be sipped. They also taught her chants that would clear and strengthen the stone, and Una showed her that those same methods could be used with all charm stones. The Rhymer's faery crystal had an unusual power to help and heal in the most serious instances, and must be used sparingly, she knew. Una had also shown her a method of touching the stone to the body to send healing there.

Instinct, or perhaps desperation, urged her to continue. She felt compelled to help this man however she could. The silence in the room was as deep as the darkness as she watched MacDuff in the candlelight, sweat beading on his brow, his breath ragged, too slow, too fast. She took his hand. His fingers flickered on hers. His eyelids fluttered. His lips were pale. He was weak, and weakening, and it frightened her.

She circled the stone over his heart, then brought the stone, softly glowing, to his abdomen to touch it there. Sweeping it over his legs and feet, she brought it back up along his body. Finally, she let the stone kiss his dry, tenderly shaped lips, then spiraled it over his brow and the crown of his head.

"Be healed, warrior," she whispered.

The stone held a brightness now that looked like tiny streaks of lightning. She blew softly over the crystal, watching its inner light flicker, and she blew the light over his chest and his face.

"Be healed, whole and strong," she whispered in a singsong chant. "Let the light of healing kindle in thy body and thy spirit. Let Heaven heal thee now."

She breathed out the last word, waited, watched. The glow in the sphere faded and vanished. She wrapped the stone in silk and dropped it back into the purse. Touching the man's shoulder, she sensed that his breathing had calmed.

"There," she whispered. "Sleep and heal."

Suddenly he moved, grabbing her wrist again with his uninjured hand, tight enough to bruise or crack her small bones.

"What was that—come here—" He pulled her close, his hand like iron, until her face was near his. "The stone—tell me where you got it!"

CHAPTER THREE

D ELIRIUM, SHE REALIZED, gave him a terrible strength.

"Sir," she said, gasping as she resisted his grip. "I only used a charm stone—"

"Charming, aye, she is. But tell me what were you doing with it—uh…" He winced, his grip lessening, tightening again. "If I die, what then for the stone?"

Did he think a charm stone could harm him? "You will not die. I will not let you."

"Only I know what it is. Only I know. I must guard the stone."

"What?" Did he mean the Rhymer's charm stone? "The stone is safe with me."

"I keep the stone," he rasped. "Precious. I alone know what it is—but now I must tell you before I die." He pulled her closer, his beard a soft brush against her cheek.

She pushed herself away with a hand on his chest. "Try to sleep, sir. All will be well."

"Not well. Must tell you. I have to trust you." He gasped for breath.

"I do not understand. I am only a healer, only here to help you."

"Stones! There is magic in that stone." Releasing her hand, he cupped the back of her head to draw her nearer. In the candle-light, his green eyes were flecked with gold and glittering with fever.

"Stop. I use the stone for healing," she said, confused. "No magic. Medicine."

"Something is magic. Listen to me. Castle—I must tell you."

"Can I deliver a message to someone at a castle? Is that what you want? You are not making sense, sir."

"Swear to me, lass. If I die, you will go there. Secret. Tell no one."

His insistence and his delirious strength alarmed her. "Sir, you will recover. You can go to the castle yourself."

"Promise me. Find the stone, bring it to the king—" His eyes were unnaturally bright. "Go to the castle, find the dove and the stone—"

"What? But I have the stone. I am confused."

"By the beach, a cave—the stones. Promise me you will go there."

"I promise, but tell me more—"

"My lady!" Behind her, footsteps crossed the floor. Gideon was just there, reaching out to grab the man's wrist. "What is this? Sir, let her go!"

Gideon grabbed the man's wrist to free her. Sitting back, Rowena straightened her kerchief. Sir Aedan subsided, turned his head to the wall. When Rowena touched his forehead, he grabbed for her hand again, but Gideon blocked him.

"Just the fever. Leave him be," she said. "He means no harm."

"We should give him the infusion of poppies," Gideon said. "Go rest, Rowena. Here, take your cloak. I will sit with him."

"Just a light dose of the Great Rest, then. I worry about giving him too much."

She would not reveal what the man had said to her. She had simply promised to help, thinking it would calm him. She would help if she understood what he was talking about. He had spoken nonsense about a castle, a stone, a dove.

Dreams, she thought, from delirium.

IN THE MORNING, she found MacDuff asleep. Careful not to disturb his rest, she was pleased to see that his stitched wounds looked less fierce and bruises were fading. His brow was warm but not hot; he no longer shivered with fever. Relieved, she passed her fingers over the curls and waves of his brown-gilt hair. As she drew the blanket up, he stirred, eyelids fluttering.

"Stay," he murmured, his fingers rippling on the blanket.

"I am just here." Feeling a pull of yearning again, she folded her hands and sat beside the bed. He slept, and she felt grateful, knowing it was all she could ask for now.

The outer door opened and Gideon peeked in, beckoning. She went to him. "A visitor is at the gate," he said. "Your brother."

"Henry! I thought he was in Carlisle with the king." Fastening her cloak against the winter chill, she hastened outside as Gideon stayed in the ward. She felt a frisson of alarm as she crossed the yard, hoping all was well at home.

Snow flurried in the air as she hurried toward the knight who had dismounted at the gate. He stood with Gilchrist while one of the young lay brothers led his horse to the stable. "Henry!" she called.

"Rowena!" He gave her an easy smile. Pushing back his chainmail hood, revealing thick blond hair spilling from a quilted cap, he bent to kiss her cheek.

"What brings you here? Is there trouble at Kincraig? I was just there last week."

"All is well. I was at Carlisle with Edward's men, and rode up to Kincraig to look for you. Sir Finley said you had come here. He is proving to be a fine seneschal, by the way. Our sisters are well too, Margaret busy in the household, Tamsin thriving at Dalrinnie—her child will not arrive for months and she is feeling better. Young Lilias Bruce is still there, as you know, and says you must hurry back to teach her more about herbs and such. And I think Andrew Murray would foster with us forever if he could. Finlay is teaching him sword skills." He chuckled.

"I can go back soon. Why would you come looking for me?"

"I was in the south meeting with the English to help negotiate prisoners of war after the battle on Loch Ryan. Then King Edward sent word that I must fetch you."

"What could Edward want with me?"

"Walk with me." Henry led her to the shelter of a roofed arcade. Shivering, she drew her cloak around her against more than the February air. A message from King Edward was usually unwelcome news. He had ordered her sister Tamsin to marry one of his knights or enter a convent, and demanded she give him a sheaf of writings that Thomas the Rhymer had gifted her.

Rowena shuddered. Somehow Edward had learned that Thomas had bequeathed special gifts to Tamsin, as well as the other Keith siblings, which could mean danger for all of them. What if he wanted the Rhymer's charm stone, which she had promised to protect?

"Edward wants you to come to Lanercost Priory, where he is staying," Henry said. "He is ill again with a malady that weakens him now and then. But he is furious with his doctors and the monks in attendance, shouting insults and dismissing them for fools. Recently he heard of your skill, so he wants you to treat him."

"Who would tell him about me? Surely not you, but who?"

"I never would. Apparently, Sir Malise Comyn told the king you saved his life when he was injured. He recommended Edward consult you if he is unhappy with his doctors."

"Sir Malise is back in Edward's court? He should still be recovering."

"Hardly a limp now. Others said he would never walk again, but you did well by him, and he told Edward so."

"Likely he did not mention how he was injured," she said wryly.

"Many know by now that a nun flattened him." Henry chuckled. "But he seems grateful and told Edward you are very skilled. So you are summoned."

"Oh dear. What more did Malise tell Edward? Henry—I think Malise saw the Rhymer's charm stone. He was in a bad way and I dipped it in water to give him a drink. I did not use it otherwise, but he must have seen it. I feared he might never walk again."

"You have a soft heart. I am not sure I would have helped him after what he did to our family and the Setons as well."

"I just hope he did not see the stone and tell Edward about it." Her siblings knew about the charm stone, as she knew what Thomas had given each of them, but for Henry, who had said little of his. "Though he might not know it came from Thomas."

"Malise will do whatever gains him an advantage. He was part of the scheme to take the pages Tamsin owns, though none of it went to plan. If Malise suspects Thomas gave you something, such as a healing stone, aye, he could have told Edward."

"But how would he know for sure?"

"Thomas made his will in the Selkirk courts. As a deputy sheriff, I have seen the record myself. Others might see it too, or hear of it."

"You should steal the document out of there, Henry." She frowned.

"Perhaps. But it remains that you must go to the king. A refusal could invite grave consequences. Tamsin faced a good deal of trouble, but thank the saints Sir Liam happened upon her and could help."

"A blessing in disguise, as they later married." Rowena smiled. "But I do not want to go, Henry. I have work here. One man here has been near death."

"Gilchrist mentioned you are treating a man wounded at Loch Ryan. He was lucky to escape capture and end up here."

"Aye. He is called Sir Aedan MacDuff. Have you heard the name?"

Henry stopped, a hand on her arm. "Aedan MacDuff of Fife?"

"Gilchrist and Gideon said he could be from Fife and might be kin to the earl."

"He is. I know him. We met at Edward's court as knights

together, but I knew of him before that. Do you remember hearing his name at home?"

"I thought the name was familiar, but I could not place it."

"You were just five then, and I was eleven. He was perhaps fifteen, but we did not meet him." He exhaled. "Father tried to arrange a marriage between you and this MacDuff, who is related to the earls of Fife. Father was impressed with the lad. But the agreement was canceled when his kin decided against the marriage."

A faded childhood memory surfaced; her first betrothal refused and forgotten. "I recall feeling sad about it, but that is all I remember."

"Aedan and his older brother—a young earl then—were wards of the bishop of Saint Andrews and Fife after their father, the earl, was killed. Aedan's brother later died in similar fashion, leaving his son Earl of Fife. The lad is Edward's hostage in England."

"How awful!"

"But not surprising. Edward seems determined to be rid of the MacDuffs."

She shook her head, saddened again—was it the ghost of her childhood self? Then she realized that if the marriage had proceeded, her husband would be the warrior now lying in the infirmary. Instead, she'd married another years later who died in battle just weeks after the wedding. Widowed over four years, she was content with the freedom to travel about and do the work she loved.

"How odd to think MacDuff and I—well, it was never meant to be. I have done all I could to help him, and pray he recovers." She glanced toward the infirmary building. "I used the charm stone for him, Henry. He was delirious and could have died. But he seems improved today."

"Then he needed the help you gave him. Just keep it to yourself, aye?"

"I will." She sighed. "I do not want to go to Edward, but if he is ill, I feel I must."

"It is your way. And trust me, we must do what this king wants, or there will be hell to pay. He is more impatient and vindictive than ever and could stir havoc at the smallest slight. If he thinks you have something he wants, it could go poorly for you. Be careful. Do not tell him about the stone."

"I promised Grandda that I would guard it, and so I will."

"Aye then. Gilchrist and I will escort you south today. I have no doubt this MacDuff will recover, thanks to you."

She touched the embroidered pouch, felt the round crystal there. Walking back through the yard with Henry, she remembered something Grandda had said.

One day, this wee stone could save Scotland. Thou art its guardian now. Keep it secret. Keep it safe. Use it wisely.

HEARING A SOFT step, sensing the light changing, the air sweeter and softer, Aedan opened his eyes. She stood beside him. He thought her a nun, with her gentle, skilled touch, her soft kind gray eyes, her kerchief and simple gray gown. Though his lips felt stretched and dry, and his stitched and poulticed cheek pained him, he smiled.

"Back again? I must be dying. Such attention." It took all his strength to stay awake, move a few fingers, smile.

"You seem improved today. I am glad," she whispered, touching his shoulder.

"Stay." Had he said that already? His mind was in a fog.

"I must go. My brother is here. I am called to the king."

"King. I must go to the king too." Dimly aware that he must find Bruce, lend his support, he shifted to sit but could not.

"Easy, sir. I must go, but you will recover. The monks will help you. Rest now."

"Stay," he said, fingers lifting. "Are you a nun?"

"I am not." She took his hand. "I cannot stay. Promise me you will heal and go home."

"Home. Promise. See you again?"

"Who can say? Guard yourself, aye?"

"Guard," he repeated. "Stone."

"What?" She sounded almost frightened. Had he said something wrong? He lifted her hand to his lips and kissed her soft, slim knuckles. It took his strength.

"Farewell, you," she said dearly, sweetly.

"Sweetling. Kind lady. I owe you."

She laughed softly and turned away, footsteps light to the door.

He closed his eyes, feeling an odd tug in his chest as she left. He wanted to see her again. Had to—the stone—he had seen its twin elsewhere, and it puzzled him greatly.

He slept.

CHAPTER FOUR

"Sire. You sent for me?" Rowena bowed her head, dipped her knee as King Edward glanced up. He sat by a blazing hearth, robed in furs and thick woolen garments, and beckoned her forward with bony fingers.

"Come here." He looked weary, his long face pale and drawn, gray hair straggling over rounded shoulders, long legs like sticks in baggy woolen stockings. But his blue eyes were sharp. "Did you bring more of that medicine we took from your hand?"

"I have some prepared, Sire. I will bring it here." After nearly a month sequestered in Lanercost Priory waiting upon the king's health and his whim, she looked forward to departing soon. If he wanted more of the potions she made, she feared he would keep her here.

Henry and Gilchrist stood nearby in the shadows, glancing at her in silence. As Edward's pledged knights, both wore chainmail in the king's presence, Henry in a wine-colored surcoat, Gilchrist in the red surcoat embroidered with golden lions that identified him as Edward's man. She was glad they had remained at Lanercost with her; she knew they too hoped to depart for Scotland soon.

"Come closer," Edward barked. She approached. "That concoction you brought the other day was helpful for the stomach."

"Sire, I am glad." Leaving Holyoak in a rush, she had blended remedies at Lanercost using whatever herbs, oils, and simples the infirmarian would spare. Learning that King Edward suffered stomach problems, she mixed infusions of mint, ginger, mallow, blueberries, and more to soothe and help heal. "If I may, Sire, I wish to return home tomorrow with my brother, Sir Henry."

"The physician left, now you too? That leaves Brother Hugo to do all the physicking! What do you say, Hugo?" He growled this at the monk who sat in a corner. "Can you prepare the same simples as Lady Rowena?"

"Sire," Brother Hugo said, standing. "With respect, if I may comment."

"Speak!"

Rowena lowered her eyes as Brother Hugo Fitzwalter stood before the king. She felt the monk's sharp, critical glance. Hugo was a cleric and infirmarian who had accompanied Edward's party to Lanercost, and who now treated the king in place of John Gadsden, the cleric and physician who had departed for his college at Oxford days after Rowena arrived. Gadsden had been respectful regarding Rowena's methods and opinions, even offering to send a precious copy of his treatise, *Rosa Medicinae*, to her at Kincraig Castle. Honored, she was sorry to see him go, needing an ally, especially one who could teach her more.

Hugo the infirmarian was a different matter. When she had first arrived, he refused to let her work in the priory kitchen to prepare a soothing syrup for the king, but John Gadsden had given permission. Still, Hugo had remained cool and unwelcoming to her. Yet since she had dosed Edward with infusions and syrups and advised a plain diet, the king had appeared to gain strength and sleep more soundly. When Hugo asked about one of her concoctions, she shared the recipe willingly. Yet he was disdainful when she revealed that an essential part of the recipe was to dip three crystals in rainwater and add the liquid.

While at Lanercost, she was grateful and relieved that Edward had not asked about her great-grandfather or the charm stone. Sir Malise Comyn had not visited Lanercost in the past weeks, and she hoped to leave before he arrived.

As Brother Hugo spoke with the king, she heard her name. "Sire, some of what Lady Rowena advises makes sense. But much of it is unnecessary and possibly harmful."

She stepped forward. "Sire, with respect—" At Edward's nod, she continued. "I am trained in traditional Highland medicine, and have seen such methods work well, helping even when naught else does."

"Your Grace, I advise dismissing the lady and summoning John the physician back again. Together he and I can provide better cures."

"Lady Rowena's potions and treatments are soothing," Edward said. "Your advice was not sought, Hugo. You may leave. Lady, you will stay." He waved toward her. "There is a matter to discuss."

She felt a twist of dread in her stomach. What did the king want? His health had improved under her watch, while the efforts of Brother Hugo and John Gadsden had made little difference. But she had not used the Rhymer's charm stone, although she had used lesser stones.

"Sire?" she asked, feeling anxious. "Your Grace does look improved, with better color and brighter eyes. You look stronger."

"Sleeping better. Eating more. The flux is less. Your potions helped some."

"I am glad." Unsure of the cause of his poor digestion, she had given him herbs that could calm and slow the stomach. He had been impatient and complained that she was not a physician, and worse, female. But he took what she offered.

"Your Grace, did you consider my suggestion to help the digestion? Smaller meals, no rich or fatty foods, less wine and spirits, and so on."

"Considered them. Not interested."

"Sire, some physicians and healers, such as the respected Hildegard of Bingen, whose works I have read, recommend that thoughts, words, and temperament can either ease or damage the body. For example, discontent and anger can harm the heart and stomach." That comment was a risk, but it needed to be said.

"Hmph. My priests are busy with prayers on my behalf. John Gadsden says the problem is the bilious nature in the blood and urine. He bled me near dry to balance it. The physicians, monks, astrologers and alchemists offer remedies and suggestions too. Naught helped more than your concoctions. You are required to provide more."

"I will prepare some this evening, Sire, and leave it here, as I wish to depart with my brother. Your physicians are knowledgeable about bodily humors and matters of blood and urine, astrology too. What I know are traditional remedies that have proven reliable. Heaven grants healing blessings through Nature in plants and other elements, and those remedies often alleviate sickness."

"Stones," he said. "You put stones in water."

"I did," she said carefully. She sometimes used small crystals.

"The monks say charm stones are suspect. Is it nonsense, or healing, or evil?" He put a hand to his belly as if in discomfort.

"I believe these things help, Sire. I do wonder if regular bleeding weakens you."

"Physicians know more than you do."

"In some ways, aye. Your Grace may have heard that the Church banned the practice of bleeding among monks long ago, though physicians still use it. Scholars and doctors are always discovering more about the body and the healing arts, and there is much to understand."

"Healing is up to God, so say the priests. However—" He leaned forward, narrowing his eyes. "We are curious about your other methods, lady. One of my knights says you possess a unique healing stone. Do you have it with you?"

So Malise must have told the king after all. She dared not risk revealing too much, having promised to keep her stone secret and safe. King Edward would turn a greedy eye on it if he knew.

"Sire," she said carefully, "I used small crystals in rainwater in the simples and syrups I gave you." She clenched her hands, hoping her answer would satisfy him. "Such things are common in Highland medicine."

"Huh! Any stone can be dropped in a cup. Look." He pulled a large ring of sapphire and gold off his middle finger and plopped it into the cup beside him, red wine splashing out. "That will not heal anyone. We hear you have something more powerful."

"Gemstones and crystals, gold and silver too, can have healing powers, Sire."

Scowling, Edward gestured to Brother Hugo to fish the ring out of the wine cup. "We ask again. You have an extraordinary stone inherited from the Rhymer. Where is it?" The question was sharp and direct.

"Sire, Sir Thomas Learmont left a few things that have meaning only to our family. He meant them for his kin, just as any grandparent might do."

Brother Hugo handed the ring back to Edward. As the king shoved it on his bony finger, the monk spoke quietly; Rowena heard some of it.

"Sire," Hugo said, "there is always a danger of poisoning with folk remedies that may have darker powers. In France, they seek out witches who claim to be healers and burn them for heresy and trafficking with demons."

"We rarely do that here," Edward muttered. The monk sent Rowena a sidelong glance and withdrew to the shadows, while the king frowned at her. "But you are advised to be careful, lady, and to answer truthfully."

"Sire." She bowed her head, startled by the clear warning. Poison! She saw that Brother Hugo did not understand certain traditional remedies—or care to.

A knock at the door prompted a young page to open it and admit a dark-haired knight in chainmail and a blue surcoat.

"Sir Malise Comyn, Your Grace," the boy said.

Dear God. Rowena sent a glance to Henry and Gilchrist. Her brother quirked a brow and Seton tightened his lips. As the knight entered, Rowena stepped back, hoping not to be noticed.

Walking with an obvious limp, Sir Malise saw her and paused with a tight smile. "My lady," he murmured, dark eyes glinting.

"Go, lady," the king said. "Fetch those concoctions now and bring them back if you expect permission to leave here."

"Sire," she said, and hurried from the room.

RETURNING TO EDWARD'S chambers in the priory carrying a wooden tray holding glass vials and small jars, Rowena saw that Sir Malise Comyn was still talking with the king. Hoping not to be noticed, she set out the vessels containing the doses she had prepared earlier, arranging them on a table covered in a patterned rug. As she worked, she glanced at Henry and Gilchrist, standing silently by, both frowning as they listened while Malise spoke to King Edward. She tried to listen too.

With good reason, the Keiths and Setons were none too fond of Sir Malise. Years ago, he had attacked Gilchrist's sister, and more recently, had pursued Rowena's sister Tamsin on Edward's orders. Yet months ago, after a serious injury, Malise had spent two months in Holyoak's infirmary. There Rowena, Gideon, and the monks had nursed him back to health. She was surprised to see that Malise had already returned to Edward's service. He seemed hearty enough now, she thought, glancing toward him.

And she had no doubt now that he had mentioned the healing stone to Edward.

He stood before Edward, his movements somewhat awkward in chainmail and the long-skirted tunic, his back injury resulting in a limp and some weakness. She had hoped such a serious injury and the need for help would have made him less arrogant and ambitious. But she now suspected otherwise.

"Sire, about the report Your Grace requested," Malise was saying. "I have the information requested about the Scotsman on the list of rebels to investigate."

"Good. Ah, Lady Rowena is back again." Edward looked toward her. "He has been singing your praises, lady."

She gulped, turning with a forced smile, again wishing she had not risked any use of the guardian stone, even though Malise had been in dire condition. Somehow he had discerned what it was. As Henry mentioned, he might be aware of the inventory in the Rhymer's last will, and could have surmised the remarkable legacy that the Rhymer left to his family—a legacy that Edward might want to obtain.

"Greetings, Lady Rowena. How good to see you again." Malise inclined his head. "True, I did tell our king that I am only walking today because of your magic."

"M—magic?" She blinked, horrified after hearing Hugo mention what could become of witches and healers.

"Not magickal arts, of course," he went on. "Just an exaggeration born of my admiration for you. And I believe that whatever you learned from your esteemed kinsman, the Rhymer, helped my recovery. So I urged His Grace to send for you if other medicines and treatments proved unsatisfactory. To my great honor, he did."

"That was not to honor you, Comyn," Edward snapped. "But Lady Rowena has provided some relief. If it was due to a remedy learned from her kinsman, certainly we want to know more."

Rowena bowed her head and stepped back. "Your Grace, I brought the herbal remedies that seemed helpful. I do not wish to interrupt the meeting with Sir Malise."

"Stay," Edward barked. "There is still a matter to discuss. Sir Malise, wait there. Lady Rowena, your treatments have helped, yet you do not ask for payment. Surely, you want some reward."

That surprised her. "Sire, I require nothing. Perhaps a donation to Lanercost Priory." She had heard complaints among the servants and a few monks about the burdens placed on the priory due to the size of the king's household.

"They have the privilege of our presence," he dismissed. "What do you want? Even loyal Scots can be rewarded. Ask for silk for gowns. A jewel. Those can be arranged."

"Sire, I require naught. I am glad to help those who are ill."

Even you, she thought, lowering her eyes. "I only want to return to Kincraig."

"Huh. But you are a young widow, living in your brother's castle, visiting monasteries to help the sick. Commendable. Saintly. But a noblewoman should not travel about on her own."

"I am usually accompanied by an escort, Sire. My brother is with me here."

"Ah, Sir Henry. The Keiths of Kincraig want to stay in our good graces, surely."

Seeing the king's sharp stare, Rowena felt unsettled. "Sire."

"We can arrange a husband for you. A good marriage."

"Husband?" She froze. Standing by Malise Comyn, she felt ill suddenly. *Not him. Not after all he had done against her family.*

"Sir Malise owes his life to you. High praise. You could do worse than to marry one of our loyal knights. It would keep you in this court where you are needed."

Lifting her chin, she felt her innate stubbornness emerge. "Sire, I appreciate your generosity, but I cannot marry. I am—" She sought some excuse and glanced at Henry, searching for what to say.

Her brother stepped forward. "Your Grace, if I may speak on my sister's behalf."

"What is it?" Edward seemed displeased by the interruption, and Malise sent a dark glance toward her brother.

"With respect, Sire, my sister cannot accept an offer of marriage. She is betrothed."

Silence. Rowena stared at Henry, the king stared at her; Malise glared at Henry and turned his flat gaze on her. Then she realized what Henry was doing.

Aedan MacDuff. There was a thread of truth in it. But mentioning the man's name here could endanger him.

"Betrothed!" Edward roared. He rose to his lanky height, wavering on creaky legs. His valet jumped forward in alarm and Brother Hugo came to his side, ready to support him should he fall. "Who is it? Scots in this court who wish to marry must have approval."

"We cannot name him yet," she said quickly. "The agreement is not final. It has been in discussion for years. I pray Your Grace understands."

"Sire, it is being negotiated," Henry said. "These matters are complicated."

"He had better be a knight pledged to our service," Edward muttered, and sat.

"He is a knight, Sire," she said.

"Sire, regretfully, my sister cannot promise to another now." Henry bowed his head and stepped back.

"Send word when it is done," Edward said. "We will offer another reward."

"Sire?" Her heart was racing. She could not bear another surprise from Edward.

He held up a finger. "Brother Hugo will visit Soutra hospital in a few weeks. You may accompany him on our royal recommendation. Then you may return here with new knowledge to continue working here. That is your gift."

"I would be pleased to go to Soutra. It is an excellent hospital." She had no desire to return to help King Edward, and no desire to go anywhere with sour Brother Hugo. But she was interested in the work at Soutra, and could hardly refuse the king easily.

"Sire," Hugo began in protest. Edward held up a hand for silence.

"Consider the marriage offer, lady. Betrothals are easily broken, and this arrangement is in your favor. The Keiths would do well to ally with the Comyns. Loyalty is rewarded when Scots are loyal." Edward's gaze was pale blue and icy. She saw grave illness in his pallor and physical weakness—and tremendous willfulness too. She knew how easily his temper was provoked.

"I will consider it, Your Grace." She needed caution, not a show of resistance.

"Sir Malise?" Edward barked.

"I would agree, Your Grace," Malise said. "The alliance would be good." He shot Henry a fresh glare.

No wonder it appealed to him, Rowena thought. By Scottish tradition, even enemies were safe if they married into an opposing clan. Marriage to her might protect Malise from the Keiths and Setons—at least in theory.

"Brother Hugo, you will send word to Lady Rowena about Soutra—you will," he insisted as the monk squawked. "Now, Lady Rowena. If you have a charm stone or anything else of the Rhymer's, those are now the property of the Crown."

She blinked. "Sire?"

"We will confiscate whatever your kinsman gave you."

"But—Your Grace, he left us nothing of value."

"More than you realize, it seems. Leave whatever stones you have with Brother Hugo. Anything else in your family's possession that came from the Rhymer must be delivered here within a month, or it will be collected. Do you understand? Sir Henry, is that clear?"

"Sire," Henry droned. She heard the tight, quiet fury in his voice.

She felt the unfair command like a blow. Edward was convinced that Thomas had left magical, faery-borne things to his family—and believed he had the right to claim them. Those were special things with unique, even extraordinary traits, items to be protected that must never fall into other hands, especially into Edward's keeping.

The very air turned tense. Edward was obsessed with prophecies and esoteric knowledge; he needed to control his future through any means, magical, otherworldly, or by force. Since he regarded the Scots as his subjects, he believed whatever Thomas owned belonged to him.

She understood that Edward, sick and growing weaker, might crave a magical charm stone if it could heal him. But Rowena would not give it up at any cost.

"I will leave the charm stones I have, Sire," she said, meaning the small crystals Una had given her years ago. The Rhymer's stone was packed in a leather satchel with her things, tucked away in the little chamber she used at Lanercost. Her heart pounded. She felt frantic to fetch it and leave for Kincraig as soon as possible.

"Send the rest," Edward said. "The clerk will draw up a writ with the orders. Sir Malise will make sure you comply. That way he can—protect the Keiths from further irritating the Crown. Now you may go home, lady. But leave the potions."

She bowed her head. "Sire." She would not thank him, her heart pounding with fury and frustration. Henry stood silent beside Gilchrist.

Returning to the table where she had left the vessels, she withdrew the small quartz stones from the purse on her belt and arranged them with the other things. Given Brother Hugo's smugness, she hoped Edward would demand that the monk use them.

She heard Edward speak to Malise then. "Give us your news," he rasped.

At the table, Rowena tipped her head to listen and saw Henry do the same.

Sir Malise produced a rolled parchment, which Edward opened and read.

"Damned Scots," the king growled. "Crowning Bruce was treason. It took you long enough to find those involved. Arrest this man and throw him in Berwick to rot. Take his property. Get a warrant from the sheriff there."

"Sire, he holds Castle Black in Fife. His nephew is the young earl of Fife, Duncan MacDuff, who is Your Grace's nephew and ward in Northumbria."

"That pup! We will not release him. The Fife castle should be forfeited."

Arranging vials and jars, Rowena felt her heart jump. *MacDuff of Fife!*

"Sire, a warrant for forfeiture must designate a new owner to keep the property under the Crown's control. Who shall have it?"

"Take it for yourself if you can. We cannot spare the men to attack it. The clerk will prepare a warrant. What do you know of this scoundrel MacDuff? Wife? Family?"

Just now, Sir Aedan was either on his sickbed or limping his way home to Fife. Rowena sent Henry a frantic glance, and he returned a frown.

"His wife is dead. He has a son. It is in the report, Sire," Malise Comyn said.

"Throw the son in the dungeon with the father."

"It is a small child, Sire."

"Gone soft, Comyn? We confined Bruce's daughter without harm. Put the boy in a dungeon and make sure he gets milk."

"The Bruce girl is twelve and in a convent. This boy is too small to be imprisoned. If the Pope hears of it, you will be censured."

"Damn it," Edward muttered. "Fine. Take the boy to live with the other Scottish whelp, that so-called earl. Find this MacDuff, arrest him, and take the property. No MacDuff related to the Earl of Fife can be free! Imprisoned, confined—or dead!"

CHAPTER FIVE

WHILE THE GUARDIANS of the kingdom of Scotland argued around him, rising voices echoing in the small stone church just outside of Selkirk, Aedan sat apart and silent on a wooden bench. He stretched out his left leg, muscles aching hip to knee along the healing scar, aware of the March wind pummeling the shuttered window above his head.

He listened as the men disputed their possible response to King Edward's most recent letter, delivered to Gartnait, earl of Mar, a high-ranking lord and one of the quieter voices in the room. If they did not find agreement soon, Aedan thought, he would speak. But as an interim guardian in a group of Scotland's elite lords acting together as regent to govern Scotland, he had a lesser say.

Yet as uncle to Isabella of Buchan and young Earl Duncan of Fife, his voice was important and respected.

"Regarding Bruce's kinswomen," said Sir John de Soules, an older knight with a raspy voice and a will like steel, "we demand that Lady Mary Bruce and Lady Isabella, countess of Buchan, be removed from their barbaric cages and taken to better confinement in a castle or convent until Edward agrees to release them back to kin and country, with or without prisoner exchange. Tell Edward that!"

"We all read Longshank's letter," countered Gartnait of Mar. "The king refuses the request of the guardians of Scotland that these women, 'including the countess of Buchan and the wife, daughter, and sisters of Robert Bruce, be taken thence to a place to be given over to the guardianship of Gartnait of Mar, Sir John de Soules, Sir Ingram de Umfraville, Sir Aedan MacDuff, the bishops of Glasgow and St. Andrews, and the sheriffs of Lothian and Dumfries. Such and similar arrangements are not amenable.'" Reading from the letter, he tossed the page, seals dangling, to the table.

"Edward has refused three times. What do we say now?" Sir Ingram asked.

Amid muttered replies, Aedan stood. "Write this," he said, and walked forward, gesturing toward a clerk brought by Mar, who scratched ink over a used parchment page.

"Since the addressee—Edward—is taking pains to ensure the cruel and unwarranted confinement of Bruce's kinswomen," he said, "herein, the Guardians of the Realm of Scotland, lords and regents, request again that the king deliver back to Scotland on good surety the countess of Buchan, etcetera," he said. "If they are not released to appointed sheriffs by—let us say the first of May," he suggested, "the Guardians promise and resolve to deliver another letter to Pope Clement the fifth detailing the uncouth behavior and great aggrievances of the King of England toward women and children who have harmed none."

"Well enough, Aedan," Gartnait of Mar said. "But Edward is convinced Isabella did grievous harm by crowning our king. He will not release or exchange anyone until Bruce begs the king's peace. And that will not happen."

"We will take our chances with a final attempt at diplomatic negotiation. Then—" Aedan paused to give the comments time to settle.

"And then?" John de Soules crossed his arms.

"We rescue them by force. But we would need men standing ready wherever the prisoners are being held—castles and convents. A great number of men."

"And a great deal of work to pull it off. But MacDuff is right,"

De Soules said. "We should send one more letter—and begin to plan assaults to reclaim the women."

Aedan resumed his seat as the discussion continued and the latest letter was composed. Flexing his shoulders, he felt weary from weeks of traveling. Only a month earlier, he had left the monastery at Holyoak; rather than return to Fife, he had headed south to carry out a promise to Robert Bruce. At Roxburgh Castle, he had seen Lady Mary Bruce only from a distance, huddled in the iron cage displayed on the parapet—a heartbreaking sight. Then he rode up to Selkirk, intending to visit Berwick afterward in an attempt to see Isabella before sailing home to Fife.

Privately he had little hope, despite the influence of the guardian lords and regents of Scotland, that Edward would release the women. The king was so determined to bend the Scots to his will that his mercy was rare now.

But what he had heard earlier in the meeting troubled him greatly: rumors of growing danger for Bruce, loyal individuals, and certain clans—MacDuff among them. Aedan felt more strongly than ever that he must make his way home to look after his kinfolk and secure the treasures he had secreted away.

Much later, his part done, he left the kirkyard while the lords still gathered in the church, intending to ride the mile or two of curving path that led to the town. Puddles in the rutted track reflected moonlight until he entered a deep aisle of shadow that cut through dense woodland. He looked forward to sleep in the tavern where he had hired the horse and paid for a room. A bed under a roof was a luxury these days, though he could fall asleep anywhere.

Still recovering from his injuries, he tired easily, limped some, and ached on rainy days. His wounds were healing remarkably well, though. Just neat pink lines remained of the stitches that had closed the gashes on his leg, forearm, and face, and the scars would fade. He was alive, healing, and grateful for it.

Grateful, too, to the young woman who had saved his life. Without her grace and ability, he would not be here today. She was not a nun after all, and she was kind and lovely. Her name was blurred in his memory—perhaps Rona or Robina—but he still thought of her. He wished he could find her, show her his healed scars, his regained strength. He wished he could repay her somehow.

At Holyoak, fevered and weak, he had watched her, had fastened his deep need to survive on her kindness, her grace, her calm strength. She was part of the medicine that had helped him. Weeks after he left Holyoak, as his head cleared, he felt as if he had fallen a little in love with her.

Perhaps what he felt was not love, but gratitude unexpressed. Yet he felt a glimmer of hope dreaming of the girl. If he found time to return to Holyoak, he would thank them and ask after her. Seeing her again would help him differentiate gratitude from infatuation or more—though he did not expect to encounter love ever again.

Tonight, he was weary, aching, and hungry. He wanted a good stew, a cup of ale watered to his tolerance, a bed, and good dreams of family, home, and the girl at Holyoak.

Then his horse neighed, snorted, lost the rhythm of his step in the lowering shadows. Alerted, Aedan slowed, glanced around, listened. Just the sound of wind through trees, an owl's cry, the horse's breath and step.

He slowed again when the horse sidestepped and snorted nervously. Drawing on the reins, he paused the horse in the shadow of the woodland to either side. The stallion he had hired in Selkirk was new to him; perhaps the animal was restive or disliked the dark. Then he heard the hoofbeats.

More than one horse, perhaps three or four; riders were coming at a fair pace. Thankful for his horse's nervous warning, he spurred the mount onward with still a mile to go. The road stretched past the forest into the open with moonlight showing the way. Soon the hoofbeats were closer.

"Halt! MacDuff of Fife! Halt!"

They were on him even as he bent to the horse's neck urging

a gallop; even as he reached for the broadsword strapped to the saddle; and before he could wheel and defend. Shouting, they surrounded him, weapons drawn. His name, so honored in Scotland and reviled in England, was yelled out. He resisted, but his arm, weakened by the long, deep scar, gave too soon.

Dragged from the horse and thrown to the ground, he rose to his feet with a roar, feet planted wide as he stood taller than the three soldiers in steel helms and red surcoats. Though his scarred leg trembled like a sapling, he stood his ground and slid a hand under his plaid to grasp the dagger hidden there. Even so, one of the three poised a sword tip at his throat, bringing the sting of blood. He froze.

"What do you want?" he growled.

"MacDuff," one said. "You are a traitor, accused of treason!"

"I am riding to town minding my own business. You mind yours and leave off." He leaned back, but two sword points pinched his neck. He liked his throat. He stilled.

"You took part in a treasonous act by aiding in the unlawful crowning of Robert Bruce. Your name alone is a crime, so says the king. We have orders to take you down."

"I am a Guardian of Scotland, a clan chief—best think before you arrest me." Feeling the snakebite of a sword point, he leaned and felt a third point press his back.

"Orders, MacDuff. Yield!"

They took him by the arms, kicking his feet from under him, his weaker leg folding. Then the side of a blade knocked against his temple and he slumped to the earthen road.

Rowena stood in the long ward room at Soutra Aisle, the Augustinian hospital in East Lothian where she had met Brother Hugo days earlier. Seated beside an old woman, she held her hand and thought about the stone hidden in her purse; she wished she had a sturdy chain to keep it even closer and out of sight of others. Even through the cloth, she felt the stone grow warm and vibrant, felt the woman's breathing ease. The stone was helping in its way, though she sensed that soon death would do its inevitable work here.

Days before, Sir Gilchrist and his cousin, Sir Finley Macnab, now seneschal at Kincraig, had left her at Soutra. She had assured them she would be fine in the company of monks and a few nuns who helped here. The men promised to return in a week if she did not send word sooner.

After spending lovely weeks at home in Kincraig with her family and friends, she had no desire to go anywhere. But when a messenger arrived from Brother Hugo with word that she was expected at Soutra, she knew she had no choice but to go.

As for Edward's demand to have whatever the Rhymer had given the Keiths, she informed her family, yet no royal order had arrived. In Selkirk, Henry wrote that he had no word of it either. Rowena hoped King Edward had forgotten—he was more ill than most knew, she was sure—or he dismissed it as unimportant, which would not surprise her. The matter of Scotland would take precedence: the king in the heather, as many called Bruce now, was rapidly gaining support.

However, she was very surprised when several of the king's men arrived at Soutra and asked to see her.

"Is the king ill? Has he sent for me, as he said he might?" she asked Brother Hugo, who came to fetch her. She could not imagine why four knights would come to the abbey hospital with a message for her. "Is there something wrong at Kincraig?"

"My lady," said the knight who introduced himself as Sir Peter Abernethy, "we have orders to take you from Soutra."

"From Sir Henry or Sir Gilchrist??" Puzzled, she felt a growing alarm.

"We are to arrest you, my lady." He seemed ill at ease.

"On what charge?" Her heart pounded, her hands shook. Had Edward finally acted on his threat against the Keiths regarding the Rhymer's legacy?

"For attempting to poison the king," Sir Peter said. "He still lives. We are here on royal orders."

Stunned, she looked at Hugo, who stood to one side. "Brother?"

"Lady Rowena, I am shocked. Abernethy, what is the meaning of this?"

"The lady has been accused of poisoning the king. Here is the order." Sir Peter produced a folded parchment with a dangling royal seal and handed it to the monk. But he did not show her, as if she did not matter. Brother Hugo read it and handed it back.

"Hugo, please, can you do something?" she asked. "Surely, you know I would never do harm to Edward or anyone."

"Of course," he murmured. "They must take you. It is their duty. I tried to warn you and the king about some of your practices. But I will do what I can." A strange look crossed his face as he turned away. It was satisfaction.

Sir Peter, with a murmured apology, helped her mount a waiting horse, side-saddled for a woman, then tied her wrists with rope attached to the harness.

"Please. I did not do this. Please—send word to my family."

"Brother Hugo will do that," Sir Peter said. But she knew that would not happen.

Led away, she rode with them over hills and meadows to a river, fear like lead in her stomach. They put her on a barge, her hands still tied, guards around her. Panic turned to illness, for water travel often made her uneasy. When the barge docked, she did not know where she was, but saw a familiar face among those on the bank.

Sir Malise Comyn. She did not know whether to hope or fear even more.

He came forward. "Lady Rowena!" He took her aside, gesturing for the guards to wait. "I rode hard to be here when I heard about this."

"Sir Malise, what is happening? They say I tried to poison Edward—two of the guards said I was a whore and a witch. Abernethy did not even reprimand them. I do not know what to do." Tears sprung in her eyes. "I did no harm. Surely you know these charges are false!"

"My dear," he murmured, "I am stunned by this order. But the king issued it himself. So I rode north to help if I could."

She had to chance trusting him, having no one else here. "You know this is wrong. Tell them you know me."

"I owe you a debt. But if I cannot arrange your release, you must consider the king's wishes for you."

"Wishes?" She blinked. Did he mean the Rhymer's legacy—or the mention of marrying Malise? Either was abhorrent. "What do you mean?"

"Edward suggested that we marry. If you were my wife, I would have more influence in this situation. Alas, you are promised, though that can be broken. And you can give Edward what he wants and earn a pardon, and favor for both of us."

Cold realization spiked through her. She could not trust Malise, though she had once hoped that helping him recover from injury would soften his hardened heart. "Is this because King Edward thinks I have something that belonged to the Rhymer?"

She was glad that Sir Peter was courteous enough to not only show reluctance to arrest a noble lady, but to refrain from searching her, or he would have found the crystal. She could only pray that Malise would show some courtesy too and leave her be.

"Lady Rowena, I am here because I care about you. If you are betrothed, I wish you luck. But that fellow will change his mind after this, if you survive this ordeal."

"Malise, please help. You said you owed me something."

"I will try. But I have my orders too. Edward insists that I find that fellow in Fife and then go to Kincraig for whatever gewgaws you possess. A lot of rushing around for not much reward. You could make this easier."

A chill doused her spirit. She was wrong to hope for mercy. "Malise—I would not marry you after what you have done to people I love. I hoped once your catastrophe had changed you, but I fear I was wrong. Help me or do not—but I cannot give you what you want. I am sorry," she added hastily, for her soft heart interfered in the moment.

"As you wish. I will do what I can, nonetheless." Yet the flash of anger in his dark eyes confirmed he was no friend, no matter what he said.

He stepped back as the guards came to lift her into the cart. As it rolled away, Malise Comyn stood watching thoughtfully.

They took her to a place called Yester Tower toward the east coast, a region of Scotland under English control. Weak with fear and fatigue, she found the strength to kick and struggle. But they dragged her into the stone fortress and down steps to a dark lower level, where they pushed her into a dark cell, slammed the door, and walked away.

Then she realized she was not alone.

CHAPTER SIX

I N THE DANK underground cell, Rowena sat wondering how things had gone wrong so quickly. She glanced again toward the chamber's other occupant. Not eight steps away, a Highlander snored, his bulky form wrapped in a dirty plaid blanket. The guards had called him a filthy Scot when they pushed her in here, and certainly he wore the wrapped woolen plaid common to northern Scotsmen. Messy dark hair and a beard peeked out of the plaid draped over his head, though his face was hidden, and his snores were loud and sloppy.

Beyond the oak door strapped in iron, she could hear English guards muttering and chuckling. A small, barred window set in the door let a shaft of torchlight into the small chamber. Those guards had dragged her in here and dumped her on the floor. Thinking back on the events that put her in this position, she pushed back the tendrils of hair that had escaped her veil and wrapped her arms around her raised knees, her blue gown spreading over the dirty straw.

She gleaned that Yester was east of Soutra near a river, which meant a few days' travel separated her from home and safety. A few days from now, Gilchrist and his cousin Finley would return to Soutra to find her gone. They would not sit idle, but would search for her. She need only wait.

But that meant waiting here for days, a woman alone in a filthy cell with a snoring stranger, and leering guards outside the door. As the snores continued, she tried to ignore the bundle of plaid in the shadows. The man had scarcely moved beyond those long, full snores. Good. She needed no trouble from him, having enough of a dilemma.

She had been betrayed. *The whore who poisoned King Edward*, the guards had said. But the accusation and arrest made no sense. She had seen King Edward at his request, had done all she could, had left him in improved health. What had changed? Had he truly ordered her arrest? Remembering Brother Hugo's sly looks at Soutra and at Lanercost too, she recalled that he had been suspicious of her methods and had mentioned the punishment of witches. She shuddered.

Hugo must have some hand in this, but why? How was the king now? She had prepared nothing harmful.

Ducking her head in her folded arms, she felt fear rise like bile in her throat. She breathed deep, clenched her fists. She would summon the steel backbone that she had developed over these last years—she had grown from the innocent, idealistic girl who had lost her young knight and the life she wanted, grown through widowhood and traveling, a woman alone, a female among males. She was accustomed to challenge. Here was another. She could wait this out.

POISONED KING EDWARD, had she? Well done, lass.

Aedan MacDuff lay still, recalling the guards' comments when they brought the girl to his cell. Wrapped in the plaid, his eyes closed, he listened to the soft sounds across from him in the stone chamber. When the guards brought the lass here he woke, but stayed silent, knowing it was the best course. She had shuffled around a bit, sat with a whoosh of skirts, and quieted.

Hearing sniffling now, he found it hard to listen to a lass cry and do nothing.

He had also heard the guards mention that she would be held here temporarily until they were ready to move her to Berwick. Lord knows what might happen to her there, especially if King

Edward had taken ill again. The king was none too healthy, Aedan knew; some said he was dying.

But if the girl had tried to poison Edward, that was trouble indeed—serious charges, a trial, perhaps hanging. Even burning, if she was accused of witchcraft, as they might do in France. Attempting to kill a king was tantamount to treason.

He gave a loud snort and rolled slightly to peer at his cell-mate, his eyes obscured by a thick fall of hair. An arched and barred exterior window streamed afternoon light into the stone cell, mingled with torchlight through the slot in the door. Golden light flowed around her. He saw a slender young woman in dark blue, knees tucked, head down, shoulders shaking.

She wore a fine blue gown, a sleeveless gray over-gown, and a pale kerchief that covered dark hair that hung in a long braid down her back. A married woman? If so, where had her man been when she'd fallen into this kerfuffle? He also noticed she was neatly shaped with slender curves and graceful limbs.

But she could have a face like a sheep. Still, the sweet sight of her body fed his eyes and his sorry soul.

She sniffled again. The sound bothered him. Snoring again for good measure, he waited. She did not move. Her tousled, plaited hair was woven with yellow ribbons. A woman of privilege, veiled like a wife—what was she doing here?

No puzzle why he was here, though. A month had passed since they had hauled him to this place. Built like a bull, he had given as good as he got. But still, here he was, needing a bath, hating the food, tossing crumbs to the mice. And trying to appreciate the unexpected chance to rest, heal, think.

Someone had arranged this, and he would dearly like to know who, and why. Edward was not fool enough to punish a guardian of Scotland, and with luck, the English were not aware that he did work for Robert Bruce when he could. Instead, his crime was the treason of aiding in Bruce's crowning—and simply being born a MacDuff.

So here he was, and he was determined to find a way out

before they could transport him to Edinburgh, a plan he had overheard. There, he would be locked in a place he could not easily escape.

But he knew Yester Castle by its dark reputation, and since it was not a large fortress, he had figured out an escape route. Taken by English a few years back, Yester was situated on a broad hill above a loopy bend in the Hope Water not far from a village. The chamber where he lay and the girl sat sniffling was an underground storage room rather than a dungeon. The exterior barred window at ground level let in light and air and showed a grassy meadow where he sometimes saw boots marching past. The window in the cell door showed an underground corridor lit by torchlight, where guards often sat vigil playing dice or sharing ale.

Yester was a partial ruin after the English attack, and an old chapel, partly rubble now, perched in view across a meadow. Edward of England had put his bullying stamp all over Scotland. But assessing the ruins had given Aedan some ideas.

Nearly a month here had also given him time to grow stronger by pacing the cell, pushing against the walls, using his weight to build back his strength. Apparently, the English used this compact stone tower to park supplies, house a small group of soldiers, and keep temporary prisoners. Watching through the door or the window, he had seen guards and prisoners come and go and had overheard some of the orders.

But he had not seen a woman held here before. Just now, the two of them were the only prisoners.

She sniffled again, followed by a sorry little hiccup. Aedan opened a bleary eye. The jug of ale they had brought him earlier had been strong and bitter and he had been damned thirsty. But he had a head for strong drink like a little girl so had been sleeping off the resulting headache. Awake now, he felt clear enough to resume devising his plan to get free of this stone box.

But he could not leave a lass alone here. They'd called her a whore, but he had his doubts. His instincts about people were good when he was not working off the fog of a bad ale.

Footsteps, then the creak and snick of the latch as the door swung open. The girl looked up; he glimpsed a sweet, kind face. When a guard stepped into the cell, Aedan closed his eyes to feign sleep.

Straw rustled underfoot. "You! Whore! You are to be moved soon. Berwick, those are the orders. You will not be treated well there, I promise. Best enjoy your time here."

"Why am I here? You have no cause to keep me." Her voice was honey, Aedan thought. Warm, dark honey. Not the sticky purr of a whore, but the calm allure of a queen or the peaceful certainty of a saint. "I was betrayed. Nor should a woman be locked in with a criminal."

Aedan pouted, hearing that. But to be sure, the woman did not know him.

"Betrayed? That lug over there would say the same. But he won't pester you. He's sleeping off his cups."

"I must send a message to King Edward."

"The king you tried to poison? Hah! You might see him if they cart you from Berwick to Carlisle. You will be taken to Berwick on a charge of treason and an attempt to murder the king. Then they may cart you down to Carlisle for your trial and execution."

"Execution?" Her voice faltered. "But I did not harm Edward. He summoned me."

"All I know is the king took ill after you were there. They say you poisoned him."

"I never did," she whispered.

Aedan heard confusion and despair in her voice. She was no whore—but she must have brought something to the king, perhaps food or a curative. Word was King Edward was desperate for doctors, alchemists, astrologers, seers, and the like to help with his illness. Some would be quacks pressing remedies in hopes of reward. Whatever this woman had done, it had gone wrong.

He heard the shush of fabric as she stood. "If the king is that ill, I must see him. I need an escort to Lanercost. Who is in charge here?"

Steps crushed straw as the guard came closer. "You will have an escort to Berwick. That is all I know. First, I have something you need now. Come here—"

Aedan heard a grunt, a soft gasp and a muffled slap, an angry growl—

Enough. Throwing off the plaid, he surged to his feet.

THE HIGHLANDER ROSE from the shadows like a shaggy brown bull. With one hand, he pushed Rowena firmly aside and with the other grabbed the guard by his surcoat, picked him up, and hurled him against the wall. She heard the guard's metal helmet strike the stone wall like a bell, and the man slid down to dump on the floor, legs apart, head tilted back.

Stomping past her, the Scotsman bent and knocked the guard hard in the jaw. "That is for your manners," he growled. "You harmed, lady?"

Staring, Rowena collected her wits and knelt by the guard. "Is he hurt?"

"Does it matter? Did he harm you?"

"He did not. And you are a brute. But thank you," she added. Taking the unconscious guard's chin in one hand, she felt his jaw and lifted each eyelid to peer at his pupils. Then she stood, brushing straw from her skirt, and turned.

Hands fisted on his hips, booted feet spread, shoulders broad, the Highlander looked fearsome, a giant. A volume of brown hair and a riot of a beard obscured his face like a hedge. But his eyes were surprisingly gentle, his frown contrite.

"How is he?"

"He will live." She passed him to go to the door.

"Do not call another guard in here," he growled.

"I am just looking out." Standing on tiptoe, she looked through the small, barred opening in the door and saw an empty table and a flickering wall torch. She turned. "No one is there. He must have been alone."

"Saw his chance, the rat." He kicked the guard's boot.

"Leave him be."

"Soft-hearted damsels invite trouble," he muttered, and hunkered down to tug the man's helmet away. The guard's head, covered in a quilted cap, flopped to one side.

"Good, he will be more comfortable," she said.

"Soft heart," he repeated, and snatched the cap as well, pulling it over his head, earpieces dangling. Then he set the bowl-shaped helmet over it and crammed it down. A wealth of wild, waving brown hair fluffed out beneath.

"Tiny wee head," he grumbled.

Rowena felt a twinge of alarm as he slid the man's broadsword from its sheath. She feared he might lop off the guard's head then and there, but he thrust the handle toward her. "Hold this."

She gripped the hilt, blade point down, and watched as the Highlander divested the guard of the red woolen surcoat sewn with yellow lions rampant. He worked the surcoat free with a muttered curse. The fellow's arms, encased in chainmail, thunked down.

"What are you doing?" she asked.

"Escaping. You and me." He stood. "I will leave his armor. It would never fit."

"Escape?" she squeaked.

He removed the helmet, set it down, and pulled the surcoat over his head. "With this, we have a chance. Damn," he said, voice muffled, head covered, one arm through the wide opening of one sleeve, the other caught.

"If you keep pulling, it will rip." She set the broadsword down to go to his aid. "Stop stretching it. This is too tight. He is a smaller man than you."

"Most are. Make it fit. Do whatever women do to make things fit."

She tugged at the cloth until his arms popped through, then gave it an extra pull as she straightened it over his wide shoulders and chest. Then she stood back.

"What do you mean, escape?"

"I mean, I am getting out of here and you are coming with me."

"I am not leaving with you. I do not know you."

He jabbed a thumb toward the door. "Do you know them? You do not. They will take you to Berwick and show you the same courtesy that cretin did. And then you will wish you had fled with a stranger this sorry day."

"I will ask them to take me to the king."

"That is foolish."

"Why? I saw the king weeks ago. He will listen to me."

"Hah!" Picking up a wide leather belt, he strapped it over his hips. Rowena noticed the empty sheath looped there; they had taken his dagger. He wore a sporran attached to the leather belt he had fastened over tunic and trews. When he pulled the surcoat over that, the red cloth strained to cover bulky clothing and brawny man.

Fixing the guard's leather strap across his broad chest, he raised the sword and slid it behind him into the strap's sturdy back loops. "Good enough," he grunted. "I need a bigger sword."

"Sword or not, we could be caught as soon we step out of here. We could be hanged for this."

"I have been planning this escape. We will be fine."

"When were you making plans? You were sleeping off the drink."

"I was thinking and listening. Nor would I leave a woman alone here while I dance out disguised as a guard."

"Disguised? You are rather…noticeable." Truly, he was a beast with wild hair, a bushy beard, and a surcoat about to split across his broad shoulders.

"Let us pray they do not look closely. Come on." He reached for her arm.

"Wait." She slipped her hand into the embroidered purse on her leather belt and took out a small pair of scissors. "Less beard would change your appearance. You might look more like an Englishman."

"I do not care to look English." He stepped back as she brandished the scissors.

"Then go out as you are and see how far you get."

He gave a reluctant grunt and lifted his chin, tugging a handful of beard for her to clip. "Hurry. But leave some of it."

"You are too tall for me to do this properly. Kneel."

"God's bones, woman," he said as he knelt, his head, still in the quilted cap, now level with her shoulders. "Will you knight me next, and shall we have wine and sweetmeats? We have no time for this."

She took hold of his beard, pushing his hand aside to slice bit by bit through the beard. Russet, brown, and gold spiraled to the floor. "Are you a knight, sir?"

"I am."

"What are you called?"

His eyes were closed. "Mine is not a name to speak aloud in this place."

Puzzled, she paused to scrutinize her work; the beard was choppy but improved. A fine masculine face emerged with a strong, elegant structure: a lean jaw, squared chin, high-set cheekbones, and long, neatly shaped nose. His hair was a riot of long brown curls partly mashed under the cap; under thick dark brows and half-lowered eyelids, his eyes were hazel green. Peeking through the shorter beard, a dimple slotted at the corner of his pursed lips, a note of amused impatience. Propping his firm chin in one hand, she began to trim his mustache.

"Not the mustache," he mumbled through taut lips.

"I wish we had time to trim your hair." She brushed back the messy waves and curls spilling over his broad brow. A scar creased the side of his cheek, thin and pink, with faint dots from old stitches. She stopped, stared.

She knew that scar.

"We have no time, lass. Are you done?"

Could it be—what was the man's name at Holyoak, months ago? She could not think in the moment, on the edge of panic, with the Highlander pressing her to hurry. As he raised his hand, she smacked it away and snipped the beard to neaten it further.

"Enough!" He scowled, his mossy green eyes touched with gold. Beautiful, she thought. Months ago, she had hardly seen them open.

"That looks better." She fluffed his beard. He lowered her hand, his fingers gentle.

Muttering gruff thanks, he stood, took up the helmet, and jammed it over cap and curls. "Too small. Damn thing might pop off."

"Bend down." She reached up to smooth the thick chestnut curls bulging out from under the helmet, then tugged up the narrow collar of his shirt and tunic, lost under the ill-gotten surcoat. "Better."

"Now you." He took up his discarded plaid, shook it, held it out. "Put this on."

She wrinkled her nose. "I do not—"

"*Ach,* it is not that dirty! Hurry, now. They will look for a lass in a blue gown. I cannot wear the plaidie with this gear and will not leave it behind. My sister wove it and she would have my head if I lost it."

"I see." She realized she had decided to go with him. He swirled the plaid around her shoulders and draped its edge over her head. Then he cupped his hands on her shoulders and looked down at her.

"Listen, lass. Be careful, follow me, and say naught, aye?"

"But—"

"Hush. Once we are away, say whatever you please." He stepped and snatched up a length of rope from the straw. "Hold out your hands."

"What are you doing?" Rowena squeaked as he wrapped and

knotted the rope around her wrists.

"You are in my custody and I am your guard. Ah! Nearly forgot." He went to the unconscious guard, fiddled at the man's belt, and returned with a dagger, which he jammed into the empty sheath. "Come ahead—er, *come ahead, you*," he repeated in a graveled voice.

A nervous giggle escaped her. "You look like a festival mummer."

"*Ach*, she cuts me to the quick. And me thinking I look a handsome English devil." He took her upper arm through layers of plaid, cloak, and gown, his grip firm. Opening the door, he peered out, then guided her in front of him. "Act frightened."

"It is not an act," she murmured.

But the Highlander was like a wall, a shield, a fortress. She was glad of it, though his name eluded her.

CHAPTER SEVEN

I N THE DIM corridor, Aedan breathed in relief to see the area empty but for a table where an oil lamp burned; someone would return soon enough. Leading the girl around a corner, he held out a warning hand. Ahead, a half-open door showed a leaden gray sky indicating rain and twilight. The day had grown long while he had slept, saved a girl, flattened a sorry guard, and mucked about changing his gear. And the woman complicated things further with beard-trimming and pretty gray eyes to distract him. He had an escape plan but had not been ready to follow it. Well, nothing for it but to try.

"This way. Careful," he cautioned as they moved to the exit. The underground rooms and passages beneath the old tower, made of rough-hewn stone on an earthen floor, held boxes and sacks rather than prisoners. If he had found other captives, he would have released them for helpful chaos and Scots justice.

With empty rooms, the guards had no good reason to put the girl in his cell. They must have thought he would jump her for his pleasure and their entertainment. But they had the wrong man.

He motioned her ahead, pausing when he heard voices outside.

"What do we do now?" she whispered.

"Walk out boldly, guard and prisoner." He guided her to the open door. The fresh cool air felt like a luxury; he had hardly been outside for weeks. A breeze mingled the scents of grass, trees, smoke, and something delicious roasting, and he guessed that guards had gathered near an evening fire where their supper rotated on a spit.

Yester Tower was a small keep with a small number of guards and was easily negotiated, but the tower's size afforded few places to hide. Aedan knew he was recognizable due to his height and build, though his stolen helmet and surcoat gave him a chance. He knew that soldiers passed through here often, so he must gamble that he would be mistaken for a newly assigned man.

Stepping outside and down stone steps to an earthen spread, he saw smoke rising beyond a hillock and heard voices. The charred smell of roasting meat was so tantalizing that his stomach rumbled.

"What now?" the girl whispered.

"Hold," he murmured, keeping her behind him, a hand on her arm. She was so finely shaped that his fingers nearly wrapped around her arm; he eased his grip. Where the smoke rose, he glimpsed a cluster of helmets as the men waited for their dinner.

Hoping they were distracted by hunger and cooking chores, he eased forward with the girl, keeping watch as he went. With luck, no one would notice the two slipping away from the tower in the dusky light.

Nearby were a few outbuildings and a stable, but he knew taking a horse to ride away would invite more trouble. Across the meadow was the ruined chapel backed by woodland. He headed there with the girl as rain pattered over his ill-fitting helmet.

A guard was walking from the woodland toward the tower. Noticing Aedan and the girl, he stopped, raised a hand, called out. Aedan paused, standing in front of the girl, instinctively protective.

"Off to Berwick? Or will you two be doing something else?" The man chuckled.

Aedan bristled. "Berwick. Riding through the night. Orders," he said curtly.

"Where is John Harley? He went to get her."

"Did ye not see him run out?" Thinking fast, Aedan landed on a tale he had heard about Yester Tower. "Scared, he was."

"Scared of the big fellow in the cell?"

"Eh, that one would sleep through anything. Nah, it was the shrieks! This place is haunted. The locals talk of it. Have ye not heard the howling at night?"

"Haunted?" The man cast a wary glance at the tower. "The sound could be a fox."

"Could be. But they say this place was built by a wizard a hundred years ago with help from the de'il and his hobgoblins. They call it Goblin Hall." He shrugged.

"Goblins? A wizard? God's foot, I heard naught of that."

"If we knew, how many would stay here? Goblins built the foundation, they say. The underground chambers are cursed by the de'il, whose hobgoblins play games at night and in storms." Aedan glanced up. "Might rain hard tonight."

"Harley ran out, you say?"

"We all ran out and left the Highlander there. That old chapel is haunted worse than the tower, I hear."

The guard looked toward the chapel and shivered. "We only use this place for storage and to house prisoners briefly. We should all leave."

"Aye! Well, best get this chit to Berwick so they can lock her up there. Keep away until them spirits calm down after the storm. Hey, smells like supper is ready." He jabbed a thumb toward the fire, took the girl's arm, and deliberately headed for the stables as the guard turned to walk toward his supper.

"Goblins?" the girl asked.

"Some, they say. We will hope that tale keeps them away for a while." Aedan headed for the chapel ruin. "Move fast and keep close."

Loping ahead, a hand on her arm, he knew her tied wrists hampered her, yet she managed, skirts billowing. Rain fell in earnest as he tugged her toward the chapel. Despite broken walls and fallen stones, it would provide shelter briefly.

Ducking inside, pulling her with him, he shoved the half-burned door closed. A gap in the front wall looked out on the tower, stables, surrounding hills, and woodland. Aedan studied the lay of the land, judging their chances. Then he urged the girl toward the shadowed end of the chapel and seated her on a stack of fallen stones.

"Stay here. I will go watch."

He found a vantage point near the entrance where he could see the group by the fire. They tucked into supper, acting relaxed, helmets off, perhaps talking of haunted Yester now. He had told the truth, having heard tales of the place, yet never thought to be here.

Soon he returned to the girl. She held out her hands, still joined by rope.

"Sorry." Dropping to a knee, he worked the knots loose. She rubbed her wrists.

"Thank you. What now?" Her honeyed voice plunged through him; that alluring sound in another time and place could have taken his defenses down quick. But he was wary and guarded, his glance straying to the view beyond the broken walls.

"We wait. When they discover we have left, they will go in pursuit. For now, we are better off here."

"How long must we stay here?" Her eyes were gray-blue framed in black lashes. Wide, earnest, calm, keenly intelligent eyes.

"In a hurry? Where would you go?" He sat on a rough block of stone, tugged off the helmet, and shoved back the wild tangle of his hair.

"I want to go home, but I should return to Lanercost to see the king."

"That is no place for you if you attempted to poison him."

"I never did. King Edward knows I would never harm him."

"Your king is a madman, and you would be a madwoman to go to him. Either way, I will not take you there."

"You do not need to take me anywhere. I will go on my own. And he is not my king, he is my patient." In the rainy half-light, she was a beauty, her face a delicate oval, eyes the gray-blue of thunderclouds. Dark hair showed in ripples beneath the draped veil. She looked familiar in a misty way, as if he had seen her in a dream.

A memory stirred, slipped away. "Are you a healer, a wise-wife?"

"An herbal healer. Not a wife. And not very wise." She gave a rueful shrug.

"It is not wise to poison a king and not finish the job."

"I did not do that!" Her chin jutted out.

"But you *could* have done it. You have the knowledge."

"Anyone who works with herbs could. But I would not."

"Pity, seeing as it was Edward."

She flashed him a steely look.

What troubled him was not only the guards beyond and the risk of being discovered. Memories accosted him, swept in, faded out. The girl was familiar.

The chapel was a sad ruin, like Scotland's very faith collapsed. He sighed and glanced toward the guards by the fire. Leaning his elbows on his knees, entwining his fingers, he considered how to get out of here and to Fife, and what to do with the girl.

"If I cannot get to Lanercost," she said, as if she knew his thoughts, "I must get home to my family and friends."

"Stay away from Edward if you value your life. When it is full dark, we will head out. A few miles from here is a river, where we can hire a boat."

"A boat?" She scrunched her nose: a bonny little nose over a bonny mouth, full and lush, and those gray thundercloud eyes, deep and long-lashed, captivated him. He glanced away. Whoever she was, he must focus on getting them out of this place.

"A boat is often the fastest way around Scotland, as you no doubt know," he replied. "We will need to move fast. I am sorting out how and by which route."

"I suppose we should travel together for a bit. May I know your name?" Her eyes were keen on his. "You said it is no name to say aloud, but we can be quiet here."

"My name alone could hang me." He met her gaze.

"Is it so? I am Rowena," she offered. "Lady Rowena Keith."

"Keith." He frowned at the elusive memory. "Kin to the Marischal of Scotland?"

"He is my great-uncle. My father was another Robert Keith, lord of Kincraig."

The realization hit him like a rinse of ice water.

Lady, we were nearly betrothed once.

"Henry Keith's sister?" He leaned toward her.

"Do you know my brother?"

"A bit. Rowena is an unusual name." His thoughts tumbled. He was not ready to tell her what he suddenly recalled.

"My mother had a copy of *Historia Regum Britanniae*. Geoffrey of Monmouth. She saw the name there."

"I have read some Arthurian tales. As I recall, Rowena seduced Vortigern."

"I hope that was not her inspiration! Mama had a brother called Rowan. He died young, so my name served his memory. Will you give me your christened name?"

"Aedan. *Aodh*," he added. "Ancient god of sun and fire. The old Celts."

"The name suits you. Sir Aedan. I—we—" She shook her head, denying some inner thought. "Did you invent that tale of goblins and a wizard?"

"Real enough at Yester. We will be fine." He winked should she frighten easily.

"I am not afraid of wizards. Some called my great-grandfather a wizard, but he was a kind and clever man—a soothsayer, but not a wizard with a familiar."

"Your great-grandfather?" He tipped a brow.

"Thomas the Rhymer," she added.

Not surprised now that he knew who she was, he nodded. "I met him once when I was young. A fascinating gentleman." Her great-grandfather had been part of the betrothal discussion years ago. The old man had impressed him. Though Aedan had been more interested in knighthood than marriage then, he had bonded to the idea of the Keith girl and the promise. "They do say the Rhymer spent time with the faery ilk."

"There were stories, but he rarely spoke of it himself. He did say that when he was a young man, he met the queen of the faeries in Elfland, as he called it. He wrote a ballad about it that he sang for us. We loved his tales, though I sometimes wondered if they were true. I had a practical turn of mind even as a child."

"And now? Do you believe in such?"

"He gave each of us some things that he said were faery-blessed. Later I came to believe that there is some merit to it." She sounded cautious. "I studied folk medicine and such."

"I am blessed to be in such marvelous company." He smiled.

"He was marvelous, not me." She tilted her head. "May I see your arm?"

Puzzled by that, he extended his right arm. She tapped his left. When he lifted it, she pushed up his tunic sleeve to reveal part of the long scar that ran there.

"Does it hurt?" She touched it gently. A tingle shivered through him.

"I took the wound in a melee," he explained. "Loch Ryan, if you have heard of it. Battle on a sea loch. A terrible day for the Scots. An enemy sword caught me just where I braced my shield. Another blade caught my leg. I fell, and went overboard, and was hauled aboard another ship. We got away."

"I am so glad you survived."

Memories flashed like stars. Cool hands on his brow. A balm poured over the gashes, stinging and soothing. A voice, honey and wine. Gray eyes like clouds. He blinked.

"You," he said.

"Me," she murmured, peering at the angled scar.

"The healing woman at Holyoak." He stared at her, heart beating fast. Rowena Keith, the very lass he had nearly married, was the bonny young healer who had treated him at Holyoak. Not Robina, but Rowena—the woman he had ached to find.

"Your arm has healed nicely, though it is just three months."

"I am much better." Sometimes the bits of one's life could suddenly converge, he thought, stunned; it was the mystifying work of angels.

"A robust man can recover quickly. Though I was concerned you might not make it. You were so ill by the time you reached Holyoak."

"Whatever you did made the difference."

She watched him, her eyes solemn gray, slim fingers resting on his forearm. He remembered that kind gaze, that soothing touch; he recalled silk stitches like tiny thorn pricks, the cleansing sting of wine, the comfort of cool cloths and warm compresses. He had clung to the sound of her voice, her presence a balm when he feared he might die. She had been a blur in candlelight then. Now he saw her clearly and felt as if his heart opened, warmed. He was very glad to find her and thankful he could help her.

"You were with the monks at Holyoak. I took you for a nun at first."

"A widow. Sometimes I help in Holyoak's infirmary. When you came there, the abbot sent for my help. I am pleased to see you well again."

"Sometimes I feel aches in rain or cold, but that is all. I am in your debt."

"You are not. I am in your debt today for bringing me out of that tower. What is that sound?" She gasped at the blast of a ram's horn followed by shouts. Aedan went to the gap in the front wall to peer out. Rowena Keith followed.

"They are sounding the alarm," he said. "They must have gone to the cell, so they know we left. Wait. Be silent." He hunkered low, watching through a gap in the wall. He set a hand on her shoulder to pull her down too. She sat, curled small beside him.

Men ran to the stables and soon a few rode out. The sky was growing dark with the threat of rain. Aedan thought it was time to move to the shelter of the forest.

"They left without looking in the chapel," Rowena said.

"They were fool enough to believe we rode for Berwick. They did not count the horses." He chuckled. "We should go into the forest. Wait a bit to be sure they are gone."

She peered through the gap, then sighed. "I am a little hungry."

"As am I. What do you have besides scissors in that magic bag of yours?"

"Some dried plants, a couple of stones. A few coins."

"Plants and—stones?" he asked quickly. A memory sparked.

"Charm stones," she replied. "They are often used in healing in the Highlands."

"I have heard of such. Did you use one when you treated me?"

The memories crowded his mind. The girl singing a chant, hands graceful in the air. A crystal glinting in the darkness. Stones, crystals—the days of his injury and illness were blurred, memories out of reach, returning without warning.

Stones. Thomas. The Keiths—

The day the Rhymer visited Fife, Aedan had been fifteen, feeling privileged to be included at a meal with the venerable soothsayer. He and his brother Duncan, the sixteen-year-old earl—how he missed him, every memory tinted with that—had been wards of Bishop Lamberton of Saint Andrews, who had tutored the boys. Now they sat with Keith, the Rhymer, other Scottish earls and barons. Aedan heard a discussion of his possible marriage to a daughter of Keith of Kincraig, kin to the Rhymer. But Lamberton argued that Aedan should study for the priesthood.

Yet Aedan had been more intrigued by the leadership council

being formed, a group of earls and warlords who would govern Scotland as regents until a new king could be found. King Alexander's fatal fall from a horse on a rainy night had left Scotland in turmoil. Edward of England was already prowling and growling at the gate, and something had to be done. Until a solution was found, the council of guardians would oversee Scotland's laws and sovereignty.

The Guardians of the Realm of Scotland was such a heroic name. Aedan's brother would be a member as an earl, despite his age, and Aedan yearned to be part of it too.

Later, at supper, True Thomas spoke to him, an unexpected honor.

Thee, lad, the old man had said, *I see a warrior and a guardian in thee. One day thee will carry much on big shoulders. Guard the crown, the blade, and the crystal.*

"Sir?" He felt bewildered. "My brother will be a guardian of Scotland, not me. I want to be a knight, but the bishop thinks I should be a priest."

Listen now. Knight, not priest. Guard Scotland and its treasure. Look for the woman with the crystal stone. The Rhymer patted his shoulder and walked away.

Guarding a crown and a crystal sounded like something out of an Arthurian tale. Though he enjoyed such stories, Aedan had dismissed it as imagination.

Now he remembered the old Rhymer's unlikely message, his vivid blue eyes, his stirring aged voice. Years later, Aedan was given the responsibility to look after the Scottish regalia—yet how strange that Thomas hinted at it earlier.

And now the old man's great-granddaughter sat beside him. Aedan stared at her with sudden understanding. The blade, the crown—and the woman with the crystal. Could that have something to do with what the Rhymer had said? The coincidence was too much. He rubbed his brow, puzzled, hoping to remember more.

"Why did you mention stones?"

He cleared his throat. "Stones and plants and wee scissors, is that what you have? We need weapons and food. Perhaps they left some supper on the fire."

"That would be a risk. We can find water and berries in the woodland."

"A fine supper for a faery sprite like you, but this great troll needs more substance."

She laughed. Good. Levity would help if they were to get through this day with their heads still attached to their shoulders.

He watched the riders disappear into the distance, relieved, his thoughts churning. He might have married this lass once—yet she was the one who had saved him, and who reappeared today. He shook his head, unable to put it all together. Did she know about the betrothal, being so young then?

"Lady, there is something you should know. You might not recall it. You were very young."

She tilted her head in a way that he was coming to know—curious, keen, her thoughts keeping pace with his. "Do you mean our near betrothal, Aedan MacDuff?"

"So you remember."

"I knew a match was discussed when I was young. My brother heard your name at Holyoak and reminded me. He thinks highly of you."

"I like him. Our paths have crossed. I liked your father too, and the Rhymer as well. They favored the union, but the Bishop of Saint Andrews objected. That was that."

She gave him a sidelong glance. "Papa and Grandda both approved of you."

"If you must throw in your lot with a rogue, at least he is a known rogue."

"A rogue who owes me his good behavior."

He huffed. "He does indeed. We have something in common, which should make the journey more pleasant for you."

"I hope the unpleasant part is over." She shivered and glanced at Yester.

"I agree." He peered through a gap in the wall. "They are gone. We can leave."

"Should we take horses from the stable?"

"I would rather hang for treason than horse thieving. The river is not far, though we might be seen walking in the open." He picked up the helmet. "I will look like an English soldier. But you—" He scrutinized her. "Take that gown off."

"What?" She set a hand to her chest.

"I may look a beast, but I am not that sort. Take off your gown and turn it inside out. I see another color there."

"This?" She flipped the gown's hem to show the underside, a lining of unbleached flax linen in a pale earthy color.

"Aye, wear it that way. They will be looking for a woman in blue, not a gown the color of dirt or suchlike."

She gave him a sour look and stood. "Turn away," she said. He did, and heard the swish of cloth as she changed. "Will this do?"

He turned back. Now her gown was a drab color, with blue seams and blue hems. She had tugged her gray surcoat over it and buckled her narrow belt, looping the embroidered bag there. The low-slung belt emphasized the graceful swell of her hips, and the gray overdress had long side openings that showed how neatly the pale gown fitted the lush curves of breast, waist, hip.

"Gates of hell," he said.

"What?" She looked up.

He flushed, wishing he had not said that aloud. "The gates of hell, some call the openings in the lady's surcoat that show the gown and the—woman beneath."

"Then look away," she said crisply, smoothing her garments.

"Turn your cloak to the outside too. That darker plaid is good. Wear my plaid over it too." He draped it over her shoulders once she swirled the cloak inside out. "The kerchief is good. Is it earned, or do you wear it for protection as an unmarried lady?"

"Earned," she answered, shrugging into the layered plaids.

"You said you are widowed?" He said it too bluntly, and suddenly wondered why he had not married the Keith girl years ago. He had wanted it to happen. Recalling that Rowena had been about five when their betrothal was abandoned, she would be perhaps twenty-seven now, while he was thirty-six.

"My husband was lost at the siege of Stirling Castle," she explained. "Captured and taken out in ropes." She held up her tied wrists.

"I am sorry I put those on you. Was he sent back into the castle?" he asked quietly, knowing the rest—one of Edward Longshank's worst cruelties toward the Scots.

"Aye. Edward ordered the Scottish prisoners back inside so he could use his new siege machine, his War Wolf, on the walls. My husband was killed."

He sucked in a breath. "I understand all too well, for I lost my wife with the birth of our son five years back." He did not share that readily, but felt comfortable giving it to her. But he wondered why a widow of good family had not remarried, as so often happened. Her healing work, perhaps. She was dedicated, he knew that.

"That must have been hard," she said, and he nodded. "John and I were married only a few weeks. And after he died—I lost the child that had just begun."

His heart surged. "Lady—"

"So I earned this veil. And it suits when I travel. Do you think they will be back soon?" she rushed on, looking through the gap.

"I hope not, but we should get away." From the first, he had felt an urge to protect her, but that intensified with the bond he now felt. Fate had brought him together with the girl he had so wanted to find, who had captured his heart. He would honor that.

But he was not sentimental or foolish enough to reveal that to her. If what he felt growing within him, heart and soul, was simply gratitude rather than infatuation—or love, if he could allow it—he could repay her by keeping her safe.

Yet he felt again the bewildering sense that angels were playing about, moving bits of his life around like pieces on a chessboard, and he, ignorant of the game. He was a pawn, a foot soldier jumping here or there to defend the queen—this lass.

"Come ahead," he said. "The soldiers will look for a big man in plaid or a stolen red surcoat, and a woman in a blue gown and cloak. They will not be looking for a wren-colored wee wifey."

"A what?" She blinked.

"I mean—you have a good guise," he stammered.

"Wee wifey, is it." She ducked her head to remove the veil, a length of pale gauzy linen. Aedan watched, baffled, as she twisted her long braids deftly around her head and secured them in place with pins pulled from somewhere. Then she wrapped the linen to cover her head, tossed the tail across her breast and over one shoulder, and gave him a beatific smile. "Better?"

Lord, aye. She was lovely, the veil a graceful halo around her face. Something tugged within his heart. "Good, then. Come on."

She followed as he stepped through a hole in the wall to walk quickly into the forest. "What if we are stopped?"

"With this English gear, I look like any English knight. And you—" He tilted his head. What a beauty, vibrant even in drab colors. He could not quite think.

"Not your prisoner. Another guard could claim custody. Not a wee wren-colored wifey either."

"Fair enough. The knight's bonny Highland bride, will that do? *A bheil Gàidhlig agad?* Do you speak Gaelic?" He translated in case she did not.

"*Beagan.*" A little.

"We will chance it. Come on."

He offered a supporting hand as she stepped over a fallen sapling. As she waded through ferns into the forest, her skirts swung in such a fetching way that he had to look away. Watching for pursuers was a better use of his attention.

CHAPTER EIGHT

AEDAN MACDUFF! WALKING beside him, Rowena felt stunned to have encountered him just when she needed help most. That blessing of luck was the work of angels, she had always been told. Whatever brought them together, she was glad to see him healed and strong. But she wondered what crime had put him in Yester's makeshift dungeon.

And she was pleased that he remembered the betrothal; it had meant something to him. The strongest bond, though, had formed at Holyoak, when she had cared for him—and began to care about him. The feeling went deep.

And she had to warn him about Edward's threats against his son and his castle, but this moment was not the time. MacDuff wanted to get them away from Yester and any pursuers. But it was good and gratifying to know that long ago, her father and great-grandfather had approved the lad—not the man—as her husband. She did not truly know him, but had begun to trust him. And her best choice was to go with him.

They walked through the shadowy woodland fast and silent, and came to a burn burbling over rocks. Kneeling, they scooped water into cupped hands, drinking deeply. Then they followed a rough path to emerge onto a green moorland under a wide sky where a pale moon floated in a lavender sky. In that eerie half-light, she saw an earthen road, the clustered rooftops of a village, and a river's silvery ribbon.

"The River Tyne," MacDuff said. "It will take us east. Wait," he said, moving her behind him. "Riders."

A group of horsemen came along the road a fair distance from where they stood. Aedan MacDuff guided her toward the shelter of a hawthorn tree, twisted and flowering. There, Rowena peered through the white-flowered branches. "English soldiers?"

"Aye, likely heading back to Yester Tower."

She waited with him in the shadow of the blossoming hawthorn. When the riders were out of sight, she looked up.

"Are they looking for us?"

"We surely gave them reason."

"Why were they holding you there, sir?"

"Treason and such. Others would call it loyalty." He glanced around as he spoke. "They may search for us together or separately, going to your castle, mine too. Edward is relentless and expects the same from his men."

She needed to tell MacDuff of the royal orders she had overheard. Her nature was to be careful and think before leaping; but if the need was urgent, as with healing duties, she acted quickly. Soon she would tell him what she knew, but MacDuff's urgency hinted he already suspected.

"Wherever they go," he continued, "they will ask about a woman who goes about healing people."

She bristled. "I am not a mystic. I do not go about just— healing people."

"Well, clearly not the king," he drawled.

"He was improved when I left him, I swear it."

"I believe you, I do. But why were you at Lanercost? Are you an English sympathizer? Should I worry?" He gave her a wry smile.

"I am not for the English. I am accused of treason too. What was your treason?"

"Various. And treason is attached to the name."

"Because the MacDuffs—"

His hand clapped over her mouth. "Do not say it."

"Mmph," she said. He lowered his hand. "I just wondered if you are kin to the earl of Fife and the captured countess—"

His big fingers covered her mouth again, firm yet gentle. He let go. "Just keep the name to yourself."

"I only wondered why you are hurrying to Fife."

"A man wants to go home, aye. Do they know your name, your home, your kin?"

"They do," she realized with dismay. "My brother was with me at Lanercost. He serves as deputy sheriff in Selkirk, but that is no guarantee of protection."

"Not from Edward. Home is Kincraig? It is a good distance from here, to be sure. Ah, they are gone."

They left the shelter of the hawthorn to walk toward the village and river. She understood why he had to reach Fife, yet she needed to go the opposite direction to Kincraig to be with her family should soldiers arrive to fulfill Edward's demands.

"Sir, I can go my way while you go yours. They may forget about us at Yester."

"They will not risk Edward's wrath. Nor should you head out on your own. Stay with me and stay safe. You poisoned a king and I helped the Scottish king. We will rank high on Edward's list of enemies."

"But I did not poison the king."

"I believe you. But someone out there thinks differently." As his long steps swallowed the distance, she hurried to keep pace. When they neared the village, she saw a dirt track that split in two directions. Aedan MacDuff took the branch toward the water, a mile or more away.

"The village—can we stop there? I do not want to go to the river. I can hire a horse in the village and ride home."

"Soldiers would be on your tail soon, and then what?"

"They might take the river instead and follow you to Fife."

He huffed. "The river does not go to Fife. Have you no map in your head?"

"I have never been to Fife."

"You will like it. Hurry. We may not find a boat if it is too dark."

She dug in her heels. "Why take the river if it does not go to Fife?"

"The river goes to the sea. The sea takes us to Fife."

"Sail on the sea?" she squeaked.

"If we value our heads, we cannot linger here or ride to Kincraig."

She fared poorly on the water and avoided water travel, but did not want to admit that weakness to this very determined man. He barreled along toward the river. When she stumbled keeping up, he braced her and continued in grim silence.

"I do not like boats," she finally said.

"That may be, but boats will take us to freedom. Hurry."

She could not go any faster. Breathless, thirsty, tired, she stopped short. "You want what you want," she said. "And I want what I want."

"I see that," he said. "And I promise to take you to Kincraig. Later."

She felt frustrated and confused. "With all your clever tongue, how do I know your promise is good?" The words were out before she knew it.

He whirled. "Lady, I am a man who keeps his word unto death," he said low, fierce. "And I am the man keeping your bonny wee neck safe. Trust my promises or not, that is the truth of it."

His gaze was intense, far deeper than his clever tongue would imply. His promise was surely as strong as his will, she realized as remorse washed through her. "I spoke too quickly. I apologize."

"Ah," he said, as if at a loss for words.

She sighed. "It might be unwise to go on my own. I only know Kincraig is well west of here."

"Just so." He sounded gruff.

She needed his help to get to Kincraig, but he needed to go to Fife first. She knew that, aware of Edward's orders. "Fine," she said. "We will go to Fife first. Then Kincraig."

"So be it. I see a boatman on the quay. Come on."

They walked down a slope toward the river bank. MacDuff headed toward a stone quay, Rowena in tow. She glanced over her shoulder toward the village.

"Is that an inn?" She pointed toward the village street and a two-story house with a painted sign. Horses were tied to posts in the kailyard. "I could stay there while you sail to Fife. I have enough coin to rent a room. Then you need not bother with me."

"You are persistent, I give you that. But you are no bother, and this region is crawling with English. I will not leave a lady alone in an inn by the riverside, let alone a lady hunted by Edward's thugs."

"We could have a meal there," she said. Anything to avoid getting on a boat.

"Rowena Keith," he said, turning. "What is it about boats, hey?"

She frowned, looked away. "Being on water makes me feel ill."

"It will be a barge here. Not much."

"I nearly drowned once," she said in a rush. "In a loch, in a storm. I fell off a boat. My father jumped in and got me. But—it was terrifying." She shrugged. "So I do not enjoy being on the water."

"I understand." He gazed at her, looked away, sighed. "We could use some food."

"At the inn, aye."

"But we must travel by water, lass, to lose those guards. First let me secure passage on the river. Then we might pick up pies. You will be fine. I promise." He smiled, reached out, cupped her shoulder.

She felt her lip quivering at his quiet kindness. "Promise."

He beckoned, and she walked with him. The quay was not busy, just a few men milling about. Further up the river, she saw a barge heading east toward the sea under the gathering twilight.

She held back by instinct, and he turned.

"We will go together to Fife and then Kincraig. We will put our trust in each other, aye?"

She sighed, preferring solid land under her feet. But he was right. Trust and togetherness were necessary now. "Aye."

He took her hand and strode toward the quay, where a man working knots in ropes attached to a post looked up. "Oy, sir! My wife and I are headed to Edinburgh and would ride the river part of the way. Have you a boat ready?"

"Edinburgh?" Rowena asked, confused, wondering what he had in mind now.

"Grizel, hush," Aedan said from the corner of his mouth.

"It is dark for sailing east now." The man looked at Aedan's helmet and red surcoat, then at Rowena in her drab garments. "English knight, sir? You talk like a Scot."

"All sorts serve the king. My bride and I would travel east by the river." MacDuff set a firm hand on her shoulder.

"The barge is out now and will not return until late. Poling the river in darkness costs more, unless you have the fee. Best return early in the morning."

"We will be here first light." MacDuff thanked him and drew Rowena away with him. "Listen now," he said as they walked away. "I know you need to go to Kincraig, but you should know that there is something in Fife that cannot wait if men are on my tail. We shall toss a coin to decide the matter once and for all, aye?" He showed a silver coin in his palm. "Do you play chance games? I make most of my decisions that way."

"You do not," she said, giving him a wry look. "Half what you say is in jest, though you are cannier than you let on."

"Am I?" He grinned and flipped the coin. "Heads! I win. East it is. After that, we go to Kincraig. I keep a promise," he reminded her. "Besides, best you stay with me. I know your crime." He tipped a brow.

"And I know your name," she replied in a saucy tone, feeling relieved that they need not sail immediately.

"It is a worrisome detail," he groused. "Are you hungry? To the inn, then. We will have to stay the night there."

Her heart quailed a bit. "What if the guards go there?"

"Ah. True." He frowned, then nodded. "Come this way." She followed him toward a dense crescent of woodland behind the inn. "I should change out of this English gear. If anyone asks the boatman, he saw only an English knight and a bonny lass."

"I thought Grizel was plain."

"Not to me." He walked toward a cluster of beeches behind the inn and stopped beneath the wide spread of an enormous beech. Stepping behind it, he took off the helmet and quilted cap, set them down, and began to struggle out of the surcoat.

"Let me." She reached up to help pull the surcoat away. He straightened his brown tunic and trews, then fastened the belt around his hips, settled the sporran, and took the plaid Rowena handed him. Draping it over his left shoulder, he tucked the front part in his belt and took a broad brooch from the sporran to fix it on his shoulder. He looked a very fine Highlander, she thought, admiring him.

She glanced at the discarded helmet and surcoat. "Shall we fetch those later?"

"They might be found." He snatched them up, then gave her a quizzical look. "Here. You take them." He held them out.

"You want me to carry them?"

"In a way. Let me think." He wrapped the surcoat around the helmet and held the bundle out again. "Aye. Wear these under your gown."

"You are mad!"

"What better disguise than a woman with child when they seek a slender lady?"

"Wear it yourself and have a plump belly from too much beer."

"Aw, and who would defend you if needed? Not a fellow overblown with beer. Take it. Please," he added.

She took the bundle and turned away, wondering quite how

to do this. Lifting her gray over-gown and the front hem of her reversed blue gown, she crammed the heavy wrapped object against her torso over her linen shift. Standing with shift, stockings, and boots exposed, she struggled to hold it close while tying the red surcoat around her. She looked over her shoulder. "Could you help tie this? But do not look."

Then she felt his hands at her lower back, felt him tug at the surcoat, taking some of the bulk and weight of the helmet. "How am I supposed to do this without looking?"

"Look, then, and fasten it snug if you can."

He pulled the cloth tight, then reached around to tuck the ends of the surcoat around her to make a sling for the helmet. As he worked, his arms came around her and she leaned back against his chest. His hands felt warm and deft at her waist and over her abdomen, tucking and snugging. A heated thrill poured through her, and she caught her breath. "Oh!"

"There." He stood back, hands on her shoulders, then away. "Is it too tight?"

"It is good." Dropping the gown and over-gown, smoothing the layers over her false belly, she felt a hot blush fill her cheeks. She turned, patting her rounded torso, arching a bit with the weight of it. "How is this?"

He blinked. "The very Madonna. I will treat her with reverence."

"You could just stop hauling her about." She smiled, pleased by the look of awe as he gazed at her.

"As you wish, my lady." His eyes twinkled.

She felt a wash of gratitude that Aedan MacDuff was proving such a steady companion. Her pragmatic nature needed to know what to expect, needed to feel on solid ground. MacDuff was quick and decisive where she was careful and deliberate, and yet she found this impulsive playacting rather enjoyable.

"I am a Highland farmer, traveling home with his bonny wee wife who is *enceinte*."

"Does the Highland farmer speak French?" she asked with a

laugh, then picked up her blue cloak and flipped it so the dark plaid lining showed outermost.

"Ready, my lady? Gentle Grizel?"

She walked in a careful circle, testing the uncomfortable burden of helmet and surcoat, supporting it with her hands. "I fear this thing will fall out."

"Thing! Your child, madam. He looks secure. And convincing."

Rowena could not help but chuckle. "You are a lunatic!"

He grinned. "Needs must, lass. To the inn."

Rowena paused, knowing she must tell him what she knew before they went further. What Edward had declared felt like a greater burden than the steel helm.

"Grizel?" He gave her a playful smile and extended an arm toward the inn.

She sighed. She was intrigued by his amiable nature, mixed with stubbornness and strength. Beneath that easygoing surface lay deep courage and an iron will beyond the norm. He was a warrior, fierce, loyal, determined, a man who cared deeply about home and family—yet he had a jester side too.

That ability to laugh in the face of adversity gave him more power somehow. He made her smile, even laugh when she could be too serious. He had a way of staying buoyant, even though he had endured great troubles. Humor, she realized, was his rare strength. She felt increasingly drawn to him, like a lodestone seeking its match as well as its opposite.

She was loath to pile more trouble on his shoulders, but it was time. "Aedan MacDuff, I must tell you something."

"What, Kincraig is that way? My lady keeps telling me so."

"Something else." The weight of the helmet pulled on her lower back, and she leaned against a tree to ease it. "At Lanercost, I overheard a discussion about you."

He folded his arms as if in defense. "Who spoke of me?"

"King Edward was angered about something you did. I heard him order your arrest and the forfeiture of your castle in Fife."

"I know. I was arrested—and now I am out. We are out. As for the castle, Edward would forfeit every Scottish property if he could, to the ruin and decimation of this land. If he sends men to Castle Black, I have soldiers installed and pray their number is enough. That is one reason I mean to get there soon as I can. Is there more?"

"I heard him order one of his knights to take your son into custody."

He stilled, his face going pale, mouth tightening. "Go on."

"At first he wanted the child placed in a dungeon, but another argued against it, saying the boy was small. Edward said for him to just give the child milk. Then he relented and ordered the boy to be taken and housed with the young Earl of Fife. His cousin, is it?"

Aedan stared at her, silent, cold, waiting.

"The knight Edward gave orders to was Sir Malise Comyn. Do you know him?"

"*Ach!* That bastard. Pardon me. He had something to do with shoving me in Yester. I saw his name on the arrest warrant, though he was not there when they took me down. But the rest of what you say—my son, my property—that is news, and I thank you for it."

"What will you do?"

"Get to Fife quickly to make my kin secure. I had that in mind already."

"I could stay here if it would help you travel faster."

He let out a breath and stared up at the tree cover in the purple dusk. "I want you with me. And I am sorry you have been dragged into this."

"I do not mind. I only regret bringing you such sorry news."

"It is good that you overheard that, because now I know what they might do. All will be well, hey. Come ahead." He beckoned, smiling, but it did not reach his eyes. The mask was back, his troubles his own.

They walked toward the tavern and he opened the door to

allow her to enter first. "Thank you, Hamish," she said as she passed.

"I like it," he murmured, then raised his voice. "Grizel, my sweetling, we will find rest and respite here on our journey home." He stepped inside after her.

A woman came toward them wiping her hands on a cloth. "Sir, lady! Welcome!"

"Good dame, my wife and I require a meal and a room. My dear, you cannot sleep another night under the stars in that condition."

She sighed. "Are there two beds?"

"I know how uncomfortable you must feel, madam. I have had three babes myself. The room has one bed. Tell your brawny man to sleep on the floor. Be seated now, and I will see that your chamber is warmed. Extra for a bath?" she went on as Aedan MacDuff shook his head.

"Could we have a basin of hot water, soap, and linens?" Rowena asked.

"Aye. We have good Spanish soap made with almond oil and roses. It costs extra."

"That is fine," Aedan said, as the woman guided them to a table.

"I hope you are not traveling far, madam. You are carrying out front. A robust boy is my guess."

"Surely it is male." Rowena gave MacDuff a wry glance as he drew out a bench.

"Are you daft, man?" the woman snapped. "Not the bench! Fetch that chair with the sturdy back for your lady! Hurry!"

CHAPTER NINE

AEDAN ATE HUNGRILY of a hot meat pie, thick with carrots, onion, and lamb, followed by cheese and wheat bread with salty butter. He noticed with mild surprise that Rowena Keith had a good appetite for a small woman, unless she was acting the role of expectant mother. The lass adapted well, he would give her that, especially with all he had asked from her so far.

And more to come, he thought, glancing out the window to keep a wary eye for anyone on the road or approaching the inn. At the first hint of danger, he would whisk Rowena up to the hired chamber quick as could be.

The innkeeper's wife returned to their table with a tray holding jugs and cups.

"Ale or wine? We have water too if you really want it." She set the tray down.

"No ale," Aedan said quickly. "Wine if it is well watered—for my lady."

"Is the water fresh from a stream, or boiled?" Rowena asked.

"My wife is in a delicate state," Aedan explained.

"We fetch water from the stream that runs behind the inn, not from the river." She set down the tray, poured clear water into the wine jug, and shook it. "Your chamber is ready. When you pay, I will give you the key." She picked up the tray and left.

"Delicate state?" Rowena looked at him.

"Boiled water?"

"Water near a town or river may be dirty. Clean water is better for health."

"Sensible enough. Do you prefer water, or will you have wine?"

"A little wine. Let me pour. Ah, it is dark red even watered. Good grapes." She poured the glistening liquid into one cup. He held up a hand.

"Just water for me, lass." She sent him an odd look, poured a cup of water, and slid it toward him. "I drink very little wine or ale," he explained.

"Some have a weakness for strong drink. If so, I applaud you for avoiding it."

"Not that. It gives me the headache," he muttered. He rarely mentioned the weakness, but felt at ease with Rowena. "Takes very little. Sometimes just a few sips. I need my head clear, hey?"

She nodded, sipped wine, nibbled a bit of the small pie on the wooden trencher. Then she glanced at him curiously. "How long were you held at Yester?"

"About a month."

"Surely they gave you wine or ale often."

"Watery stuff, bitter and awful. Enough about that." He grabbed a chunk of bread, dragged it through the butter, and took a bite. "Good bread. We are close enough to the English border here to get wheat bread."

She tore off a small piece and buttered it with a spoon. "It is rare in the north." When she popped the still-warm piece in her mouth and gave a little groan of pleasure, Aedan wished suddenly she did not love it quite so much.

"It does not grow well in northern Scotland, where the soil is loamy with peat and too rocky. We have some better success in Fife. But the English have cut off imports and supplies to Scotland where they can, so bread is even harder to get."

"Sassenachs can keep their wheat. Oatcakes and bannocks are good fare, so we do not miss bread in the Highlands. Your castle in Fife, is it—"

"Hush." He glanced around. "An easy reach tomorrow, I hope. With luck we can shake off any who follow. Later we will go where you wish to go."

"Aye, dear Hamish," she said.

He smiled a little, enjoying the pleasant wee game. Looking past her through the window, where pewter-colored clouds swept a storm along, he saw riders on the road. "We should go up now." He stood and brought her to her feet. "Careful, Grizel dear."

She cupped a hand beneath the burden she carried under her gown, set the other hand to her back, and took a few waddling steps. Aedan felt a quick sense of how much he owed this lass, not the least for her willing ruse here.

As they approached the stairs, Aedan turned to the innkeeper's wife, standing nearby. "Good dame," he said, and handed the woman more coins than required. "No one disturbs us, aye? My wife needs her rest."

As he spoke, the inn's door blew open, and three men in chainmail stepped inside, damp winds billowing their cloaks. Aedan turned away and urged the Keith lass upward quickly. Realizing that the helmet was tilting her off balance, he set a hand to her back. Behind him, he heard the men talking but could not make out what they said.

"Let me be, Hamish MacDonald. You will trip me up on these steps!" Rowena said, loud enough to be heard.

"What you will, Grizel, my bluebell," he said, smiling.

"Bluebells are poisonous," she muttered.

"I know, my dear."

ROWENA SMOOTHED THE blankets over the narrow, sagging bed, patted the pillows, and sat, rubbing her lower back, glad to be rid of the helmet and surcoat that she had wriggled out of and dumped on the bed. She looked up to see Aedan MacDuff tilting a brow at the discarded things.

"You will need to stuff that under your gown again if someone comes here."

"I trust Hamish will guard against visitors."

"He will. Did you have to make him a MacDonald, then?"

"Friends of English, some of them. He could not be Hamish MacDuff."

"Indeed." He drew the sword from the scabbard at his back and sat, the leather stool all but disappearing beneath him. Then he pushed long fingers through his hair and beard, a thoughtful, troubled gesture. A frown shadowed his hazel green eyes.

Hearing thunder and a distant crack of lightning, Rowena went to the room's small square window and opened the wooden shutters while rain pattered against the building. "Are we safe here?"

"From thunder and rain? Most likely." His frown was distracted.

"From the guards under our feet?"

"I think so." He rose, took a dry reed from a batch, bent to light it from the squat iron brazier where flames crackled, and lit two tallow candles to brighten the room. Then he crossed to stand beside her at the window, resting a hand on the wall. A damp breeze blew inside, sifting his hair, wafting her veil.

"The air feels good after being confined for weeks," he said.

"I was only in that cell for a short time. I cannot imagine weeks there."

"Eh, I am used to dungeons. But when rain cleans the air, it feels very good." He drew a long breath, exhaled.

"Used to a dungeon? How often have you been in such a place?"

"Now and then. Are you worried you have thrown in your lot with a rogue?"

"Fairly sure I have," she said.

He huffed a little laugh and was quiet, a tower of a man, broad and brawny. The top of her head barely reached his shoulder. Yet she felt no threat in his presence, just his steadfast shelter. A sweet, curious thrill sank through her. She sensed a thread of danger too, dark and low, but never turned toward her.

"Aedan MacDuff," she murmured. "Why are they after you?"

"My name tells you that." Even quiet, his voice thrummed.

She frowned. "I know MacDuff is an ancient clan, and they say there are no Scottish kings without Clan Duff—the kingmakers." She looked up at him.

He drew a sharp breath and closed the shutter. "The rain will wet us both."

"We will not melt. Tell me. Are you one of the kingmakers?"

"Not me." He turned toward the table that held the basin, towels, soap. "We should wash before the water cools."

Sensing he was reluctant to discuss the MacDuffs, she nodded. "I will step outside until you are done." She turned for the door.

"Grizel, you forgot your wee condition. Let me go out first. You do not want to use that water after me."

She had to admit that. "Aye then. Just outside?"

"Nearby. I want to hear what those fellows are saying downstairs." He opened the door, then closed it behind him.

Stripping out of her gray over-gown and the blue gown with its plain lining, Rowena stood in her linen shift, shivering a bit. She dipped a cloth into water that was nicely warm, then used a dab of the soft soap that smelled of roses, ash, and almond oil. Rinsing and drying, she loosened her braid and combed her fingers through the damp, rippling length of her dark hair.

As she pulled the blue gown over her head, not keen to sleep in her shift as she otherwise might, she heard a light knocking. MacDuff opened the door and retreated with a murmured apology.

"Come in," she said, sliding the gown over her hips, the hem swirling around her bare feet. He entered, closed the door, and stood there looking awkward.

"Did you hear what the guards were saying?" she asked.

"Some." He watched as she worked fingers through the waves of her hair. "I did not hear much. A patrol, perhaps from

Yester. But they do not seem in a hurry. I smell roses," he said. "You—are glowing."

"Just the candlelight. And the soap smells of roses." She blushed. "If you want to wash up, I can wait outside."

"We cannot risk anyone seeing you. Turn away so I can clean up. Though I fear you have seen all of me already."

"Not *all*." She laughed softly, sat on the bed, and angled away. She heard the rustle of cloth, then splashes as his tall shadow danced over the limewashed wall. From the corner of her eye, she saw that he had stripped to the nude, his back to her, linen toweling wrapped inadequately around him. Candlelight gleamed over his broad form and long back, over smooth rippling muscle, and glinted gold in the mop of brown curling hair that touched his shoulders.

She glanced away, glanced back. Over years of helping injured men, she was accustomed to seeing the male body, though generally not all at once. And she had thought desire numbed, willed all but gone after her brief marriage and the shock of widowhood. In fact, she felt more like a nun than she would have admitted. Yet at the sight of this man, her body remembered suddenly, warmth spinning through her. She looked away again.

On the wall, MacDuff's shadow rubbed the cloth over his shoulders, his back, over swaying hips while he hummed under his breath. What she heard surprised her, for it sounded like a monk's chant. Even softened, his voice was harmonious, deep, and mellow. She breathed in, closed her eyes.

"Och, the feet," he grumbled, raising one foot, then the other, hopping about.

Rowena glanced over her shoulder. With cupped hands, Aedan MacDuff sluiced water over his hair and beard, then rubbed another cloth vigorously over his head, curls springing and spiraling. He was humming again, low and rich.

He glanced at her then, and she looked away. "Pardon," he said. "I was so happy to have a wash that I forgot myself."

"You have a nice voice."

He sniffed his arm. "I smell like roses. Stay turned away, lass, for decency, aye?"

She heard rustling cloth, then footsteps. Thinking he was done, she turned back as he began to drop his loose linen shirt over the trews drawn up and tied at the waist. His torso was long, lean, muscled, golden in the candle's glow and arrowed with a dusting of dark hair. Another thrill pulsed through her, warmer now, more insistent.

He poked his head out. "I should rinse the shirt. It does not smell like roses."

"You could. It should dry by morning." She thought then of the night to come, the small room, one bed, the two of them, and hours until dawn. Her breath quickened as she looked at his torso, the strength there, the breadth of his shoulders and chest, the hard toned torso, the taut waist—

She had promised to trust him. Now she needed to trust herself. These feelings were not usual to her. There was something about him—the humor, his easy manner, and now just the beauty of the man—that pulled her to him, that had her craving to be near him. Those feelings crowded her thoughts in this little room.

He shrugged off the shirt, dunked it, splashed about, then wrung it out. Draping the shirt near the brazier, he turned back. "Do you mind a shirtless man?"

"I am used to such," she said.

"Ah. The healing work." Taking up the plaid, he draped it loosely over his shoulders and sat on the low stool, leaning forward, arms on knees, hands clasped. "Tell me this, Rowena Keith. What happened at Soutra? Though that is how you came to Yester where we met again. Luck—and fate," he added with a curious glance.

Aware he teased her gently, she wrinkled her nose. "Fate," she said. "Could be, for truly I do not know how all this came about. I was invited to Soutra by a monk I met at Lanercost. I had no maid with me, for she took ill at the last minute. Sir Finley

Macnab—our seneschal at Kincraig—escorted me with a friend, Sir Gilchrist Seton. I felt sure I would be safe in a monastery—I always have been. They were to return in a week to bring me back to Kincraig, but Edward's men came for me before then. I thought perhaps King Edward had summoned me back to Lanercost. But I was taken to Yester."

He barely moved. "How did they treat you?"

"Well enough. Tied." She held up her wrists to show the pink marks still there.

"Beg pardon again, Lady Rowena."

She shook her head. "The ropes helped you get us out of there."

"Aye. When did you last see Edward?"

"I was there March into April, returned home, and then went to Soutra. And Yester. A knight in Edward's service met me there. Sir Malise Comyn."

He swore under his breath. "A busy fellow."

"He—wants something from my family," she said carefully. "He seemed unhappy about the accusations and said he would try to undo it if I—well, he said he would try to help. He was courteous and apologized. I almost believed him."

Aedan narrowed his eyes. "What did he really want?"

"You know his ways, then. Whatever it was, I might have had to pay it—but you were there. I thank the angels for that."

"Thank them from me as well."

"I had helped Sir Malise last winter when he was severely injured, and he claims he owes me his life. So when he was there at Yester, it felt like a betrayal."

"You are a trusting soul. Perhaps it is the healer in you."

She shrugged. "It could be. He fell and injured his back, and they brought him to Holyoak. A nun pushed him off a parapet," she added with an impish smile.

He laughed, shook his head. "I heard something about that. Likely he deserved it. So, you healed him, as you healed me."

"Not me. The body heals itself with the person's inner spirit and God's help. Those who know cures and treatments assist." She glanced down, aware that she had used the Rhymer's crystal for Malise, but only to dip in water, which she might have done for anyone, regardless of who they were or what they had done.

"I know you did more than simply assist me, lass." His gaze was steady. "But it might have been a fever dream. I thought you used a stone and sang a chant."

She looked away. So he remembered the faery stone. She had used it more completely to help Aedan MacDuff, much more than for Malise.

Yet Malise had told Edward, who wanted the stone. She sighed. "You healed well, being a strong, healthy man." She felt herself blush again. "You never answered my question, Sir Aedan."

"Question?" He folded his arms, leaned back, the plaid covering only part of his broad, gleaming torso. He watched her through hooded eyes. She wished she could read his thoughts, but he kept a barrier of humor, of ease, a man who seemed to take life lightly—while hiding a deeply serious nature. She was beginning to see it now.

"Kingmaker," she repeated. "Is that you?"

CHAPTER TEN

"NOT ME. MY nephew—and my niece, acting in her brother's place." He leaned forward, forearms on knees, hands clasped, damp curls framing his face. He was very handsome, she thought, distracted; his appeal was powerful in that small room. "Young Duncan is the earl of Fife. His father—my brother—was killed weeks before his birth. So he was born in England because his mother fled to her uncle—King Edward. Duncan is fifteen, Edward's ward, and has never set foot in Scotland."

"I did not know. Then his sister, Lady Isabella, is your niece."

"Aye, but raised in Scotland, a ward of the bishop of Saint Andrews. My brother was twenty-six when he was killed in an ambush, so I took on some responsibilities since his children were little."

"How awful to die so young," she said.

"The same happened with our father and our grandfather. Being close to the throne of Scotland brings privilege and danger, especially with the English conflict. Fathers who are killed young leave small sons in roles that require warriors."

"Sadly so. What responsibilities came to you?"

"A position that belongs to the Earl of Fife. Guardian of the Realm of Scotland."

She gasped. "The council of earls and bishops that govern Scotland?"

"Aye. My position is an interim, if young Duncan ever returns. Now that Bruce is king, the regent role of the guardians is changing." He shrugged. "And I have other duties. My brother's death and his heir's absence left much to manage in Fife. But I would do anything to help fill my brother's boots—and his son's too. I have never met my nephew, but he has my loyalty in Fife and Scotland. And my niece too. Isabella means a great deal to me. I care for her as if she were a daughter."

"Her captivity must be very distressing for you. I heard about her fate. But I did not realize—the rest of it, that Edward would take revenge on the MacDuffs because of their role in crowning Scottish kings." She shook her head in disbelief.

"Aye. It is infuriating. Heartbreaking." He looked away.

Her heart broke for him, for his kin, in that moment. Outside, thunder rumbled, shook the walls. She desperately wanted to reach out to him, but kept still.

"Then you were arrested for being a MacDuff."

"Anyone who shares the blood-right of crowning the king of Scots is a threat in King Edward's regard." He set his hands on his thighs, then stood. "And I have done deliberate treason in English eyes."

Rowena looked up. Standing over her, he seemed a giant, filling the room with presence, as if his head might touch the raftered ceiling, his wide, gleaming shoulders press the walls apart.

"What treason?" she asked.

"I am a MacDuff of Clan Duff," he said, low as thunder. "I brought Isabella to Scone to crown the new king. I made sure she arrived. I am proud of my so-called treason. But I failed her otherwise."

"You would never fail her." Rowena felt certain of that.

"Bruce sent his kinswomen up to Kildrummy, planning to send them to safety in Norway. I was with Bruce in the southwest. We were not there when the women were captured. I failed my niece."

Her heart surged at that, and she stood, wanting to go to him. Yet she sensed his pride would not accept it now. "Neither of you knew that would happen. I have heard that their release is being negotiated."

He snorted. "No time soon. I have been part of the discussions. Our latest offer was refused. Edward does not want diplomacy. He wants to twist the knife in Bruce's back and use these women as a warning to all Scots. Lady Mary is ill but holding on. Isabella, they say, is very weak. Even if Edward relents, she may not survive long enough to be released."

"Aedan—" His name came so naturally then. "I am so sorry. Surely there is hope. You have a hopeful nature."

"Sometimes. Not for this." He shoved a hand through his hair. "I cannot fail my clan or Fife. If you understand that, Rowena Keith, you understand me." Thunder rolled again beyond the window. She barely heard it, focused on him.

"I want to," she blurted. His words were stirring, his meaning rich with loyalty, honor, love for his kin. "You are doing all you can. All will be well."

"Hold that hope, lady." He sounded bitter.

A burst of wind and rain sounded then, and the shutters blew open. Startled, Rowena went to the window with Aedan, both grabbing the shutters. The window had no glass or parchment, so rain blew inside. They closed the shutters together, the wind pushing hard. Aedan pressed his hand over hers as they held them closed.

He looked down at her. "I am glad you are here."

"You needed help closing the shutters." She gave him a little teasing smile.

He laughed. "I seldom talk about these matters. But you already know some of my secrets. As my—nurse," he said softly.

"I know you like being the strong one and the jester. Then you need not show much of your true self, your thoughts. Feelings."

"Sometimes." He was silent, fingers over hers damp with

rain. The wind shoved, then quieted. He let go, and the shutters stayed closed. Leaning a shoulder against the window jamb, he gazed down at her. "I owe you another apology. You want to go home. I know that. But here we are. I am sorry to keep you from what you want."

What she wanted, she realized in the moment, was this: standing here with him, listening, learning, growing closer. She had a few friends, Brother Gideon and others, but she had learned to keep distant because of the need in her work to keep apart from pain and emotion. Her widowing had wounded her in deep ways, but she had moved on by clinging to a natural inclination for caution and solitude.

Aedan had shared something close and important to him. She wanted to do the same, felt trust and safety growing. "I need to go home to be with my family," she said. "King Edward has ordered us to relinquish some valuable things that belonged to Thomas the Rhymer. He will send men to Kincraig."

"You can hardly help them face down the king's men, lass."

"I have been away too long." She felt tears rise, sting, recede. "But you must reach Fife quickly. I understand that."

"And I would never send you off alone to wander about with no map in your head." His smile was rueful. "We have a bond, and I will honor it."

"Fugitives, aye."

"Cranky Edward is displeased with both of us. And there is the forgotten betrothal, and a healing with chants and stones and such." His voice pulsed through her.

She looked away. "You said the stones and chants were a dream."

"Did I?" He was silent, not the jester now, but the deeper man within, brilliant and thoughtful, guarding his secrets while discerning hers.

Rowena met his gaze, but as much as she wanted to know more about him, she could not open her guarded heart so easily. But she had to be honest with him. "I should tell you—I used a charm stone to help you at Holyoak."

"I thought so. I thank you for it. Do not fret, I am not a superstitious sort."

"It belonged to the Rhymer," she said, surprising herself at sharing so readily.

"Not the usual wee stone, then."

"Grandda gave it to me when I was studying with my aunt to learn about herbs and remedies, chants and charm stones too. Here, let me show you." She went to the bed, where she had left her embroidered purse, and took out the Rhymer's stone.

Her fingers trembled. This was her closest secret, yet she wanted—she needed somehow—to share it with him. She held it in her open palm for him to see. Highlights gleamed in crystal and silver, reflecting candlelight and a lightning flash.

"It is beautiful. Like a jewel." He stared at it, frowning deeply, his expression something other than simple admiration.

"It is more than that, so Grandda said. I do not understand all it does, but I have seen it help illness when nothing else did. Grandda told me to use it with caution, keep it secret, and protect it. He said I was—the guardian of this stone." She looked at him.

"Guardian," he repeated. He met her gaze, hazel-dark eyes somber, brows drawn. She handed him the stone and he cradled it, rolled it in his fingers. "A precious thing. You circled this over me, sang a chant. I thought it was a dream."

"I hope it helped."

"Something did. Thank you. It is a beautiful thing." He gave it back, his fingers cupping her palm. His touch sank through her like fire, emanating not from the stone but from some pull between them that was growing stronger. Standing close in the candlelight, hands joined over the polished crystal, she felt the draw of him deep in her body, in her belly, her knees.

"King Edward wants this. He ordered me to send it to him."

"How did he know about it?"

"Malise," she said, and explained quietly, quickly, about the gifts Thomas gave the Keith siblings, how they promised to keep them safe and secret, how Tamsin had been pursued for the Rhymer's written prophecies. It was a surprising relief to tell him. Sharing it with MacDuff, with his easy manner and sharp focus, made her feel calmer.

"I thought the stone might help Sir Malise, so I dipped it in water, but that was all I did with the stone in his case. He was so badly hurt."

"Not everyone would have helped such a scoundrel."

She watched the light flicker in the stone as if it had a soul. "But it is my work, and I am not a vindictive sort. I did not think he saw, but he must have, for he told Edward. I would never regret using the stone to help someone, but I fear I made a mistake with him."

"And now the king wants the stone for himself."

"Aye, this, and everything Thomas gave our family. Edward had a writ drawn up and told Malise to carry out the order. Malise mentioned it when I went to Yester. If we refuse to give up the legacy Thomas gave us, Edward will collect every item by force."

"So you want to warn your family."

"I was home earlier, and told them. But we thought Edward would not follow through on it, and Henry did not intend to obey the orders. But now that I know men will come for the things, I must go home to be there." Her voice wobbled.

"Soon, I promise." He traced his hand down her arm, a touch like soft lightning. She drew a breath. "What can I do beyond seeing you safely there?"

Hold me, listen to me, love me? She could not say what flashed through her thoughts. "There is more. Malise wanted to marry Tamsin, but she refused. Now—" She sighed. "Edward expects me to marry Malise. He thinks a widow should either become a nun, or be married off with no say about it."

"Too often it is the way. What did you answer?"

A hot blush rose from breast to brow. "Henry was there. He said—we were negotiating my next marriage, so I could not promise to another."

His brows shot high. "Ah! Sorry, I had not thought—are you betrothed again?"

"I am not. He meant the arrangement you and I nearly had once. It just came to him to say it, though he did not share your name," she added. "I told Malise I would never marry him. Ever."

He huffed a little laugh. "Good. The old betrothal will save you trouble, I hope."

"You do not mind?"

"Why should I mind?" He smiled. "I wanted to marry you once."

Surprised, she blinked. "You were a lad. We never met."

"But I liked the idea of joining the Keiths. You see, I—wanted to be part of a family. After our father's death, my brother and I did not see Mother often after she remarried and went to live in Perthshire. Because my brother and I were heirs of Fife, we stayed as wards of the Bishop of Saint Andrews. He disapproved of the betrothal. He intended me for the priesthood. Clergy in the family can be so useful," he drawled.

"But you became a knight."

"I studied theology at Saint Andrews, but swords and chivalry were more to my liking, and the bishop saw I was suited to it. So I rode off as a knight. I married, and we had a son, and I lost a wife." He looked away.

"I am sorry." She set a hand over her heart. "But you have a family."

"I do, with my sister and our aunt, who look after my wee son. It grows late, lass. We need sleep." Thunder boomed distantly as he spoke. "Bed or floor?"

She blinked. "What?"

"Bed for you, floor for me." He waved toward the bed. "That looks too small. I would break it, crash through the floor, and fall on the guards downstairs."

"One way to be rid of them."

He laughed and dropped his plaid on the floor, kneeling to spread the cloth, bare torso golden in candlelight as he moved.

He lay down, wrapped part of the plaid over himself, and folded his hands behind his head. Rowena settled on the bed, arranging the blanket, plumping two small pillows.

"Are you comfortable? Here." She tossed one of the pillows toward him.

"Oof," he said as it hit him in the face. The scar on his arm caught the light.

"Your arm looks good," she said, leaning to peer at the puckered scar. "I meant to look closer earlier, but there was no time."

"Fine. A bit stiff now and then." He flexed his arm, fisted his hand, sinew and muscle shifting beneath smooth skin. "The other scars are healed too. All is well."

"May I?" She moved to the floor, sitting like a child with crossed ankles, spreading her skirts, and leaned close as he tilted his face to the light. Brushing back his damp brown curls, she touched his cheek. "It looks good. Your leg is stronger too?"

He began to pull at the waist of his trews. "Here—"

"Oh, do not," she said with an embarrassed laugh.

"You have seen it. Here, just the side." He loosened the draw cords and pulled down the fabric to show part of his hip and upper leg, the plaid covering the rest. The skin of his thigh was pale and taut, the partial track of the scar pink and rippled.

Time flowed back to the night months ago when she'd sat with him, willing him to live, doing all she could. "It looks well-knit."

"Good work well done." He tugged up the trews. He was such an honest soul, she thought, with no arrogance and so at ease that she felt relaxed too. Yet they were all but strangers except for an oddly intimate bond in the past.

"Does it hurt? We walked a fair distance today."

"Aches a bit. Could be the rain." As if to punctuate his words, lightning crackled and rain pounded anew on the rickety shutters. "I owe you and your wee stone too."

As he tightened the waist cords, Rowena noticed the firm pattern of muscle flexing across his abdomen, and felt keenly aware of how close they sat, and of a sweet tension rising between them. She wanted to be even closer. The thought felt nicely wicked, unexpected, and compelling.

"What are you thinking?" he asked, eyes keen.

"Just—the coincidences between us. It feels as if we were meant to meet."

"Perhaps we were." His voice reverberated, low and delicious.

A tremor of anticipation swirled within her as she met his gaze. Suddenly the two candles flickered and went out, and she gasped. Aedan reached for her hand in the dark and she startled.

"Lady, I am no threat to you."

"I know." Her voice was strangely wobbly. "This day has been so strange. Thrown in a dungeon, running off with a stranger—"

"We are not strangers." He held her hand. "The troubles will pass, and you will soon be home, I promise."

"You, as well." She pressed his hand, needing that soothing touch, that subtle thrum of power and attraction spiraling through her.

"You are a lass to admire, I think. A practical one, steady and cautious, a lass who does not falter, who helps others. And who keeps her heart to herself."

"Sometimes," she said, echoing him earlier. "And you are steadier and more certain than me. Humble and kind, too, though you hide your feelings. And you make me laugh." She smiled, tentative in the darkness.

"A bargain. You heal me, I heal you—your seriousness. It is the least I can do." He brushed a tendril of hair from her brow.

Thunder sounded like boulders on the roof. She looked up. "The walls are shaking."

"We will not blow away. Though we might reach Fife faster that way." His thumb caressed her palm, sending shivers through her. Then he let go.

Her hand felt cool, lonely. What she needed she could not ask for—it was not in her nature. But she deeply wished for the comfort of an embrace. She was ever the one comforting another. Yet when he touched her, it stirred a yearning that grew. She wanted more than comfort and companionship. Widowed so young, romantic affection had been only a brief light in her life.

He touched her shoulder, stroked her arm. She felt it everywhere, an easing of tension, a building of awareness. Thunder rumbled. Water dripped at the window. She wished he would never release her. But he did, and sat back a little.

"When I was at Holyoak," he said, "I was not aware of much. Later I wanted to thank you, but you had gone. I wanted to apologize. I seem to remember thrashing about and pulling on you."

"You were agitated, but you were fevered. I was worried for you."

"Listen now. I will repay you for what you did. I will," he insisted as she shook her head. "If only with loyalty and protection. And a poor joke or two."

A little sob caught in her throat. "I just need to go home to be with my family should the king's threat come to our gates. But so do you."

"Crossroads, lass. I ask a little patience. And do not hie off on your own, hey? Good." His quick smile lifted one corner of his mouth, wicked and delightful. His lips were full and lovely. She wanted to taste them—

"We should rest," he went on. "Though I could talk with you all night."

She could too, wanting to know his fears, hopes, all of it. "We must wake early."

He stood, nimble for a tall man, and reached down to help her to her feet. Then he raised her hand to his lips and dropped a light kiss on her hand. It rippled through her like a strand of lightning. She caught her breath.

"Pardon. That was loutish."

"That was chivalrous." Her hand was poised, almost begging

another kiss, and now she yearned for a true kiss, lush and deep. Yet she would not cross that gap here, nor would he. "I will take that as a pledge, Sir Knight."

"Do. If you prefer, I can sleep outside the door."

"Stay," she said quickly.

"Fine then. Good night, Grizel, bluebell."

"Good night, Hamish." She sat on the thin straw mattress, which gave off hints of lavender and must. Aedan shuffled about making his simple bed on the floor.

In the reddish glow of the brazier, his profile had a finely drawn masculine handsomeness, his chest and arms sculpted and gleaming. Beyond the unkempt hair, scruffy beard, rough clothes, brawny build, and the brusque humor that masked his thoughts, the reddish light revealed the quiet power of a man who endured much, yet carried all with steadfast ease. She glimpsed the beauty of his nature, made of courage, integrity, and humility. She felt a sense of safety, of gratitude—and something deeper, something expansive. Months ago, she had cared for him. Now she cared about him, and realized it was deepening.

"I hope you can sleep there," she said.

"I can sleep anywhere, lass." He lay back, quieted.

She busied herself with blanket and pillow and rested too. Sometimes her pragmatic nature surrendered to romantic ideals. She had spent one day with him, and her thoughts were straying in ways that rarely happened with her. She hardly knew him, yet felt as if she had always known him.

A bond existed with him that she did not have with any other. It expanded, insisted. She had to express it somehow.

"Aedan MacDuff," she said, "I think you want others to believe you are a lout. But you are a good man. You just do not want anyone to know. But I see it."

"Ah, she plumbs my secrets. I look like an ox, but I am a pup seeking affection."

"Well, I could trim your hair. I have scissors," she offered.

"You terrify me." He crammed the pillow under his cheek,

turned on his side.

She pulled up the blanket, listening to the rain on the roof, a sleepy sound. Before long, a new noise began, louder, distracting. *Drip, drip, splash, drip—*

"Damn." Aedan sat up. "The roof is leaking. In my face." He scuttled away, dragging the plaid with him. *Drip, drip.* With a muttered oath, he moved again.

"Aedan." Rowena peered toward him. "Come up here."

"I am fine." The drips splashed on the floorboards, on something soft, cloth or man. He swore softly and swiped the edge of the plaid over the wet floor.

"Aedan MacDuff, come into this bed. We both need to sleep."

Tap. Tap. Drip. With an exasperated mutter, he rose and sat on the edge of the bed. The mattress sank under him as he stretched out with his broad back to her.

He was brawny but no ox, she thought, tugging the shared blanket over him. Taller than most, solidly muscled, he lay with his feet hanging off the end of the bed and the mattress sloping under him. The angle tilted her toward his back.

"See, you did not crash through the floor," she said.

"I dare not move."

She giggled. "You said you could sleep anywhere."

"I was mistaken." He sounded chagrined. "I like hearing you laugh."

His simple, sweet words brought tears to her eyes. "Sleep, Hamish."

"And you, Grizel, bluebell."

Savoring his warmth and closeness, she felt so grateful. "Thank you."

"For what?" He sounded drowsy.

"For being there when I needed you."

"Magpie," he murmured. "Hush it."

"Magpies are bad luck and bluebells are poisonous."

"I will take my chances. Hush."

HE WOKE, STARTLED in the darkness and sudden quiet. The rain had stopped. About to doze, he heard other sounds—low voices, the clomp of boots, a door creaking. Then horse hooves in the yard. The guards were leaving. *Good.*

At his back, Rowena slept peacefully. He lay still, not wanting to disturb her rest or risk tipping the narrow straw mattress off its rope frame. Listening to her even breathing, he tried pondering his way back to sleep.

Fatigue sat heavy on his shoulders, but he was keenly aware of the girl, her warm body pressed to his back, her rose-scented hair just at his shoulder. Earlier that evening, when he had opened the door as she was dressing after her wash, the candle-light behind her had revealed lithe curves through her shift.

God save him, he was too alert to every aspect of her, had even kissed her hand before he could stop the impulse, though he owed her his utmost courtesy and protection.

More awake than he wanted, he wondered about her lost husband, her kin, her great-grandfather too. He marveled that his wounds, so serious, had healed more quickly in her care than any he had received in the past.

Rowena turned in her sleep with a small murmur that rocked through him with sudden heat. He drew a breath, tried to sleep. But she gasped and pressed against him as if frightened by a dream. Afraid to roll back on her, he shifted and raised his arm, and she came easily, naturally, into that circle to rest her head on his chest.

When she whimpered again, he patted her shoulder. She moved her head, her hair a silky, rose-scented cushion under his bearded cheek. He inhaled.

She sighed and slept, curled against him. His body surged; he angled away. For months, he had felt a strong urge to find this girl. Now she was cuddled close, trusting him. He would honor that trust; more, he wanted to understand the pull he felt.

He had been a widower long enough to yearn for love, companionship, a wife and family again, but he staved off any hope, any plan, until he felt free to dream of such things. But as she snuggled beside him, he realized that, beyond his obligation to her, he was quickly growing fond of her. He kissed the top of her head as impulsively as he had kissed her hand.

Still awake, he thought of how they had met and how curiously fate and circumstances had reunited them. An elusive memory half-surfaced and he pursued it. From the moment he had recognized her at Yester, memories had tapped at him and began to return. He recalled Rowena at Holyoak, kind-hearted, capable, lovely, circling a star over him. Now he knew that star had been her crystal charm stone.

Fevered then, wondering if he might die, he had not feared death; he believed that a good soul with good intentions, despite mistakes, would find salvation. What frightened him was the uncertain fate of his son, his kin, his secrets if he died. His small son was his paramount concern, though he could rely on his sister and others to care for him.

But what would become of the Scottish regalia that Bruce had entrusted to him? With war and travel, covert work and injuries too, he had told Bruce it was hidden in Fife, but had not given him exact details—Bruce trusted him and did not ask where it was hidden. Worse, if Edward sent Malise to Castle Black to take it, English soldiers might poke around far too close to where he had hidden Scotland's precious symbols of kingship. He had to consider moving them, and soon.

His eyes flew open in the dark. He had told someone else where it was.

At Holyoak, he had pulled Rowena close and told her something about the regalia of Scotland and the treasure of Fife. And he recalled now that he had seen a stone very like her healing crystal elsewhere. Its twin was part of the hidden regalia.

That was no coincidence. But what could it possibly mean?

Rubbing a hand over his face, he knew he could not let Rowena Keith out of his sight. Not yet. He had to know the truth about that stone—both stones. And he needed to remember what he had told her about the treasure of Scotland. Did she know its location? And if so, had she told anyone else?

Chapter Eleven

B EFORE LIGHT, THEY left the inn and ducked into the forest when Aedan reminded Rowena that the boatman would expect to see a king's knight and his wee wife, so they must change. She was just as glad to be free of the helmet wrapped under her clothing, and draped his plaid over her drab reversed clothing against the cool air of the summer morning.

"Are you ready, Dame Grizel, my bluebell?" he asked as he adjusted the helmet and smoothed the snug fit of the red surcoat.

"A bluebell is still a poisonous flower, Hamish," she said with a soft laugh.

"Just so, *ma belle.*"

Dawn bloomed pink and silver over the river as MacDuff paid the boatman, then guided Rowena to step down to the barge. As the platform wobbled under her feet, she gripped his arm for a moment, then let go, embarrassed to show uncertainty.

She sat on a bale of hay while Aedan spoke with the boatman. Mist clouded the calm river, birds sang and flitted above the trees, and all seemed peaceful. Though she felt anxious about traveling over water, she was glad that she had shared with Aedan some part of why she was so hesitant.

As the boatman and his son poled the barge eastward along the river, Rowena leaned away as several goats came close, nuzzling and chewing at the hay where she sat. They belonged to a surly farmer in a sagging hat who sat near her. At the front of the barge, Aedan MacDuff conversed with the boatman and his sturdy son as they poled along, the flat vessel moving along on a swift current.

Sensing the motion of the barge beneath her, Rowena felt a lurch in her stomach, and with it, a familiar dread. She was never fond of being on the water, ever since the childhood misadventure when she had tumbled out of a boat crossing a loch, and had sunk, flailing and fearful, hampered by a heavy cloak. She surely would have drowned that day, but her father had jumped in to bring her to the surface just in time.

Here, MacDuff had assured her that the river ride would not be long, and she clung to that. Aware of the urgency driving him toward Fife and sensing tension in him that morning, she would not add her troubles to his.

She glanced at him now as he raised a foot to a wooden crate and rested an arm on his knee, watching the river flow past, talking quietly with the boatman. In the red surcoat and helmet, with his height and natural confident demeanor, he had a determined authority. The wind blew through his rich walnut-brown hair and billowed the hems of the surcoat and the brown tunic beneath it. Rowena studied his handsome profile, once again glad of his company. But she wondered how long he planned to stay once they reached Fife. Surely, he would need to be there, and so she would have to find her way back to Kincraig.

A deep need to go home pulled at her, sucked her under at times as she worried about her sisters, her brother, her friends there, and the king's looming demand. Her family knew she had gone to Soutra, certainly—but they might not know that she had been taken to Yester, much less had escaped with MacDuff. She did not want them to fear for her. The sooner she reached Kincraig, the sooner they would know she was safe—and the sooner they could decide together how to respond to Edward's unreasonable demand.

The barge moved past a shoreline thick with trees as the sun rose higher, bursting through the leafy cover and glittering over the water. Looking at the rippling water proved too much for her stomach, so she watched the goats instead as they roamed and bustled and knocked into her knees. The farmer grinned at her.

"'Tis a good river for trout. I was fishing this morning. Do you fish? My wife likes it. Jumps in the water and grabs 'em. She is a Highland girl, my wifey."

"I have never fished, sir," she replied.

"Fishing early in the morning makes for a fine supper. See!" He reached down, grabbed a basket, and opened it to show her his glinting catch, some still flapping about. "Want a few for your supper? I have more than enough."

"Uhh—nay, thank you." She turned away, hand over her mouth. The sight, the smell, the thought of a fish supper only worsened her private struggle.

THE GIRL HAD been glowing and content last night, Aedan thought, glancing at her. Now she looked deathly pale and oddly skittish. Neither of them had slept enough, and he knew how much she wanted to return to Kincraig, but was willing to delay that, knowing his need to reach Fife. What troubled her now must be her fear of water travel. Something was obviously affecting her.

Perhaps it was best to get her off the water. While the barge plowed through a river flux with last night's rain, he decided to disembark before reaching the coast and take an unexpected route that could throw the English further off their tracks.

He turned to the boatman. "Tyningham is not far. My wife and I will stop there."

"Not going all the way to Belhaven, then? There is a good tavern there. My brother owns it. I could get you a good price if you wish to stay there."

"Tyningham," he said. "We will hire horses and head to Edinburgh from there." Might as well throw the fellow off the scent should soldiers question him later.

"Right, then," the boatman grunted, and poled along.

Wading through a sea of bleating goats toward Rowena, Aedan reached out a hand. She stood slowly.

"Grizel, dear," he said, making sure the others heard, "we will disembark soon and head north to Edinburgh."

"Edinburgh?" She sounded wooden. "How much longer on the river, then?"

"An hour or so."

"Oh." She set a hand to her mouth.

He gave her a keen look. "All is well?"

"I am fine." She pushed one of the goats away.

Certain she was not fine, and suspecting the cause, he took her arm. "Come with me." He led her to one side of the barge, away from the farmer, the goats, the boatman and his son. "You dislike traveling by water. Nor did you eat before we left."

She blanched. "No talk of food, please."

"Come here." He put an arm around her shoulders and drew her close, planting his feet firmly and holding her still to give her a solid wall of sorts. "I used to feel that way as a boy. It is very unpleasant."

She looked up. "You?"

"Aye. It was embarrassing. You have my sympathy. Luckily, the problem cleared as I got older and rarely bothers me now. An old sailor once told me that watching something in the distance that looks straight and steady, like a castle or trees, can help. Better, standing like this?"

"A bit."

"Look away from the water. Look ahead." He took her hand, snugging her fingers against his chest, another anchor. "See that castle on the hill? Watch its tall tower rather than the water."

She stared up at the castle, and nodded after a few moments. "That does help."

"Stand here with me. We will be off this thing soon enough."

"I wish I had some mint. It calms the stomach."

"We will find some for you at Tyningham."

"On land, I will not need it." She gave a frail laugh. "Tyningham?"

"A friend is there. I need to ask a favor." He patted her hand. "We will dock soon."

"I am sorry for the trouble."

"Eh, I do not mind standing here with you. Those goats stink."

ROWENA WAS GLAD to stand with MacDuff away from the goats and the fish basket, and glad of the fresh wind on her face as the barge moved along. Once the castle on the hill was out of sight, the barge's motion crowded her senses again. She leaned anew against the rampart of Aedan MacDuff, and he settled his arm around her as if it had always been so between them. After a while, he pointed to another building on a hill in the distance. She fixed her gaze on the stability of its pitched roof, chimneys, and gray stone walls, which helped more than she expected.

"What is that place? It is not a castle."

"Tyningham. My friend's manor house. Then we are for Edinburgh," he added, with a glance for the two boatmen.

Knowing he invented that part of their journey, she did not reply, focusing on the stable profile of his friend's house and leaning into MacDuff's calm solidity. When the barge pulled to the bank to dock at a wooden platform, MacDuff lifted her by the waist to set her on the dock, then stepped out with her. He gave the boatman additional silver, thanked him, and led her to an earthen path.

She flexed her toes in her leather boots, glad to feel firm ground beneath her feet. To the left, she saw a square bell tower and the rooftops of houses. Toward the right, a narrow path cut through trees and went upward toward the house on the hill.

"Wait," Aedan told her. "The boatman does not need to see where we go."

"That is Tyningham?" She gestured toward the old stone church and buildings.

"The village and manor house go by the same name. Once

the barge is out of sight—ah, there he goes. This way." He led her toward the inclined path.

"Will your friend be home? Will we be welcome?"

"Welcome, aye, even if he is not there. The path is steep. Can you manage?"

"The sickness passes quickly once I am off the water." She took up her skirts and swept ahead of him to follow the zigzagging path. Above, the house stood on a cliff with a wide view of the river and surroundings. The clay-tiled roof was bright in sunshine, and soon she saw the top of the wooden palisade that enclosed the bailey.

"What if he is not home?"

"I am known here," he said as they approached the palisade and its high gate. "Halloo the house! MacDuff here for Sir Brian Lauder of Tyningham and Bass Rock!"

A bolt was thrown and the gate opened a crack. An elderly man with a gray head and white beard peered out.

"Ye're not MacDuff!" He began to shut the gate.

"Wat Johnston! It is me." Aedan removed his helmet.

"Hah, Aedan, is it! Come in!"

Aedan ushered Rowena through the gate and into the bailey within the palisade, then grasped Wat's hand. "Where is Sir Brian?"

"Here, but leaving for the Rock soon. It is good you came now and not later."

Rowena glanced about. They stood in a modest bailey yard fronting a two-story fieldstone house; a stable hunkered on one side and outbuildings crammed along the palisade elsewhere. The compound sat high on the hill, so the windows would command a far vista all around, from the river to the distant sea before and land behind.

"Aedan!" A woman rushed toward them, green skirts flowing around her. She was small and plump, with round cheeks framed in a wrapped veil, and a big cheerful smile as she held out her arms to greet him.

"Lady Ellen!" He kissed her cheek. "I am sorry to arrive without notice. I was hoping to find you and your husband at home."

"You are lucky to catch Brian here. He is leaving for the Rock today and may be gone for weeks. I sent one of the grooms to tell him you are here. And this is—?" She turned to Rowena, brown eyes sparkling.

"Lady Ellen—Lady Rowena Keith. I am escorting Lady Rowena home to Kincraig by way of Fife. I hope we are not interrupting your day."

"You are always welcome here! Lady Rowena, it is good to meet you."

"Aedan!" The man striding toward them was lanky with wavy red-gold hair, a reddish beard, and a smile as bright as Lady Ellen's. "Good to see you! I heard you got caught again. Did they let you go, the fools? What is this English kit you wear?" He clapped Aedan's shoulder in the red surcoat.

"Took this off a fellow at Yester, where I was stuck for a bit. But here I am and heartier for it. Sir Brian Lauder of The Bass, baron and worthy knight—this is Lady Rowena Keith of Kincraig."

"Ah, my lady, welcome to Tyningham. Keiths of Kincraig, is it? Your father and mine were allies over the years," Brian Lauder said. "In fact, years back, Sir Robert arranged a marriage between my brother and your sister Margaret. Sadly, my brother did not survive to join your family. I trust your sister is well?"

"She is, thank you. Recently she married Sir Duncan Campbell of Brechlinn."

"The justiciar? Good man. And how is your brother Henry? Still in Selkirk?"

"He is well also, and deputy sheriff there."

"Excellent. We need loyal men there. Come in. Aedan, we have much to talk about. After our midday meal I am off to the Rock. You are welcome to sail with me if you like."

"I hoped for an invitation," MacDuff said as they walked toward the house.

"Sail?" Rowena asked, as Lady Ellen took her arm.

"WE CAN VISIT here in my solar until the meal is ready," Lady Ellen said as she sat with Rowena in a small room off the main hall. The house was not large, its raftered ceilings low over whitewashed walls in rooms made cozy with curtains and cushions and embroidered hangings. The lady's solar was fitted with seats beneath windows of painted glass and open shutters. A little black dog slept by the hearth, and Rowena noticed baskets in the center of the room filled with books, wooden document boxes, leather boots, rolled garments, and other items.

"We are packing," the lady explained. "Tyningham is our home much of the year, though Sir Brian often goes out to the castle on Bass Rock. I will go there in a few days, after one of my daughters arrives to visit. The Rock is such a drafty place, and I dislike sailing back and forth, as we must do for supplies and such. The castle is garrisoned by Scots, so it is more like a fortress, and the seabirds are so noisy! I prefer being here, but I want to be with my husband when I can."

"Of course. Where is Bass Rock?" Rowena sat at the lady's invitation.

"Just off the coast. It is a great rocky island that was granted to the Lauders by an earlier king of Scots. Do you know of it?"

"I do. I heard it has a fortress, but I thought it was a prison, not a lord's castle."

"Both now." Ellen sighed. "My husband inherited it, but Robert Bruce has sent some English prisoners there. Brian keeps watch over them. May I ask how you come to be traveling with Sir Aedan?" The lady smiled and took up a small embroidery frame as she spoke, fingers flashing a needle and red thread in and out.

"A long story," Rowena said. "I should apologize. We arrived suddenly and you are so busy here. And so kind to show us hospitality."

"Aedan MacDuff is like a brother to Brian Lauder. Aedan

fostered here for a few years as a lad, and later, he married Brian's sister. But I suppose you know that."

That surprised her. "I know he is a widower with a son, but he has shared little more than that. I did not know he fostered here." So his wife had been Sir Brian's sister, she thought, which made Brian Lauder an uncle to Aedan's son as well. They were like family to Aedan, and she was glad of that.

"They have known each other twenty years and more. Lady Alisoun died shortly after her son was born, alas. It still saddens me, and reminds me to be grateful for my son and daughters. The girls are recently married and our son is a new knight riding with the English to fulfill his pledge."

"You must have a lovely family. Indeed, how sad that Sir Aedan lost his wife. The lad is well?"

"Aye. Five years old now, living in Fife. Aedan will be anxious to see him."

"I am sure he will." Aedan had confirmed that he had a son, but had said little of him otherwise. Nor had he mentioned the Lauders of Tyningham and the Bass. Suddenly she felt more like an acquaintance than a friend, though she had begun to feel that, and perhaps more. But she reminded herself that he did not owe her explanations.

"You wear a veil. May I ask—are you married, my lady?" In Ellen's sweet smile, Rowena sensed curiosity.

"I have been widowed for over four years. When I came into some trouble recently, Sir Aedan kindly offered to escort me home. Lady Ellen," she said quickly, feeling a touch of guilt, certain Aedan would confide their situation to Lauder, his close friend. "You are so kind, and I want to be honest. Sir Aedan and I were both in English custody, you see, and we escaped together. So we are each going home."

"Oh dear. Brian had heard that Aedan was arrested, but you as well? How awful! So you may be pursued?"

"They may look for us, aye."

"You are safe here. Any place held by Brian Lauder is a haven for Aedan MacDuff. So, in prison again, was he? Goodness!" She shook her head.

"Again?"

"He takes risks, but he is a capable soul and the king relies on him. I trust you know which king I mean." Ellen raised her brows.

"I do. And I agree, Sir Aedan is a steady sort. I marvel at how he can be so cheerful even when things seem at their most bleak."

"That is his nature, that cheerful constitution. It is a marvel indeed, considering what he has faced in life. But he puts on a good face."

"A jester's mask," Rowena said, and Lady Ellen nodded. "He has told me a little about himself. It seems he has a good deal of responsibility."

"The MacDuffs of Fife have closely supported the throne of Scotland since we had kings in this land. With that comes danger as well as privilege. He would be inclined to take you under his protection. That is his way. What put you there, a lady of rank?"

"I am not sure, to be honest. I am trained in healing remedies, and sometimes help in infirmaries. There was an accusation—from a great lord, an unfair charge that caused my arrest. I had met Sir Aedan before, months ago when I treated his injuries."

"That was you? We heard about that. I am even happier to know you! So you are one of the cunning folk, as we call healers where I come from. Aedan is well today thanks to you."

She shook her head. "His healing is a tribute to his strength and vigor."

"And your skill. I think he would give his very life to repay you for that. He is loyal beyond loyalty, our Aedan. But you will have seen already what a fine man he is."

"I have," Rowena said.

"We will eat soon, but first, may I ask if you need anything?" Lady Ellen smiled. "You seem to be traveling with just the clothes on your back."

"We did leave in a hurry, and I came away with very little."

Ellen gestured toward the baskets and boxes on the floor. "I have so many garments, and some no longer fit me. I would be pleased if you would help yourself."

Rowena blushed, noticing that the flaxen lining of her gown was torn and smudged. "Thank you. I could use some things, truly."

Ellen took her hand. "Aedan and Brian are like brothers, and I feel as if we can be good friends too. Come, look at what's here and take what you need."

CHAPTER TWELVE

"WERE YOU TAKEN leaving Berwick?" Brian Lauder asked. "I thought you were headed that way last month."

"Near Selkirk, where I attended a meeting of the Guardians. Edward's men discovered I was there, and jumped me in the dark."

"He is after all the MacDuffs, I fear. And you are an easy fellow to spot."

"They shut me in Yester Tower for a month, but I took a helmet and surcoat off a guard and left their hospitality."

"Good! Did the council settle the negotiations regarding the captive women?"

"Not yet. I went there to stand in for Fife, but not all of us could gather, with some too far away, others captured—Edward has the bishops of Glasgow and Saint Andrews now." Aedan shook his head. "Sir Malise Comyn was one of the signees on the king's letter refuting our latest attempt to regain the women."

"Has he recovered? He had quite an injury, I heard."

"Bit of a limp now, but smug as ever. A nun took him down, but it did not knock the arrogance out of him, I know that." He sighed, thinking of what Rowena had said.

"I had heard something about a nun!" Brian chuckled. "And your niece needs you there during these discussions. Your voice may help."

"I am doing all I can. But Edward is as inflexible as ever. He seems satisfied that he is doing enough simply by replying to us."

"You do not hold out hope, then."

"Not much. Lady Mary Bruce is coping, but they say Isabella is ill. The council has requested a physician, and Edward must comply or risk a reprimand from the Pope. Bruce is still excommunicated for killing John Comyn before he took the throne, so he cannot appeal directly to Rome in this situation. And naught will change Edward's heart of stone."

"He has little honor left, though I hear he was different in earlier years. Showed more mercy, had a sense of fairness and courtesy. My father remembered him as a better man. But this fervor to rule Scotland has brought out the worst in him."

"The need to force Scotland into subservience is like a poison in him." That irony did not escape him, considering Rowena's situation.

"What charges put you in Yester? Treason for escorting Isabella to Scone and taking part in the crowning of Bruce?"

"That, and being a MacDuff."

"I wonder what Malise Comyn has to do with this. He is Edward's man, but he is also kin to the Abernethys in Fife, who took down your brother. The attackers were exiled, one of them executed, so it could be that."

"Such grudges do not go away easily. But I need to look the other way. There are more important matters than revenge."

"True. But you should know that Sir Peter Abernethy, the attacker's son, is back in Scotland. Just be careful, Aedan. Malise Comyn and Peter are cousins."

"I am always wary, lad. We all must be these days."

Brian sat up as two maidservants entered the hall carrying trays of food. "Supper is ready. The ladies will come in soon. I must ask—how is it you are with the Keith girl?"

"She was brought to Yester on charges of treason as well. And she is the very healer who helped me months ago at Holyoak. I did not expect to see her again. We have much in common, as it happens." He shrugged to make light of it, though it meant much. "When I left, I took her with me."

"Why would the English arrest a Scottish healing woman?"

"She is accused of poisoning King Edward. She had occasion to give him some remedies. It did not go well."

Brian frowned. "Did she do it on purpose?"

"I would have, and you might. But that lass would not hurt a flea. My guess is someone arranged her fall. She is a great-granddaughter of Thomas the Rhymer, you see. Edward is likely drooling over that."

"The Rhymer! Is she the Keith girl you were once betrothed to?"

"Almost betrothed. Aye, the same. As I said, much in common."

"Curious! Would you marry again, Aedan?"

"Someday, perhaps. Not yet."

"Indeed, you have much on your mind and your shoulders. How is your lad?"

"Good, last I saw him, a few months past." He leaned forward. "I must get to Fife, but I dare not hire a boat to cross the firth nor go by land, in case of pursuit."

"If you want a boat, take my longship and my captain after we reach the Rock."

"I appreciate that. You do not need it?"

"We use longships often here along the east coast, as you know, especially useful as we go back and forth often to the Bass Rock. I have two ships, and one is yours if you need it. I may go with you to Dunfermline, as we often fetch supplies there."

"Excellent. I am in a rush to get there," Aedan admitted. "At the council meeting, they said my nephew may never return to Fife as earl. He has been raised to believe in English might over Scottish right. And truly any of us who might have the blood-right of crowning could be in danger from Edward."

Brian sucked in a breath, pushed a hand through his red-gold hair, and shot his friend a grim glance. "Which includes you, your sister Marjorie—and your lad."

"Exactly." A muscle punched in his cheek. "When Lady Rowena was at Lanercost in Edward's presence, she overheard Edward order Malise to take Castle Black—and my son."

"Jesu! We must get you there quickly. I am glad you came here for help."

"You have always been like a brother to me." Aedan smiled, though it felt flat with worry. "There are other matters I must tend to in Fife as well."

Brian gave a grim nod. "I know Bruce gave you something of value at Scone, but I will not ask." He lifted a hand. "They watch me too, the English. The less I know about your business, the better for all of us."

"Something of value, true. And I may have to move it, but I cannot take it over water. Too much risk of losing it."

"Huh. And a risk of pirates if they think a boat carries something they want. But a twelve-oar longship going for supplies will not catch attention."

"Once I do what I need in Fife, I must get Lady Rowena safely to Kincraig. After that, I will find Bruce and see what he has for me next."

"Ever the guardian, my friend. But this Keith girl adds more responsibility."

"Not much. I owe her."

"Ah, here are the ladies. Now we will eat. Hungry?"

"Always!" Aedan stood as the women entered. Rowena had changed, he noticed immediately, wearing a dark blue gown that skimmed her form and flowed with each step. He could look only at her, as if she had a glamourie around her, a spell of beauty and kindness and an allure of magic so strong, suddenly, that he stepped forward.

He was weary and easily distracted, surely, but the attraction felt deeper, compelling, as if he were caught in a glorious dream, reluctant to awaken. He had to resist that enchantment. Now was not the time.

THE WIND BLEW back his plaid and ran brisk through Aedan's hair as he stood in the bow of Lauder's longship. The sea lapped in frothy peaks, spray dampening his face while seabirds swooped and the sails snapped overhead. The boat skimmed low and swift through the water, just eight men pulling the twelve-oared ship. Ahead, Bass Rock rose massive and ancient. On its dark landward face, a flat plain supported a castle, while the summit and sides were covered in turf and more birds than a man could count.

He felt invigorated by strong winds and the powerful sea, ready for whatever might come next. But when he glanced toward Lady Rowena, he saw she was pale and silent, hunched at one side of the boat. He stepped over ropes and sacks to sit beside her on a cross bench.

"How are you feeling? We are nearly there."

Her eyes were shadowed, cheeks sallow as she nodded, pushing at her dark hair as it whipped free, her white veil crumpled in her hand like a towel at the ready.

"You can cure nearly anything, but not this, hey?" he asked. "That great rock is the only steady thing ahead. Watch that. Does it help?"

"Not this time." The prow rose and fell on the waves, and she tipped sideways. Aedan put a bracing arm around her. "I will be fine once we land."

He looked up as Sir Brian approached and noticed the man's concern. "The water is a bit rough. She dislikes sailing," Aedan explained, and stood.

"Lady Ellen is the same, so I understand. The light is falling fast. You can stay the night on the rock rather than try to cross the firth this evening." Brian looked at Rowena. "We have a *médecin* of sorts at Bass Castle. Perhaps he can help."

"Seems the best cure for this is just to be on land. A physician, truly?"

"One of our Scottish guards worked as a barber-surgeon before he was pulled into knight service. Bruce sent him here, and when I learned of his training, I put him on that duty. We have a few prisoners on the rock, English lords who must stay healthy. Bruce intends to exchange them."

"Ah." Perhaps the captives were important enough to trade for his niece and the others. But Aedan knew better than to wish for stars to fall in his lap.

Brian glanced at Rowena. "Your lady could stay on Bass while you go to Fife. Then you could take her to Kincraig when you return. We could send word to her brother to come fetch her from the Rock if you prefer."

"Henry Keith will want to know she is safe. We could send a messenger." Aedan wanted to keep her with him; he had told her something about the hidden regalia, though he was not sure quite what she knew. He trusted her, but the men pursuing her—including Malise—would not hesitate to harm her to find out what she might know.

The captain called to Brian, who made his way to the bow, and Aedan turned back to Rowena. "My lady—"

"I heard. If we could send word to Henry at Selkirk and at Kincraig too, that would be helpful. But I would rather go with you to Fife than wait on Bass Rock."

He was relieved to hear that. "We will go to Kincraig soon, I promise."

"I will hold you to it. Oh—" She set a hand to her stomach as the boat rose and slapped down on a swelling wave. Aedan merely shifted his weight with the motion, for sailing did not bother him. But he felt awful to see her suffer with it.

"Steady," he said. "I will not let you fall in."

"I will hold you to that too," she managed, hand to her mouth.

He stood still to support her, and began to hum low in his throat. That became a melody that he sang softly so only she could hear. It was one his aunt, of the purest voice, sometimes sang when she took him and his sister down to the beach below the castle to watch the sea. Now he sang a refrain and a verse or two in Gaelic.

Hì ri bhò hò ru bhì
Hì ri bhò hò rinn o ho
Ò hì shiùbhlainn leat

"What is that?" Rowena asked. "It is lovely, but I do not understand the words."

"Something my aunt sang when I was a boy. About a man who drowns at sea, and his lover cries and keens for him."

"Oh dear." She put a hand to her mouth. "You have a beautiful voice. Would you sing a bit more—in English?"

He went on, adding a verse.

O hey, I would go with you
If sand be your pillow
If seaweed be your bed
If fish be your candles bright
If seals be your watchmen
O hey, I would go with you—

She listened, leaning against him. "I love it, though going into the water is not something I want to think about just now," she said when he finished.

"The song is just to say that if it all goes wrong, I would be here for you."

"Or down there," she said, pointing to the waves.

"Or down there. Look, the Rock is close."

The longship entered the shadow of the rock and the oarsmen slowed their pace. Rowena came to her feet and took Aedan's offered hand. She wanted off this boat, that was clear. But tomorrow the journey would be hours over the water and possibly rougher than this short trip. He felt guilty about that, especially when she looked up at him with a trusting smile.

CHAPTER THIRTEEN

S UNLIGHT HEATED THE summit of the great rock and the wind pushed at her, though she planted her feet firm, gown filling, veil and braids blowing back. She set a hand to her head and turned away from the wind. Seabirds—gannets, she saw, white with black-tipped wings—skimmed overhead and sank out of sight beyond the rock to seek their nests or glide over the water.

Rowena smiled, shading her eyes with a hand. Seen from the height of the massive rock, the sea was beautiful, endless. She enjoyed views of the ocean, the bays and firths, the lochs and rivers she had seen in childhood and later. Traveling on water was another matter, her reaction something she could not easily remedy.

But sailing was the only way off this rock island, and soon she and MacDuff would go over the waves to Fife. This morning she had climbed to the meadowy area high on the rock hoping to find some curative among the growth there. The rock supported stretches of grassy turf, wildflowers, mosses, herbs, and plants. Much of the broad rock surface was glazed in bird droppings too, but she avoided those as she gathered a straggling bouquet that included mallow with pinkish-purple flowers, a few long stems of sea beet, some lovage, parsley, soft mosses, and wild lichens.

Hearing a shout above the constant rush of the sea, she turned to see Aedan walking up the steep slope from the castle. He waved and she did too.

Already she felt comfortable with him, trusting him quickly though she normally kept a reserve around strangers. But as he had pointed out, they were hardly strangers, with a brief and unique acquaintance. Once she had done her utmost to save him; later, he had been there when she most needed help. It seemed almost miraculous.

Desperation and danger had furthered trust and familiarity, and she realized that when she was finally home, she would miss him greatly. She smiled as he came closer.

"Sir Aedan! Have you come out to enjoy the sun and fresh air?"

"I came up here to find you, but the air and sun do feel good." He grinned. The wind whipped through his thick brown curls and the sunlight added sparkle to his eyes. He had given up his English surcoat and wore his tunic, trews, and plaid, garments that seemed far more natural to him.

The wind filled her veil and billowed the hem of the dark blue woolen gown that Lady Ellen had given her. When the wind batted her veil free, she reached for it just as Aedan snatched its tail and handed it to her. He brushed back strands of hair that blew over her forehead, and she straightened the veil to try and wrap it over her head again.

"Leave it," he said. "The winds will just undo it again. You look fine without it."

The shiver that went through her had naught to do with wind. She tucked the veil into her belt and waved the wildflowers in her hand. "I wanted to see what plants I could find here. They are unusual sorts. I have never seen this kind of mallow before."

"Bonny," he said, looking at her rather than the straggling plants. "Best come down from this great rock before the wind takes you over the edge." He grasped her elbow to lead her down the rough incline back toward the castle.

"I have a request for you from Sir Brian's *médecin*," he said, "who heard you have some skill. He wants your opinion on one of the men held in the dungeon."

"I can try to help."

"I thought you might agree. Also, Brian told him you had some trouble on the boat, so the fellow offered to give you some ginger for the sickness."

"Ginger! How kind. It is rather costly."

"An expense covered in the accounts here, no doubt. I also wanted to let you know that we sail this afternoon, so you may be glad of the ginger."

"I might. How long is it from here to Fife?"

"About three hours, more if rain moves in." He pointed toward the distant sky, where gray clouds gathered on the horizon. "What plants do you have there?"

"This is mallow, good for wounds and digestion, and this one is a kind of parsley. These long fronds are a small beet plant that rather likes salty climates, as it grows near beaches and sea cliffs. I thought to dry them and bring them back to Kincraig. I have a little cottage there where I make some remedies. It used to belong to my aunt, who left it to me," she added softly.

"She taught you well. I think we ate that weedy-looking bit for supper last night."

"The sea-beet? We did, with the baked fish. It tastes rather like spinach and is nicely salty. When I recognized it, I wanted to see if I could find some."

"Will any of those help your sickness?"

"Not much. Perhaps the mallow, though it thickens when boiled, so it is not very appealing on an upset stomach."

"I wish I could help, lass, but I know little about cures and things."

"You did help when you told me to find straight lines in the distance. I had not tried that trick before. I just wish I did not have this—flaw."

"Flaw? You have none. Me, I have more than enough for both of us."

"You! Not a one. Well, fewer than you think," she teased, laughing. He chortled, wind blowing through his curls, ruffling his beard.

She felt a thrill of joy over so small a thing as his low, easy, lovely laugh. She had never known anyone who made her smile as much as Aedan MacDuff did. Wondering at that, she stared at him. He tilted a brow in question.

"I am devilish impatient sometimes," he said.

"So am I. Patience is not my virtue."

"You have been more patient with me than I could ever ask. And I am sorry we must go over the water again to reach Fife."

"I know you need to get there to see your family. Your wee son."

"My lad, aye." He smiled. "His name is Colban. He is five. He is my heart."

"I can tell. Your sister looks after him?"

"My sister Marjorie and my aunt, Lady Jennet, live with him at Castle Black. I thought it would be a safe place for them. But Edward wants to change that." He frowned, watching the rippling white-tipped sea beyond the great rock.

"You are very concerned about their safety."

"Our ilk is under threat from the English. I will do all I can to protect them."

"You are more than a guardian of the realm, sir. You are a protector in your soul, with a way about you that just makes others feel secure. I feel that too." She blushed.

"Do you? Good. I want you to. And you, lass, have a healing way about you. I feel better in your quiet company. Look at us, hey." He gave her an impish smile. "Stuff of legend, we two."

She smiled, could not help it. "I know herbal cures. But you, MacDuff himself, watching over all of Fife for the good of others. It is impressive."

"Eh, my nephew is true earl and my uncle is true chief. Uncle Duff is imprisoned in Wales, thanks to Edward. I am just there to help."

Rowena paused on the slope, and caught her loosening braid as the salty wind whipped at her hair, her gown. "Tell me. If

Edward has your niece, your nephew, and your uncle—he must want to take you down as well, and your son. Is it so?"

He drew a long breath, looking out to sea. "That is the way of it."

"What you do for your clan takes remarkable bravery."

"Not really. It is what I need to do, and so will do. Last year I offered coin for my uncle's release. Edward refused my bargain. But he was reminded of my existence and asked questions. I did not need that."

"You have much on your shoulders, Aedan MacDuff."

"Good they are big, hey." With a quick smile, he plucked a mallow blossom and slid the flower into her hair, fingers smoothing there. A sweet chill ran through her as his gaze caught hers and held. She took a frond of sea beet and stuck it behind his ear. Leaving it there, he led the way down the slope.

"I was surprised to see such a lush meadow on this rock," she said as they went.

"Plants grow well up here. When Brian and I were lads, his father brought a small flock of sheep to graze. Sometimes they would fall into the sea. We dove in and rescued one or two, and were lucky not to drown. His father was upset about the risk we took. But I always thought the sheep appreciated it."

"I am sure they did. You spent a good bit of time here?"

"I did. His father fostered me for a few years. A good man, and a good place for me. Before that, because my father was dead and my mother married again and was living elsewhere, my brother and I fostered with the Bishop of Saint Andrews. I think I told you he wanted me to be a priest, as my brother was already earl."

"You were too spirited for priesthood, I imagine." Shading her eyes, she looked toward the coast to see the ragged blur of a castle and a town. "So the Lauders have held Bass Rock a long while?"

"Since the time of King Malcolm Canmore. Long before that, an acolyte lived alone here. Baldred, he was called. See those ruins over there—that was his wee house." He pointed. "He was made a saint for staying here to pray for our sorry souls. He should have been sainted for putting up with noisy seabirds and eating sea-spinach."

"Sea-beet. Scotland could use such prayers now."

"Indeed so. Watch your step." He took her hand, his fingers firm, then let go. She reached up to pluck away the sea-beet frond flopping over his ear.

"Will we find the *médecin* in the dungeon?" she asked.

"Aye, if you do not mind going to such a place again."

"I do not mind." *Not if you are with me.* But that felt too bold to say aloud.

AEDAN STOOD BY while Rowena examined the prisoner and spoke quietly with Sir Walter Forbes, the barber-surgeon, who was knowledgeable, calm, and showed respect for Rowena's comments. Aedan was glad to see that.

"For his cough and fever," she said, "you might try the rare mallow that grows here. I picked some this morning. Simmer it down to a syrup—it can help a cough and stomach ailments too, if needed." She handed him a few of the mallow plants she had plucked.

"Good suggestions, thank you. I have seen lovage growing high on the rock too, useful for wounds," Forbes said.

Aedan watched as Rowena nodded thoughtfully, standing beside the prisoner, a young man with flaxen hair and clammy skin. Seated on a cot, he coughed and looked exhausted. The compact stone cell held a narrow bed and small table beneath a barred window that emitted weak light. The place was damp and dim. He knew what life was like in such places, how easily it was to take ill.

"Another suggestion," Rowena said. "Bring him outside more often. He needs fresh air and sunshine. The salty sea air will help his cough as well."

"I must ask permission to do that and it may require extra

guards outside."

"Where is he going to go? Jump off the rock?" she asked bluntly.

Aedan suppressed a smile, enjoying this clear, direct aspect of Lady Rowena's nature. He was not sure Forbes appreciated it, for the fellow looked sour.

"Outings are not common practice with dungeon prisoners, though it could be arranged."

"Good. In fact, all the prisoners should be allowed outside regularly for air and sunshine," she replied. "If you want these men to be healthy, do arrange it. Try to add sea beets and parsley to their diet as well. It grows abundantly in the grassy areas here, and will help the prisoners—and everyone here."

"I can get the plants, but I need permission to take the prisoners outside," Sir Walter said.

"As the lady pointed out, they can hardly escape," Aedan said. "You could let them wander outside all day and not lose a one. Perhaps they could do some fishing and be well occupied and useful."

"I will speak to Sir Brian."

"You will find no objection there, is my guess," Aedan said, and Walter nodded.

Rowena bent toward the prisoner. "May I see your tongue, sir, and your teeth?" He obliged as she peered. "Aye, sea beet will help. You will feel much better soon, I think. What is your name?"

"Sir Austin Grey," he said in a hoarse voice. "Son of the Earl of Aylesford."

"His father is an advisor to King Edward," Sir Walter murmured. "Sir Austin is heir to the earl and a companion to the Prince of Wales."

Rowena gave the young man a kind smile. "I hope you will not be here long, sir," she murmured. "Sir Walter, I could do something else for him if we had a cup of water."

"Here." Sir Walter poured water from a pottery jug into a

wooden cup, and Rowena took it. She opened her belt pouch, removed a translucent white stone the size of a small plum, and dropped it into the water. She passed her hand over it in light, fey-like gestures, as if she cast a glamourie over the young man. Watching the dance of her fingers, Aedan felt bespelled himself.

"Is fresh water transported to this isle?" she asked.

"The only fresh water source here is rain we catch in barrels," Sir Walter answered. "And barrels of fresh water are brought from the mainland each week."

She nodded, casually circling a flat palm over the water as if lost in thought. Suddenly remembering moments at Holyoak, Aedan continued to watch, curious.

"Austin Grey needs water," she said. "His body thirsts for it. Everyone here needs more, I think. Sir Aedan, might we ask Sir Brian if more barrels can be brought here?"

He nodded, leaning a shoulder against the open door of the cell. "I will do so."

She plucked the stone from the water and set it on the table, then handed the cup to Sir Austin. He sipped it slowly.

"I have heard of using stones in healing, my lady," Sir Walter said, "but I have not seen it done. I wonder if they are just superstition, or if they have some effect."

"They do have some benefit. Those who know stones choose them carefully and then prepare them by infusing them with charms and healing chants. The stones leach their nature into the water, which can lend strength to those who drink it," she explained. "Stones can help cool fevers and soothe aches. They can calm the mind and the spirit if dipped in water or wine that is then swallowed. Sir Austin should have some each day for a week at least. Here," she said, handing the stone to Sir Walter. "You may have this one."

"Lady, I cannot take your stone if it is special to you."

"I have others. Take it," she insisted. He did.

Standing by the door, Aedan remembered how Rowena had used a special stone months ago to treat him. In fast, foggy images, he recalled seeing a translucent white stone dropped into water; hands moving gracefully; her voice, chanting softly; and cool, wet stones on his fevered skin. The woman with the crystal, as Thomas had once mentioned. The stone she had shown him at the tavern, the Rhymer's stone, was wrapped in silver bands, different than the stone she gave Walter Forbes.

Waiting, Aedan admired her skill, her calm, her humility, her simple beauty—long dark hair, creamy flushed skin, full and tender lips, eyes of stormy gray.

He just wanted to gaze at her, take in her gentle grace, like a balm for the soul. Being near her made him feel better, calmer somehow. In a way, she was like a balance for him, her calm and compassion filling gaps in his sometimes hasty, troubled spirit.

Last February, in a fevered fog, he had leaned into her healing strength while his body, his very spirit, recovered. He fell in love with her a little, a mingling of gratitude, relief, awe. Now, standing by while she worked, he felt that rush through him again.

This time, gratitude and admiration were riper, fuller, more real, filling him. He was falling in love not with an ideal, but with the woman standing a few feet away. Sucking in a quick breath, he wondered if that was indeed so—and what to do about it.

She bid Sir Walter and Sir Austin farewell, and as they thanked her, Aedan recognized the spark in Austin's eyes. The young knight had fallen a little in love with her too, lured by her calm magic, leaning on her every word, his eyes sparkling, cheeks flushed. Sir Walter took her hand and thanked her again. Aedan had thought him sure of his own worth and skeptical of hers, but his gesture now was warm.

She turned, her quick smile just for Aedan, gentle and intimate, as if they shared a secret. Crinkling his eyes in affection, he marveled. She glowed from within, peaceful, alluring, beautiful, and unaware of it. He had never met a woman like her. The little sparkle in her eyes could knock him over. That soft hand could heal all his ills.

As they left the cell, Aedan turned.

"Sir Walter," he said, "were I you, I would do whatever the lady suggests. I am alive today because of her skill."

CHAPTER FOURTEEN

F OG AND RAIN rolled in, and with it came the pirates.

Rowena saw the other ship emerge through a curtain of mist as it sailed into the firth from the North Sea. A bolt of alarm shot through her and she stood, sensing a threat, looking around for Aedan and Brian, who stood talking with the captain at the other end of Lauder's longship. She waved, called out, but they did not turn immediately.

She had been watching the thick, pale fog float on the whippy surface of the water under darkening clouds while Brian's longship sailed into the heart of the firth. Miserable, she chewed on dried ginger and trained her gaze on the tall mast at the center of the low-slung, clinker-built longship.

The other stable element nearby was Aedan MacDuff, who stood strong and still as he spoke with Sir Brian and Tom Robertson, the captain, and even as he took a turn at an oar with the crewmen. He was becoming a reliable anchor in her life; without him she felt a bit afloat herself on the ship.

Now she saw the other longship, larger and coming fast as it plowed through the waves toward Lauder's vessel.

"Aedan!" she called over the sound of wind and waves. He turned and she gestured. Seeing the other ship, he spoke to Brian and the two of them made their way toward her better vantage point.

"The flag it carries is not English, nor one I recognize," Aedan said. "Nor does the prow carry a dragon's head, so it is not Viking—but the legendary Viking dragon ships have not attacked Scotland in living memory, I think."

As the ship swerved its course to sail closer, Brian swore. "Pirates! They sometimes prowl these waters, but usually at dusk. The fog makes them bolder today."

Her heart slammed as the ship came into sharper view and she saw several men lined up in the larger ship, bows at the ready. Behind her, Tom Robertson called out and the oarsmen rowed harder, alert to danger.

Then several of the pirates raised nocked arrows. Now the ship was so close that a tall man could leap from one vessel to the other. At Aedan's quick signal to her, Rowena backed into the shadow of the prow, while Aedan and Brian placed hands on the hilts of the daggers at their belts.

Suddenly ropes soared across the gap between the two ships and iron hooks caught the side of Lauder's boat, claws sinking into wood. The longship lurched and was pulled close, bobbing on the waves as the two boats nearly knocked against each other.

Rowena felt her stomach sink, sour with fear and renewed nausea. She clutched the rim of the prow and watched as Aedan strode to the side, hand on the hilt of his dagger. Brian Lauder came with him, while Tom Robertson called again for the crewmen to pull hard, though just eight oarsmen manned the twelve-oared boat on this trip. The longship jerked, held fast by the hooks, as wood pierced by iron cracked with a sickening sound.

"Hold!" Robertson ordered.

Rowena felt ill again with the lurching motion of the boat. She sank to a bench, limbs trembling, fear adding to nausea as the smaller longship bobbed in the water.

"Who are you? What do you want?" Aedan bellowed, as two of Lauder's oarsmen left their benches and tried to pry the claws loose without success.

The boat dipped again as three pirates stepped over the gap

and into their boat, hands on daggers. Behind them, archers trained arrows on the longship.

"What do you want?" Brian repeated.

"Whatever you have, sir," said the older of the invaders. Broad, gray, and gruff, he kept hold of his dagger's hilt. "Whatever you are carrying, give it over now!"

"Who the devil are you?" Aedan growled.

"Meikle John Reid," Tom Robertson said. "A pirate in these waters. Out of Flanders now, but an Aberdeen man, if I am not mistaken."

"That is so," Reid replied proudly.

"A Scotsman? Why attack your own?" Brian demanded.

"We do what we must," Reid answered smoothly. "Just out looking for goods to trade. No harm will come to you—or yours." He looked at Rowena, turned back. "Give over your goods and coin. Give us your names, too. You might be useful to us."

One of the pirates came forward and grabbed Brian by the neck of his tunic, holding the tip of the blade at his throat. Reid trained his dagger point on Aedan, while the third crossed to Rowena. Though she backed away, he took her arm in a rough grip.

With a growl, Aedan surged forward. Reid's blade went up, and an arrow swooshed to slam at his feet. He stopped, glowering.

"I am Lauder of the Bass Rock," Brian gasped, with a blade under his jaw too. "We are only traveling for the day to get supplies in Dunfermline. We have no cargo."

"But you have fat purses and a pretty lass," Reid said. "If you have nothing else of value, we will take those."

Dizzy, heart slamming, Rowena strained against the man's grip on her arm, but felt faint suddenly. She saw Aedan send her a keen glance, then away.

He reached into his sporran to remove a cloth pouch. "Take this. Let the lass go."

Reid snatched it, weighed it in his hand, looked at Lauder. "And you?"

Rowena knew Brian had enough coin to purchase grain, foodstuffs, and more. She watched anxiously, aware that Tom and the crew were still and wary.

"Come on," Reid said, and Brian untied the leather pouch beneath his cloak. It jingled as he handed it over.

"All I have. Now be gone."

"Or what?" Reid looked at some wooden boxes. "What is in those crates?"

"Vestments for the bishop of Dunfermline and his priests," Brian said. "Gifts embroidered by my wife. No use to you."

Reid nodded, turning. "This your wife?"

"Mine," Aedan snapped. "Leave her be."

"Pretty thing." Reid went closer. Rowena leaned away. The boat seemed to spin under her feet. "Give us your purse, hinny." He stretched out his hand for the pouch at her belt.

When she did not answer, he snapped the cord that attached it and took the purse. She launched forward with a cry, reaching for it, though the other pirate held her back. The Rhymer's charm stone was in that pouch—she could not lose it.

Seeing that, Aedan roared but could not move, for another dagger was pointed at his throat now.

John Reid laughed, holding the bag out of her reach. "Something precious in here?" He opened the gathered neck of the bag to look at its contents. "The wee vixen wants her scissors and ribbons and—what, flowers? And a wee jewel!" He plucked up the charm stone, polished and glossy. It winked in the cloudy light.

"Give that to me!" She stretched out her free arm.

"Not a chance, darlin'." Reid slid the things back into the pouch and tucked it inside his shirt.

"Give it to her! Take this instead," Aedan barked, sliding a hand inside his plaid and the neck of his tunic, extracting a second pouch of leather. Tilting his head away from the point of the blade, he held it out. "Have it, you bastard, and leave us be."

"Take that," Reid told the man beside Aedan, who grabbed it. "We will have all this and the lass too, since you have little else to offer and I am not in a killing mood. This fog depresses my spirit, but this bonny lass will cure it quick enough."

Aedan was fuming now. Rowena saw the rising temper in his flared nostrils, pulsing jaw, eyes flashing dark and dangerous.

"Leave!" Aedan boomed. "We must get my wife to town. She is ill and needs a physician. Leave her be, or regret it!"

As he spoke, his tone fiercer than she had ever heard from him, she felt a new wave of dizziness as the ship swayed. Her legs weakened under her and she set her free hand to her chest, again feeling faint.

"That fine woman? What could be wrong with her?" Reid asked.

Rowena bent over as the contents of her stomach erupted, spewing over the man holding her arm.

"That," Aedan said.

Recoiling, the pirate released her just as Reid whirled. Aedan shoved the man beside him, grabbed the man's dagger, and launched for Reid. Throwing himself on the older man, he slammed him down to the curved floor of the longship.

Unable to stop herself, Rowena retched again, this time covering the boots of the pirate beside her. He yelled and jumped back, losing his dagger. As Aedan pinned Reid down, Brian jumped on the third pirate. At the same time, an oarsmen leaped on the distracted man beside Rowena. A couple of other crewmen followed, jumping into the fray to help subdue the three pirates.

Now arrows sailed through the air like needles, punching into the ship, clattering on wood, a few striking crewmen. Swift and sure, Aedan rolled Reid and dragged him upright to use him as a shield against the arrows. That quelled the barrage as Reid's men halted, uncertain. Aedan dragged the man to the side.

"Take your men and go *now*, if you want to live!" he shouted, grasping Reid by the neck of his shirt, arching him backward.

Dropping to her knees, dizzy and weak, Rowena hunched beside a crossbench and watched Aedan and John Reid grappling, pressed against the boat's curved side. Hearing a clunk, she saw something drop out of Reid's shirt as he moved—one of the pouches. Another pouch fell away as he pushed Aedan, whose plaid came loose. He kicked it away, twisting to keep his hold on John Reid.

Cautiously Rowena crawled toward the purses to try to recover them while no one was looking. All around, men shoved and shouted; a moment later she heard a great splash as someone pitched over the side into the water. Looking up, she was relieved to see Aedan still in the boat, holding Reid partly over the side. Now another man went into the water—a pirate, she saw, heaved over by Tom the captain.

Easing forward, she grabbed the two fallen pouches, feeling the weight of coins. Both were leather—her embroidered bag was not there. Subsiding between two benches, she peered out, wanting to be sure Aedan was safe.

Amid the chaos, oarsmen worked to loosen the grip of the iron hooks pinching the side of the boat, freeing one, then the other. Then Tom Robertson sliced through the lashing ropes. The boat surged free.

Rowena nearly tumbled to the floor with the sudden motion, still dizzy. A few feet from where she crouched, Aedan and Reid struggled, the older man shoving hard, twisting about. Then Aedan grabbed Reid's shirt as they pitched over the side together.

As they disappeared, Rowena screamed, her voice lost in the commotion. Tom Robertson shouted to his men, only five or six scrambling to the benches.

"Row! *Row!*"

The crew pulled and the boat launched ahead, and Rowena stood, shouting to Brian, hoping he had seen Aedan in the water with the pirate leader. She ran to the side of the boat just as Brian shouted to Tom to halt the oars.

Any thought of the Rhymer's guardian stone left her. She thought only of the man lost under the water's tumultuous surface. Sinking to her knees, she stretched out an arm and cried out his name.

AEDAN SUBMERGED AGAIN as Reid dragged on his shoulders for purchase as both struggled. Water enveloped him, slowing time. Hearing a siren's voice, he saw light above, and pushed away from Reid, who floundered and came up too. Aedan rose out of the water, gasping, sputtering, to see the long curve of the ship's side ahead. For an instant, he saw Rowena, her face a pale oval, dark hair streaming as she leaned over the side. He powered toward her as Reid came up, pulling at him. Aedan kicked him away.

"A ship! A ship!" the pirates were shouting from their ship. "John! Come back!"

Confused, Aedan swerved to see another ship approaching through the fog. This was no longship, but a large galley with forecastle and broad square sail, the sort sailed by English. Even so, he was relieved to see it.

Reid noticed it too, turning to swim for his boat. The mere sight of another ship, let alone an English war galley, was more than enough to send them on their way.

Sputtering, Aedan swam toward Lauder's ship as someone extended an oar toward him. He reached, missed, as a wave rocked through and lifted him, then slapped him down again. Sinking and rising, he reached again for the oar tip and missed.

Someone dove in and swam toward him—Brian, he saw, emerging to grab his arm and pull him toward the ship. Within moments, Tom Robertson reached down to help both men back inside. Collapsing in the belly of the boat, Aedan felt the ship lurch as Brian clambered in too, both of them sinking to the deck, coughing.

"My thanks," Aedan gasped, sitting up, shoving back wet matted curls.

"I saved a sheep once, why not save you," Brian said breathlessly. They came to their feet, dripping, laughing. Aedan glanced around to see Rowena standing apart, watching, a hand to her chest, face pale.

Hearing shouts, he looked where Brian pointed to see Reid's ship sailing eastward and away. Then he searched for the galley that had sent the pirates scurrying off, and saw it approaching through thinning drifts of mist.

"Look," he told Brian. The broad English sail bore three huge lions, and the mast carried Edward's red and gold flag. Men onboard the ship wore red surcoats over chainmail. He also noticed bows, arrows, glinting swords, tall pikes.

"English." Brian groaned. "Whoever sails there, we owe them our escape." He went to Tom, who was calling out to the oarsmen to row hard and away.

Hearing Rowena's voice, Aedan looked down to see her beside him. He opened his arm and she came into its circle. He did not care who saw that or what they thought. He just needed her close.

"Aedan," she said on a little sob, holding up his discarded plaid. Lifting on her toes, she draped it over his wet shoulders. Welcoming its warmth, he leaned his cheek on her head, then saw Brian Lauder's glance. Smiling, his friend looked away quickly.

"Are you harmed?" Aedan asked her. "Are you ill?"

"Better now that you are safe." She put an arm around him as if to support him, but he knew her need for an anchor too. "Do not worry about me," Rowena went on. "Your cheek is cut and bleeding! And that eye may turn black." She touched his cheek, fingers gentle.

"Eh, he got worse than me," he said as her hand came away with blood. His cheekbone ached, he realized. "It is naught."

She traced cool fingers under his eye. "I should tend to it."

Angled away from the view of others, he took her hand and kissed it. She blinked, a blush seeping into her pale cheeks.

Cradling her hand in his, he felt affection pour through him.

"I should see to the others," she said, pointing toward two men who sat at the side of the boat. Brian crouched beside them.

"You should." He let go, and she crossed to kneel with them and talk quietly.

If she felt unwell, she did not show it now, though Aedan saw how drawn and pale she was. Perhaps her empty stomach helped; he nearly laughed, recalling what had happened. Then he realized she felt better because the needs of another had eclipsed her own. A deep fondness flowed through him again.

Suddenly he remembered what he had tried to do when struggling with John Reid. He patted his soggy tunic. Her purse—where was it? During the fight, he had grabbed Reid's shirt for the pouches the man had stuffed there.

Just before they tumbled into the water, he had managed to grab her purse and drop it inside his tunic above the cinch of the belt. But in that fierce dunking, it could have been lost in the sea.

Feeling a lump caught in a tangle of wet cloth against his lower back, he groped and brought it out. Rowena's soggy embroidered purse, closed tight by wet, knotted cords, threads seeping dye. He breathed out, relieved. Alas, his pouch and Brian's too were either lost in the water or in Reid's possession now.

Approaching Rowena, he waited while she fastened a make-shift sling on an oarsman's arm. Rising to her feet, she gave Aedan a shy smile. He extended his hand, and her expression turned to delight.

"My purse! How did you get it?" She tugged at the knotted wet string.

"Took it off that rascal as we went overboard. Else the fishes would have it."

"The stone!" She drew it out of the wet sack, crystal gleaming, silver washed bright. "I do not know how to thank you."

"I told you if all went wrong, I would be there for you." A smile played at his lips.

She laughed. "You did. Wait here." She stepped away, bent beside a bench, and returned holding something in her hands. As a wave slapped the boat, she tilted, caught herself. Aedan took her arm as she handed him two leather pouches. "These dropped on the deck while you and that man fought."

"What luck!" He hefted the pouches in his hand. "This one is mine, and the other is Brian's. Excellent. Once more, I am in your debt."

"I just happened to see them fall. But I did not see your other one." She looked about. "I hope it did not have anything of value."

"Some coins, a pilgrim's shell, simple things. This is the important one. Gold coins, and a key I could not lose."

"You traded that purse to help me. I am the one indebted to you again."

"Fortunately for you, I am a courteous knight." He gave her a lopsided smile.

"Thank you." Resting a hand on his arm for balance, she rose on her toes to kiss his bruised cheek. Yet as he looked down, she came up, and their lips met.

The boat seemed to rock under him, and his fingers tightened on her arm as his lips moved over hers for a moment, the surge in his body stronger than that of the sea.

"Oh!" she said, dropping down.

Astonished too, he was silent, feeling his heart somehow widen. He looked into her beautiful gray eyes and saw starlight and silver in them. "Rowena—"

"Sit down, Aedan MacDuff, and let me look at your eye." When he sat, she leaned to look, fingers cupping his cheek. "Is there an apothecary in Dunfermline?" she asked.

"Is your stomach unwell?"

"I will be fine once we are on land. I want to find something to soothe your cuts. My purse—the herbs were drenched."

"At Castle Black, my sister and aunt may have what you need. But I will be fine by then too." Something went topsy-turvy within, and he realized it might be his heart as he looked in her eyes. "Besides, Lady Rowena has secret healing ways, I think."

"She does." She lowered her hand and stepped back, and Aedan rose to his feet. Then she kissed her fingertips and touched them to his cheek. "There. My cure."

Aedan laughed softly. "That ought to do it." Wanting to truly kiss her, a delightful lunacy in the aftermath of excitement and her faery-like touch, he heard Brian call out.

"Aedan!" Brian hurried toward them. "The galley!"

He had forgotten about the other ship, thinking only of the girl. Whirling, he saw the English galley closer and very large, wide sail billowing, flag whipping on the mast. Several men stood within. The one by the prow shaded his eyes against the cloudy sky. His blue surcoat was unnaturally bright in the fog.

Aedan groaned. "Malise Comyn."

CHAPTER FIFTEEN

"Comyn," Brian muttered. "We should hurry ahead, but a crewman is injured."

"I will take his oar, but if they pull even with us, Malise must not see the lass." Aedan noticed Rowena watching the rapidly approaching galley, and called to her.

"Both of you need to keep out of sight," Brian said.

"True. Lady, sit in the prow and pull your hood up," Aedan told her. She did.

He went to an empty bench to pick up an oar and set to, with a nod for Tom Robertson and the men near him. Another glance over his shoulder showed the English ship closing fast, powered by more oars in the water and a bigger sail.

"*A-hoi!*" came the shouted cry, a Flemish word used often out on the ocean. Malise Comyn cupped his hands to his mouth. "*A-hoi* the ship! Haul over!"

Brian motioned for them to slow while Tom Robertson called to the crew, who slowed but did not stop. The two boats aligned, bobbing on the waves. Aedan looked toward Rowena, satisfied that the shadow of the high-curved prow and the slope of her hood would shield her face. In the distance, he saw the pirate ship fade into the fog. He turned back to the work of rowing.

"*A-hoi!* Do you have trouble?" Comyn shouted. From his position on the larger ship, he stood above them, looking down.

"Pirates!" Brian shouted. "Meikle John Reid and his rogues!"

"That rascal! Brian Lauder, is that you, sir? Where are you headed?"

"Dunfermline and back again!" Brian called in response.

Listening, Aedan drew the oars toward him and away in a rhythm.

"Who is the woman?" Comyn asked next.

"Wife!" Brian shouted.

Aedan was grateful for that, though if Comyn came close enough, he might recognize Rowena—and him too. Though he felt a powerful urge to confront the fellow for his reasons and Rowena's, he would not endanger the girl. He ducked his head and continued to row as they glided beside the English ship.

"What is your business in Dunfermline, Lauder?"

"Supplies!" Brian shouted over the noise of waves and sails. A length of several feet separated the two ships now. "Wife wants to pray at Saint Margaret's tomb. Where are you bound, sir?"

"Stirling Castle—king's business!"

"You ought to pursue Meikle John!" Brian called. "If he wants to be useful," he muttered within Aedan's hearing.

"I have royal orders to go to Stirling and meet with De Valence, Edward's chief lieutenant in Scotland."

Malise did like to sound important, Aedan thought, and might give away too much because of it. He bent to the oar, listening.

"Then I will head back to Fife," Malise continued. "Tell me! Have you seen Aedan MacDuff? You know the man!"

Aedan's stomach sank. Brian paused. "Not recently!"

Bless him, Aedan thought, pushing the oars forward and back. If Comyn went to Fife, he would look for his son. Aedan wondered how much time he had to see to his family's safety and also get Rowena back to her kin.

"MacDuff escaped custody. We are searching. He has a castle in Fife."

"Fife, aye. But he would head west to join Bruce, I think!"

"He has a woman with him. We are looking for her too. A Keith of Kincraig. Edward wants her brought to him!"

"Must be serious! Head west to find MacDuff—he will not go home if he thinks he might be followed. You will waste your time in Fife. Will you go to Kincraig too?"

"Nay, I cannot waste the king's time! I am not welcome at Kincraig," Malise answered. Listening, Aedan almost laughed. "If I find MacDuff, I will find her."

"If I hear news, I will send word to Stirling."

"Look for me in Fife soon enough! Farewell!"

"Farewell, sir!" Brian drawled. Aedan heard the sarcasm in it, but Malise did not, for he waved as the galley sailed past.

Aedan bowed to the oar, pouring fury and frustration through muscle as he went forward and back in steady loops. He had to move his family out of Castle Black quickly, and help Rowena as well.

Regardless of what Malise had said, Kincraig was not safe either. All he could do was keep her close until he knew more. Somehow, he would guard against the threats piling on her, though he did not yet know how to resolve them.

LATER, AS SUNLIGHT warmed away the fog and the longship carried them fast across the firth, Aedan stood near the mast and watched the shoreline of Fife growing closer. *Home.* His heart filled, expanded. Soon he would see his family, and see to the rest of it.

Glancing back, he saw Rowena seated on an empty rowing bench, face raised to the wind, veil blowing back, dark hair slipped loose. Her profile was delicate, beautiful, her cheeks pink from the wind. Perhaps she felt better, he thought, with land in sight.

"Aedan, lad," Brian said, joining him. "The galley turned west to head up the river toward Stirling."

"Fair riddance," Aedan muttered. "If they had decided to dock at Queensferry and go up to Dunfermline, that would bode ill for all of us."

"I only hope he takes my advice to ride in search of Bruce—

and you."

"The king may want Lady Rowena even more than he wants me. We cannot know which direction Malise will take. We must stay on guard in case he comes back to Fife. Remember, Rowena overheard that Edward wants my son taken hostage. "There is too much damage he could do wherever he goes. And he knows it."

"What will you do?" Brian asked.

Thoughtful, Aedan studied the shore. "Do you know the fishing village on the point, that way? I have friends there. If we sail in close enough for them to recognize me, they will send a boat out to fetch us. It is close to the castle. I must get home quickly."

"Aye. When I leave Dunfermline, I can take your family back to Bass Rock with me. They can stay as long as they like, or go over to Tyningham. Lady Ellen would be pleased to see them."

"Thank you. We could meet you there—day after tomorrow? Aye. Lady Rowena and I will head to Kincraig from there."

"If Malise goes to Castle Black, he will find a garrison, your family gone, and you and your lady well on your way."

"Not my lady," Aedan murmured, watching the sea.

"You would not mind if she was, I think."

Aedan's smile was guarded. "What man would not? Even you called her wife, and you happily wed as any."

"I did not say whose wife she was." Brian grinned. "You claimed her as wife when the pirates asked. A wonder she has not wed again after her widowing, though Her kinsmen could find a very good match for her. Worthy family and a worthy lady."

"I gather she keeps busy with her healing work," he said carefully.

"Ah. If I may say"—Brian glanced at him—"my wife wondered if you might offer for the lady's hand. Ellen thinks you have great worth as a husband."

"Huh, with the English on my tail and Edward eager for my head! "But thank her for the compliment. Did she put you up to the suggestion?"

"Possibly. It would do you good to marry again. You could rekindle the betrothal."

"I suppose I could." He said it lightly, not quite ready for that suggestion.

"That lass there," Brian said, "would be a boon for you. Her kinsmen and her character cannot be bettered—and you both seem well matched. Her patience especially recommends her for putting up with you."

Aedan huffed. "That may be." He watched the rippling waves, thoughtful, realizing he felt the urge to let go and move on, but unwilling to admit it aloud.

"I loved your sister," he finally said.

"I know." His friend was silent for a moment. "Alisoun would not want you to remain a widower. Nor would she want her lad to be motherless all his life."

"My sister does well with him. But I take your point." Aedan turned then, sensing a change. Rowena came toward them, dark blue gown blowing back, outlining her lithe figure. He savored the sight of her feminine curves, her glossy dark braid, the sunlight soft on her skin, warm on her shoulders, bright on her widow's veil.

Brian asked her about the oarsmen she had treated, and while they spoke, Aedan's thoughts whirled, considering Brian's suggestion. If Rowena was his wife, he could protect her, be her companion on this mad journey now and into the future. If she was his wife, he would not have to leave her at Kincraig, perhaps never to see her again. If she was his wife, she would know his secrets and keep them. And he would protect hers as his own, always.

Always. That was the part of the truth of a strong marriage, he knew. Always loved, always protected, respected, supported, understood. Always had not been part of his first marriage. Those years had been too short, the years since too long.

Marriage with Rowena Keith would endure and grow. He felt

it his bones, his blood, his soul suddenly. Their match would be strong, a union of trust and love.

If he had such a wife, his world might right itself at last.

She smiled up at him, catching his gaze, her eyes the same gray-blue as the sea that flashed all around them. Yet he looked away, his heart and his yearning too obvious.

Then she slipped her hand inside his elbow as if seeking an anchor as the ship surged on the sea. He pressed her hand to his side to lend the stability she sought.

"Aedan MacDuff," she said, "you are very quiet."

"Just wanting to see my lad."

"Before we arrive, let me thank you again. You have been so good to me."

"Always," he said.

"I THINK WE have been sighted," Rowena said a little while later. Shading her eyes, she watched a few men gather along a strip of beach, waving. "Who are they?" "Fishermen from the village above Castle Black," Aedan said. "Friends all. The big man, blonde in the red plaid, I have known since I was a babe." He waved and shouted. "Erik *Beag!* Bring a boat out for us!"

"MacDuff, is it you!" Erik shouted. He and another man pushed a rowing boat off the rocky beach into the water. They jumped in to row to the longship.

Brian took Aedan's hand. "We will meet you at Dunfermline, then."

"I am grateful to you. Take care—and keep an eye out."

"I will. Lady Rowena." Smiling, Brian inclined his head. When she took his hand to wish him farewell and thank him, he blushed to the roots of his red hair.

The smaller boat came alongside and soon Aedan lifted Rowena in his arms to help her step into the boat, which dipped slightly. Erik, golden-haired and brawny, guided her over a wad of nets to sit on a crossbench in the narrow stern. Aedan stepped down too as Erik slapped him on the shoulder.

"Aedan MacDuff! *Fàilte!* Welcome, man!" They murmured in Gaelic, and then Erik gave Rowena a broad smile. *"Fàilte gu Fìobha!* Welcome to Fife, lady!" His English was lightly accented. "I am Erik Ogilvie and this is my brother Andrew. Sit there and soon you will set your bonny foot in Fife."

She smiled, and Aedan settled on a center crossbench to pick up an oar and dip it in cadence with Erik and Andrew as they sped to shore.

The craft was a currach used for fishing, she knew, common enough on lochs and rivers, and though she had ridden in them on occasion, she had not seen one used on the sea. The long, sleek body of thick oiled hide was tightly shaped to an inner skeleton of curved and fitted branches for a swift, lightweight vessel that could hold half a dozen men as well as nets and fishing gear. It was a good boat, quick and well-balanced.

She sat with hands gripping the sides, but soon realized she felt remarkably safe. The water was calm, the boat light and fast, the men capable, and the shore near. A few men and women stood on the beach, children and dogs running about; inland beyond rocky hillocks lay a cluster of huts and cottages.

Rowena looked left and westward, where the narrow, rocky shoreline wandered into the distance. Far off, she glimpsed the top of a castle's crenellated tower and parapet. That must be MacDuff's castle, she thought.

Aedan pointed that way as he chatted in rapid Gaelic with Erik and Andrew. His broad back was to her, but she sensed that he was relaxed, his earlier tension gone as if he had shed a heavy cloak. Aedan MacDuff was home at last—and his relief lifted her own spirits. She smiled as the little boat skimmed along.

What might come next, she could not say. But for now, all was well.

Erik pointed toward the castle and spoke to Aedan. Though she did not understand his rapid Gaelic, Rowena recognized *"Caisteal Dubh"* and *"bàta."* Boat.

Aedan glanced at her. "We can continue on the water, or we

can walk if you like."

The currach had been a gentle ride so far. Besides, the boat was fast and she knew Aedan was anxious to be home. "Over the water is fine."

Lifting his brows in surprise, Aedan murmured to the others and they bent to the oars as the craft followed the curving shoreline. At times the curragh slapped crosswise over small waves, but Rowena held on and smiled, reminded of Aedan's habit of hiding his reaction that way. Just now his smile was wide and genuine, his laughter as delighted as she had ever heard from him.

Soon the castle loomed above the shore, a massive structure of red sandstone on a green hill. The incline swept down to a sandy crescent scattered with stones and seaweed, the rocky hillside and beach forming a small cove. Above it all, the castle was blocky and forbidding, with round towers at the corners and thick walls pierced by narrow windows.

As the boat pulled into the shallows, Erik leaped out to drag its bow onshore, and Aedan helped Rowena step onto the beach. He turned to speak with his friends, and she walked up the beach a bit, gazing at the rugged beauty of cove and castle. Clusters of pebbles and round stones stretched over the damp sands like a sprawling mosaic so that she stepped carefully. Then she turned to see the men walking nearby.

"*Àite brèagha,*" she managed to say in simple Gaelic. A beautiful place.

Erik grinned. "It is! You and MacDuff will be very happy here."

She lifted a brow. Did he think she was MacDuff's bride? She almost smiled.

Aedan murmured to him in Gaelic, and Erik replied with a laugh, patting MacDuff on the shoulder. Moments later, Erik and his brother waved and rowed away.

She waited on the beach for Aedan to return. "Your friends are lovely men," she said. "Erik said we would be happy here and spoke in Gaelic. What was that?"

"He said it was nice to meet you and hope you have a nice visit."

She huffed. "He said more than that."

He chuckled. "Truly, he thought I brought home a bride, seeing your veil and all. I said you were a widow and a friend. So he said I was a *baobach*, a dimwit, if I did not marry such a fine widow when I need a wife." He tipped his head.

"Ah. *Baobach*. A word to remember." She gave him an impish smile.

He laughed. "Come up to Castle Black."

"It is not black, but red."

"Local red sandstone, pink when dry and quite red when damp. In Gaelic, the place is called *Caisteal Duibh, duibh* for black and for MacDuibh or MacDuff. Now we call it Castle Black—it does not catch English attention as easily. They despise anything called MacDuff, person or thing. Well, Edward seems to," he clarified.

"It is a handsome castle, and may the English stay well away from it." As she spoke, she walked with him up the beach, going carefully over damp stones slick with surf and seaweed. She bent to pick up a pink stone, turning it in her fingers. "What a pretty stone. A bit of pink rock crystal made smooth by water."

"You have an eye for those. Does it have healing power?"

"Many such stones have a special quality. This may too." She tucked it into the purse still damp from its earlier dunking. "This place is beautiful in a rough way, as if torn out of the earth. That rocky wall under the hill has crevices and openings—are there caves under the hill?"

"A few." He reached out to offer a hand over a slippery patch of rounded rocks. "I will show you later. One has been used as a dovecote for generations."

"Is that the cooing sound? Doves in the caves?"

"Aye. There are large and small caves there, though some fill with water when the tide is high or storms drive the surf up. A family of travelers stays in the dry caves in the winter months. They are good folk and we let them be. Come up the hill. The castle will have seen us by now." He led the way up the grassy sward.

"I see guards on the battlement." At the top of the castle, she saw two men waving, helmets gleaming in the cloudy afternoon light.

"Guards there, kinfolk and servants likely watching from the windows." As he spoke, shouts sounded from above. "And here comes a wee lad."

Running past the wide base of the castle toward the hilltop, she saw a woman, a child, and two dogs bounding toward them.

"Aedan! Aedan!" the woman called, lifting her skirts to run.

"Da!" the child screamed.

CHAPTER SIXTEEN

"D A!" THE BOY ran on fast little legs to overtake the dogs, then stumbled, laughing, rolling partway down the hill, scrambling to his feet. One of the dogs leaped over him, rounded, nosed at him, then ran in tandem with the boy.

"Colban! Here to me, lad!" Aedan squatted on his haunches, arms spread wide to welcome the boy and the dogs tumbling into his arms and all over him, laughing, barking, the dogs licking faces, bounding over to Rowena, who stepped back, smiling, staying out of the way of the happy tumult. She got her share of licked hands too, though the dogs, one large and one small, wheeled back to the man and boy fast enough.

"It is good to see you!" Aedan managed to stand, little boy hanging off one shoulder, the taller hound bounding up, pawing his chest, panting with delight. "*Ach,* you lot," he said to both dogs, "give me a moment with my lad, will you? Look how tall he has grown! All but a man, and his da not here to measure his great feet for new boots!"

"I have new boots, see!" Colban stuck out a foot to show him. "Sir Patrick had them made for me."

"Sir Patrick? Do you mean our neighbor, Patrick Wemyss? Marjorie, lass!" Aedan grinned as the woman stopped on the hill just above them, hands on hips, her smile wide and dimpled, her cheeks rosy. Her hair, as golden-red as a bright sunset, was braided in a halo around her head beneath a simple kerchief.

"Aedan MacDuff, where have you been these weeks?" She smiled as she spoke. "I am glad to see you hale and whole and still with the living, since we had no word."

"No time to scare up a messenger! They did not get me yet, and I see the lad is hale and whole too, and I have you to thank for it." He reached out an arm and she ran to throw her arms around him and the boy too, dogs leaping about.

Rowena stood by, silent and smiling, one hand fending off an affectionate dog. Her eyes stung with tears to see such love, bright and clear, in their greeting. She felt a tug within, a wish that she too was part of that warm, laughing embrace. But she folded her hands, feeling as if she stood outside in the cold, watching through a window as a joyful family sat round a cozy, crackling hearth fire. She yearned for the same, missing the dream of the family she might have had once.

Her family at Kincraig was warm and close. But she had lost her dream of her own little family and had tucked that away. Yet now she saw Aedan MacDuff as the center of his, his big heart and cheerfulness like a glow enveloping them. She smiled, taking in that joy and strength, wishing she were part of it too, with him.

"Greetings, lady," Marjorie told Rowena. "Aedan, who have you brought us?"

He released his sister, set his son down, and held out his hand to Rowena. "No need to be shy. This is Lady Rowena Keith of Kincraig. I am escorting her home. This is my sister, Lady Marjorie MacDuff, and my son Colban."

"Welcome to Caisteal Duibh!" Marjorie wove between circling dogs and held out her hands to meet Rowena's grasp. "Colban, where are your manners, aye?"

"My lady!" Colban bounced toward her and bowed like a knight in a royal court. "I am Colban MacDuff," he said, straightening and puffing out his little chest, "son of Aedan, son of Duncan, son of Colban, son of Malcolm, son of—stop it, Cheese!" He pushed at the dog nosing into him.

"Cheese!" Rowena laughed, petting the dog's head. "It is

lovely to meet you, *Colban mhic Aodh mac Duibh*. And Cheese, you too," she said.

"The big one is Cheese and the little one is Bean." Colban took her hand, looking very serious as he bowed again. Then he looked up at his father. "Does she have the Gaelic, Da?" He spoke in English.

"Just a little, but we forgive her because she knows the old ways."

"Then I am glad she came to stay with us, and I will teach her the Gaelic."

"Ah, but the lady must go home and I promised to take her there, so we can stay only a day or two. And you will travel soon too, with your Aunt Marjorie and Great-aunt Jennet. I will explain all," he added to Marjorie.

"You had better," Marjorie said. "Our lady aunt is eager to see you. Come."

AEDAN SAT AT dinner, pleased and satisfied. Family again. It meant all to him. All. And with Rowena here as well—he sucked in a breath to stop the thought before it could take him too far into the dreams he had set aside years ago, dreams that clamored now.

They gathered for an early supper in the great hall, a raftered room with whitewashed walls and planked floors. Cushioned chairs sat beneath tall, shuttered windows and the long table was flanked with benches. Swords and shields were hung on the walls between lengths of plaid in bright patterns, with plaid curtaining the windows and covering cushions too. At the center of the great room, a tall iron fire basket radiated heat. Altogether, the cozy atmosphere meant home to him, and he would protect it however he could. Just now that meant moving his family away for a while.

Silent, he watched them fondly: Marjorie, his younger sister, widowed ten years, and her child lost too young. Yet she had an unmatched grace and lively spirit, and like Rowena, had carried on, despite tragedy, to find her work in life; Marjorie was a skilled weaver. He knew all too well the toll that losing a spouse took on the heart and spirit. Alisoun had been gone five full years, leaving him lonely. But his son was the treasure of his life, and he treasured Marjorie and Aunt Jennet for their steadfast, caring natures.

Seated beside him, Lady Jennet set her hand over his, affection crinkling her blue eyes. "Finally home. I am so relieved. We worry about you so when you are gone."

"Here, but not for long. That is what I wanted to talk to you and Marjorie about."

"Not yet. We just want to enjoy having you with us. Supper first, then a game with the lad, and later we will talk."

"Aye," he agreed. His uncle's wife, Jennet Ogilvie, an older cousin to Erik and Andrew, was still a beauty as she aged, with elegant bones, pale hair peeking from under a white kerchief, and ice-blue eyes that had warmth even when she acted stern. She was not a widow in fact but in spirit, for her husband, his uncle Duff MacDuff, actual clan chief, had been an English captive for several years.

Jennet brooked no fools and was the pragmatic, efficient heart of the little family they had formed at Castle Black after Alisoun's passing, when Aedan had an infant son and owed his knight duties to Edward. Jennet and her husband took Aedan, Colban, and widowed Marjorie in at Castle Black, and together they parented the little boy. Colban's aunt and great-aunt had become a mothering presence for his son, and he was grateful.

"Da, watch me! Watch!" Colban said, and Aedan looked up to see him stand on the bench and walk, foot in front of foot, arms out for balance.

"Very good—" Aedan began.

"Colban, we sit during supper," Marjorie said.

"Sit *now*, Colban MacDuff, and stop that horseplay," Jennet said.

He sat, but shifted to a crouch, curled his fingers, and growled. "I am a gargoyle!"

"Gargoyles are rain gutters," Aedan pointed out.

"Do not say that, he will spit water next," Marjorie said as Aedan chuckled.

"He reminds me of you at that age," Jennet said. "Always acting the wee jester."

Rowena, sitting across from him and beside Colban, laughed suddenly, sweetly.

"Ah, you know our Aedan, my lady," Jennet said.

"A little," she replied.

"A little is enough and sometimes too much," Marjorie said, a twinkle in her eye.

"Erik Ogilvie called him a *baobach*," Rowena said. The women burst out laughing.

To cover a smile, Aedan picked up the goblet of green Venetian glass that held watered wine, for his kinswomen knew his habit. Sipping, he savored the light taste and watched Colban with quiet delight, growling gargoyle, wee lad giving Marjorie a hug, hungry little boy spooning up stew. The last time he had been here, Colban was just beginning to learn letters and numbers from a local priest who taught some boys and girls in the parish. Already he seemed older.

Marjorie spoke with Rowena, admiring the dark blue gown borrowed from Lady Ellen, sliding the fabric between her fingers. Aedan leaned forward.

"Marjorie is a weaver," he told Rowena. "Her plaids are very fine indeed." He patted the tartan draped over his shoulder and tunic.

"I would love to see your work," Rowena told her.

"There are lengths of it hung on the walls here, and I will be glad to show you what is on the loom. Aedan, that old plaid is filthy and torn—and damp too. I will give you a new one."

"This has been to hell and back, and today I fell in the sea and used it for a towel, so it has not quite dried. I hoped you could repair the weave."

"Or turn it into a horse blanket!"

He laughed, then looked at Colban. "Lad, I wonder if you could play a game while I chat with your aunts about something."

"We could play a table game if you have one," Rowena offered.

Colban had a hand under the table as he slipped bits of food to one or two dogs. "Do you know Ard-Rì? We have a silver board with polished stones, black and white."

"High King? I know it. Will you capture my king, or shall I capture yours?"

"I will get to the king's square first! All your knights and soldiers will fall. But I will help you pick them up again," he offered.

"Thank you. Show me your board while your da and your aunts have a chat. Come," she said, standing, holding out a hand.

Aedan stood when she did, and watched them, entranced. She had a natural manner with the boy, kind and respectful. Colban had taken to her easily, and the dogs followed her too.

"Aedan. Aedan!" Jennet repeated. "What is this matter we must discuss?"

He stepped away from the table as two maidservants entered the room. "They will want to clear the table. We can talk over there on the window bench. Ah, those are fine new cushions."

"I covered the old pillows with scraps of plaid," Marjorie said. "I could make cushion covers out of your old plaidie too."

"A horse blanket suits a knight's plaid better than a seat cushion."

"Either way, *baobach,* you would sit on it," she replied.

"BUT WHY LEAVE tomorrow?" Marjorie asked after he explained the threat from Edward and Sir Malise, adding that Sir Brian would take them to Bass Rock for safety.

"Day after tomorrow," he clarified, "we will go to Dunfermline to meet Brian Lauder." He glanced toward Rowena and Colban, who sat on the opposite end of the long room focused on moving black and white polished stones over a silver board.

As if sensing his glance, she looked up at smiled. Just then,

Colban slid one of his white stones into place and crowed.

"Aedan," Jennet prompted. "You were saying?"

He cleared his throat. "Just for a few weeks until the matter is settled. Sir Brian and Lady Ellen are good friends and you are welcome on the Rock or at Tyningham."

Jennet set her needlework aside and folded her hands calmly. "The Bass is a prison now, they say, and remote. Think of your son. He should not live in such a place."

"I am thinking of my son," he said. "I fostered with the Lauders, remember?"

"Aye. But to leave here—my loom is not easily moved," Marjorie said, "and I have plaids that are promised."

"Those may have to wait. Bass Rock is safer for all of you just now."

Jennet huffed. "How could this castle be unsafe, guarded and secure as it is? Even when the English burned Wemyss Castle, between here and Dunfermline, they did not ride here. They will leave us be. We have had troubles enough."

"Edward has always threatened the MacDuffs, Aunt, you know that. He keeps our nephew in England as his ward, truly a hostage. And he has caged Isabella in a heinous manner, while your husband, our chief, sits in a dungeon," he said fiercely.

"And they captured you, but you escaped. Now they want Colban!" Marjorie said.

"So it seems. The Bass Rock is the one place you can be secure."

"Sir Patrick will come by tomorrow," Marjorie said. "He often brings news, and may have heard word of Edward's plans in Fife."

"Patrick Wemyss?" he asked.

"Aye. The other Patrick, old Abernethy, is still exiled. But we hear his son Peter is back," Jennet said. "I hope he will not stir up that old feud."

"He would not dare. Patrick Wemyss is a sheriff in Fife. He is a good man and can be trusted."

"And well he should be," Marjorie said firmly. "The Wemysses and MacDuffs have long been allies. The English burned Sir Patrick's castle three years back, if you recall. Edward made some recompense by awarding Sir Patrick the sheriffdom. But he has no funds to rebuild, so he sometimes stays here, and is always welcome."

Something in her voice, and her quick blush, caught his attention. "Always welcome?"

"Does it bother you?"

He lifted a hand to beg peace. "Not me. I like Patrick Wemyss, always have. It is good to know he has been watching over our castle in my absence."

"Are we truly under threat here?" Jennet asked.

"It is possible, so we need measures to prevent it. Apparently, Edward gave orders regarding my kin and this castle, and entrusted them to Sir Malise Comyn."

"I do not know him," Jennet said.

"I have heard that name," Marjorie said. "Sir Patrick said Malise Comyn was nearly killed by nuns." Beside her, Lady Jennet gasped.

"Something like that," Aedan said. "Suffice to say he may try to take Colban and wreak havoc here. So you must go elsewhere for a while."

"Aedan is right," Jennet said. "But we would be gone for only a bit, aye?"

"As soon as it is safe, you can come back. The lad looks tired," he said, glancing across the room. "Lady Rowena needs rest too after this day. Where will you put her?"

"She can have the guest chamber," Jennet said. "And your bedchamber is always ready for you. You both look weary."

"It has been a busy week of days." He stood. "Colban, how goes the game?"

"Lady Rowena's king is surrounded! I am winning!" Colban lifted his arms high.

"Be careful. Your opponent is a clever lady," Aedan warned.

"Why, this very day she defeated a band of naughty pirates. Perhaps she will tell you about it at bedtime."

"Pirates! I want to hear about the pirates!"

"Then go off to bed so she can tell you about her unique strategy." He leaned out of the way as Rowena threw a little black playing piece at him. He caught the stone deftly and set it on the table at her elbow, his arm brushing hers.

"I will be back," he said as he went to the door. "I need to find the seneschal in the garrison."

"Your cousin will either be at supper or on the battlements at this time of day," Jennet said. "I am surprised he did not come over to greet you, but the lad takes his work very seriously."

"Good. We need Michael Balfour's vigilance, especially now."

CROSSING THE YARD with long strides, glad of the sea wind blowing through his hair, refreshing the old plaid that Marjorie disparaged, he took the outer steps leading to the battlement to where two guards strolled.

"Hey lads!" he boomed, waving. "Halloo!"

"MacDuff!" one called as both turned. "Welcome home."

"Good to see you. Where is Sir Michael?"

"At his supper!" one called back.

He went to the corner tower and took a few narrow steps inside the breadth of the stout curtain wall, a warren of rooms that could easily house fifty men, though only twenty made up Castle Black's small garrison. He passed sleeping quarters and meeting rooms, and took another door into a separate building jutting into the bailey to enter the garrison dining hall.

The dim vaulted room held several tables where knights and guards ate supper or played at dice and bones. Each one lifted a hand or said a greeting. Then he spied the young man he sought coming toward him.

"Aedan!" Michael Balfour said, holding out a hand. "I heard you had returned, but I did not want to disturb time with family." He grasped Aedan's hand.

"Michael, you are a cousin, lad, and always welcome with us."

"Thank you." The knight, ten years younger than Aedan, was black-haired and brown-eyed, with a short dark beard that did not hide the dimples that enhanced a charm that would have done him well in a royal court in more peaceful days. But Michael wanted to serve Scotland and Bruce, and despite his age, he was a capable leader. Though they had not seen each other often as boys, when Aedan heard of Michael's prowess, he invited him to Castle Black. Soon he was so impressed with his cousin's skill and wisdom that he had asked him to serve as seneschal to direct the garrison and ensure the safety of the castle and its residents.

They climbed to a parapet and stood in a corner overlooking the sea that surged to the beach a hundred feet below the castle. Aedan explained Edward's threat, warning that an attack could occur if Malise Comyn arrived.

"My son and my kinswomen will go with Brian Lauder to the Bass Rock tomorrow. Then I mean to escort a friend to Kincraig in Lanarkshire, but I will be back."

"We will need more men if Comyn intends to follow the king's orders. Patrick Wemyss has offered to assign men here. We should do that."

"Aye then. My sister mentioned Sir Patrick, and I had the sense—is there something there?"

Michael smiled. "They are smitten with each other, if you ask me. As sheriff and neighbor, he keeps watch over us here and shares news when he has it. But he has not mentioned this business with Edward and Comyn. However, he did tell us that you were taken not long ago and had managed to escape. We had feared you might have disappeared into a dungeon for years."

"I might have, but I did not like their plan, so I left. I met a young woman who was also held, and brought her with me."

"Is she the one you will escort to Lanarkshire?"

Aedan nodded. "I owe her a favor. So," he went on, "I am grateful to Sir Patrick for his help in my absence."

"Aye. Colban is fond of him too. I should tell you, sometimes I allow the lad to knock about with wooden waster swords. He is a quick learner. Lady Marjorie and Lady Jennet are not in favor, but agree you would want him to play at swords as he grows."

"It has to be part of his education. I appreciate it. Sooner or later, many of us will need to knock about with swords." Aedan sighed.

FOLLOWING THE BOY and his aunt up the stone spiral stairs, Rowena felt the pull of fatigue as she climbed. The voyage across the firth, then sickness, a pirate attack, and an encounter with Malise—all had taken a toll. Rest would do her good, and she felt sure she would sleep well. She felt immediately welcome and at home here.

Marjorie led them up the levels, Colban following with a bouncing step, and Bean, the little brindled gray terrier, running up with them, stretching to make it up the stairs. Rowena proceeded carefully on the wedge-shaped steps that wheeled around a massive stone pillar soaring four levels to the parapet. Aedan had remained in the hall with his cousin and seneschal, Sir Michael Balfour, a quiet, rather beautiful young knight. Lady Jennet sat with them, doing needlework by candlelight, taking part in their conversation.

The older lady was calm, composed, elegant, strict but kind, Rowena thought with admiration. She could see why Aedan and his sister adored their aunt, who had a firm hand over the household. Marjorie had a delightful freshness despite long years as a widow, which she had revealed to Rowena while they chatted at supper. Rowena also admired her ability to match her brother's wit, and Marjorie was skilled and creative too. Her handsome plaids decorated the hall and were worn by many; they were in demand at local market fairs too, she had learned.

She loved being at Castle Black, and had not expected that. No wonder Aedan had wanted to hurry home to rescue his family from any hint of danger.

As for his little son, Rowena had already fallen in love with Colban, with his honey-colored hair and blue eyes, perhaps inherited from his mother; he had his father's features, his curls, his laugh, and sense of mischief.

"I want to show Lady Rowena her bedchamber, can I?" Colban asked Marjorie, and looked at Rowena. "It is just above my room, up these steps."

She smiled, holding fast to the rope slung around the stone pillar as she followed the others. The tenacious little dog, rough-coated and ready, scampered repeatedly up and down, then up again in excitement. One moment Colban was chattering to Marjorie, who climbed ahead. The next moment the terrier yelped, slipped down a step, and rolled into Colban, tripping him.

With a cry, the boy tumbled into Rowena, who caught him as he fell awkwardly across the wedge steps, taking her down to her knees with him. Holding the boy in one arm, her hand clinging to the rope to keep from tipping backward, she fell hard, smacking her knee and twisting her foot on the hard-edged stone. But she hardly noticed, intent on catching him.

"There," she said, breathless. "There we are."

"Oh! Colban—my lady—" Marjorie ran down, bending to help them stand again. Bean had fallen a step or two below and clambered back up, shaking her coat, panting, and licking Colban's hand.

Brushing her fingers over him, looking for injury, Rowena noticed then that his hand was limp. He whimpered. "My arm—"

"He's hurt," Marjorie said.

"We will get him to his room and find out for sure. Can you walk, lad?"

He nodded tearfully, holding his arm as they went up a few steps to the level platform. Marjorie opened a door and ushered them into a room that held a draped, postered bed with a green plaid coverlet. Marjorie lifted Colban to the bed, and Rowena moved close as the little dog ran in after them, jumping about. Marjorie set Bean aside and calmly told her to sit.

"May I see?" Rowena asked Colban, who nodded. Gingerly she took his hand in hers, noting the bruise forming on his forearm as she carefully pushed his sleeve up.

"This—is—my room," he said tearfully. "Aunt Marjorie sleeps in this bed. My bed is in there—" He pointed with his free hand toward a second door that opened on a small circular room inside the round corner tower. It held a narrow bed.

"What a cozy sleeping chamber," she said, as she examined his arm. "Where does it hurt?" She asked questions and he pointed here and there, but when she asked him to turn his wrist, he could not, wincing. She looked at Marjorie.

"Can we cut his sleeve? He may have broken something."

"B-broken?" Colban said, as Marjorie turned away and came back with small shears to open the sleeve along the seam.

"I will fix the sleeve for you later," Marjorie promised. "Show us your arm, dear."

He did, snuffling, lip trembling. "It hurts. But knights do not cry."

"They certainly do," Rowena said, as she probed along the forearm. "I will not tell and neither will your aunt, so cry if you like. Can you turn your arm that way? Ah, that hurts? Stop, then."

She turned to Marjorie. "I think there is a fracture, but it could be a bad sprain. I can splint it and wrap it and give him some healing herbs. Would that be fine with you?"

Marjorie blinked at her, wide-eyed. "You know how to treat it?"

"I do. But his father should hear what happened first. I will need some linen wrapping and a few things." She detailed some of the herbs to make a poultice. Marjorie nodded, promising to fetch those and fetch Aedan as well, then flew from the room.

Rowena spoke calmly to Colban, and soon he laughed tearfully about the dog running on the steps, and how sad silly little Bean would feel if she knew he was hurt.

"We do not need to tell her," Rowena said, putting a finger to her lips.

Aedan pounded up the steps and rushed into the room, Marjorie behind him. "What happened?"

In his eyes, Rowena saw what she had not seen before in this strong man—fear and love twined together. She saw how deeply he loved his son. *He is my world*, he had told her once. Then she saw him master it, straighten his shoulders.

"Hey, lad. A wee tumble? It happens to us all. How is Bean, did you save her? I know you did. Brave lad." He ruffled Colban's honey-colored curls.

If Rowena had never thought of loving Aedan before that moment, it came to her swift and sure and deep then, watching him laugh with his son.

CHAPTER SEVENTEEN

"He tripped on the dog, I think," Rowena said. "He will be fine, aye, Colban?"

"Aye," he said, lip quivering.

"Rowena caught him and kept him from falling all the way down. There was water on the steps, and the dog slipped a little," Marjorie said. "Earlier the servants filled a bath in your chamber, Aedan, and must have missed mopping up."

"I see. Such things cannot be helped, but thank heavens the boy will be fine. And you, Lady Rowena? Did you fall as well?"

"I am fine," she said, flexing her ankle, which had begun to ache.

"My arm hurts, but Lady Rowena says she can fix it."

"She can indeed," his father said, "and we are grateful she is here to help you."

"Are you an herb-wife?" Marjorie asked. "One of the cunning folk?"

"I am," Rowena said.

"She is the very healer who tended me at Holyoak," Aedan said. "She is the reason I am here today."

"Truly! We are so fortunate and so grateful to you," Marjorie breathed.

Lady Jennet came up the stairs just then, with Sir Michael behind her, hurrying through the open door. "What is going on?" the lady asked.

"All is well," Rowena said, and while the others talked, she prepared a quick poultice with a few herbs in cold water, and rinsed the boy's arm. With the linen strips and a wooden spoon Marjorie brought at her request, she splinted and wrapped his arm.

"What more will you need, dear? We are so grateful to you," Lady Jennet said, having just heard of Rowena's ability.

"If we could have some willow and chamomile steeped in hot water, perhaps with mint or lavender, that will help calm him and help the ache a little." Nodding, Lady Jennet went downstairs to get the things.

"Does it seem broken?" Aedan asked quietly.

"Perhaps. We may as well consider it so, and give it some stability and coddle it so it will heal, whether broken or sprained."

"What a lucky lad to have a lady medécin as a guest here," Aedan told Colban.

"A what?" he asked.

"That is like a physician," Marjorie said.

"But I am not that," Rowena said. "I work with herbs and stones and such."

"She knows a great deal and you are in very good hands," Aedan said.

"I want to leave his arm splinted for the night," she said. "Tomorrow I will make a wax sleeve for him before you leave with Sir Brian."

"Wax sleeve?" Marjorie asked. "What will you need?"

"Linen dipped in limewash and some warm wax that I can shape around his arm. That should protect it nicely." As she moved around, she could feel a deep ache and tenderness forming in her ankle and foot, which she had twisted when she'd grabbed the boy and held onto the rope to keep from tumbling farther down. But she could tend to that herself later, and would not call attention to it here.

Soon, with his arm wrapped and the excitement subsiding, Colban began to yawn. Aedan carried him into the little round room with the narrow bed and set him down, then stood back as Marjorie and Rowena helped ready him for bed in a simple shirt. Marjorie helped him wash his face and such, then left the chamomile and willow drink beside his bed.

"I want to hear about pirates," Colban said.

Rowena, tucking an extra pillow under his arm, laughed softly and agreed. She sat carefully on the bed beside him.

"Once there was a longship that carried your father and Sir Brian and me, too," she said. "And a huge pirate ship came out of the fog! We were so surprised and your father and Sir Brian were very brave, fighting off the pirates who wanted our gold."

"What did you do?" Colban asked, eyes wide.

"Tell him what you did, my lady," Aedan said, quirking a smile.

"I—felt kind of sick, and I—" She paused, wondering what to say next. She looked up and saw Aedan, Marjorie, and Lady Jennet still standing by the door. He folded his arms over his chest and cocked a brow, waiting.

"And I—spewed my dinner all over them! And then they went back to their ship!"

Colban burst out laughing. Aedan guffawed, and his sister and aunt laughed too.

"Did you? Did she, Da?"

"She certainly did," he drawled. "And they jumped into the sea and were never seen again."

Marjorie was still laughing, and Lady Jennet wiped her eyes.

"Aedan," Marjorie said. "We love Lady Rowena."

He grinned, then turned to her. "Thank you, Lady Rowena. Let me sit with him now until he goes to sleep. Marjorie sleeps in the larger room so she will be nearby all night. You need rest."

"I will show you to your room, dear," Lady Jennet said.

She nodded and stood, favoring her ankle, hoping no one saw her slight limp. At the door, she turned, glancing back.

Aedan bent over his son, speaking softly. Her heart nearly burst with love to see that. She turned away, not wanting anyone to notice what shone in her eyes.

HER ROOM WAS very like Colban's, placed just above his on a level in the round corner tower. The larger chamber held a big bed, and the small circular room had another modest bed tucked beside a chair and table. The smaller bed looked so inviting, with pillows and a handsome red plaid blanket, that she settled there after washing up. She was pleased to find a basin with a jug of clear water, and glad to find a tiny private latrine room as well. Those small spaces would be stacked on the tower's outermost wall, utilizing a chute that would extend down the cliff to the sea.

She examined her foot, the ankle bruised and sore, and applied some ointment that Lady Jennet had brought earlier for Colban. Then she undressed to her linen shift and lay down, blowing out the candle, and was soon asleep in the snug space.

And she dreamed that Thomas the Rhymer came to her, walking through a forest ripe with fog. *Thou art where thee must be,* he said, *doing what thee must do.*

But Grandda, I do not know what to do. Tell me.

The crystal has its home, the sea comes in, the doves cry out, the faery stones are safe. Thou has found thy guardian.

But Grandda—

She woke to a noise, unsure for a moment where she was. Sitting up, she heard a slight, persistent sound. She stood, hopping a bit on her stiff foot, took the blanket from the bed and wrapped it around her shoulders to step out into the darkened room, illuminated only by bluish moonlight streaming through a narrow outer window.

The noise came again. She opened the door and looked out on the stairs. No one was there. Shuffling back through the room, she heard it again, a scratching, then a series of whimpers and more scratching.

It had to be one of dogs, but the stairwell was empty. The only doors in the room led to the latrine chute and her small sleeping chamber.

The sound seemed to be coming from the wall. Puzzled, she followed it in the darkness to find a plaid panel hanging there, with something like a door handle behind it. Pushing the plaid aside, she found a hidden door.

The scratching sounded again. She tugged on the iron ring and cracked the door open a bit. Suddenly a terrier squeezed through the gap and leaped up to greet her. "Bean!" she said. "What are you doing in there?"

Thinking it must be a closet of some kind, she peered into the darkness to see a short flight of steps that turned a corner. A moment later, she heard footsteps and saw a blare of golden light, then big bare feet coming down the steps. Holding a candle, Aedan descended toward her. She stood back while Bean jumped about with absolute joy, licking Rowena's hands as she bent to pet her and rub her ears.

"Come here, you pesky—here, you!" Aedan stepped through the doorway, reaching down for the dog and grabbed her up. Her little body squirmed with delight in his arms as she licked his face all over and then hung over his arm to cock her head and look at Rowena.

Straightening in the gap of the doorway, holding the dog, he saw Rowena too.

Startled for an instant, she was not sure this was Aedan.

Tall, broad, in a long tunic and bare feet, stood a powerfully handsome man with dark, damp hair, beautiful long-lidded hazel eyes, and a familiar smile. Yet something was different. He set the candle, held in one hand, on a nearby table.

"It is me," he said, rubbing his bare chin.

"Oh! You shaved!"

"I did." Hazel eyes crinkling, he gave her a wide smile, his teeth excellent, lips full, swollen a bit with the cut from earlier that day. A pink blush spread into his clean, smooth cheeks. His skin was fine, the sort that colored easily, marred only by the scar that ran from cheekbone to ear. "And I am sorry the dog woke you just now. She got away from me. She must have sensed you were here."

"You shaved," she repeated, still stunned, oddly trying to recognize him.

He rubbed his jaw. "You look surprised. Not good?"

"It is good. I just—had not seen your face before." She reached out to touch his jaw, softly bristled, then touched the scar she had stitched months ago, and grazed over the new bruise he'd acquired from a pirate.

His skin under her fingers, after the scraping of the blade, was warm and surprisingly soft. His chin surprised her too, with a gentle cleft like a recurve bow, determined and yet whimsical. She touched a finger to his swollen lip.

He pulled in a breath. So did she, and dropped her hand away.

"My lady aunt ordered a bath set up in my chambers, and she intended to order one here for you too, but Colban fell and we came running." He slicked his damp hair back, dark curls catching his fingers. "After Colban went to sleep, I went back to my room and bathed and shaved. It was time."

"The shave will help. They are searching for a big man with a bushy beard."

"True. Also, I thought you might like it." His gaze caught hers.

"I do." A blush filled her cheeks. "Has Colban seen you without a beard?"

"Last year I shaved once to show him, and let him watch the process so he would not be confused or startled."

"What did he say?"

He twisted his mouth awry. "He said, 'Da, your chin looks like a bum!'"

Rowena laughed, cupping a hand over her mouth. Aedan set a finger to his lips.

"Hush or you will wake the household." He grinned.

"It does rather look like that." She brushed her thumb over his chin again.

"Out of the mouths of babes." He scowled playfully. "And here I thought I was handsome and virile, like Sir Lancelot of old."

"You are very handsome," she said. And virile, a thought that sent soft lightning through her. Suddenly shy, she petted Bean's head, scrunching the dog's ears. "I heard a noise and wondered if someone had come to fetch me for Colban."

"He is asleep, and so is Marjorie. All is well."

"I was going to go up in a little while, but I do not want to disturb them."

"Let them rest." In his arms, Bean stretched for more head rubs, and squirmed enough that he set her down, then gave her a little push through the doorway. "Up you go." He shut the door quickly. "She will squeeze right back through here if I leave it open."

"Where does it lead?"

"To my chamber. These two rooms are connected." He watched her for a moment. She felt a tug, hard and sure and nearly physical, between them. Her heart beat so loudly she thought he might hear it. "I should go," he said. "You need to sleep."

"So do you." The pull to be near him felt insistent.

He grasped the iron latch, turned. "Thank you. I am glad you were here for the lad. If you had not caught him, he could have been injured more seriously."

"The arm will bother him for a bit, but will heal."

"Such things happen. When I was young, I often fell, tripped, climbed, jumped, broke, or bruised myself. Aunt Jennet threatened to pack me in wool and shut me in a box until I was older. I believed her, and worried whenever she got the yarns out."

She laughed. "Colban is very like you. He even has a dimple in his chin, I see that now. He is a happy child. And so happy you are home."

"I am not home enough. But Marjorie and Aunt Jennet are good for him. He likes you too." His voice softened and his eyes sparkled. "Go rest."

"I will look in on your lad early in the morning."

"Aye." He pulled on the latch. "Good night."

"Good night." She did not want him to leave.

Aedan opened the door, then closed it so fast she thought the dog had bolted toward it. He turned, reached out, and pulled her into his arms.

The kiss was sudden, tender, deep—not the impulsive kiss shared on the longship, but a kiss of passion and certainty. She melted like butter at the first touch of his lips, at his hands on her waist.

He drew back in a natural question, and she answered by circling her arms around his neck, pressing to him. His hand cradled the back of her head, her hair spilling loose down her back as she leaned into his sure embrace. The wonder of that swift, surprising kiss and the sense that it declared something honest and real between them thrilled through her, crown to toe.

She had wanted this, scarcely realizing it, but her body knew before her mind or heart just how much she wanted this with him. A soft moan escaped her, pleasure and desire, and his next kiss covered it. Cupping her face in his hands, he pulled away, touching his brow to hers.

"Och, lass, we cannot—"

"We can." The words surprised her, out before her usual reason could take over.

"God in heaven," he murmured, and pulled her hard against him to kiss her again, the firm response of his body stirring her body too, so that heat shivered through her. He leaned back, his height such that her toes all but came off the floor.

But then he set her on her bare feet. "I did not mean to disturb your rest."

"You are not disturbing it," she whispered. "Suddenly I am not tired."

"Ah, and what shall we do about that, hey?" He brushed her hair back, tipped her chin up, kissed her.

"You could stay for a bit," she said in a rush.

"Could I?" It was not a request—it was pondering. "I am not sure."

"I just—do not want you to go yet." She felt a new urge to act on her feelings before the moment was lost to doubt, to reason. She was learning something from him, feeling her protective caution beginning to shake loose, like leaves from a tree.

"Rowena," he said, taking her hand. She turned, hoping he would sit with her—but a sharp pain stung through her ankle and she winced, unable to put weight on it.

"What is it?" He took her elbow.

"Just—naught."

"When you have said that before, it was something. You are in pain. What is it?"

"My ankle," she admitted. "When I moved just now, it gave out a little. I twisted it on the steps when I grabbed Colban. Clumsy of me."

"Not clumsy. Those steps can be treacherous, and Marjorie said there was a water spill. Can you walk?"

"It will be fine." She took another step, felt a shot of pain, halted.

"Let me see." He dropped to his haunches.

She drew up the long hem of her linen shift and stuck out her bare foot and ankle. In the flickering candlelight, she saw the darkening bruise on her outer ankle and part of her foot.

"No walking about the hills for you, lass."

"It will heal. I put some ointment on it and will bandage it."

He took her foot in the palm of his big, warm hand, and she rested her hand on his shoulder for balance. "I could bandage and splint it for you." He grinned up at her.

"Truly, it will be fine soon."

He set her foot down and stood. "Sometimes it is good to ask for help. Who heals the healer, hey?"

She blinked at his honesty. She was accustomed to treating others, solving their issues, but rarely asked for help herself. Yet

Aedan had been there for her at Yester, on the water, and elsewhere, just when she had been most vulnerable. His help had felt natural, easy to accept.

"I will rest it and see how it does," she said, and took a careful step. Another knife of pain stabbed through her foot. Wincing, she hopped.

"Come up," he growled, and swept her into his arms. She set her arms around his neck as he tilted his head, looking at her quizzically, wondering. Then he kissed her again, holding her in his arms as he stood. These were not the tender kisses ventured before, nor the shy kisses of years ago with her youthful husband, a sweet memory packed away in her heart, memories she had all but released.

These were powerful, startling kisses, welcome as a hearth on a cold night, kisses brimming with heat as his lips moved with hers, slaking and giving. Soon she was breathless, feeling their two hearts pounding together as one kiss became another and still another, luscious and deepening with every breath. He turned with her in his arms, and she knew that at the slightest hint from her, he would set her down, step away, end the freedom of this moment.

She did not want that. She wanted strong, honest, deep kisses, wanted his love to surround her. She wanted to shake off the caution she had worn like a caul, and let passion rise in her impulsively. The craving cascaded through her. The pain disappeared, forgotten in the circle of his arms.

Cupping his new-shaven jaw, she tilted her head to open to the slipping tease of his tongue, felt her body ache, surge for more.

He sucked in a breath, pulled back. "Lass, you are all I could ever—but I cannot."

"But—"

"I mean I cannot hold you like this for long. My knee—that wicked scar."

"Oh! Set me down, do. In there." She indicated the sleeping

chamber.

"Aye, my love." He nuzzled his nose to hers. "Though what we may be tempted to do in there may not be the best course yet."

My love. She heard that and little else, just savoring the sense of being enveloped in his bold spirit, his strength. Something was shifting within her, changing. She cared for him so much, more than anyone she had ever—loved, she thought. The feeling was more than being held secure. It was an urge to reach out and surround him too. She had been the cautious and practical one among her sisters since childhood, reinforced by the tragedy of her first marriage, and made stronger by her work as a healer. But now she needed, wanted, to break free, not let caution hem her in again.

CHAPTER EIGHTEEN

CARRYING HER, HE knocked the door open and strode in to set her on the bed. The small, dim tower room with its curved walls formed a snug space in the light of a single candle as she sat. Aedan sank beside her, the rope-slung bed creaking and sagging under him. She laughed a little at that, remembering the bed in the tavern where they had talked and laughed, where she had begun to truly grow fond of him, of his size and strength and humor. She reached up to cup her hand on his newly bared cheek, the skin warm and gritty under her palm. He kissed her again, lightly this time, and set an arm around her.

Her heart pounded. She yearned, wanting him and yet, she was hesitant, her thoughts tumbling—push and pull, courage and fear.

He rested his cheek on her head. "This is madness, this between us, so quick, so sure. What is it?"

"I wonder too. Whatever it is, I like it," she whispered. Cozy against him, she was aware of a fire building within her. "But I am not sure what I want just now." Though her body knew, she was not sure she was that bold after all.

"You want me to tend to your ankle," he murmured. It was as if he offered a reprieve, a chance to breathe, consider. "Foot," he said, tapping his knee.

She shifted on the bed to set her foot across his knee, adjusting her shift over her legs. Cradling her foot, he traced his fingers over the bruise and the swelling. An aromatic scent wafted up, a trace of the healing ointment she had rubbed there earlier.

"Do you have bandaging?" he asked.

"I brought some here should I need it for Colban." She stretched toward the small table by the bed and he reached past her to grab the linen strips. With her foot propped on his knee, he wound the lengths around her ankle with nimble fingers.

"You have done this before," she said in admiration at his easy skill.

"Aye. When I was running in the hills with Bruce and his men, there was no surgeon or healing woman if someone was injured in a skirmish. We did what we could. There." He tied the end securely around her ankle. "Try that."

She stood, carefully walking away and back to test. "That does help," she said, sitting beside him again.

"So. That is some of my debt erased, I hope."

She huffed. "You have no debt to me."

He kissed her brow. "What is this, then? Not repayment. Not only lust, though there is surely that," he said with a lilt. "Whatever we both want, lass—this may not be the time to pursue it."

"I know—but I like wondering," she said, and craned up for a kiss, her words suddenly lost in his lips. She caught her breath as his hands slid from her waist up her ribcage, fingers stretching easily to capture the sides of her breasts. She arched as he explored, kissed her, cupped and teased until she moaned against his mouth. His hands stilled, slid down, his lips parting from hers.

"But we must think what—" he began.

"I do not want to think" she said quickly. "I am usually so cautious—but I just want to feel—wanted and—" She needed courage to say what came to her. *Loved—by you.*

"You are," he murmured. "I care for you. It feels as if we are playing a game of Ard-Rì, and the board has spun about. My pieces are yours, yours are mine."

"What do you mean?" She wanted to be close, to feel his

hands upon her, his lips on hers. She nudged her nose to his. He kissed her, came away.

"I mean, in my clumsy way, that I want to think about this—just when you want to push on and think later." He touched her hair, tugging playfully at a loose wave over her shoulder. "You are careful, thoughtful. Beautiful. And I can be a rogue. But I want to be careful with you, not hurt you, or make the wrong move."

"I am not delicate, sir."

"You are stronger than either of us knows, I think. So here we sit, my bluebell and I," he said, putting his arm around her again, "both wanting this. But I will not treat this woman hastily. She is too important to me."

"You are important to her too," she admitted. "Very much so."

"Listen. You are in my thoughts every moment now. You are in my heart, do you know that? It has been so for months."

"Months? Since Holyoak?"

"When you left, I wanted to find you to thank you for saving my life. But not just that. I could not stop thinking about you. I wanted to see you again. And I wondered—if you—felt something too." His hand soothed over hers. She rubbed her thumb on his. "I did," she said. "I thought about you long after I left. I needed to know how you were. I wanted to see you again. Seeing you at Yester—felt like a miracle. You were there just when I needed you."

Head tilted, eyelids long, he looked thoughtful. "Fate."

"Fate," she agreed. "It felt that way. Feels that way," she amended.

"When I thought I might die, lying there," he said, "I told you something. Perhaps you do not remember."

"I do. You spoke of stones and—doves and secrets. I did not understand it. But you were fevered and seemed desperate. What you said did not make much sense, but once I felt sure you would live, I did not worry about it. It was not mine to know, but yours.

Nor did I share it with anyone."

"Do you recall what I said?" He took his hand away, cool air instead of warmth.

"A little of it. But you did not need me to remember it once you were better."

"Need you," he murmured. "I do now." He pulled in a breath. "I wanted to find you when I left Holyoak—because I was a little in love with you."

She caught her breath. "It can happen with healers and patients. But it is gratitude more often than not."

"Remember the young captive at Bass Rock? I watched him fall in love with you. Just a few moments in your care, and he was yours, my lady."

"If so, he is over it by now."

"I will never be over it," he said. "I believe I love you, Rowena Keith."

"Love?" she whispered. Her heart pounded, grew, soared.

"So I fell in love with my healer, hey. It happens. And it was more than gratitude."

"Aedan—"

"I have loved you—perhaps for years, in a way. When I was a lad, I loved your pretty name on a bit of parchment. Fancied myself a knight destined to wed that pretty name, daughter of a great Scottish house. I—even made plans for it."

"But that agreement was broken. You must have forgotten it."

"I never did, though we had not met. I wondered if you had married, if you were happy."

She stared at him. "I never knew."

"Nor would you." He shrugged. "No matter. I just wanted you to know now. And I wanted to know if you—felt something at Holyoak, as I did. Even though you were not aware we had a canceled betrothal."

"At Holyoak," she said, "when I heard your name, I had the oddest feeling, as if I had forgotten something. It must have been a memory of that betrothal. I did not want to leave you, even healed, and I wanted to see you again. That wish came true."

"Fate and the angels have had their way with us."

"They have. And so here we are." She angled to look up at him, breathless, marveling, feeling as if doors had flung open in some vast new place of starlight and dreams and treasures untold, if she dared take the risk.

"At the bidding of the angels." He snugged her close, an arm around her. "Enough thinking. I am a man who far prefers doing to thinking."

"You!" She gave him a wry glance. "You are as thoughtful a man as I have ever known."

"Eh, I can have no secrets around this one." He tipped a brow. "Alas, this bout of thinking and conscience has undone my plans."

"What plans?"

He hooked a finger under her chin and tipped her face up to kiss him. She leaned into the slow caress of his lips. Then he let go. "Plans for another time," he whispered.

"Aedan, stay," she breathed.

"And who is the impulsive one?"

"Me." She threw her arms around his neck and drew him toward her again. "I think I began loving you in that awful dungeon when you made me laugh when I was scared. And I loved you even more when you went in the water and I was afraid I had lost you. And I loved when we were Hamish and Grizel—"

"Hush, Grizel. Enough thinking." He wrapped her in his arms and pulled her into a deep, luscious kiss that spun through her body like honey and lightning. He laid her back on the bed, and as it sagged, they laughed. She rolled atop him, delighting in kisses, in his hands sliding along her shift, bunching it up, lowering his head to kiss her where she had not been kissed before, ever.

Then he stilled. "What the devil. Listen."

"What is that?" She lifted her head. Barking, scratching, yelping.

He lay back and groaned. "Bean. I have to let her out."

She rolled away, sighing, as he sat up and got to his feet.

"We have done a powerful lot of thinking tonight, my dear. When next we meet, we will not talk and think so much, hey."

"When next we meet, we may be slathering wax over a wee boy's arm."

"Well, then, time after that," he said, then bent to kiss her and left the room.

As she heard the door to his hidden stair shut, she remembered confessing that she had begun to love him, and he had said the same. It was true, she did love him. It filled her like a fountain. But between them and a hope of happiness—if that could indeed come about—lay a score of troubles that might prove impossible to solve.

Chapter Nineteen

T HE GREAT HALL was bathed in morning sunlight and chaos as Aedan entered the room. An array of boxes and piled garments and sundry items were spread over a large table, where his sister and aunt stood with two maidservants folding garments and packing smaller items. The women barely glanced up as he came near.

At the other end of the room, Rowena stood beside Colban, who was enthroned in a high-backed wooden chair, his arm in a cloth sling, the two dogs lounging protectively at his feet. Colban smiled and waved at his father.

He waved too, then paused near Marjorie and Jennet. "Are you bringing all these things to the Rock?"

"There are five of us," Lady Jennet said. "We will take Jane and Sheila to help us there. We do not want to burden Sir Brian's household."

"He will appreciate that. But all this?" He gestured toward books, bags holding skeins of colorful yarn, folded fabrics, and a box of carved animals and game pieces.

"Colban needs things to do, and so do we," his sister explained.

"Brian has a small library in the castle that you can use. He also keeps some sheep on the Rock if you run out of wool," he drawled.

"Shear them for me, and I will dye and spin the wool," his

sister replied.

He grinned. "I hope you can sail to Tyningham to see Lady Ellen if she does not come out to see you."

"We could go to market on the mainland with her," Lady Jennet said.

"Just be safe. It is all I ask. How is the lad now? He seemed in pain earlier this morning. Lady Rowena was just looking in on him when I went to meet with Michael and the garrison." He had spent an hour or more with the men discussing the need for more watchmen on the battlement and more patrols around the region.

"Colban seems better," Marjorie said. "Lady Rowena examined his arm and wrapped it securely. She insists he rest today since we travel tomorrow."

"Good advice." He crossed the long room and Rowena looked up, her eyes sparkling as she hid a smile. He suppressed a smile too, aware that his sister and aunt watched. No need to give them ideas; he knew they wanted him to marry again, for they had never been shy about bringing up the topic.

He huffed softly, imagining their delight if they only knew his thoughts.

"Da!" Colban said, as the dogs at his feet stood to greet Aedan while he bent to pet them. He murmured quietly to Rowena, who murmured in return, glancing at him and quickly away. What had occurred between them last evening had faded like a dream in the sunlight, but at that moment, he vividly recalled it. Her rosy cheeks said she felt the same.

"Da, look!" Colban proudly supported his arm, propped on pillows. "Lady Rowena wrapped my arm in wax! I am a candle!" He held his arm high, hand waving like a flame. Rowena gently lowered it to the pillow again.

"He is your son," she said, laughing.

"We have enough candles, lad," Aedan said. "But let me see. Is it truly wax?" He took Colban's small hand.

"Lady Jennet melted down some beeswax candles this morning so we could wrap his arm," Rowena said. "Tallow is less dear than beeswax, but does not smell as good."

"Only the best for you, lad," Aedan said. "Your arm has a good casing there."

"It will help protect his arm while the bone heals," Rowena said. "I dipped some linen strips in wine to keep his skin clean, then wrapped warm sheets of wax over that. Once the beeswax cooled, it became stiff enough to protect him for a while."

"Thank you," Aedan said, setting Colban's forearm carefully on the pillow.

"I will write a note for Sir Walter Forbes at Bass Rock," she went on. "He can remove the bandages in a fortnight or so, and apply a fresh wrapping of linen and wax for another two or three weeks, and again after that if he thinks it is needed. If they are still on the Rock then," she added.

"They may be. We cannot know."

"With your permission, as his father," she said, "I want to give Colban some watered wine, warmed and spiced, mixed with willow and a few herbs to help with pain. That will help him sleep."

"Whatever you think is needed."

She nodded and turned to speak quietly to Colban, who listened eagerly, watching her with bright, adoring eyes.

So Colban was another, Aedan thought, who was falling in love with his beautiful caretaker. For an instant, love swamped him too, simple and warm and expansive, for the boy and the woman both. He touched Colban's head, caressing the silky, tousled hair. He hated to leave him again and did not want to send him away, but his family would be safer in the lair on Bass Rock. Just for a little while, he told himself.

Rowena glanced past him. "Sir Michael just came in looking for you, I think."

"Michael!" He walked toward him. "What is it?"

"Riders, sir. Patrick Wemyss just arrived with several men."

"Ah, good! I was hoping to see him while I was here." Aedan left the room with his cousin and hurried down a short flight of stone steps to the oaken door of the keep to go outside and down wooden steps to the yard.

More than several men waited in the yard. As the Fife sheriff dismounted and turned, wearing chainmail and a dark tunic draped with a plaid in red and black, he waved and crossed toward Aedan. A chainmail hood covered most of his gray hair, framing his long face with its neatly clipped silvery beard and pale blue eyes crinkled and keen. As Aedan went to meet him, he counted the men on horseback. Twenty at least, he saw, feeling sudden hope that they were here to assist.

"Sir Patrick," he said, extending a hand. "Welcome. Good to see you."

"And you," Patrick Wemyss said, "especially good, considering what we heard lately. Yester Tower, was it?" He shook his head disparagingly.

"Aye, just a storage tower. Not the best for my reputation as a dangerous rogue."

"Better than a pit in Edinburgh or Berwick."

"My thought as well, so I walked out."

"They are looking for you. I had word of it. And as sheriff in lower Fife, I am instructed by the English crown to arrest you if I see you."

"Ah." Aedan glanced at the phalanx of mounted men. "And have you seen me?"

"I believe not. The Aedan MacDuff I remember has a great bushy beard," Patrick said, as Aedan snorted in laughter. "I saw Brian Lauder in Dunfermline. He told me of your dilemma and said you might need extra men and swords here. Just in case."

"Just in case," Aedan echoed.

"I understand King Edward sent Sir Malise Comyn to lay claim to this place."

"So it seems. I hear he intends to round up my wee son as well."

"Jesu!" Patrick shook his head.

"It will never happen," Aedan said firmly. "The boy and my

kinswomen will go with Sir Brian to the Bass Rock."

"Good." Patrick nodded, his eyes tracking to the keep. "They are still here?"

"Aye. Come up to the hall and visit. Your men can go up to the garrison quarters, and the grooms can lead the horses to the stables. We have plenty of room. This castle was built a hundred years ago to house a large garrison, but we are not many now."

"These men will be under your charge for the nonce, so direct them however you need. Most of them are Fife men and all are glad to help MacDuff."

"I appreciate that. Sir Michael will be in charge. I will be leaving for Lanarkshire, as another matter needs my attention. Will you stay the night?"

"If I may. Then I can escort your group tomorrow to meet Lauder. I expect you will want to visit the abbot in Dunfermline as well. He has a guest you will want to see. I came here to bring you that news as well."

"What news—what guest?" Aedan cocked a brow.

"Bishop Lamberton arrived at the abbot's house days ago. I knew you would want that news."

"Excellent. Dear God, I worried for him." He felt as if a weight had come off his shoulders at the news that William Lamberton, Bishop of Saint Andrews and Fife, was safe. Captured months ago by the English, he was an outspoken rebel who widely shared his views regardless of the risks, and had even taken up a sword in defense of Bruce and Scotland. Furious, King Edward had outlawed the bishop and demanded his arrest, and so Lamberton had been sought, found, and shut in an English dungeon.

Yet to Aedan, William Lamberton was far more than a rebellious Scottish bishop. He had taken Aedan and his brother, the young Earl of Fife, as his wards after their father was killed, and had become teacher, mentor, and a fatherly influence.

"So Edward released him. I had not heard."

"I did not know either until he arrived at the abbot's house in secret. He will stay there until his next move is clear. Word has been sent to Bruce, and Lamberton wants to see you."

"I will go there as soon as I can. Good that Edward backed down," he mused. "But he knew he could not imprison a bishop for long without offending the Pope, who is none too pleased with the English or the Scots as it is."

"Aye, Bruce is still excommunicated for his actions last year. Edward should be excommunicated too, if you ask me. But Edward is facing his mortality now, as he is very ill, they say. He is not one to change his mind, but he had to release Lamberton and Wishart, the other bishop he had in custody, or hear from the Pope. Not even the King of England can ignore the authority of the Church."

"How does this bode for the Scotswomen in his keeping? My niece and others."

"I asked Lamberton if he knew more about their situation. He heard that only the two bishops, not the women, would be released."

Aedan blew out a frustrated breath. "I am not surprised."

"Nor was I." Patrick walked beside him as they crossed the yard toward the keep. "Is Lady Marjorie in the hall?"

"She and Lady Jennet are there, packing for their journey." Aedan smiled. "Colban too. He broke his arm yesterday, and will be pleased to show you his bandages."

"*Och,* poor lad. I will make a fuss over it."

"He would enjoy that." Aedan clapped Sir Patrick on the shoulder.

The door opened as they approached the wooden stairs leading to the keep's high-set entrance, and Marjorie stepped out.

Sir Patrick paused, and Aedan followed his gaze as he looked up the steps. The sun brightened, slipping out from behind a cloud, and suddenly Aedan saw his sister as if in a new light. She was lovely, though he rarely noticed it. Now, her cheeks were flushed, her smile shy and rosy, her large eyes dark blue. A smattering of freckles over her nose gave her a sweet, youthful innocence, though she was near thirty. The thick red-gold braid that peeked out beneath her widow's kerchief shone like rose gold.

"Sir Patrick!" She folded her hands as she looked down the height of the stairs.

"Lady Marjorie," he replied. "So good to see you again."

"Aye so. Will you stay and visit, and share our midday meal?"

"If you like, I will."

They stared at each other, went still, both smiling. Aedan looked from one to the other. Marjorie was a widow, but she glowed like a girl. Patrick was her senior by fifteen years or more, long widowed, with grown daughters and small grandchildren.

Always protective of his sister, Aedan looked from one to the other. Just a moment in time, yet he saw the gaze that lingered between them, saw the smiles they tried to hide.

She is in love, he realized. Surely this had happened while he was away. They had known Patrick Wemyss for most of their lives, but Aedan had not seen a connection between his sister and their neighboring laird until now—or was he simply unobservant? Glancing at Patrick, he saw a change in the man he had known for years—a calmness, a new warmth in his eyes that sparkled when he looked at Marjorie MacDuff.

Just then, Lady Jennet appeared in the doorway behind Marjorie. Catching Aedan's eye, her slight, meaningful nod said she knew and was pleased.

All in an instant, longer to say than see, yet he knew it as clearly as if they had announced it. The air around them seemed filled with sunbeams.

His widowed sister, devoted to caring for his son, dedicated to her weaving art, had fallen in love with a steadfast and worthy gentleman who returned the feeling. Marjorie deserved happiness, peace, and contentment, and had finally found it—or perhaps it had found her.

Watching them, Aedan felt a tug within. After lonely years as a widower following a quiet, even tepid marriage, he was ready for something more, something lasting and strong—ready for himself and for his son too. He wanted to claim that with Rowena, if she wanted that as well.

In that swift moment, he felt a powerful urge to be the one in Rowena's life who made her feel loved, treasured, and safe. He wanted to protect her, provide for her, encourage her in her work. He wanted to join his life to hers if she would have him.

That was the source of the tug he felt in his chest and abdomen—the insistence of truth, the love burgeoning in his life, as if his soul knew already and he was waking to it.

Drawing a breath, he clapped Patrick on the shoulder. "Come up to the hall, my friend. Colban will be delighted to see you. And there is someone I want you to meet."

SUPPER WAS A quiet hour of good food and conversation as Aedan, Patrick, and Michael discussed the cause of Scotland and Bruce, while his sister, aunt, and Rowena talked of herbal remedies, weaving, and household difficulties, while now and then directing Colban's developing table manners. He had been permitted to have supper with the adults, since his father was there on a rare visit. Amused and pleased by his son's charming spirit, Aedan also found that the slightest gesture or frown from him put the lad on his best behavior quickly. Colban might be a natural jester, but he was smart and eager to learn.

Talking with Patrick and Michael, Aedan told them what he knew about English plans and Bruce's whereabouts, though some information could not be shared without Bruce's approval. His thoughts went to his mission regarding the regalia entrusted to him last year. He needed to be sure it was still safe where he had hidden it, and then decide what to do with it. That could wait until the castle was asleep.

Throughout the meal, Aedan noticed the glances exchanged between his sister and the Fife sheriff—polite murmured comments, voices warm with laughter or gentle praise, looks that seemed casual but held meaning. He saw subtle blushes, eyes quickly lowered, and smiles pressed away.

Rowena saw too, once giving Aedan a wide-eyed stare, silently eloquent. He held her gaze, and her answering nod was clear. She saw the love the pair thought they kept to themselves. Yet it was no secret to those near them.

He wondered if his growing feelings for Rowena were that clear to others. Brian Lauder suspected it; Erik Ogilvie assumed they were married. Covering a private smile, he sipped from his goblet of watered wine. The mixture was more potent than he liked, so he reached for a jug of water beside his bowl—the stew of lamb and vegetables had been especially good that night—to pour a slosh of water into the wine and drank again.

Perhaps the dilution came too late, for a pesky headache was beginning. He rubbed his temple, but seeing Rowena's glance, reached for an oatcake instead, not keen to bring attention to his aversion to wine. Scraping the thick, crisp cake through a pot of soft butter, he nibbled. Perhaps a bit more food would diminish the ache, he thought, as he turned to Patrick.

"Have you had reports of English ships in the firth lately?" he asked.

"Now and then," Patrick replied. "They sail through on their way to Stirling Castle. Brian Lauder said you encountered Malise Comyn on a galley heading that way."

"Aye, and may we see the last of him," Aedan replied.

"With luck," Patrick said. "I heard recently that Peter Abernethy was seen riding for Stirling with several men."

Michael Balfour nodded. "We heard the same."

"If Sir Malise and Abernethy meet at Stirling, that is a poor pair. May they keep well away from Fife," Patrick said.

"They are cousins," Aedan said. "And Scottish lords who support Edward over Bruce are no friends of ours."

"Aye," Patrick agreed. "Hard to forget the murder of your brother at their hands, though it be fifteen years and more."

"Two were caught and punished, but they were not alone," Aedan said.

At the other end of the table, Lady Jennet said it was time for Colban to go to bed, but the boy protested, eager to remain with the adults.

"To bed, you lad," Aedan said. "Lucky you are to be sitting with us so late, but you need your rest. That arm bone needs rest too."

"Your da is right, sleep will help heal you," Rowena said. "I can take the lad upstairs. I want to look at his bandaging again." Colban agreed to that, and she stood and ushered him out of the room, promising to tell him a story if he liked.

"What stories do you know?" Colban asked as they walked away.

"My great-grandfather told wonderful stories. The Queen of Elfland was his good friend," she added. Aedan smiled to hear her laughter ring out as Colban ran to the stairs, eager for a story. "Hold up, or you will fall again!"

Lady Jennet looked at Aedan. "Queen of the faery ilk?"

"Her great-grandfather was Thomas the Rhymer," he explained.

"True Thomas! I want to hear her stories too," Jennet said as the others echoed agreement.

"I must go over to the garrison quarters to talk to my men," Patrick said, and Michael stood to go with him. Aedan wished them good evening, taking another sip of the watered wine when Marjorie and Jennet asked him to stay.

"Aedan," Marjorie said. "I am glad you brought Lady Rowena. I quite like her."

"I do as well," Lady Jennet said. Both watched him intently, leaning forward.

"She is a fine lady." To hide his expression, he took another sip.

"You will have the headache if you finish that," Lady Jennet warned. "It was quite strong, I thought. Sir Patrick brought it from the abbot. A gift to our household."

"I already have the headache from the stares you two are

giving me. What is it?" He both dreaded and welcomed what might come of that question.

"That lass," Lady Jennet said. "Is she the one you were promised to when you were young?"

"Almost promised," he corrected, and took a small sip. He could not bring himself to look at their determined faces.

"You should have married her," Marjorie said. "Is it so, Aunt?"

"It is," their aunt agreed.

"What is this?" Aedan said. "Matchmaking? She has been here but a day."

"Marry that lass," Marjorie said bluntly. "She is—"

"You do not waste time, sister."

"—the one for you," she spoke over him. "She is lovely, kind, skilled, intelligent, and she has the backbone to put up with you."

"Why, thank you," he drawled, suppressing a smile. The two looked so serious.

"She is the bride your mother approved," Lady Jennet said. "And you are the bridegroom her father chose for her."

"We did not meet then. We were children," he argued, but he agreed with them. "And my mother was not much interested in whom I married, but whom she would marry. She chose an earl and left Fife for Perthshire and a castle thrice this size."

"Tell him," Marjorie said to their aunt.

"Tell him what?" he asked.

"Very well. I chose her for you," Jennet said. "Your mother simply agreed. I thought it best if you believed your mother decided on your behalf."

"You mean, believe that she cared?" He pulled in a breath, exhaled. His head truly ached. "I appreciate that, but I have learned since that she was never the mother to me that you have been, Aunt, and to Marjorie and our brother too, God rest him."

"Then listen to me and ask for that young woman's hand," Jennet said.

"You need her," Marjorie said. "Colban needs her. You could

be happy again."

"I am happy, doing good work to support our new king."

"Chased, tossed in prison? Injured in battle? Running, hiding?" Marjorie asked.

"Helping," he said firmly. They had scant idea what he had done or was willing to do, and he meant it to stay that way for their peace of mind.

"She is the one for you," Lady Jennet said. "I had a moment of the Sight about that betrothal years ago, I did. I saw you married to a black-haired beauty, saw her strong and true by your side, but had never seen the Keith child. Lamberton wanted you for the priesthood, which never happened, and you married another. That was good. Alisoun was a sweet girl and I loved her."

"We all did," he said.

"But years later, your path crossed with Rowena's," Jennet said. "That is fate."

"Fate," Marjorie repeated with a nod.

"I am being ambushed. Help," he said faintly, glancing about.

"You are," Marjorie affirmed.

"If I need a wife," he said, sitting forward, tapping the table for emphasis, "then you, sister, need a husband. Do I rail on about that? I do not. I am a saint accosted by wild matchmakers."

"A saint in need of a wife and a mother for your son," Marjorie said. "And God willing, I will have a good husband someday soon." Her smile was mischievous.

"As your brother, and the man's friend, I approve."

"Thank you. And I approve of your lady."

"Not my lady," he said.

"Yet." Marjorie held out her hand. "Give me a coin, sir."

"For what? Pirates took my coin purse," he groused.

Lady Jennet opened a leather bag on her belt to extract a coin. "Give it to her."

Amused, puzzled, he handed it to his sister. "Will you tell my fortune? A future with a beautiful wife who has enough steel in her bones to tolerate such as me?"

"That one has steel in her backbone, though she hides it," Lady Jennet said.

"There," Marjorie said, pocketing the coin. "You have paid a matchmaker to find you the perfect wife."

He grinned. "No wonder I have a headache, with you two."

"Watching you and Lady Rowena," Lady Jennet said. "I see what is in your eyes when you look at her."

"And what is that? Sunlight?"

"Hope. And a spark you have not had for years—very like love."

He tapped a piece of oatcake on the table. "And in her eyes?"

"Love like sunlight." Jennet smiled and glanced at Marjorie. "You too, my dear. I am old enough now to speak my mind. I want to see you both married before I die."

"My lady, you always speak your mind," Aedan said. "And you are not that old."

"Ask Lady Rowena to marry you," his aunt returned.

"What if she does not share your opinion?"

"Ask her, or ask her family," Marjorie said in agreement with Lady Jennet. "Though she is a widow—she told me so when we chatted—so she can decide for herself without waiting on her kinsmen. Just as I can," she added with a lifted chin.

"I have no objection to Patrick Wemyss, so decide as you like. But I believe Lady Rowena is content as a widow because she can devote herself to healing arts."

"If you know that about her, then it is a good sign that you are getting to know one another."

"We are." He was careful not to look up, lest his feelings shine in his eyes.

"She is good for you, if you would see it. She knows your mind. And knows you make light of things even when you take them to heart." Jennet twisted her mouth awry. "She sees through you, lad."

"She does," he admitted. "I rather like that."

"I am sure you do. And you are good for her," his aunt said.

He looked up. "How so?"

"She relies on you. She seems more assured when you are near. For all her calm as a healer, and for all her backbone, she hides an uncertainty within," Lady Jennet said. "But she is steadier around you. Fear throws her off balance at times, but you can teach her how to stand straight, in a way."

"Off balance," he repeated, thinking of Rowena aboard ship. "True, sometimes."

"I have my grandmother's Sight. You know that."

"I do, and I have tried to listen to that. Ladies, we can banter this about all we want, and I am grateful for your thoughts. But I am not in a position to marry."

"You are. You just refuse to see it," Jennet said.

"I am dedicated to serving my king. And that means taking risks."

"Risk is not exclusive to men. Women take grave chances all the time. Consider childbirth."

"I know," he said curtly, having lost a wife to that.

"Your work for the king put you in that infirmary, and in Yester dungeon, where you met Lady Rowena. She took a risk to follow a man she did not truly know," his aunt said. "She has a strong and worthy spirit. You would be a fool to let her go."

"I have my reasons to play the fool. But some of what you say is true."

"It is all true," his sister said. "Marry her before she is out of your life."

He nodded, thoughtful, silent. Then he smacked his hand on the table. "Very well, I will try. Good night, my dearies." He stood, pleased to see them gape as he left the hall.

CHAPTER TWENTY

ROWENA SAT BESIDE Colban in the darkness of his tower room, a twin to her own above it. She touched the child's curly hair as he slept peacefully. Hearing a tap on the door, she looked up as Aedan peeked in and put a finger to her lips. "All is well. I will stay here for a while."

He nodded. "Thank you," he murmured. "I will be in my chamber working on some documents. Fetch me if he needs anything, or if you need something." As he closed the door, she saw him rub his brow as if something troubled him. Perhaps it was the headache again; he had sipped the strong wine at supper, which had a peculiar effect on him. While he never complained, she had seen it.

After a while, leaving Colban asleep with one of the dogs to guard him, she headed down the winding stone stair, going carefully to spare her ankle. It had improved with ointment and snug bandaging, but she did not fancy twisting it again. She passed a small library and the solar that contained Marjorie's loom and baskets of yarns, cloth, and stitchery, then took a corridor through a door to the separate building that confined the kitchen, always wise in case of fire.

She hoped to find some herbs that were helpful for headache, wanting to make a hot infusion to bring to Aedan before he tried to sleep. The large kitchen was dim and all but deserted. One woman in a dark gown and pale kerchief stirred the contents of a kettle over one of the hobs in the great arched fireplace. As Rowena's footsteps sounded on the slate floor, the woman turned.

"Lady Rowena!" Lady Jennet said.

"My lady! I did not expect to see anyone here."

The older woman smiled. "I was talking to Cook about the needs at the castle since we will be away for some weeks. The garrison is larger now, and so must be accommodated. Tomorrow in Dunfermline, I will arrange for supplies to be delivered each week. I am sure you know how it is to run a household."

"I do, though I live in our family castle, my brother's property now. My sisters and I have managed the household together since our mother's death, and then Papa's."

Jennet stirred the kettle. "I knew Robert Keith of Kincraig. A good man."

Rowena tipped her head. "You did? Oh," she realized. "The betrothal?"

"The one that never was, aye. You are close with your siblings?"

"We are. But my sisters have married and will be living elsewhere, so Kincraig will be managed by our brother Henry, who is not yet married. But I can help him."

"Do you think you would marry again, and move away as your sisters have done?" Her tone sounded careful, Rowena thought.

"If I ever married again, I would want to divide time between Kincraig, which I love dearly, and wherever my husband's property might be." She was careful too.

"Ah. Aedan said you were recently on Bass Rock?" Jennet changed the subject.

"I was. It is isolated but beautiful in its way. Have you been there before?"

"Not since Aedan was a lad. Can I help you find something here in the kitchens?"

Rowena nodded. "I was hoping to make a warm posset, and

need a few herbs for headache. Do you have more mint and willow, chamomile, and perhaps yarrow or feverfew?"

"We have those." The lady tilted her head. "Do you have a headache?"

"I thought Sir Aedan might benefit from it."

"Ah, so you noticed at supper."

"I did. I hope it would be welcome if I prepare something for him."

"Very welcome, I am sure, though he would not ask. Over here." She led Rowena through the cavernous room, white-washed with a vaulted ceiling, to open a large wooden cupboard. Inside were multiple nooks with tiny painted labels, the niches filled with packets and small jars containing dried herbs, ginger, pepper, and other herbs, spices, and more. Rowena inhaled the blended scents.

"This is a lovely collection!"

"We try to keep many herbs and such to hand." Lady Jennet removed a few packets. "Here is peppermint, willow, yarrow. And some dried all-heal if you want some." She piled the packets into Rowena's hands. "Use what you like and we will put the rest back in the herb cupboard. We have some oils too, mint, lavender, and others that might help."

"Thank you. I would like to boil some water." Rowena turned.

"There is water already heated on the smaller hob. I prepared elderberry syrup recently if that would help. And we have raw honey, drawn from the hives last month."

"That would be excellent." She laid the things on the scrubbed oak table, took the little pottery bowl that Lady Jennet handed her, and measured out some herbs while Aedan's aunt fetched the syrup and honey. Quickly, Rowena added small portions of herbs to the water heating in an iron kettle and began to stir the simmering mixture. She closed her eyes, inhaling the warm, sweet, tart scent of the rising steam.

"This will help Aedan," Lady Jennet said. "It is kind of you to think of it."

Rowena stirred the concoction. "It is something I can do for him. I owe him so much. He took me out of Yester, did you know? If I had stayed, I dread to think what might have happened."

"He told us," Jennet said. "Aedan feels he owes you for healing him when he was sorely injured. We all appreciate that so much. And the infusion will help tonight. He has an aversion to dark wine. Even as a lad, when we gave him watered wine, as one does to help small children become accustomed to it—it never agreed with him. His father was like that, as I recall."

"You knew Aedan's father? Were you married to his Uncle Duff then?"

"Aye, just married. But Aedan's father was killed while a young man, when his children were small. Colban, he was called. The names stick in this clan—Duncan, Colban, Aedan, Duff, all repeated through."

Rowena stirred the posset. "Aedan said he and his brother lived with the bishop."

"They did, while Marjorie was with her mother, just an infant. After a few years, Marjorie came to Castle Black to live with us—my husband is chief of the MacDuffs by tradition, being close kin to the earl. When they were boys, Aedan and his brother were wards of the bishop, then came here to Castle Black. Later Aedan fostered with the Lauders, as part of the tradition of training up a lad to become a knight."

"He told me a little of that. He took on a great deal of responsibility after his brother died."

"And he handles it well. Interim guardian, overseeing Fife, and acting as clan chief with my husband captured." She sighed. "I maintain hope that Duff will be released."

"Hope is all you need, sometimes, for all to be well," Rowena said. "Aedan is happy here. You have made a good home for him and his son."

"He has much on his mind and his shoulders, but he puts on a good face. You see through that," Jennet added. "He is pleased that you do, I think."

"I am glad." Rowena smiled. "Is there a goblet or a jug I can use to bring this to him? I will knock on his door and leave it without disturbing him."

"Take a pottery jug. He will have a cup in his room, if he can find it."

Rowena laughed. "You know him too."

"My dear, I know him better than he likes sometimes."

BALANCING THE JUG with its steaming contents as she slowly climbed the steps to favor her foot, Rowena came to the level of her chamber. Though she was aware that Aedan's room was on the next level, she was not sure which door was his. Remembering the private stair, she went through her chamber to the doorway hidden behind a length of plaid. Moving up the steps carefully, she saw his door partly open.

She knocked softly, pushed it open, stepped into a darkened room, and heard snoring. The double chamber was much like hers and Colban's as well, a large room and a smaller chamber. Here the larger space contained a bed with upright posters and draped curtains, with a table, chairs, and cupboard nearby. The smaller space held a simple bed. This was not the master's chamber in the castle, she realized; Lady Jennet would have that.

"Aedan?" She saw him lying in the curtained bed, snoring softly. He had removed his tunic and lay in trews and shirt with a blanket pulled lightly over him.

Not wanting to wake him, she set the jug on the table beside the bed, gasping when a little of the hot liquid spilled. But he did not stir, eyes closed, snores rumbling. She knew sleep was the best remedy, though the herbal potion would help as well.

She remembered her first sight of him at Yester: a large man emitting loud snores under a bulky plaid. At Holyoak, she had encountered the brawny warrior, earthy and handsome, taut with muscle, weakened by injury and fever. She had treated and soothed him and felt reluctant to leave him. A subtle bond had begun there to flourish now, as compassion and attraction deepened to feelings she could no longer ignore.

Perhaps a buried memory of their near-betrothal stayed with her, for she had thought of him often after Holyoak. When she overheard King Edward and Sir Malise scheming to destroy him, she felt a fierce urge to warn him—then fate had sent her to Yester. Now she was losing her heart to him, and glad of it.

Reaching out, she touched his dark curls, warm and puppy-soft, clustered over his brow. In sleep, his face had a lean, elegant strength, softened by the tender curve of his lips, the long eyelashes under arched brows, the velvety scruff of his shaven face.

Had she truly noticed the tough, nimble beauty of his hands and long fingers? She grazed her fingers over his hand, lifted away—but he grabbed her fingers.

"What," he mumbled, eyes opening. "Rowena! Is it Colban?" He began to sit up.

"Colban is fine. Lie back." She gently pushed his shoulder. "I did not mean to wake you. I just brought you something to drink."

He sat, swinging his legs over the edge of the bed, running long fingers through his hair, then over his face. His bare torso was golden and powerful in candlelight. "I am glad you woke me," he said. "I did not mean to sleep for long. There is something I must do. What is that?" He gestured toward the jug on the table.

"A warm posset. I thought you might have a headache."

"You saw that? Aye, you did." He answered his own question, then ruffled his hair and gave her a half-wink. "What is in it?"

She explained the contents. "With honey and Lady Jennet's elderberry syrup."

"Some would call that a child's drink," he muttered.

"If a man drinks it, then it is a man's drink."

He lifted the jug and sipped directly from it. "Not bad. A bit flowery."

"It has lavender in it. But even if you smelled like rose soap and wore flowers and ribbons in your hair, you would still be a most virile and manly rogue."

"I trust that is a compliment," he drawled, and sipped again. "This should fix any weakness in me." He drank and set the jug down.

"I see no weakness in you. Well, sometimes your jests can be thin."

"Now that hurts." He beckoned. "Come here."

As she stepped forward, he widened his knees to bring her close, so that she stood a breath away. She began to stroke his temples gently, then combed her fingers through his tousled curls, flexing and pressing to ease the headache away. Aedan closed his eyes, silent, hands resting on her hipbones, thumbs circling.

"Feels good," he murmured. His gaze met hers, keen and lingering, an intangible touch that thrilled through her as much as his hands on her.

She leaned toward him and nudged her nose to his in invitation. His hands tightened, fingers stretching over her lower back to snug her closer, and answered tenderly, the caress of his lips so luscious that the sensation sank to her knees so that she leaned against the mattress. His lips tasted, drank of hers, and she opened to him as he leaned back, propped on an elbow, bringing her with him. She went willingly, lifted in his big hands to rest partly on his bare chest, her hands on his smooth shoulders. Gliding her fingers over his chest, feeling the soft cushion of hair and the thumping heart beneath, she pressed against him, his natural response rigid beneath her hip even with layers of cloth between them.

With a low groan, he rolled to his side with her, kissing as they went, hands roaming, hers sliding over his rib cage, smooth and warm and thick with muscle, his pulse pounding beneath her touch. She leaned into the depth of the feather-stuffed mattress covered in plaid, the wool a slight tickle against her cheek. As

Aedan moved a hand to cover her bodice, she shifted toward him with a little moan to give him access to her body, to her heart.

She sighed against his coaxing lips, the slip of his tongue, and her body pulsed against his nude torso as she glided her hand along his back. The cloth of her gown and shift hampered her—she tugged at the knotted ribbons along the side openings to loosen the cage of laces. His hand found hers on the ribbons and tugged too. Then his fingers slipped inside, over the linen shift beneath, fingertips finding her breast, teasing the nipple so gently that she sucked in her breath and moaned again.

"Lass," he said, his lips separating from hers as he whispered. "We—"

"Hush you," she whispered, and her hand slid down his back to pull at the waist of his trews. "Just hush. I think we both want this."

"You know I do, but if you—"

"I do, now hush," she said, roused and sure as she surged over him. She felt the certainty of what she wanted within as if she had always known she would find him. The childhood wish, the healing wish, the steadiness he brought her, the calm she gave him in return—suddenly seemed to merge, and she knew this was deeply good.

Now he kissed her again and his hand cupped her breast under fabric, warmth and passion spinning wild through her as his thumb rolled her nipple, and she arched back with a little cry.

"So much cloth," he murmured, his lips tracing down her throat, fingers tugging at the edge of the dark blue bodice to kiss along her collarbone. A whirlwind of heat, of need and sensation, drove her to press against him. As he pulled at the cloth, frustration outdid need—she sat up and yanked the gown up and over her head to toss it aside.

"Lass, when you decide something, it is a glorious thing to behold."

She laughed and lay back, feeling free, savoring cool air over her nearly bared body under the shift, feeling more entirely herself than she ever had before in the cavern of the curtained bed, in the warm circle of his arms as he lay back with her. He kissed her again, deep and slow, then traced his mouth down her throat again and down, his fingers easily drawing aside the loose neck of her shift. As his lips found her breast, she gasped, letting her body plead for what she wanted so very much now, with him.

Thoughts whirled above her body's urging like swifts in flight, never landing, far away—she knew herself, knew her tendency to think and reason, but she would not allow it to douse the heat within her or cool this precious fire.

She pulled him to her, urging him to roll with her, moving her hips against his. He groaned deep, the sound lost against her lips. As he slid a hand under the shift, along her leg, thumb tracing the inside of her thigh, fingers reaching over the curve of her slender hip, she ached for his fingers tips to seek that clefted part of her none had touched or known since the month of her wedding, long ago, lost in time. Knowing what would come, she paused, brow to his shoulder, gasping a little, wanting this so much now, yet needing to breathe in a moment of clarity.

He kissed her temple, his bristly cheek grit and velvet. "What is it, love?" he murmured, his voice soft thunder, resonant and beloved. "Enough?"

"A moment—" She lifted her face, kissed him. "Not yet enough, my love," she whispered, then tugged at his trews, which came out of the way quickly. He pressed against her, hot and hard and tender. Decision, as he had said, felt glorious.

Then his hands and his will and his lips found her fully, touch and love and freedom all blending as she arched against him, feeling a lush whirlpool take her over, spin thoughts away from her as breath and body took over. And then he shifted and she opened to him, widening her legs, arching and tilting as her body allowed him to slip within, merging, feeling overtaking thought— for that was what she needed most, wanted most. Feeling a blend of soul and craving and grace, too, she rose with him, coaxed him deeper into her, certain in her very core that they belonged together, surging with him now as if they had never been apart, ever, in their lives.

"ROWENA," AEDAN SAID later, against the silky press of her hair along his cheek.

The candle had nearly gutted out, the steam had left the jug, the chill of evening settled in the air. He woke tucked with Rowena under the plaid, snug and satisfied, feeling such satiation in body, heart, and soul that it felt profound there in the dark.

The low-burning candle told him they had slept for a few hours. Glancing down, he saw Rowena's dark eyelashes flutter and open. "Mmm?" she asked. "Morning?"

"Still dark. But if you are awake, I want to show you something."

She circled her hips against him. "What?"

"Before you came up here and sweetly distracted me—"

"I only came up here to bring you a posset," she replied in a sleepy voice. "Then we both got distracted."

"Ah, true. But I need to tend to something before we leave for Dunfermline." Tossing the blanket aside, he sat up.

"What is it?"

"Come with me and you will see." He left the bed and reached for the shirt he had discarded earlier, climbed back into his trews, and pulled on a long tunic and low-slung belt. Rowena slid off the bed and tugged her gown over her head, while Aedan draped a plaid over his shoulder, then turned to help her tie the side lacings of her gown. She sat to fasten her boots, kicked off in a hurry when the candle still burned high.

"How is your ankle? Can you walk down to the beach?"

"I can." She flexed her foot. "The bandage and boot lacing help."

"We need to be quiet and quick. I do not want to wake anyone here."

"You do not want to answer questions," she guessed.

"Aye." He took up a metal lantern of pierced metal with a sturdy wooden side handle, inserted a new candle taper lit from the spent candle, and turned.

"But your questions, love, I will answer. It is past time I showed you what is kept here. This way." He indicated the door to the hidden stair.

Chapter Twenty-One

I N THE DARK of the staircase, he opened a door she had not noticed before, hidden in a corner. This led down a steep winding stair. She followed, grateful for the light of the lantern. When Aedan opened a door at the bottom of the steps, she stepped with him into a tunnel of earth and rock so narrow, she could touch both sides at once, where tree roots curved out of the rough earthen walls.

"Does this go under the hill to the beach?"

"And out to one of the caves. MacDuffs built this tunnel long ago."

They came to an arched opening in the rock and when Aedan bent to pass through, Rowena did too, stepping into a cavern lit only by the faint glow of the candle in the lantern. She saw a rough-textured dome of a large cave like the inside of an inverted bowl. From somewhere she heard the distant rush of the sea, and closer, a burble of water.

The dome swept down to an uneven floor with two exits, natural arches in the rock, at opposite ends of the space, one leading toward the beach. At the center of the cave, several rocks formed a circle around a small pool where water bubbled.

"A natural spring?" She looked at Aedan, delighted.

He held the lantern high. "It comes up from below. They call this Saint Margaret's Well—a healing spring, supposedly blessed by the sainted queen over two hundred years ago. The water is very pure and is believed to have curative powers. People come from all over Fife to drink the water and take some away in jugs and buckets. I thought you would want to see it."

Thrilled, she sank to her knees, dipped her hand in the shallow pool, and poured the water back. "Is this what you wanted to show me?"

"This, and something else. Stay by the pool while I make sure the way is clear. Dip your foot and have a drink of the water."

"Do you drink the water?"

"Oh aye, we have always done that. My aunt stores this water to dilute the wine, but today there was none left in the cupboard."

"And you had the headache," she noted.

He shrugged, assent or doubt, and went over to a niche in the wall, reaching in and returning with a small bottle of green glass, plugged with wax. "We keep containers here for folks who want to take some of the water." He winked, then left through the outermost exit.

Sitting beside the pool, Rowena removed her boot, stocking, and the bandages around her ankle, then dipped her foot into the cool water, swished it about, then dried it with the hem of her gown. Cupping some of the water in her palm, she drank, finding it chilled and clear.

Rewrapping the bandage and lacing her boot, she filled the little green bottle with water, plugged it, and fit it into her belt purse. Then she removed the Rhymer's crystal from its silk wrapping to dip it in the water and set it on a rock ledge below the surface to let it absorb whatever power the pool might hold. The stone sparkled as if it was filled with stars.

Aedan came back, calling softly to her, and she scooped up the stone and followed him along a short passageway in the rock to a wide outer exit.

Outside on the shingled beach, moonlight reflected in the dark waves of the firth. As a breeze fluttered through her hair, she realized she had left her veil in Aedan's bed chamber.

But she knew then she no longer needed it as she once did. She felt new somehow, hopeful. Shivering, she wrapped her arms around herself and felt eager, suddenly, about the changes shifting through her life so quickly now.

Aedan took her hand and indicated the stretch of the beach. "Can you walk far enough to visit the other caves? I need to look at some things."

She flexed her ankle. "My foot truly feels better. Lead on, sir."

Moving across the beach, he ushered her inside a wide cave entrance where she heard birds rustling and cooing. As Aedan swept the lantern light around, she saw neat rows of niches cut into the stone walls, and inside the small crevices, birds bobbing and fluttering.

"A dovecote," he explained. "The birds are here much of the year."

"Do the MacDuffs use these caves often?"

"Aye, as have all the locals. The caves have served us for generations, so we take care of them. Come this way." He led her farther down the beach.

The next cave was another vast domed space swept clean by wind and water. "We call this the court cave. Generations of MacDuff chiefs and earls have held meetings and councils here. Long ago, Fife was a kingdom, though now it is an earldom within Scotland. My nephew will hold that rank of earl all his life, even if he stays in England."

"So you are guardian of these caves and the beach too."

"So it seems." He walked ahead into a space as large as any grand hall.

"Is that furniture?" Rowena saw a stack of chairs, tables, and sundry things propped at the back of the cavern.

"Those belong to families of traveling folk. They roam Fife and Perthshire and often winter here. And they help to protect something special." Now he guided her along another narrow passageway to an interior cave where lantern light revealed designs cut into the rock. Pausing, she recognized birds, animals, fish, weapons, wheels, rods, and other objects, all with similar decorative curling shapes.

"Beautiful!" she breathed.

"And ancient." He traced his hand over the chiseled lines. "Here is a crown or a headpiece, this one is a horse. Over there are birds, and a chariot and harness."

"And a longship!" She studied a linear design of a long vessel with oars.

"These were likely carved by people who lived in the caves long before the Scotti settled here from Ireland. The Romans called the first people they discovered in Scotland the 'Picti' because they painted pictures on their bodies before going into battle. Perhaps those people carved these, but only they knew their meaning."

"You are a warrior and a scholar, Aedan MacDuff." She slipped a hand inside his elbow as they left the carvings and walked out to the beach again.

"There is one more cave I need to visit if you can walk farther."

"Anywhere you like. My ankle feels good at the moment."

"The well did its work. I hope your wee stone soaked up some of its magic too."

"I think it did." As they strolled along the gritty beach in moonlight, Rowena saw Aedan hold out his plaid to shield the lantern's light. "Will the flame blow out?"

"The light could be seen from boats that might be out in the firth at night. I thought I spotted a vessel earlier, but clouds are covering the moon so I am not sure of that. Here is the cave. It is on a bit of a slope, so do be careful." He went up the incline, reaching back to help her enter the cave.

"More carvings?" she asked. "Another pool?" She wondered why he wanted to look at carvings and a healing spring before dawn, when all seemed secure here.

"Something else important." Carrying the lantern, he went to the back of the cave, then stepped into a vertical crack in the dark rock wall to all but disappear. She followed the light as it moved ahead over glossy dark stone.

"Come through," he called, as she edged along a passageway so narrow that she had to turn sideways, surprised that Aedan, with his broad shoulders, fit through. Stepping around a curve, she entered a tall narrow space. Aedan set the lantern on a ledge, where it created glowing fingers of light.

He reached into a hidden crevice to draw out a long shape muffled in plaid and tied with leather thongs, and set it on the floor with a heavy *thunk*. Kneeling, he unwrapped the cloth to reveal a wooden box strapped with iron bands and three locks.

So this was why he came here, she realized. Not to see a pool or ancient carvings or primordial caves. The caves were significant and he was proud of them, but this box was something else entirely. Something profound. Chills ran down her spine.

Then she remembered being at Holyoak with Aedan while he tossed in a fevered state and pulled her close to whisper something desperately.

I must keep it safe. You must find it. Stones. Magic. She had thought it was the fever in him. More of it came back to her, and she turned.

"Stones," she said. "The castle, the dove. The stone, the magic. All here."

Aedan paused briefly but did not look up. Taking a small key from his sporran, he inserted it into the latches with nimble twists. He sat back on his heels and looked up.

"So you remember."

"I recall part of it, but I did not understand it."

"Now you will." He opened the lid, peeled away more fabric, and leaned back.

Peering over his shoulder, Rowena saw gleaming gold and silver and a long blade of shining steel. "What is this?" she asked, breathless.

He stroked a hand over the items nestled in wool and silk, a gesture of reverence. "The regalia of Scotland."

"But—how is this here?" Sinking to her knees beside him, she gazed at the objects nestled in plaid and silk: a golden circlet with fleurs-de-lis in beaten gold attached to the band; a silver rod with a polished sphere and decorative finial; and a magnificent sword that took up the length of the narrow box.

Aedan lifted the hilt from its fabric bed. The blade was brutal and beautiful, sharp and shining, with a grip wrapped in tooled leather, and a straight cross-guard. And the pommel—

She gasped. "The stone!"

"I thought you might recognize it," he murmured.

Set in the pommel above hilt and cross-guard was a round, polished sphere of nearly transparent crystal, held in place by silver bands etched with designs.

She touched the cool crystal with a finger. "It looks like the Rhymer's stone!"

Aedan nodded. "When I saw your charm stone, the resemblance struck me. We need to see them together."

She stood and plucked the crystal from her purse, holding it out to him. In the flickering light, the charm stone reflected golden sparks from the lantern light.

He got to his feet, lifting the sword from the box to hold it near the charm stone. The pommel crystal flashed golden incandescence from the lantern as well, the light shimmering within.

"Even the silver bands are similar, as if done by the same smith," Aedan said.

"They are like twin souls, these crystals," she said.

"*Krystallos.* Quartz," he said. "The Greeks called such stones *krystallos* and thought they were chunks of ice turned to clear stone. The Saxons and Scots called them *querertz.* I read that in a treatise on natural *scientia,*" he explained with a little smile.

"Grandda told me the same! He would have liked you, I think. He also said his charm stone came from the faery realm, which explained its healing magic. Now I wonder—he said something about faery stones, though I did not understand at the time. Perhaps both stones came from the Otherworld. They are so much alike."

"Could be." He balanced the point of the sword on the floor, grasping the hilt, looking like a king himself, tall and magnificent and powerful.

"Where did this sword come from?" she asked.

"It was kept in Castle Black, but its origins are uncertain. You see, the Scottish regalia was stolen by the English and carted off to London," he explained, "so when Bruce needed to be crowned quickly, new regalia was needed. A goldsmith crafted the crown in a hurry, ordered by the Bishop of Scone, who had hidden some things from the English—this scepter, some banners. But a crown and sword were essential for the kingmaking ceremony. When I brought my niece to Scone, I brought the sword too."

"Why was it at Castle Black?" As she spoke, she dropped her stone into her purse.

He tilted the sword, looking down the gleaming length of the fuller that lessened the weight of the steel and channeled blood in warfare.

"It is said in our clan that this ancient sword was used by King Macbeth of long ago. He was kin to the MacDuffs, you see. After his death in a clash with Malcolm Canmore, who killed him to grab the crown—he was husband to the sainted Margaret," he added, "a MacDuff brought the sword here. But we do not know where Macbeth got it."

"And you brought it to Bruce. It seems so fitting."

"Scone is the place for the regalia, but that is not safe now. Bruce entrusted these things to me. I could not leave them in the castle hall, and could not reveal to anyone that I had them. So I brought them down here."

"Aedan," she said, as the truth struck her, "you are truly the guardian of Scotland. A member of the guardian council, aye, but more than that, you guard the symbols of sovereignty here, hidden in this humble place."

His fingers flexed on the hilt. "You and I know it is here.

Bruce knows, but he does not know exactly where it is. I will tell him when next I have the chance."

"But you needed to see that it was safe. That is one reason you rushed here."

"When I heard Edward intended to forfeit Castle Black, I knew it was possible. I worried this might be found if his men explored the caves. And that would—" He shook his head.

"Be disastrous," she supplied.

He nodded, and raised the sword, hoisting its point to the ceiling. The crystal in the pommel twinkled like a star, giving the blade a luster of power.

"They cannot have this," he said. "This is the sword of a rightful king of Scots. It did not need to gather dust in our hall any longer. The time had come for it to be of use again." He lowered the blade. "Macbeth was a strong and good king, revered for bringing peace and plenty to the Scots, did you know? Poets composed verses about him. I read one of those when I was at Saint Andrews. But Rowena, there is more to this than we know, with these twin stones."

"Surely it will come clear someday. It has to."

"Did Thomas mention another stone that might be significant for Scotland?"

"He said—there was another, but I thought he meant another guardian, which confused me then. It never occurred to me that he might mean two separate stones."

"Two stones," he said, "and two guardians. He meant both. But why?"

He lowered to one knee, as a knight would kneel before a king in loyalty and respect, and laid the sword in its place, wrapping it together with the other pieces. For a moment he bowed his head. Then he shut the box, locked the latches, wrapped the wood in the dark-patterned plaids and thongs, and stood. Hoisting the box up, an action that needed raw strength, he slid it back into the deep horizontal niche in the rock, where shadows absorbed it.

Rowena stood silent, spellbound by the moment and the meaning, awestruck by this man who carried such immense responsibility with earthy humility and grace. This man that she loved and respected beyond any she had ever known. Her heart surged.

"Aedan MacDuff," she said, "there is no man more suited to this responsibility."

"Ah," he said, wiping his hands, "just luck that I knew of this cave. But it is damp at times, not a proper reliquary for the sword of Macbeth and the rightful King of Scots, and the regalia as it exists now. I did what I could."

"You did well. I am grateful that you trusted me with this."

"I *trust* you," he clarified. "I love you and I honor you."

"I love and honor you," she whispered. "Trust and truth go with that."

"They do. But I am sorry to have drawn you into my wee wicked scheme." He glanced at the dark niche. "Someone else needed to know about this, should I fall off a boat or suchlike before I see Bruce again."

She laughed softly. "You trusted me at Holyoak too, not knowing me."

He cocked his head, smiled. "A beautiful lass with kind eyes and a pretty stone that looked oddly familiar—you were heaven-sent. You were my only hope when I thought I might die. Later I knew I must find you, for I had told you a grave secret. And I had fallen in love with you a little. I am glad to share this secret with you." He kissed her. "Shall we go? The dawn will break soon and we have a busy day ahead. After a busy night, hey."

"Very busy," she agreed, kissing him, then being pulled into his arms.

"This cave is not the place for what I suddenly have in mind," he murmured. "But we should go up to the castle before the others awake."

She preceded him, turning sideways to pass through the deep, high crack in the rock that led out to the cavern. Together they headed up the incline toward the wide cave entrance. He reached out to lend her a hand but stopped.

"Get down," he said. Dropping to his hands and knees, he crawled to the entrance and peered out. After a moment he drew back.

"God's very bones," he muttered.

She dropped beside him. "What is it?"

"Look toward the water. But stay low. We must not be seen."

She peered out and saw what he had spotted. "A boat!"

"A galley. With Edward's damned sail."

Out on the water, the galley was visible against the dusting of pale pink color along the horizon. She could make out the ship's silhouette, the billowed sail with gold lions on red, the dipping oars, and the shapes of men moving along the deck.

She gasped. "Malise?"

"Must be." He looked out again, and she inched closer to him, shoulder to shoulder. "He may be patrolling through here looking for any sign that we might be at Castle Black. Coming back from Stirling, he might have noticed Brian's longship at the quay at North Queensferry."

"Perhaps he will sail back across the firth and away. He cannot dock here."

"But they could send a small boat to shore if one is stored on the galley." With a muttered curse, he sat back. "We need to get to the castle, but we could be seen on the beach. Is your ankle strong enough for you to run?"

"Thanks to Saint Margaret's healing waters, I think so."

"Ready?" He opened the lantern to blow out the candle. Then they moved cautiously out of the cave, keeping to the shadows as they crossed the beach beneath the overhang of the cliff, hurrying into the cave below the castle. There, Rowena peered out to see dawn glowing on the horizon.

"The galley is still out there," Aedan said. "But they are turning. With luck, they will cross the firth and go as far as Berwick and England. I do not relish meeting Malise Comyn again on land or water. Come on—keep close to me."

"Always," she said, as he reached for her hand.

FOLLOWING AEDAN UP the secret stair, Rowena stopped near her chamber's hidden door. "I should go," she whispered.

"Come up here for something," he said, gesturing toward his room. "Aw, not that, love, unless you want to," he said, lifting a brow.

"That would need time—I can only stay a moment. The others will wake soon."

In his bed chamber, he crossed to the smaller room. Curious, Rowena peered into a simple room containing a table, chair, and standing cupboard. He opened that.

"Since I am sharing all my secrets, the treasure of the Mac-Duffs is here."

"You jest! It is a small cupboard."

"It is a small treasure," he replied, and rummaged inside. She heard some rustling and the snap of the latch of a small casket, the sort that might hold coins or jewels. Returning, he ushered her into the larger room and held out one hand. A long, sturdy silver chain lay coiled and glinting in his palm.

"For your crystal. It was my grandmother's chain. Your purse was nearly lost in the sea, but with this, you can keep it on you always."

"What a pretty thing," she said as he poured it into her hand. "I will wear it inside my bodice." Taking the stone from her purse, she slid the chain through the small bail in the silver setting.

Turning, she lifted her thick braid aside as he clasped the chain around her neck. She cupped the pendant in her hand, its cool surface gathering the warmth that always made the stone feel familiar and dear.

"The day Grandda gave me the crystal, he said I was its guardian. And he said there was another—either stone or guardian. He often spoke in riddles."

"He gave me a bit of a riddle too. I felt honored that he even spoke to me, a lad. He said one day I would be a knight and a guardian, but I did not understand the rest of it." He smiled briefly. "He told me to look for the woman with the crystal stone, but it made no sense. I forgot about it until I saw your charm stone."

"Then he knew about the twin stones and knew we would be the guardians. Oh, and he said I should look for a man with a crown. I thought he meant a king."

"There is another man with a crown. Me." He wiggled his fingers. "I have a crown tucked away, and we have the two crystals."

"For some reason, fate brought us together. Thomas must have known. But why? Though he did hint that the stone could save Scotland."

"That seems unlikely." He sighed.

"I must go." Rowena glanced toward the window, where dawn was breaking bright. "What if Thomas knew you and I would meet and perhaps—" She stopped.

"Marry?" His simple word echoed her thought, and her heart thumped.

"That was the plan years ago, and fate reunited us."

"Fate seems insistent with us. And Thomas knew about our betrothal."

"But he did not know the rest. It all sounds—almost magical." She felt her cheeks heat pink at the thought, the possibility, of marrying Aedan.

"Lady Rowena," he said, "for all your caution, you are a bit of a dreamer." A little smile twitched at his lips.

"My great-grandfather taught us to accept magic—it was so natural to him. The charm stone has a kind of magic. And my sisters have the Sight, I know that. I may be a practical soul, but I have seen strange things that are very real."

"Something else seems almost magical to me," he said, "yet it is very real. Fate is telling us something, Rowena. So I have another gift for you."

He opened his other hand. In his palm was a small golden ring. He must have fetched it with the chain, she realized. She caught her breath. "What is this?"

"Looks like a ring."

"I mean—it is lovely. But what—is this?" She lifted her gaze to his.

"A token of betrothal. Of marriage." He sounded awkward, this brawny and confident man. Her heart went out to him.

"It is beautiful." The ring was elegant in its simplicity—a plain golden band with a phrase etched in tiny letters around the outside, its only decoration.

"I would marry you here, now, or anywhere you like. Will you—accept the ring?"

"I will," she said in a rush. "Oh, I will. It is beautiful. What does it say?"

He turned it in the light. *"Io sui de druerie,"* he read. "In French, it means 'I am a love gift.'" Pink stained his cheeks beneath new beard growth. "In a way, this has been a long time coming."

"It has. I feel as if I have known you forever."

"Aye," he agreed. She held out her right hand, knowing the Church had decreed that promise rings belonged on that hand and could be moved to the left with marriage.

He slipped the ring on her finger, then kissed her knuckle, as he had done in a tavern one night, a sweet thrill she had not forgotten. When he tugged at her waist to pull her to him, the kiss was so tender that tears started in her eyes.

She stretched her hand out to look at the ring glinting in the dawn light. "Where did you find this? It is perfect."

"Ah, no one ever knew this, but I had it made when I was fifteen." He took her hand, rubbing his thumb over the golden circlet. "I thought our betrothal would be sealed, so I went to a goldsmith in Dunfermline to have a ring made. I had a gold coin and gave it to him to melt. You were just a child, but I asked for a ring to fit a woman. I thought you might wear it on a ribbon until you were older and we were wed. But then it was over, and I put it away. I did not even give it to my wife. To me, this has always been your ring."

She caught her breath. "You are a romantic. You are so many things, Aedan MacDuff." She gazed up at him. "A warrior, a guardian, a jester, a scholar. A dreamer and a romantic soul."

"I might even earn sainthood if I carry on like that."

She laughed, dashing away a tear. "And I love you. I love your strength and kindness. You make me proud. You make me laugh."

"Only sometimes," he qualified. "I am not sure when it began, but I know I love you with all my heart. My soul loves you, loves your soul. I want to marry you."

"I want that too, I do. When I truly know something, I know it for certain. Besides, I think we made our decision last night." She glanced at the bed, its rumpled blankets holding the memory of what they had discovered together hours ago.

"We did. This is the next step. I admit, since Colban was born and Alisoun passed, I never thought I would marry again. But then I found you again."

"I was only married for a few weeks, though I had my work and dedicated myself to that. But at Holyoak, when I saw you, everything changed somehow. We have both been hurt, and we both loved before. But this—this feels different."

"It does." He touched her cheek. "We will talk later and say all that must be said. But know that we are good for one another and it is a miracle, in a way, to find one another like this. It is enough, Grizel, my bluebell." He kissed her brow.

She laughed on a little sob. "You are a good man all on your own, and I am so glad I found you." She rose on tiptoe to kiss his lips. "I want to stay, but they will search for us soon. What shall I tell them?" She held up her hand, the ring gleaming.

"Naught yet, but if they see that, say whatever you like."

"Remember your sister and Sir Patrick. We all saw it when

they thought they were hiding it."

"Well, they may know about us already." He grimaced. "I had quite the lecture from my sister and my aunt, who pressed me to marry you. Sir Brian spoke of it too. They say I would be a fool to let you go. And I am no fool."

She remembered Lady Jennet in the kitchen—so warm and familiar, treating her as if she was part of the family. "Your friend Erik thought we were newly married."

"He did, but he is a bit thick about such things." He grinned.

"Did you decide to give me the ring because of what they said?"

He chuckled. "It was on my mind, love. But let them think it was their idea."

"And Colban? Will he be pleased?"

"The lad adores you. I expect his hearty approval."

"My family will be happy for us as well. My sisters have wanted me to marry again, thinking I was too focused on my work. And my brother always favored our betrothal, though he was a lad then. But others will take issue with this."

He frowned. "Edward and Malise."

"The king wanted me to agree to marry Malise. But Henry told them I was promised and quashed it."

"It is a ruse no longer. Malise can be troublesome, but the sooner we reach Dunfermline and head to Kincraig, the better. I want that fellow as far away from you as possible. The bottom of the firth might do, but that galley is too seaworthy."

"I want to reach Kincraig before Edward sends men there to collect Thomas's things from us—I want to urge them not to comply. If Malise arrives—"

"As soon as we depart Dunfermline, we will go there. I promise."

"Aedan, how long before we are no longer hunted by the English, looking over our shoulders for Malise or someone else?"

"Hard to say, lass. Edward's death could undo it, but he seems indestructible Though if you had just let him—"

"Do not even think it!"

"Aye well. I intend to see all this untangled. I swear it." He lifted her hand with the promise ring and kissed it.

Chapter Twenty-Two

AEDAN WOULD TAKE no chances as their caravan rumbled toward Dunfermline.

A caravan indeed, made up of guards, horses, a curtained van carrying the women and the boy, and an open cart filled with bags and belongings. Aedan rode beside Sir Patrick, and several guards surrounded the van and cart. The journey took most of the afternoon, but the women were content, his son enjoyed the adventure—and Rowena was glad to ride rather than sail. In Dunfermline, he knew the guards would take the van and cart to the quay to meet Brian Lauder at the longship and load the things aboard. The women wanted a little time in the town and would take Colban while he and Sir Patrick met with the abbot and the bishop.

As they rode, he was ever watchful of the view of the firth to his left and the hills to his right. Soon the town with its abbey and market cross were visible in the distance, and he began to relax a little.

He would not rest easy until his kinswomen and his small son were well on their way to Bass Rock with Sir Brian—and he and Rowena were riding to Kincraig Castle at last. What might come after that, he could not say.

Finally, they followed a drovers' track beside a wide stream with dense forestland on the other side, and reached the town's main thoroughfare. They headed up a hill toward the abbey, stopping on the lawn stretching between the church and the abbot's house.

In a way, he felt at home here too, and breathed in relief as he dismounted and walked toward the van. Rowena peeked out of the curtain—and in that instant, she was all he saw, until Colban peered out beside her, and the sun seemed to come out in his day, though the sky was as gray as Rowena Keith's eyes.

Massive stone pillars and high rounded stone arches, carved and painted with geometric patterns, soared to a wooden vaulted ceiling. Rowena craned her head to look up at a broad stone pillar incised with chevrons. As she touched the stone, her skin took on the colors shining down from the stained glass in the clerestory above. Smiling, she turned slowly, taking in the peace.

Having the ancient church to herself for a little while was an unexpected joy. Aedan and Sir Patrick had gone into the abbot's house, while the guards took the cart the three miles to the quay at Queensferry. Lady Jennet, Marjorie, and Colban had gone to the market square to visit some of the shops, but Rowena had decided to wait for Aedan, who said he would meet her inside the church.

Her steps echoed on the slate floor as she moved down the nave toward its east end. The tranquility was palpable and restorative. For centuries, this place had absorbed prayers, plainsong, and hymn beyond measure, and she felt its healing peace now.

As she walked, an old Irish hymn came to her as if it reverberated from the very pillars. She began to hum, trailing a hand over the enormous pillars as she passed.

"Be Thou my vision, oh Lord of my heart," she sang softly. Then she saw the extension in the chapel wall where the tombs of Queen Margaret and King Malcolm Canmore sat. On a marble plinth, Margaret's tomb was shaped like a huge reliquary covered in bright paint and golden trim.

Afternoon light poured like rainbows through stained-glass

windows, and as she walked, the song came to her again. She sang quietly, her voice soft in the silent church.

"Be thou my best thought in the day and the night," she sang in a near whisper, "waking and sleeping, be my light—"

"Be thou my breastplate, my sword for the fight," sang a deep voice behind her. "Be thou my armor, my true might."

She whirled. Aedan was there, his face touched with amber light from the high windows. His voice was mellow and rich and beautiful.

"Oh!" she gasped, hand to her heart. "Oh, you do have a beautiful voice."

"I sang plainsong as a lad. It made my aunt proud. The abbot wanted me in the monastery just to keep his monks in tune. Not for me, but I did like the singing."

"Plainchant is a heavenly sound."

"Good for any soul, hey." He brushed back a waft of her hair, spiraling loose of its braid. She had given up the kerchief, and the freedom felt good.

When she was with him, she just wanted to smile. Even when things went awry, what existed between them now felt new and good and strong. She felt she was learning something from his cheerful strength to add to her more serious nature.

He leaned to kiss her brow. "I came here to tell you that I will meet with the abbot and Patrick and Bishop Lamberton for a bit. If you want to go to the market fair, I can take you down the hill to find Marjorie and Aunt Jennet and Colban."

"Is there an apothecary shop in town? I need to replenish some herbs and such."

"There is. What mysterious cures do you have in mind?" He grazed his fingers over her cheek, slid his hand along her jaw. His touch went through her like soft lightning, and she lifted her head as his fingers shaped her jaw, then he leaned to kiss her cheek, sliding to cover her lips with his. She looped her arms around his neck and curved toward him as he pulled her tightly to him.

"Kissing in a church! I must have missed a wedding," came a

male voice.

Rowena broke away to look past Aedan, who turned. A man stood in the shadow of a pillar, wearing a black tunic and shoulder cape with a large silver cross hanging down on a thick chain—not a cleric, she realized, but a bishop. He was a short man with a belly like a barrel, iron-gray hair shaved at the crown, and a whimsical grin. He rather looked like an elf, Rowena thought. She loved his laugh as he came forward.

"Reverend Sir!" Aedan said. "Lady Rowena, this is William Lamberton, Bishop of Saint Andrews and Fife."

"Excellency," she murmured, taking his offered hand, bowing her head a little.

"So this is Lady Rowena, Sir Robert's daughter!" Lamberton took her hands in both of his. "Aedan told me about you." His dark eyes twinkled as he looked at Aedan. "So, this is the healer you spoke of just now in the house? The one you nearly married?"

"She is, sir."

"Something has changed here, I think. Or did my eyes fool me just now?"

"Your eagle eyes never miss a thing, Reverend Sir. I wish you had made more noise when you entered," Aedan laughed.

"You would not have heard. And before the tomb of sainted Queen Margaret! Though she had eight children and was no stranger to love and passion with her warrior-king," he added with a chuckle.

Aedan laughed too, a warm echo. Blushing, Rowena looked from one to the other, sensing the affection there. She could see that the bishop who had raised Aedan and mentored him to become a scholar and a fine man had also taught him the example of cheerfulness. She could not help but smile at both.

The bishop scratched his balding head. "I owe you both an apology. I was wrong."

"Wrong?" Rowena asked, puzzled.

"You should have married each other. I stood in the way, but

I was mistaken. I see that you, my lady, are just the one for this brawny lad."

"How do you know that, sir?" Aedan asked.

"Look at those eyes, shining like stars." He gave Rowena a jolly smile, his cheeks pink. "Love! I see love and joy there. This is just what I needed today. I spent months in an English tower wondering if I would ever see Scotland again. I have just returned and the best thing I have seen, other than Scottish soil and sky, is you two."

She was beginning to adore this man. The bishop was outspoken about his views on Scottish independence and had not hesitated to wield a sword to lead his followers, resulting in his arrest. She saw that feisty spirit in him.

"So," Lamberton went on, "when is the wedding? Shall we do it now?"

"Now?" Rowena blinked in surprise.

"I have not done a proper wedding for years. Bishops, you know," he said to Rowena. "But I would perform this one."

"We only just decided," she said. "We would want family with us."

"She is a planner, this one, and will put your sorry soul in order, lad," he told Aedan, who chuckled. "We can fix the betrothal today and post the banns if you like."

"Lady Rowena?" Raising his brows, Aedan looked at her.

"I am agreed," she said, her glance lingering on his.

"Good! I will have the abbot's clerk write up the banns and post them on the west portal. Remember, you two," the bishop gave them a knowing glance, "by Scots law, if an unwed couple knows each other with consent, their marriage is already fixed in the eyes of God and therefore the law."

Rowena blushed fiercely; the bishop seemed to miss nothing.

"With the banns posted, we can arrange a wedding whenever the lady wants," Aedan said, avoiding a direct answer to that remark.

"Now to other matters," Lamberton said. "Aedan, we are

ready to meet. I heard news in London that I want you to take to the Guardians when you can."

"Aye, sir. Lady, will you go down to the market while I am gone?"

"I will stay here a little longer. It is so peaceful. And I owe Saint Margaret my thanks and prayers," she said, thinking of the little bottle of healing water in her embroidered purse. "If you are not back soon, you can find me with the others."

"Margaret will hear your prayers." The bishop smiled and went toward the door.

"So," Aedan said, taking her arm, "according to Scots law, we are as good as wed."

"I would like a ceremony with family, would you?"

"I would. Whatever you wish, we will do."

"If you wish it too." She rose for a kiss. "Hurry back."

IN THE ROYAL chapel that extended past the altar, Rowena knelt beside the marble plinth that supported Margaret's large, beautifully decorated tomb. Every Scottish child knew that Queen Margaret answered Scottish pleas and assisted women especially. Long ago, as an English princess stranded in Scotland, Margaret married King Malcolm Canmore to become an exemplary queen, wife, mother, and pious soul who died of heartbreak when her husband and eldest son perished in the same battle. Years later, another son, also a king, built the chapel and petitioned Rome to declare his mother a Scottish saint despite her English origins. She was dearly loved, Rowena thought.

Rising from her prayers, she whispered thanks for protection from her troubles of late and asked blessings for those she loved, adding thanks for the healing water, and a final wish for peace in Scotland. But she knew that without some of these troubles, she might never have found Aedan. Now she could not imagine life without the vital, somewhat unpredictable man, who made her feel loved and changed for the better.

She wondered how long Aedan might be, and if she had time

to go to the market square and come back before he returned to look for her.

Hearing a door and footsteps out in the nave, she was startled. Was he back so soon? But the rhythm of the steps did not belong to Aedan; she knew his gait now. Another man was coming this way—two, she realized, perhaps three, for she heard uneven steps, the chink of chainmail and the thunk of heavy footfalls.

Fear flashed through her; she dared not be discovered here unless she knew who they were. Slipping behind Margaret's tall, canopied tomb, she stood in the narrow space between the marble catafalque and the wall.

"No one is here." The voice was familiar. She narrowed her eyes. Another man answered in a low, indistinct murmur, and the first man spoke again, louder.

"What do you mean, the abbot refused to see us? We are here by king's orders!"

Malise Comyn! Gasping, Rowena covered her mouth to smother the sound.

"The clerk said the abbot was meeting with Scottish officials and then would be at his prayers. He told us to return tomorrow." The second voice was clearer now, unfamiliar, but Scottish as well. The other had not yet spoken. Their steps and voices echoed as they walked up the nave.

"Abernethy! Did you ask after MacDuff?" Malise demanded.

"We did, but the clerk said he has not been here for months. The clerk would not even permit Brother Hugo to see the abbot."

"Even me," Hugo confirmed.

Shocked, Rowena leaned to hear more. The fact that Brother Hugo and Abernethy were here with Malise meant only trouble. The English galley had not sailed away after all. If they saw Brian Lauder's longship in the harbor at North Queensferry, that might prompt them to search in Dunfermline if Malise was unconvinced.

"The clerk refused even when I said our orders were from the king. He was unimpressed," Hugo went on.

"Because they regard Bruce as their king now, the fools," Malise said in a sour tone. "This church seems deserted. If MacDuff did come to Dunfermline, he would be recognized, but they might protect him. That clerk likely lied to you."

In the shadows, hearing footsteps, Rowena prayed they would not come closer.

"We saw Castle Black from the water, but I want to ride there," Malise said. "I suspect MacDuff and the Keith girl did come to Fife, though Lauder said otherwise. He knew something, I suspect."

"The lieutenant at Stirling said MacDuff could be anywhere," Abernethy said. "Perhaps they went west to Kincraig."

"I am not welcome there, but you can go there, Abernethy. You need to hire horses. Promise the Crown will pay later and let the stable worry about getting the coin."

"What about the MacDuff boy?" Brother Hugo asked.

"That has to wait. I want MacDuff and the girl. They have gone to ground somewhere, but where?"

The footsteps faded as they walked away. Rowena waited, trembling, sick about the threat that had come to this peaceful place—and she dreaded what might happen if Aedan encountered them, for he would not hesitate to confront them on behalf of his son, his home, and his loved ones.

All seemed quiet, so she slipped out of the chapel to peer down the nave. At the far end of the church, she saw the glint of steel and a flash of color as Malise and the others stepped into a side chapel. Somehow, she had to get out without being seen so she could warn Aedan. Moving on silent feet, she ducked behind a pillar and paused. Both arms of the church had side doors, but she might be visible if she ran to either.

Then she heard the sound of the main door and a flurry of footsteps on slate. "Rowena! Rowena! Are you here?" A high, light, dear voice called out.

Colban! Heart in her throat, a fierce need to protect the child eclipsing all else, she moved away from the pillar and rushed down the nave.

CHAPTER TWENTY-THREE

THE BOY STOOD in a beam of golden light from a high window and called her name again. "Lady Rowena!"

The men heard too. A knight—Abernethy—ran out of the side nook and snatched the boy up as Malise and the monk followed. Colban yelled, arms and legs flailing, his shrill cry smothered by a gloved hand.

"Let him go!" Rowena called, running down the central aisle, skirts flying. Her only driving thought was to stop them, grab the boy away—

Whirling, Malise reached out, but she skirted around him to confront the knight holding Colban. Incensed, she pulled at the man's arm while he struggled with the writhing boy. Abernethy pushed her away even as Colban managed to kick him so hard that the man grimaced.

"Let him go!" she shouted, pummeling his arm. But Malise grabbed her back toward him, trapping her, though she struggled.

"Lady Rowena! How good to see you," Malise said into her ear. "Be still."

"Let the boy go!"

"I thought he was a town brat—but he knows you. Who is he?" His voice had an ugly edge. "Who are you, boy?"

"Do not touch him!" She twisted in his grip.

"I am Colban MacDuff," the boy piped up, "son of Aedan, son of Colban, son of Duncan, son of—"

"Colban MacDuff!" Malise held Rowena in a hard grip, his arm across the front of her shoulders. "We have been looking for you and your father."

"My father is a warrior and he will come after you if you hurt Lady Rowena!"

"I am eager to see him. Where is he?" His arm was an iron band around her, but Rowena kicked backward. He grunted, barely avoiding the blow.

"Rowena—mmph!" Colban shrieked as Abernethy clapped a hand over his mouth.

She reached out, hindered by Malise, while Colban watched her with large, frightened eyes. He flailed his uninjured arm, which Abernethy grabbed back.

"He has a broken arm, can you not see that?" she demanded.

Abernethy, a muscular man whose chainmail hood framed a square face, dark beard, and rather large brown eyes, eased his hold, frowning as he looked at Colban.

"Go easy on the brat, but keep him quiet," Malise snapped. "I need to decide what in God's name to do now. I was not expecting this," he muttered.

Abernethy set Colban on his feet but kept a grip on the boy's bunched tunic. Colban kicked and twisted, distracting the fellow, who sidestepped and held on. Rowena twisted against Malise's grip, but felt her ankle wrench. She cried out.

"Quiet," Malise growled. "I have to think."

"You wanted us, now you have us," she hissed. "But this is a holy place and it would be a great sin to harm us."

"As great a sin as Bruce committed, killing my cousin in a church in Dumfries?"

"That was for the good of Scotland—you have no such worthy reason. Let us go. We are too much trouble."

"Trouble indeed," Malise agreed. "God's bones!"

"Where?" Colban looked around. "Are God's bones over there?" He pointed to a tomb and effigy in a side chapel.

"Shut up," Malise said.

"Take them to the ship," said Hugo. "The king wants both of them."

"He wants the boy taken to Northumbria, and the woman brought to him," Malise said. "We cannot go in both directions at once. We will take her."

"What do we do with the boy?" Abernethy asked.

"I have not decided yet."

"If I do see Edward, I will tell him all I know about you," Rowena told Malise.

"He might like to see you and dispense justice in person." Hugo spoke now, moving toward her. "The king was furious when he heard what you tried to do. He would never listen to you now."

"Hugo! You know I did not poison him. You watched every-thing I did when I was there, yet I was accused. I wonder if you know something about it!" She glared at him.

"Do you accuse me instead?" He shook his head. "Get them to the ship, Comyn."

"Are you in charge here?" Malise snapped. "How in hell are we to do that? Go outside and see if anyone is about. No one will notice another monk. Go!"

Scowling, Hugo went to the door and pushed his way out.

"Colban, listen. All will be well," Rowena said, seeing the fright in the boy's eyes. He nodded, glancing again at the door. She knew he feared and yet hoped, as she did, that his father might arrive with friends at his back.

"If you want to spare that child, tell me where MacDuff is," Malise said in her ear.

"If you want to be spared, leave Dunfermline now," she retorted.

"A threat?" He laughed, then drew a dagger from his belt sheath and pressed it against her throat. "Tell me where he is, or you and the boy will suffer."

"Stop this." She angled away from the steel point. "Malise Comyn, I know you better than you think. I saw you at your weakest—you were not a bad man then. Not then, when you were suffering and in need. You said you owed me. What of that now?"

He stared down at her, nostrils flaring. "I paid my debt to you when I arranged for you to go to Yester. The order was for Berwick. You were to suffer the same fate as Bruce's kinswomen." He laughed, flat and bitter. "I intended to take you out of Yester myself, but you had escaped with MacDuff! I owe you naught, lady."

"What was your plan at Yester?"

"I was concerned about your welfare. In fact, I returned to Yester with a priest, intending to find you. Why do you think that wretch Hugo is with me?" He leaned closer. "He agreed to marry us according to Edward's wishes. But we can still do that."

"I would never marry you. I told you that already," she said, writhing in his grip.

"Think! If you were my wife, I could plead for mercy. Otherwise, I must follow Edward's writ. Marriage would solve your problem. Henry said you were betrothed, but there is still hope for you."

She lifted her right hand. The ring glinted in the low light.

"What is that?" His eyes narrowed.

"My betrothed gave it to me. He was my father's choice for me years ago. Thomas the Rhymer's choice for me too." Heart pounding, she hoped the sanction of her father and the Rhymer would give him pause. "The banns have been posted." She hoped so.

"Who is the man," he growled.

"My da gave her that ring," Colban said. "I heard them talking this morning." Rowena blinked, not knowing that.

"MacDuff?" Malise snapped.

She lifted her chin. "My hand was promised to Aedan Mac-Duff years ago."

"What! When Edward hears that, you will lose any hope of his favor."

"Sir Malise, we do not need to follow his orders or his laws. Scots are not his subjects," she said. "Release us and go your way. Remember I helped you. Please, for the boy's sake—"

"You do not understand Edward's temper. What the devil!" This as Hugo burst into the church, bumping into Abernethy and Colban, who cried out.

"People are coming this way! Men, ladies, and monks will come for prayers soon."

"Did you see MacDuff? Big fellow. Brown and brawny as an ox."

"I did not see him. But if they enter the church—we have to get out!"

"We cannot just walk her out and let the boy go—wait," Malise said. "Hugo, do you have it? Use it."

"Use what?" Rowena strained against Malise's grip as he took hold of her jaw, his fingers biting into her cheeks, his arm locking her arms to her sides.

"Who knows you are here? MacDuff?" he asked low.

She could not lead him to Aedan. "The abbot. The bishop. And Wemyss—the sheriff of Fife," she managed, despite the hand clamped over her jaw.

"Damn," Malise muttered. "Hugo, now would be excellent," he hissed.

The monk approached as Malise pried open her mouth with his gloved thumb. Hugo set something cold to her lips. Glass or ceramic—then liquid drizzled into her mouth—the thick, sweet burn of heavy wine—mead, she realized—with an oddly bitter undertaste. The potion seeped under her tongue. She struggled, and for a moment felt as if she could hardly draw a breath. Wooziness began to creep its cold through her.

Dizzy, gasping, she knew then. Mead, as a carrier for the strong, bitter tincture called the Great Rest, a powerful sleeping potion of dried, crushed poppies originally brought back by crusading knights. Mixed with cloves and other herbs, the substance was common in wealthy infirmaries. Brother Hugo, an infirmarian in Edward's court, would have access to it.

Chasing under the tongue, the liquid would rapidly penetrate the body. Though dizziness swamped her, she saw Hugo move as if through fog. He went to Colban.

"Not the boy," she said hoarsely, "he is too small for a dose of—"

Colban thrashed and shrieked, then suddenly ducked down, so that Abernethy lost hold of him. The boy slipped between the knight's legs and raced to the door, still partly open after Hugo rushed inside. He slipped through the gap and was gone.

"After him!" Malise yelled, holding Rowena, whose limbs began to fail. As her knees buckled, she felt Malise grab her under her arms. "Peter! Fool, go get him!"

"What am I to do with him?"

Malise growled in disgust, and Abernethy ran outside.

"What a disaster! Hugo, help me get her out of here." Malise picked her up in his arms; she was losing strength to fight. Her senses were slipping, but she could still hear what was said.

"The side door," Hugo said. "I saw a cart out there. We will wrap her up in her cloak like a parcel from the market."

"Damn and damn," Malise said.

"You are damned," Rowena slurred. "Aedan MacDuff will—"

"If he comes for you, he will walk into a trap. I will see to it."

"We could just leave her here with the boy, and run," Hugo said.

"You are as much a dimwit as Abernethy!"

As he carried her toward the side door, Rowena felt strangely floaty. As they passed the altar, she noticed the chapel behind it where the queen's beautiful tomb shone in the afternoon sun.

"Lady, help us," she mumbled, and sank into darkness.

"ROWENA!" AEDAN CALLED, standing in the entrance of the church. He strode down the nave, steps echoing, and paused to turn slowly around. The west door opened and he turned in relief. "Rowena—"

"Colban!" Marjorie entered the church. "Are you here?"

"Where is Rowena?" Aedan walked toward her, seeing Lady Jennet and Patrick coming in after her. "I thought she would be here. And you are looking for Colban?"

"He should be here," his sister said. "He ran ahead of us a while ago, and said he wanted to find Rowena, who we thought would be in the church."

A cold chill went through him, but he dismissed it. "Neither of them is here. They must be in the market square. You must have missed them."

"They are not in the market, I assure you," Patrick Wemyss said.

"I let him go on his own, thinking he would be safe." Marjorie seemed on the verge of tears. "But where is he?"

"We will look everywhere, my dear," Patrick said. "We will find him."

"Rowena is gone too," Aedan said. Worry dragged at him, but he had a thought. "She wanted some time in the queen's chapel. Let me look there."

His footsteps echoed as he went past the altar to the chapel extension. In the rainbow light of stained glass, he paused before Margaret's tomb to nod briefly to the painted effigy of the queen. She had been a beauty, he thought.

"Where is my son, lady? Where is my wife," he whispered, that last word coming so easily to his lips. Dread sat heavy in his gut. Something was very wrong. He felt it.

Yet nothing seemed out of place. He turned to leave, then noticed a space behind the huge tomb. Peering around the plinth, he saw a small foot.

"Dear God!" He sank to one knee and looked around the corner. Colban ran into his arms so fast, he nearly lost his balance.

"What is it? What happened?" Aedan asked, holding him.

"I was hiding—I ran, and came back, and I saw them—and I hid in here. I heard your footsteps and I kept hiding."

"Who was here?" Aedan lifted his son in his arms, holding

him close for a moment. Then he left the chapel to stride through the church calling for the others.

"Quickly, to the abbot's house." He had a strong feeling that the church was not a safe place. He hurried outside and across the lawn to burst into the house.

A flurry of action soon had Colban installed in the abbot's best chair with a cup of milk and an oatcake. Desperate to know what Colban had seen, Aedan waited, not wanting to frighten the boy. But Rowena was gone, and fear had its claws in him.

"Tell us what you know, lad," he said quietly.

Colban nodded. "Men came into the church. Knights. And a monk all in black."

Aedan glanced at the abbot and the bishop, standing near Patrick and Marjorie. The abbot shook his head; the Dunfermline monks wore brown robes.

"Was Lady Rowena there when you saw these men?" Aedan asked.

"Aye. They grabbed me and her too. I fought and so did she but they would not let us go even when she asked them."

"And then what?" He began to feel an incandescent fury. "Did you hear their names? Did Lady Rowena know them?"

"She called one of them Milo, I think. Or Miles."

"Malise," Aedan groaned. He glanced quickly at Patrick, who scowled. "Colban, did they hurt you, or harm the lady?"

He would kill them hard and swift if they had. He waited.

Colban shrugged. "When they grabbed me, it hurt. But I kicked one of them. Then the monk gave Rowena something to drink. And he was going to give me a drink too but she yelled at him. And then I got away. I ran."

"Where did you go?" Marjorie asked.

"I ran to the market to find you, but I did not see you. The other man was chasing me so I ran back up the hill and came in here. He came in too but did not find me. I was sure he saw me, but he looked away. So I waited and then you came." He smiled up at Aedan, looking like an angel, an elf, and a scared little boy all at once.

"You will be fine now. All will be well."

"Rowena said that too. Where is she?"

"I do not know, but I will find her."

A servant came into the great hall. "Father Abbot—Sir Brian Lauder is here." As he spoke, Brian entered, his face creased with worry.

"I just came from the quay," he said. "Comyn's galley was there. They were loading supplies on the ship and did not seem rushed. I was about to ride up here to find you, but the harbor master arrived to ask what goods we were delivering or taking away. Now I wonder if Comyn sent him deliberately to delay us."

"Could be. Is the galley still there?" Aedan stood.

"Gone," Brian said. "Before I could do anything, they sailed out."

"Was Rowena with them?" Aedan growled.

"That was why I hurried here. One of my crew said they saw a woman on board. Blue gown, dark hair. They thought they recognized Rowena."

Aedan swore. "Is your ship ready to leave? Patrick, can you sail with us?"

"I can. If wrongdoing was done in my sheriffdom, I have authority to go after these fellows with you. I can bring some guards with us."

"Good. Quickly, aye? Father Abbot, can my son and his aunts stay here until we return? I cannot send them to Castle Black now and we have no time to stop at Bass Rock until we find Rowena. I will be back as soon as I can."

"Of course, they are welcome here," the abbot said. "Go!"

CHAPTER TWENTY-FOUR

WEARY, SICK, AND frightened, Rowena hardly remembered sailing over the firth, the sleeping potion strong enough to keep her dozing fitfully. By the time she felt more alert hours later, the galley was sliding into a busy port beneath a castle that overlooked the horseshoe curve of a broad river. Berwick-upon-Tweed, she heard someone say. There were several men on the galley—Malise, Hugo, Abernethy, soldiers, oarsmen.

Where were they taking her? Berwick was just above England, and three hours or more from Fife, but she had hardly been aware of the time that had fled past.

Aedan! Colban! Where were they, what had happened? She vaguely remembered being in the church at Dunfermline, and remembered Colban running out, and Hugo approaching her. But she had lost the rest. Confused, she looked about, relieved to see that Aedan and Colban were not on the galley with the others. Setting a hand to her chest, she felt the crystal, safe on the silver chain Aedan had given her.

She felt sick and dizzy, and leaned back, her hair blowing about in the sea breezes. Then Malise approached, taking her arm without a word to march her down an angled platform to the stone quay. Glad to be off the boat, she soon quailed as she realized he was leading her to yet another boat, a smaller one. She dragged back.

"Do you need another dose of Hugo's tincture? Do as you are

told," he said.

She did, knowing his threats were real. Soon several men joined Malise, and the oarsman began to pull the smaller longship out into the river.

Sir Peter Abernethy had guided her to a cross-board and sat beside her. "This is the River Tweed. Up there is Berwick Castle." He pointed to a castle on a hill overlooking the waterway. Then, with a curt apology, he tugged at the knotted ropes around her wrists to make them secure. She leaned back against the stern of the boat and he tucked her cloak around her. He stood.

"Do you want some ale?" he asked.

"Please." Her mouth was dry, her voice hoarse. "Where are we going?"

"Carlisle Castle. The king wants to see you."

"But he is at Lanercost," she protested.

"Not any longer." He turned to leave.

"Sir Peter—did Colban get away?"

"That wee lad! I decided not to look for him."

"Thank you," she said, realizing he had let him go. He nodded and walked away.

She closed her eyes, unsure what would come next. If Edward wanted to see her, suspecting she tried to assassinate him, he might be angry enough to declare some awful fate for her. She thought of the Scotswomen in cages and shuddered.

And she knew that Carlisle Castle, Edward's stronghold on the border between England and Scotland, was just a few miles from Lanercost Priory where the king had set up his household. She had heard that Scottish captives disappeared into Carlisle forever.

Lifting her hands, wrists joined by the damp knotted rope, she pushed her bedraggled hair out of her eyes as Sir Peter returned.

"My lady." He handed her a wooden cup that she took awkwardly. Thirsty, she drank, finding the frothy ale refreshing at first. But it had a bitter aftertaste; the stuff they called the Great

Rest had been added. She dumped it out.

"Tell Brother Hugo not again," she said. "I know the taste."

She noticed the monk standing nearby with Sir Malise and knew they could hear her in the smaller longship. Hugo shrugged innocently and turned his back.

Though she had sipped only a little, she felt the effects again. Thankful she had not downed the whole of it, she leaned her head against the rise of the stern, dizzy again.

Soon Malise came toward her. "Brother Hugo says he just wanted to ease your suffering on the journey, since you were so sick on the galley. So you should be grateful."

"I was sick?" She did not remember that. But she noticed that her blue gown had some messy streaks—and she saw similar stains on Malise's surcoat. She smiled.

"I do not travel well on water."

"Wish I had known that," he snapped.

"So do I. You would have left me in Dunfermline."

"You would have come with us if we had to drag you over land. Boats are faster. We will reach Carlisle tonight and you will face the king."

"What will he do?"

"He will not be interested in your troubles." He sat beside her. "Listen. Edward wants you brought to him. Aye, there is a charge against you, but if you agree to certain things, I can still help you."

She did not answer. The boat was skimming fast, and she felt the sickness begin again. She gulped fresh air to delay it.

"Give me your promise, and all this will be gone."

"I am not a fool." She slid him a glance.

"You are foolish to refuse a marriage that would solve your problems." He lifted her hand to examine the gold band and let go. "You escaped with MacDuff because there has always been something between you."

"That is not your concern." She turned a shoulder to him.

"He puts you in jeopardy with the king. Pledge to me instead so I can help you. Otherwise, you take unnecessary risks."

"I do not take risks." But she had done so with Aedan, and would never regret it.

"Once Edward learns the name of your betrothed, you will have signed MacDuff's death warrant. And there is the other matter."

She did not look at him. "What other matter?"

"Have you gathered the Rhymer's things to relinquish to Edward, as ordered?"

Feeling an urge to touch the silver chain at her neck, she kept still. "I have not been to Kincraig since Edward made that petulant demand."

"Soldiers will be sent there to take those things. It will not go well for your kin."

"You want those things as badly as Edward does. But they will not benefit you."

"A king's writ is a serious thing."

"Edward's writs can be ignored on Scottish soil. They are not legal."

"Are you a legal mind now, not just an herb-wife and silly female?"

"One of my sisters recently married a justiciar. Ask him what is legal in your actions here."

"Well then. A legal marriage would benefit both of us. Brother Hugo can take care of that on this very boat. That would cancel your promise to MacDuff."

"You are persistent, I credit you that." She swept her hair back in the breeze.

He stood. "We will be on this river for a while, then we will ride the rest of the way. You have a little time to think it over."

"I have done enough thinking." The words brought Aedan to mind so keenly that tears pooled in her eyes. She blinked them away, and rested her head back, feeling again a heavy, unnatural urge to sleep.

When she woke, she heard Malise and Abernethy talking

nearby. Straining to hear, she kept her eyes closed.

"Still following us? Good! But they cannot be allowed to sail too close. Not yet."

"How do we prevent that?" Abernethy asked. "They have been behind us all the way, and now they are sailing the river too. They could be on us if we do not hurry."

"Find a way to stall them if they get too close. They must not catch us until we reach Carlisle. Then we catch them." Malise turned. "Ah, Lady Rowena. Good news!"

She stared up at him. "News?"

"Your lover is on our tail. Look there." He pointed behind them on the river.

Aedan? She struggled to sit up and look. The light was fading toward dusk, glinting on the water. Blinking, she saw the shape of a longship well behind them.

She thought it looked like Lauder's longship, but she could not be sure. "That could be any ship on this river."

"That one has been behind us steadily since Fife." He smiled. "I told you I would set a trap for MacDuff. And you are the bait."

BRIAN LAUDER'S LONGSHIP, propelled by a full complement of oarsmen and a billowed sail, was fast, but the larger galley had cut powerfully through the water all the way from Fife. The English ship was a misty, distant sight when the angle of sea and coastline allowed, but Aedan had not lost sight of it.

He stood in the bow watching, determined. No matter how much distance the other ship had on them, he had no room in head or heart for defeat. He felt grim, flat, all trace of humor lost. Malise had grabbed his son, who thankfully got away. He had taken his wife—she was that to him now.

Aedan would catch him. He saw no other course but that.

Brian joined Aedan then. "They have pulled into the harbor at Berwick—you saw that. And they are far ahead to catch on water, but we can keep them in sight and follow wherever they take her."

"Aye, but where the devil is that?"

"To King Edward, most likely. Patrick says he recently heard Edward has gone to Carlisle. A long way for a day's journey, but it could be where they are headed."

"Could be." Aedan thought again of the difficulty Rowena had while traveling on water. The thought brought a new ache of worry and stoked a fire of anger in his blood. He clenched his fists and watched the sea. They had been on the water three hours now, and he had kept a keen eye on the distant form of the English ship.

As the galley turned into the water at Berwick-upon-Tweed, the northernmost port on the English coast, Brian's longship followed. The crew navigated the curving port and the water flowing around fingers of land as they entered the River Tweed. Soon enough, they saw the galley—docked and empty but for some crewmen and soldiers.

Brian sent men to inquire; they returned to say the English lord from the galley had hired a smaller boat to head down the river as far as Kelso, where they planned to change to horses. The riverman did not know their destination, but he confirmed that a woman was with them.

"She looked ill, we heard," the crewman reported. "They half-carried her into the smaller vessel. The riverman noticed, finding it odd."

Aedan turned away, mastered fury, turned back. "We follow," he told Brian and Patrick. "If they sail, we sail. If they take horses, so do we. I will not give this up."

"Nor will we," Patrick said.

"My longship can sail the Tweed for a long way before the waters become too narrow to allow it," Brian said. "We will catch them."

The oarsmen bent to the task as the ship skimmed along the river in the gathering twilight, proceeding more slowly than on the open waters of the sea.

Before they left Berwick, Aedan looked up at the castle in the purpling dusk. His niece Isabella was trapped there in a horrible iron cage—he had intended to visit her somehow but fate had intervened. He did not see a cage along the profile on the high parapet as they passed beneath the castle.

At Selkirk, just before he was ambushed and taken to Yester, the guardians of Scotland had word that Isabella was removed daily from the cage to sit in a chamber with a servant woman, then returned to her cruel confinement. He could only pray that Isabella had some small moments of comfort.

Near Kelso, the waterway became a challenge even for their sleek longship. Lashing in at a riverside dock, they heard that a group of Edward's knights, a monk, and a woman had docked and hired horses and a cart to head west for Carlisle. Hearing that, Patrick hired horses in the town—making sure to charge the cost to the English Crown, as his sheriff's rank permitted—and they took to the road too.

WHEN ROWENA WOKE again, she was in a haycart drawn by a horse, surrounded by Malise, Peter, and guards on horseback. Not certain how she got there, she was glad when they drew into the yard of an inn. The light was leaving the sky. Twilight was late in summer, and though they had been traveling for hours, the lavender light would last until nearly midnight. Tired and hungry, she thanked Sir Peter when he lifted her out of the cart. Without a word, he handed her over to a large woman who came out of the inn.

"Ropes? Is she a criminal?" the woman said.

"Not your business to ask," Abernethy said.

"Fine. I want no trouble here. But she is a woman and no matter what she has done, she has likely had enough of men for a while. Give her to me."

Not long after, refreshed a little, Rowena was back in the cart. Riding beside the cart, Malise spoke to Abernethy, and hooted, a pleased sound that startled her.

"Aye, sir, they are still following," Abernethy said. "Far off.

On horses now."

So Aedan was still on their tail, Rowena thought. Thank the saints he and the others had not lost the route in the change from water to land. He had not given up—and she knew with every fiber of her being that he would never give up looking for her. He was a guardian, a protector to his bones. And he loved her.

Knowing that filled her with hope, with love, and with fear.

As the cart rolled on, each turn of the wheels rumbled his name. *Aedan, Aedan, Aedan MacDuff.* Stay safe, she thought. And keep away. But she knew he would not.

Finally, as twilight darkened to indigo sparkling with stars, the silhouette of Carlisle Castle loomed. The escort rolled through the gate, though Rowena was left to wait under guard while Malise disappeared into the keep, asking for the captain of the castle. The effects of the potion were clearing, but she felt dull-witted and just sat.

Malise returned to beckon to Abernethy. "The king is not here. They say he headed out, intending to invade Scotland again. He felt strong enough to don his armor and ride a horse, determined to lead his army in battle. Insistent, they said."

"Where is he now?" Peter asked.

"The royal camp is a few miles north, near the border of Scotland," Malise said. "Hurry. Those rogues cannot find us until I can introduce them to King Edward."

TENTS AND TORCHES stretched through the darkness as Rowena walked with Malise, Peter, Hugo and a few men into the royal camp a few hours later. They had left horses and cart with the king's guards once Malise showed permission to enter, signed by the lieutenant of Carlisle.

Unsteady on her feet, wrists still confined, Rowena felt Abernethy's guiding hand on her arm. Ahead, Malise Comyn stopped to talk with a few men—lords by the look of them, in fine tunics over shining mail, with gold chains and even fur-lined cloaks; although the summer days now flowed into July, the evenings were cool.

She shivered a little as she and Abernethy waited for Comyn. Then he and Sir Peter took her along a path to a cluster of small tents on the edge of the field near a woodland. Along the way, she noticed Malise's pronounced limp after the ordeal of travel. She frowned, wondering then if he resented that she had not cured it entirely.

A woman came toward them, tall and tough-looking, wiping her hands on her apron, a kerchief pinned on her head. "It is late, Sir Malise. Who is this chit?" She tipped her head toward Rowena. "A lady by the look of her, and no whore."

"A lady to you, Dame Bessie. She will stay in your tent. A guard will sit outside for the night."

"Guarded?" Bessie scrutinized her. "She looks poorly. Is that your doing, sir?"

Rowena blinked, pleased that Dame Bessie took a dim view of Malise.

"No one mistreated her," he said, though Rowena gave a doubtful huff. "She has had a long journey today," he continued. "We all have. She will stay here. In the morning, she is to be brought before the king. So clean her up."

"I want extra coin for this favor. Something is not right here and I want naught to do with it." The woman took Rowena's arm. "Audience with the king, hey? Then she is no whore. The king is too weak to crawl out of bed, let alone—"

"Just do what you are told," Malise snapped.

In the tent, the woman cut the rope from Rowena's wrists, muttering, then gave her a cloth, a bowl of water, and a corner for privacy. Undressing to her shift, Rowena washed while Bessie shook out her clothing to refresh it.

"Sit there and let me comb the tangles from your hair." She began to glide an ivory comb through Rowena's long hair in a surprisingly soothing manner. "Braided or brushed loose? Combed out, it is lovely. Are you wed, do you need a kerchief?"

"Braided. I—am betrothed." She gazed at her hand, where

Aedan's gold ring glinted in the candlelight. She was a widow—and now a wife again. But she could not admit that, or soon be widowed again.

"What a pretty chain. What kind of stone is on it? It sparkles."

Rowena set a hand over her chest, realizing that the Rhymer's crystal, twinkling in the candlelight, was noticeable through her shift. "Just a trinket."

"Why does the king want to see you? There are no other ladies in this camp. I hear his young queen may arrive with her ladies, but I have not seen them yet."

"I am a healer," Rowena said. "Perhaps he wants to see me for that reason."

"He needs healing, that one! I only see him from a distance. I do the laundry and some chores in camp and rarely go to the royal tents. But he is weak, anyone can see it. Yet he comes out here to stir war with the Scots, even in his condition. I hope you can help him, lady."

Then no rumor of poisoning had reached the washerwoman's ears, or she would have said. Nodding, silent, Rowena wondered if she had been summoned to help—or to be reprimanded and unjustly sentenced despite her innocence.

Again, she thought of Aedan as she had done so often that awful day. Where was he? Had he followed them to the royal camp by now? Would he keep away and stay safe, or would he try to rescue her and step into danger?

She remembered Malise's chilling words. *I set a trap, and you are the bait.*

INCONSTANT MOONLIGHT MADE the way more difficult to follow, but Aedan and the others made progress, sighting the other group now and then—distant moving shadows on the road or the crest of a hill, too far to catch but near enough to see. At a tavern, they learned their quarry had stopped there too and had moved on, perhaps an hour or more. Lingering long enough for ale, water, bread, and wedges of yellow cheese, Aedan and the others took to the road again.

He was deeply grateful for the help of friends who neither complained nor questioned their mission that night. Without sharing his thoughts with them, he was by turns terrified, furious, heartbroken, and determined. He sensed they felt the same.

The cadence of compline bells tolled in the air from some monastery in the hills. Aedan knew that marked the hour of prayers before bed for those monks, and he was grateful for some sense of the time. Riding on, they stopped in a woodland grove to share what remained of the bread and cheese, then rode a little farther until Carlisle Castle was visible in the distance, a powerful fortress on a high round hill overlooking a river that gleamed in the darkness.

They rested in forestland within sight of the castle gates, choosing a spot where they would not be seen. Then, exhausted, they rolled up in plaids and dozed for a little while, taking turns to keep watch. The hired horses, quiet and robust with strong hearts and much patience, slept too.

CHAPTER TWENTY-FIVE

"THIS WAY," A king's guard said the next morning as he led Rowena, Sir Malise, and Sir Peter toward the royal tents. Larger and more finely appointed than the dozens of other tents scattered over the meadow, the royal tents were marked with flags showing Edward's lions rampant. He was there, then. Rowena's stomach flipped a bit.

Walking through the camp, she noticed a large roped-off area where several knights and soldiers practiced with swords and pikes, while others groomed and exercised horses. On poles around this area flew various banners—among them, the dragon banner, a cylindrical red cloth dragon that filled with wind when carried aloft.

Edward's knights raised the dragon banner before them only when the king sent them out to declare no mercy. Chivalry ceased to exist under that banner. She shivered at the gruesome reminder that this was a war camp focused on conquering Scotland. She walked on, her cloak billowing in the wind. On impulse while dressing, she had turned it to show its plaid lining: her own banner declaring her a Scotswoman.

Lifting her head proudly, she walked beside Comyn. He had not bound her wrists when he fetched her from the washerwoman's tent—a relief for her stiff hands, irritated skin, and peace of mind. She did not care to go the length of the camp with her hands tied; her presence already attracted attention. As she passed, men turned, paused. A noblewoman here was unusual, Bessie had said. Or did they know what she did not?

Dread rolled through her as she wondered what awaited her in the king's tent.

Approaching the largest tent, Malise rudely poked her waist to hurry her along, then took her elbow in a sham of courtesy. She tried to pull away, but he held tight.

The guard pulled back the curtained doorway. "Your Grace. Sir Malise Comyn and Sir Peter Abernethy with—a lady." Malise did not give her name. The guard motioned for them to wait outside while he disappeared into the shadowed interior.

"Abernethy," Malise snapped, "go see if Brother Hugo is with the king. I have not seen him today." Abernethy ducked inside.

"Malise," Rowena said. He looked at her in surprise when she spoke. A question was tearing at her; she had to ask. "Is Aedan MacDuff following? Where is he?"

"I sent men out this morning to look for them. I expect you will see him soon."

"You used me to lure him here."

"I am hopeful my trap will work," he said. "Edward will be pleased that I snared MacDuff so easily. Hunting both of you was tedious. Had I known you were on Lauder's longship in the firth that day, I could have boarded it and saved this inconvenience."

"I wish you had done so. MacDuff would have thrown you into the sea."

He laughed. "Before you see the king, I should tell you something first."

Fear spiked through her. "What is it?"

His dark-eyed gaze slid about the area and returned to bore into her. "Edward did not send me to find you because of the charge of poisoning. Not quite."

"Then why am I here?" She tried to jerk her arm away, but he held fast.

"He sent me to find you because he is ill and knows he is dying."

"What!" She glared up at him. "But I would have returned if I had known. I told the king I would come back if he sent for me. But you twisted it—to this!"

He shrugged. "Somewhat. You were accused, you escaped. He was not told all."

"You abducted me, you were willing to hurt a child—does he know that? Are the charges false?"

"The charges are real and you will answer to them." He glanced around. "I had to get you here quickly, but I guessed you would not travel with me."

"That is true. But now that we are here, I will help Edward if I can." She looked away. Helping this king, despite what he had done to the Scots, to her first husband, to Aedan and his family, pulled at her. But years ago she had promised herself, and Aunt Una, and Grandda Thomas, to help others. It was part of her, and hard to deny. But she would not use the Rhymer's crystal. She would not.

"His health is fragile. Do not excite him by pleading your innocence. He may have forgotten what he was told of that. But if he is reminded and becomes angered over it, a temper fit could kill him."

"Ah. Now I see," she said. "If Edward dies, you would not be rewarded. You dragged me here so you could earn praise and reward for your service. And you used me to lure Aedan MacDuff, another prize for you. What else do you want?" The sudden realization drove through her like ice. "You want the crystal."

"The Rhymer's charm stone. The one you used for me. I hear you wear it."

Stunned, she stared. "What—"

"The washer-woman told me you wear a valuable crystal jewel. Did you think she was your friend—or mine?" With a finger, he hooked the silver chain around her neck and slid it upward. She clutched it in place and locked her gaze with his.

"This is not what you think it is," she said.

"She still denies it! Give it to me. Better yet, agree to be my wife and you will be pardoned. I will see to it. We will both reap reward."

"Nay, and nay." She held the stone against her. Another thought came clear then. "And you want me to treat Edward with the stone, so you will get the praise for that too. Even more, you want him cured. If he dies, you lose the advantage you crave."

He sucked in a breath; she had hit on a truth. "We cannot let the king die. You are here to help him."

"If he were to die, you would have no more protection for your past deeds and ill intentions. If Edward is gone and Bruce wins the day, you, a disloyal Scot, would suffer."

"I believe," he said, "the king would be very interested to know who your betrothed is. He trusts you, or did—so that would be a betrayal. Edward does not tolerate betrayal well." He cocked a brow.

She quailed, knowing that was true. If Edward heard she would marry Aedan, he would be enraged. And if Aedan walked into the trap Malise had set, she feared the consequences.

The guard pulled back the tent flap. "The king will see you now."

"WORD WAS, DAYS ago," Patrick Wemyss said, "that Edward decided he must show sovereign strength and lead troops to attack Scotland with the dragon banner flying. He means to terrorize the Scots and crumble their resistance."

"He has enough temper and mania to believe that would work," Aedan said. He reined in his horse on a hilltop beside Patrick, Brian, and the few guards with them. The red sandstone walls of Carlisle Castle were bright against the summer green of the surrounding hills. Yet something was not right, he thought. He did not see the king's personal banner flying on the parapet.

"A pack of damned Scots will not be welcome down there," Brian said, gesturing toward the castle. "We would be arrested—

or slaughtered."

"The king may have ridden out already if he means to try to invade Scotland. If so, they have made camp somewhere. Malise will go there. But where?"

"There must be a war camp within several miles, likely along the Scottish border," Patrick agreed. "We could ride north and see what we find."

"Wait. Something may happen. Patrols have been going in and out of the castle all morning," Aedan said.

The sun climbed as they remained on the hillside behind a screen of scrub and trees. Looking out over the long meadow and a vast woodland beyond, he noticed men riding along a track that cut a winding path through the meadowland. They were heading for Carlisle.

Aedan shaded his eyes against the sun. The men were English soldiers by their gear and shields. Just another patrol. One of the knights paused on the road to look around, shading his eyes as Aedan did. For an instant, Aedan felt their gazes connect.

"We have been seen," Brian said.

The lone rider cut away from the patrol to head across the meadow toward the hill where the Scots sheltered behind some trees. Sir Patrick swore low and set a hand to the sword at his back.

"Hold." Aedan recognized the design of a shield he had not seen for a while—a white field with a band of red and gold vertical stripes. *Keith.* As the knight rode, he pushed back his chainmail hood, revealing a gleam of golden hair in the summer sunshine.

Aedan guided his horse to the hilltop and lifted a hand.

"What are you doing, sir?" Patrick hissed. Aedan rode past him and down the slope to the meadow, his horse loping through the grasses toward the advancing rider.

He rode closer, lifting a hand in a sign of peace. "Henry Keith!"

"Identify yourself!" Henry reined in, hand on the sword hilt beside his saddle.

"I know your shield. Sir Henry Keith, I trust? It has been years."

"Do I know you? Think before you answer, Scotsman. I am deputy sheriff in Selkirkshire, and here under King Edward. Who are you?"

"MacDuff. Sir Aedan MacDuff of Castle Black in Fife."

Henry startled visibly, his horse echoing that in a sidestep. "Aedan MacDuff! I did not recognize you."

"I shaved." Aedan touched his chin.

"Where is Rowena?"

"I came here to find her, so I have the same question." He guided his horse closer.

"I had a message from Lauder of the Bass regarding her," Henry said. "A shock to learn she was falsely accused and taken to Yester, then escaped and somehow ended up in your company. What the devil, sir! If harm comes to her—"

"No harm would ever come to her in my care, sir. She was safe with me in Fife until Malise Comyn got hold of her. Edward ordered him to bring Rowena to him. My friends and I have pursued them day and night to this place."

"Malise, that bastard!" Henry rode closer. "Edward is camped with his troops a few miles from here. He has it in his head to invade Scotland again."

"I have naught polite to say about that."

Henry huffed. "I saw Malise this morning at the royal camp. I had no idea he might have Rowena. She will be there unless he has moved her. He sent a patrol out here, and I came with them. We were told to search for renegade Scots. I presume that describes you and your friends."

"We need your help, Henry."

He shifted the reins to turn his horse. "Fetch your friends. I will take you there."

As THE GUARD beckoned them into the tent, Rowena jerked out of

Malise's hold to step ahead of him. Immediately the stifling atmosphere inside the tent struck her. Two braziers rippled heat in the July warmth, and the tent was cluttered with furnishings, carpets, stacked chests and boxes, a tabletop thick with documents. Guards stood in every corner, a clerk scribbled at a table, and Brother Hugo sat in a corner studying a book. He glanced at her with no hint of surprise.

Edward sat in a wooden chair, high-backed with armrests, the chair draped with furs and robes, but he looked uncomfortable. Gaunt and pale, he leaned awkwardly on the chair's arms. His eyes were red-rimmed, his hands trembled, and he was shivering. When he saw her, he straightened.

"Lady Rowena. So you came."

"I did, Sire. What can I do for you?"

He gestured for her to approach, but held up a hand when Malise moved too. "Stay back, Comyn. Lady, did you bring potions? What you left us is gone."

"I did not, Sire. I came in a rush with no time to prepare."

"I suppose Sir Malise fears I will die any moment. I will not. I just need what you gave me before to give me the strength to do what I must do."

"May I ask what that is, Your Grace?"

"The Scots need to see a mighty monarch at the head of an army. They refuse to show obedience and even crowned a so-called king—Bruce," he snarled. "I rode out today wearing armor, riding my warhorse. I want them to see that I will not back down. Tomorrow I will drive my army farther into Scotland." A spasm of pain crossed his craggy face.

"Sire, I cannot aid you for that cause. You know that I am Scottish."

"Aye, but a woman." He waved a hand. "Get me those tinctures."

"I do not have them, Sire, nor means to prepare them."

With a bony finger, he beckoned her closer. "Then give me that charm stone that healed Comyn when he was doomed," he said low. "Where is it?"

"Sire, if I could find ingredients to make a potion," she said, hoping to deflect him. "If Brother Hugo has anything—"

Edward snapped his fingers and Hugo came forward, frowning.

"Brother, you have potions and tinctures here. Share some ingredients with me." Rowena listed some herbs she might need.

"Sire, there is little here," Hugo said, addressing the king. "I have some ingredients at the castle if the lady will go there. A war camp is not the place for her." He shot Malise a dark look as if to reprimand him.

Rowena would not agree to go to a castle where so many Scottish prisoners had vanished. "I feel the king's need is more immediate. What do you have here?"

"Only what his doctor, John Gadsden, prepared. The king seems to think whatever you made for him was helpful. Willow and something—peppermint, perhaps. Or did you include something more—precious?"

"I left the recipe with you. You know what was in it."

"Whatever you have, Lady Rowena, give it over now. That includes the stone," Edward snapped. "Hugo, go back to your corner. Bring the doctor's remedy later."

"Sire," Hugo said, and backed away.

Edward leaned toward Rowena. "Give me the Rhymer's stone," he hissed. "Where is it? Sir Malise said you would bring it. He is to be commended for his help."

She shuddered with resentment, yet against all reason, she felt tempted to use the crystal—an old man needed its power. King or tyrant, he was suffering. But she could not do that. There was a limit, she realized, though it wrenched at her.

And she was loath to expose the crystal here; Edward would steal it; Malise would use it to gain privilege; and she had promised to protect it always.

But there was something else she could offer, nearly forgotten in the frantic, frightening rush from Fife to this place. "Sire, I have another treatment that could help."

Reaching into her embroidered purse, she brought out the little green glass bottle that she had filled from a queen's pool in the cave beneath MacDuff's castle.

"How the devil do we get in there?" Aedan asked no one in particular.

Hidden in a strip of woodland, he stood with Henry, Brian, Patrick and the sheriff's guardsmen. Through the leafy tree cover, he saw dozens of tents sheltering hundreds of English soldiers. The large tent at the center flew the king's royal banner. Beyond it, he saw clustered flags that included dragon banners for patrols to carry.

"We need a reason to walk in there," Patrick said. "Even then, it will be difficult to take out a girl accused of trying to kill the king."

"Poisoning—impossible. Not my sister." Henry shook his head.

"If we could prove she is innocent, we could argue to take her away, provided Edward would let her go," Patrick said. "Since Henry and I both have sheriffdoms, we have some authority to try that."

"Accuse Malise of abducting her and argue for her innocence," Brian said.

Aedan straightened as a solution occurred to him. "Henry was sent out with others to find Scottish renegades. Take me in there with you."

"Capture you?" Henry asked.

"You would give yourself up?" Brian stared at him.

"Trade me for Rowena."

"They would kill you," Patrick said bluntly.

"I will take the risk. Barter me for Rowena. Edward might agree."

"And then what would you do?" Brian asked.

Aedan stared at the camp. "Patrick, marry my sister," he said.

"Take care of Colban. Henry, see that Rowena is happy. I trust you all."

"You are a fool," Brian said.

"A fool in love does foolish things, they say. Aye, Henry," he said, seeing the surprise on the man's face, "I love her. Take me in." He held out his hands to be bound.

"Some of us could rescue her and the rest could fight beside you," Patrick said.

"Get her safely away, yourselves as well. I will think of something. I have escaped dungeons with walls eight feet thick. That camp is all cloth tents. I could tear through one of those with my teeth." He smiled. His friends did not.

CHAPTER TWENTY-SIX

"BROTHER HUGO, BRING me a cup." Rowena held up the small bottle, which glittered pale green in candlelight and afternoon sunlight.

The monk, scowling, brought a goblet of thick, clear glass with a gold band and a base of swirled green glass—a treasure from some exotic place. He gave it to her.

"If I may, Sire." She set the goblet on a table beside the king's chair.

"What is in the vial?" Edward barked.

"Water." She held it up to show the liquid. "I drew this water myself from a pool in a cave, fed by a spring blessed by a sainted queen. Healing miracles have occurred there. Folk come there to drink it and claim their ills are cured, and take it away."

Here was another risk. Edward might expect a miraculous healing, but she did not know for sure what the water would do. Yet she had experienced a healing—her ankle likely needed weeks to heal, yet felt stronger each day.

"What pool? Which saint?" Edward demanded.

Would he accept it once he knew? "The pool is in Fife, Sire. The saint who blessed the spring was Queen Margaret of Scotland, later made a saint."

Edward glared. "Scotland!"

"She was English, Your Grace," she said in haste. "Her father was a prince and her uncle and kinsmen for generations were kings of England. Your ancestors too."

"Huh. I know. English queen in Scotland."

She pulled the wax from the bottle and poured some water into the goblet. The small bottle did not contain much, another risk if he did not feel better quickly. She offered him the goblet in two hands. The binding rope had left pinkish rings around her wrists. His eyes flashed there, then to Malise standing a little behind her.

"Would you care to drink, Sire?"

He wiggled his fingers and she gave him the glass. He sipped, set it down.

"Well?" he said after a moment. "I feel naught."

"It needs time to do its work, Your Grace."

He tapped his fingers on the arm of the chair. "I want the Rhymer's stone."

"Sire, I cannot—" She hesitated. Even if she was willing to use the stone for him, she would not perform a healing as if she were a jester or an alchemist at court.

Behind her, she heard footsteps and voices raised at the door of the tent. Edward looked up with a sharp glance. She whirled.

"What is that?" the king demanded. "Sir Malise, go find out."

Outside the tent, a commotion of men shouted, moved, pushed. As Malise ran out, she saw familiar faces through the wide cloth gap. Henry! And—*Aedan!*

BUT FOR HIS hands bound in front of him, Aedan would have flattened Malise as soon as he burst out of the royal tent. As it was, Henry and Patrick each kept a grip on his arms. But Aedan pushed forward and managed to trip Malise as he came out, so that the man stumbled.

"Sorry," Aedan said, "I forgot your limp."

"What in God's name are you doing here?" Malise demanded.

"Bringing Aedan MacDuff, as you wanted," Henry said.

"The patrol's instructions were to fetch me once you had him in custody."

"I am delivering the prisoner to King Edward personally, in my capacity as a deputy sheriff," Henry said smoothly. "This is Sir Patrick Wemyss—sheriff of Fife."

"We have full right to deliver a prisoner to the king," Patrick said. "Did Edward request to see him? Or just you, Comyn?"

Malise sputtered. "You may have the rank, but your loyalty to Edward may be far less than your loyalty to Bruce. Bring him in. Guards, stand back. The king wants to see this man." He waved Aedan and his supposed captors into the tent.

Aedan was satisfied. This was just what he wanted—the chance to stand before Edward and Malise together, especially when he saw Rowena there near the king, who sat looking slack and old.

For the rest of his life, he would swear that when she turned, there was a golden glow all about her, like a saint, like an angel. Aedan stepped into the tent, oblivious to stares and exclamations, ignoring Malise, who flapped his hands, explaining to the king— Aedan discounted even Edward, glaring at him with fiery blue eyes. They were all a noisy blur.

He saw only Rowena, and his heart near burst in his chest.

She ran to him, threw her arms around his neck, and embraced him. "Aedan—dear God, Aedan!"

"Lass," he whispered. "Love. Are you well? Are you hurt?"

"Fine. You, are you hurt—what happened? Why are you here? They will kill you!"

"It was the only way in here. You may not like this, sweetling, but I am here to bargain my freedom for yours."

"Do not say it," she breathed.

"What is this!" Edward was on his feet now, bellowing. Aedan realized the king had been shouting and he had not heard, nor had Rowena turned. "Come here!"

Rowena turned, took Aedan's arm, and walked him—Henry and Patrick behind them—toward the king and Malise.

"Sire," Aedan said, not waiting for anyone to speak for him, "I am Aedan MacDuff of Fife. I understand you wish to see me. And

I wish to see you," he added.

His heart pounded hard and fast. He knew the gamble he was about to take. Rowena stared up at him. They all stared. The silence was brittle.

Edward stayed on his feet, though he seemed a bit wobbly. "What could you, a MacDuff, possibly say to the King of England? Caught like a fugitive—we should have you thrown in a dungeon!"

"Sire, you did for a bit, but I left. Would you punish an ambassador representing Scotland? The Pope takes a dim view of such things, I hear."

"Ambassador?" Edward sat.

"I am interim Guardian of the Realm of Scotland in place of my young nephew, Duncan MacDuff, Earl of Fife, who you hold hostage." His voice was strong and resonant in the surrounding silence of the overwarm tent.

"Guardian?" Edward frowned. "You?"

The old king must have forgotten, for he had known. "Sire, I am not an earl. But in my nephew's absence and as his nearest kinsman, I act on his behalf. His sister, Lady Isabella, is currently a victim of your hospitality. I believe the Pope has been advised of the treatment you have accorded the royal women of Scotland."

Aedan knew the impact the Pope's disapproval could have. He also knew that a sick and aging king would want his sins forgiven or at least overlooked. Edward would not relish a papal reprimand at this point in his life.

All part of the gamble. He waited.

The king had turned even more pale and drawn. "What do you want, MacDuff?"

"Sire, weeks ago, the council of guardians sent another plea for terms in the negotiation regarding the captive Scotswomen. Our terms and our offer of compromise were refused, without discussion or countermeasures."

"We will not release those women until Bruce relinquishes his claim to the throne of Scotland. That is why we are invading again. The point shall be hammered home." Edward projected his voice louder than before.

"Sire, hammer your point. But not on the backs of women. Not when Rome is watching you and reading letters detailing your behavior—and your sins."

"What compromise does the council offer?" Edward said. "We do not recall that any terms were delivered."

They were, Aedan thought. Was Edward trying to crawl away from it now? "We demand the humane release of the women back to Scotland. Until that time, the ladies held in cages on public display must be removed to convents for the sake of their health and dignity. That was the latest message of the council. I witnessed the letter."

The king stared at him, fingers drumming. His eyes flashed to Rowena, then to Malise, Henry, and back to Aedan.

"Who can verify that this man is a Guardian of Scotland and acts in that capacity?"

"I can," Brian said, stepping forward from the back of the tent. "Sir Brian Lauder, Lord of Bass Rock and justiciar of Lothian. Sir Aedan is on the guardian council."

"I can," Patrick said. "Sir Patrick Wemyss, Sheriff of Fife."

"I will. Sir Henry Keith of Kincraig and nephew of the Marischal of Scotland."

Edward looked at Malise. "You?"

"MacDuff is on the council of guardians," Malise groused. "He also escaped one of our prisons, and Your Grace wanted him brought to justice."

Edward waved his fingers. "What about you?" he asked Rowena.

She caught her breath at the unusual request for a woman's word in such a situation. "Your Grace, Sir Aedan is as he says—an interim guardian of Scotland, acting chief of Clan Duff, and uncle to the current earl and a captured Scotswoman. And he is one of the best men I have ever known. We are betrothed to marry."

Aedan's heart surged. He wanted to reach for her hand, but

his were bound.

Edward cast a sharp look at him. "You are betrothed to Rowena Keith?"

"We were pledged in childhood." He glanced down at Rowena, who moved closer, her arm brushing his.

"This needs thought." Edward cleared his throat, then began to cough. A fit began as he gasped for air. Rowena stepped forward.

Aedan saw a monk in black move forward too. "Sire, let me give you something."

Edward waved the monk away. "Before this guardian came rudely into our presence, Lady Rowena was about to give up the Rhymer's charm stone. You know about that, MacDuff?"

"I do. And I know it does not belong to the Crown of England."

"If you want your terms met, it will. That is my price."

Rowena gasped. "Not the stone!"

As she took a step, Aedan moved to hold her back, but she slipped past.

REACHING EDWARD, ROWENA clasped her hands and shook her head. "Please, your Grace, the healing stone must never be in the hands—of others. That was Thomas the Rhymer's request."

"I want it. You can bargain that stone for the comfort of those women to fulfill MacDuff's request. Surely you would approve that."

She looked over her shoulder at Aedan—and for a moment could not look away. Standing among other men, he was magnificent, taller than most, shoulders wide and proud, eyes keen, his whole being radiating strength, capableness, confidence, kindness, too. She felt the love that warmed his eyes as he gazed at her. It did not matter that his plaid and tunic were plain and shabby compared to some here, or that his hair was curling and unkempt, or his jaw shaded dark with days of beard. He was beautiful, a greater man in his quiet power than many. He always would be so in her eyes.

Those eyes crinkled with a small, private smile for her. She melted, and suddenly the strength he lent her filled her with resolve. He would not ask or expect anything from her. Whatever she decided, he would accept.

She turned back. "Sire, if trading the stone means the ladies who are suffering will be released to better comfort, I—" She paused. Tears came to her eyes. She felt compassion for the women and loss for herself, yet knew she had little choice.

"Sire, she has the stone even now. Just take it!" Malise said.

Before she could react, Malise grabbed her shoulder, snatched the silver necklace and yanked it away from her. The chain snapped and the crystal pendant flew free. Malise caught it, holding it up triumphantly.

"Here! My king, I give it to you freely, no bargain! I give it to you!"

He went down on one knee, pulling Rowena with him as he tossed the silver chain and shining pendant to the king, but his weak legs gave way, so that he fell forward in clumsy haste—directly on the king. Edward fell too, his chair cracking and collapsing. Rowena tumbled as one of Malise's feet swept her ankle.

All around were shouts and tumult as guards moved forward to protect the king.

Then Rowena saw Aedan throw himself at Malise, tackling him to yank him off Edward, who writhed on the floor.

Even with his wrists tied, Aedan reached down to pull Malise off the king. He surged to his feet, holding Malise by the scruff of his tunic as if he were a deerskin. Then he tossed the man aside, reaching down to offer his joined hands to Edward.

"Sire, may I?" Bending, he carefully assisted the old man to stand.

Edward rose, wobbly, as Brother Hugo and one of the guards rushed to help the king. An attendant brought another chair and Edward sat heavily.

"Guards! Get him out of here!" Edward pointed at Malise. A guard pulled him to his feet and began to shove him toward the curtained doorway.

Brushing at his clothing, Edward held up his hand, cupping the stone in his fingers, its surface gleaming in the light.

"So this is it? The Rhymer's charm stone?"

Her heart nearly broke to see it in Edward's hand. Rowena got to her feet, silent.

"Does not look like much," Edward went on. "What does it do? Is it worn like a jewel, or dropped in wine?"

"Sire, I put stones like this in water, then you would drink the—oh! Queen Margaret's healing water! Sire, may I have the goblet?"

"Go on," he drawled. She heard disappointment. He expected more and saw just a pretty crystal banded in silver. Given his temper, she wondered what he would do next.

Taking the wax plug from the little green bottle, she poured the rest of the water into the goblet. Edward plunked the crystal into the cup.

She reached out to swirl the flat of her palm over the top of the goblet.

"What are you doing there?" the king demanded.

"I am asking the stone and the water to heal you."

"Either you are mad, a witch, or both."

"Your Grace," Aedan said. "I have seen the lady do this before. I can attest that it has healing benefit. She saved my life with it."

"Saved your life, did she? Malise's too. Huh!" Edward motioned to Henry and Patrick. "Untie the guardian's wrists lest we be schooled by the Pope."

Rowena lifted the stone out of the goblet by its broken chain, glad to have it in her hand again. She gave Edward the goblet, hoping he would not ask for the stone back.

The king drank. Sitting back in the chair, he closed his eyes. Pale-faced, cheeks drawn, his eyes shadowed gray, he did not move. She looked up as Aedan stepped beside her, his hands free. He set an arm around her shoulder and she stood close, waiting.

"Sire?" she finally asked.

Edward's eyes popped open, sharp blue. "The illness in the stomach feels—calmer. Something about it. I want you to send kegs of that water to me."

"We could do that." She glanced at Aedan, who lifted a skeptical brow.

"Brother Hugo, come here," Edward barked. "I want you to learn all you can from Lady Rowena about stones and healing water. There something to this. I feel—refreshed. We shall see if this lasts."

"Sire, you have had a trying day," Hugo said. "This magical healing is nonsense, perhaps even dangerous heresy. You should avoid it. I will give you a dose of the treatment you have been taking for months. It is more reliable."

Rowena stepped forward. "Brother? What is that, may I ask."

"Hugo has something that relieves aches and brings on sleep," Edward said.

"A sleeping potion?" she asked sharply. "The same that you gave me?"

"I prepare a tincture that benefits the king's health." Hugo stared hard at her.

Then she knew. Hugo had been giving Edward the blend of the Great Rest, a powerful mixture of poppies, cloves, valerian, and more. "Sire, that tincture must be meted out carefully and never used often. It is powerful enough to produce weakness and even death. I fear," she said, glancing at the king, "I fear Brother Hugo has not just been dosing aches and pains. He has been poisoning you."

"Poison," Edward said. "What is this, Hugo?"

"He may not realize it, depending on his training," Rowena said.

"This was prepared and recommended by John Gadsden, who learned of it in Constantinople when he was on Crusade,"

Hugo defended.

"You make it yourself? Is the king ever slow to wake, or very weak?" she asked.

"Sometimes, but he is very ill, as you know."

"It helps sleep," Edward said. "We will have more tonight. But we may not need it. The crystal and the water have done something—remarkable."

"Sire, if Lady Rowena was blamed for poisoning you, she was wrongly accused," Aedan said. "Whatever happened was done by someone else's hand." He looked at Brother Hugo. "Easy enough to blame a lady who was there to help. You wanted to be sure you did not catch trouble for it yourself when you saw the king weakening."

"I have reduced the dose since," Hugo said. His cheeks were flaming red.

"Hugo, we will discuss this later," Edward said. "We will have justices consider it. If that sleeping potion has caused illness, there will be harsh consequences. But you two," he said to Aedan and Rowena. "You are both free to go."

"Sire?" Rowena leaned into Aedan, the stone still clutched in her hand.

"Take the stone. Hugo will just get rid of it if you leave it here. Send Queen Margaret's healing water, but make sure the stone is dipped in the water before you send it on. Do whatever you must do and get it done quickly. It—is needed."

"Sire," she breathed out, filled with relief. Aedan dropped his arm away and she reached for his hand, wanting that constant. He was her rock, her protector, the man she loved with the deepest love and compassion she had ever known, the man she would protect, however she could, in turn.

"Sire, what of the captive Scotswomen? If you do not keep the stone, what will become of them?" she asked.

"We will consider their conditions. There is much inconvenience and expense keeping those cages. People come to stare, say the reports, they trample the grounds, they make it difficult for soldiers to move in and out of those places. There are extra visits from physicians because of their health. It is very annoying. Letters from the Pope—we are full aware, MacDuff, of his disapproval. Other kings and potentates as well—letters from the King of France and the Holy Roman Emperor—no one seems to agree with this. Allowing the women to live in convents may be necessary."

"It may be best, if I may say so," Aedan remarked.

"You may not say!" Edward snapped. "You and your council may wait upon our decision. Lady Rowena, how long will the effect of that water last? There is a reviving of the spirit, it seems."

"I am glad to hear that, Sire. I cannot say how long it will last."

"There are matters that require our royal presence. The Scots must see Edward of England riding under the dragon banner in armor on a war horse, expecting obedience."

"Sire, we are Scots, if you please," Rowena said, knowing it was bold. "And should you do that in your state of exhaustion and illness—it could be the last time you do."

He looked at her for a long moment. "I know that. Go."

Outside the tent, Aedan took Rowena's arm and hurried with a long stride, while Brian, Patrick, and Henry followed. He wanted to leave this place as fast as possible. Rowena hastened beside him, and in deference to her ankle injury—though she did not seem to be limping—he slowed.

And saw Malise Comyn in the company of three or four guards, arguing with them. Aedan made a sharp right turn on the path to head toward him.

"What are you doing?" Rowena asked.

"Finishing what I should have done in the royal tent."

Malise had his back turned as Aedan walked up to the men. The king's guards looked up in astonishment at the interruption as Aedan tapped Malise on the shoulder.

"Pardon me, sir," he said.

Malise turned and scowled. "MacDuff! Best get out of here quickly before I bring the whole of the Scottish and English justice systems down on your head. You got away neatly today, sir. But it will not last."

"One favor," Aedan said.

"Hardly. What do you want?"

"This." Aedan hauled back and punched him so hard that Malise went down to his knees, cupping his hands over his face, blood pouring between his fingers.

Aedan shook the tension and ache from his hand. "Thank you, sir. I look forward to whatever the justice system has to say about you and me, and which of us has inflicted more ill and damage on the other. I will gather my witnesses. You do the same."

He turned on his heel and walked away. Behind him, he heard the guards laughing as they brought Malise to his feet and led him away.

His friends stared at him, mouths open. Henry grinned, ear to ear, and clapped him on the shoulder. Brian laughed, while Patrick applauded.

What he cared about most in that moment was Rowena. He turned to her. "Was that chivalrous, do you think, or the act of a brawny ox in need of taming and tethering?"

She looked up at him and smiled. "A little of both, I think. And I think—I rather enjoyed that." Suddenly she laughed, a chime like sweet bells that went into his heart like the twinkling lights in the stone she treasured.

And he treasured her. "Love," he said, "so long as you are pleased."

"I am. But there are other things that will please me more," she murmured.

"Tell me about them," he whispered. "But not here."

He bent to sweep her into his arms and kissed her, soundly and surely, in the dust and mud and commotion of the enemy king's war camp. Her lips were soft and lush under his, her promise truer than any he could imagine—but for his own.

"I am a fool in love," he murmured, sweeping back a drift of her dark hair.

"We must do something about that. Surely there is a treatment for it. I have the same malady, as it happens."

"Perhaps that wee stone can help." He took her hand and walked with her, while the others followed, chuckling.

"Oh, I have something even better," she said, taking his arm, kissing his hand, and then hurrying beside him out the gate and into the meadow where the horses and freedom waited.

EPILOGUE

Scotland, Kincraig Castle
September, 1307

"WITH EDWARD LONGSHANKS gathered to God on the seventh of July," Aedan said to those seated or standing about in Kincraig's great hall, "it is true we can breathe a bit, if just for a short time."

Standing beside her new husband, Rowena looked up. "We do have cause to celebrate now that his son Edward, now king, has left Scotland, taking his army with him."

"Some of his army. He left his English lieutenants in place, and his knights and soldiers still garrison our captured Scottish castles. He will be back," Aedan replied.

Henry approached, goblet in hand, to stand with them near the hearth, where a crackling fire radiated warmth and light on an evening gone chilly with autumn. "The younger Edward has gone south to see to his father's burial in Westminster, and to meet with his advisors to discuss the troublesome matter of Scotland. He promised his father to gain absolute dominion in Scotland. Whether he will keep that promise remains to be seen."

"We will be ready, but I doubt this Edward is up to the task," said Sir Liam Seton, husband of Rowena's sister Tamsin. Beside him, Tamsin sat content and beautiful as she held their newborn son bundled snug in her arms. Just six weeks old, his tender tuft of pale golden hair matched his mother's. Rowena longed to hold him again before Tamsin and Liam departed for Dalrinnie Castle.

"Edward will be back, but Scotland will prevail," Tamsin said quietly. "But it will take a few years. I have seen it." Her shy smile was almost apologetic. "I believe so."

"And I believe you," Liam said quietly, dark-haired and serious as he watched his wife, his gaze soft with love. Rowena sighed, seeing that, so happy that her sister was content at last. Tamsin had inherited the Rhymer's visionary gift, and had begun to understand it. If she said Scotland would endure, her words carried truth.

Glancing around the room as the others talked, Rowena felt content, too. Married recently, now a wife and stepmother, she wished her family could be together whenever they pleased. She knew that tonight's gathering would be rare as long as there was strife in Scotland. She was grateful to be home after the events of the past months. She was grateful her siblings were here too: Henry, as lord of Kincraig in residence for a short time before his duties took him elsewhere; Tamsin, with Liam and tiny, mewling Robert, named for their father and the king, and already called Robin; and Margaret with her husband of a few months, Sir Duncan Campbell, justiciar in the north. Rowena had only met him days ago but found him not just very handsome, but quiet, wry, and likeable.

All too soon they would return to their homes. Aedan would travel, too, for he had promised to continue his work for the King of Scots as well as the Guardians of Scotland. The council would eventually take a new form once Robert Bruce drove the English out and established a firm seat of government as monarch.

A fortnight past, Bishop Lamberton had arrived at Kincraig with Marjorie MacDuff, Lady Jennet, and Colban, though the Keith siblings were not all there yet. The bishop was on his way elsewhere and could not stay—but as promised, he had performed their wedding.

The wedding was double that day, for Marjorie and Patrick Wemyss were married in a shared ceremony beside Rowena and

Aedan. The day was full of laughter, love, and happiness, though Rowena was sad to bid farewell to Aedan's kin when they returned to Fife. But she loved that small Colban wanted to stay with his father and new stepmother.

She smiled to herself, thinking of that. Even now, Colban was tucked in bed in Kincraig's keep. Though he had begged to stay up with the others, he yawned so fiercely as he pleaded that Aedan had carried him up to bed while Rowena stayed to tell him another story about pirates.

Before she left the room, sleepy Colban had confided that he had four mothers—Alisoun, whom he had never known, then Marjorie and Jennet, and now Rowena.

"Could I call you my lady mother now?" he asked in a shy voice.

Her heart expanded, tears rinsing her eyes. "I would be honored, Colban MacDuff," she said.

She could hardly believe that only months ago, she and Aedan had faced the unknown, all they knew in danger. Now life felt secure, the future bright again. While her family talked, she yawned behind her hand, sleepy in the late hour, but not wanting to disband this wonderful company.

Her sister Margaret, so lovely with her vibrant red hair and the glow of love around her, seemed more lively than most of them as she leaned to whisper to her husband. Duncan smiled and stood, clearing his throat.

"Now that supper is done, we can share some news," he said, "I recently had a message from King Robert. Some of you know that Robert Bruce is leaving the southwest to make his way north. He plans to stop at Brechlinn in a few days, since it is a convenient place to meet with Scots lords from the central and Highland areas. He would like Liam and Aedan to join him there as soon as can be."

"Excellent," Aedan said. "I have news that he will want to hear with his own ears." He smiled at Rowena, but his deeper glance held meaning.

She knew he thought of the hidden regalia, which Bruce might decide to leave in Fife or move elsewhere. The sword with the crystal stone, and her charm stone, were twin stones. Each stone had played an unusual role, as it turned out, in saving Scotland. The sword's stone had come to the new king—and the healing stone had played an unexpected role too, for Malise Comyn had tripped because of the stone, injuring the king—who had died days later, freeing Scotland in his way.

Thomas the Rhymer had been correct after all. And with Longshanks gone, all Scotland could breathe more easily and begin the long road to recovery, redemption, and independence.

"I would be glad to join you to meet with Bruce," Liam Seton was saying.

"I can stop there briefly as well," Henry said. "Robert gave me a new assignment. I will be leaving my post in Selkirk to join Edward Bruce, Robert's brother, in Ireland."

"That is so exciting, Henry!" Margaret's eyes twinkled. "Henry—you have never said much about what Grandda Thomas gave you as part of his legacy."

"I have not. But I will say that while in Ireland, I should look for the faery ilk rumored to be thick upon the ground there. They may know what I should do."

"Henry, tell us!" Tamsin said.

"Someday, dear." He grinned. "Truly, I am not sure yet."

Rowena leaned toward Aedan. "After you go to Brechlinn, I hope you will come back to Kincraig for a bit before Bruce sends you away on some new task."

He reached for her hand. "For a bit, sweetling, I promise," he murmured. She knew him now, so well, in so many ways—and knew he kept his promises.

"Tamsin's vision will prove true, I think," Henry went on. "The younger Edward will want to show his might as a new king. But he lacks his father's hatred for Scotland. He is—insouciant, they say. He lacks his father's cunning. Bruce is a determined and strong king, and Scotland will grow stronger and more unified under him. But we all know that victory will be neither easy nor quick."

All murmured agreement. Listening, Rowena was glad that here at Kincraig, they could all find respite in the comfort of home, family, and friends.

At the far end of the great hall, the door opened, and she whirled to see three newcomers—a knight, a gentleman, and a woman. For a moment, she recognized only Sir Gilchrist Seton—then realized the others were his twin brother and their sister. She moved toward them to greet them just as Liam Seton took the length of the room in long strides to greet his siblings.

"Gilchrist—and Gideon!" she said, as she approached. "And Agatha! How wonderful to see you all." She hugged each in turn. "I have not seen you since we were at Holyoak. I feared you might not be able to join us here."

"We had some delay," Gilchrist said. "As you can see, Gideon and Agatha have made some decisions, and needed extra time before we could leave for Kincraig." With a wide and handsome grin, he indicated his twin brother—their smiles identical—and their dark-haired, beautiful younger sister.

"Indeed!" Rowena grasped Gideon's hand and took one of Agatha's as well. "Gideon, the last I saw you at Holyoak, you wore a monk's robe and a shaved tonsure, and were still undecided about taking your final vows."

"I made that decision since." He gestured toward his clothing, a simple long garment of dark brown, with a long plaid pinned over his shoulder in a pattern similar to those worn by the other Scotsmen in the room. "I will tell you all about it later."

"Good," Rowena said. "And Agatha, I am so pleased to see you. This is my husband, Sir Aedan MacDuff." She embraced the young woman, who had just greeted Tamsin and Liam, admiring the new baby.

"Dame Agatha." Aedan took her hand cordially. "I am glad to meet you."

"It is Lady Agatha again, I suppose," she said. "I recently

resigned from my position as prioress and decided to leave the order altogether."

"I know you were considering it," Rowena said.

"It was the incident at Dalrinnie last fall that made me realize that I wanted to be with my family again. My brother Gideon felt the same as a lay brother at Holyoak. We discussed it endlessly, and decided together."

"Ah, the nun!" Aedan said. "You are a legend where I come from, my lady."

With a curious glance, Agatha tilted her head. The light caught the long scar that traced from her left eyebrow to her mouth. Rowena noticed the scar anew—but the young woman was so beautiful in face and in spirit, radiating calm strength, that the scar seemed to all but disappear.

"A legend?" Agatha asked.

"The one who took down Malise Comyn," he said, inclining his head.

"I heard you took down Malise." She made a little fist and imitated a punch.

"I bow to your greater accomplishment," he said, bending low.

Gideon laughed. "Rowena, I see you and Sir Aedan found each other again, and with a lovely outcome."

"Quite." Aedan shook hands to welcome Gilchrist and then Gideon. "Thank you again for your help at Holyoak when I was ill, and for escorting Rowena."

"Alas, we did not reach her at Soutra before she was taken away. Finley and I searched frantically until we had word that she was safe," Sir Gilchrist said. "Where is Finley?" He glanced around.

"On the parapet with a couple of the garrison," Rowena said.

"Kincraig and all Scotland remain under constant vigil," Aedan said. "The conflict is far from over. But it brought many of us together." He gestured around the room.

"Come sit and rest from your journey, and have some refreshment," Rowena urged. She led them to the trestle table where a maidservant had just refilled jugs of wine and set out platters of bannocks and cheese.

A while later, Gilchrist sat back. "We have some additional news," he said. "I managed to leave Carlisle without much notice in the kerfuffle following Edward's death. And I heard some word of the captive Scotswomen. Aedan, I know your kinswoman is there—and yours as well, Duncan Campbell, your brother's wife, aye?"

"You have word?" Duncan asked, as he and Aedan sat forward.

"The ladies kept in cages, Lady Mary Bruce and Lady Isabella MacDuff, will be moved to convents in England once negotiations are agreed between the new King Edward and Robert Bruce. Edward will honor his father's promise about the women, since several witnessed MacDuff's request of the old king."

"Aedan informed the council, who submitted another letter," Duncan Campbell said. "We are all indebted to you for exacting that promise, sir."

"Not me," Aedan said. "I took it to old Edward, who was ill, so he conceded."

Because he wanted the Rhymer's stone, Rowena thought. "What of Malise Comyn?" she asked. "He and a monk were taken away, but where are they now?"

"They are in the Tower in London, both accused of hastening the old king's death," Gilchrist said. "Apparently the monk was dosing him with a medicine that weakened him. And Malise somehow injured the frail king. All that, with Edward's chronic illness, was too much."

"To be fair," Rowena said, "he was already dying. No one could have changed that. When I saw Edward in the royal camp, I remembered what Grandda Thomas once told me about healing."

"What was that?" Tamsin asked.

"He said that no matter what a healer does, naught is stronger than death once God wills it. I saw it on Edward's face. He knew."

After a moment of quiet, Gideon spoke. "You did all you could, Rowena. Heaven decided in its own way—the only remedy for what seemed an incurable illness."

"And the only remedy for Scotland," Gilchrist murmured.

Rowena glanced at Aedan. His gaze met hers, held. She knew he had the same thought as he leaned toward her, seated beside her at the table.

"Thomas said your crystal might save Scotland one day," he murmured.

She nodded. "And the crystal in the ancient sword went to the one man who could help save Scotland too, as king."

He took her hand. "The twin stones—Thomas knew. And he knew we were part of it." She smiled up at him, then heard her name.

"Rowena," Gilchrist said, "I heard that you will soon have official word about the charges against you. You can expect them to be canceled. Sir Malise and the monk will be held accountable for the king's death."

"Thank you," she said in relief, setting a hand to her chest.

"I will look into that to be sure it is sealed and done," Duncan Campbell said.

"And share your news, brother," Gideon reminded his twin.

Gilchrist nodded. "I saw Bruce in the southwest before I came up here with Gideon and Agatha. Bruce wants me to act as an ambassador to northern England. I will be granted a forfeited castle along the Scottish Border. Gideon has agreed to go with me. Our sister Agatha as well." He grinned at them.

"That is outstanding news, all of you," Liam told his siblings. "Agatha too?"

"I left the priory, but I am not sure where to go," she said. "Liam, I know you would welcome me at Dalrinnie, where we grew up. But that is your home with Tamsin now. I want something different—some challenge. I am happy to manage

Gilchrist's castle and see what comes of that."

"She needs adventure, having been stuck in a convent for years," Gideon said.

"If you want adventure," Aedan said, "there is no wilder place than the Borders."

"In the safe company of her twin brothers," Gilchrist said.

"I wish you all a promising future," Rowena said. "For those going to the Border, or to Ireland with Edward Bruce, or the Highlands with Robert Bruce—and here at Kincraig as well. Blessings to everyone—and Scotland too!" She lifted her goblet in salute as they drank together.

Smiling, she leaned against Aedan's shoulder, the feeling of love and camaraderie warming her even more than the hearth. He bent and kissed her head.

"I love you," he murmured. "Always."

"Always," she whispered.

Author's Note

King Edward I, called Longshanks—and who called himself the Hammer of the Scots—died an ignominious death on July 7, 1307. Insistent on a fresh foray against the Scots while leading his army, he donned armor and rode with his military escort, making camp as they traveled north from Carlisle. They covered but a mile or so each day, the king exhausted and very ill with what historians have called chronic dysentery, though it might have been one of several ailments; we will never know. On his last day, Edward summoned enough energy to armor up, mount up, and travel a short distance until he collapsed on the road. Back in his tent, said the chroniclers, the king died in the arms of attendants who lifted him to give him some refreshment.

With the passing of Edward I, whose vitriol against the Scots was unparalleled, the wars of independence in Scotland did not end immediately but took a more hopeful direction. Edward II was not as dedicated as his father to pounding Scotland into submission, though he made a valiant effort to lead campaigns for years. On the field of Bannockburn in 1314, King Robert Bruce and his army faced the English and finally turned the tide. Bruce and the Scots prevailed, and Scotland began to emerge once more as an independent entity under a Scottish monarch.

Among the many results and changes wrought by that victory, the captured Scottish noblewomen held in England in cages and convents since 1306 were finally released. They did not all survive their long ordeal; notably, Lady Isabella MacDuff, just nineteen when she was captured, was not listed in the release documents of 1314, and is presumed to have died by then. She is not mentioned in extant documents after 1310, though it is believed that she and Lady Mary Bruce had been transferred by then to confinement in English convents.

In my books, I do my best to adhere to the chronology, historical figures, maps, and fascinating details that history preserves. I love the challenge of weaving fictional characters and their dilemmas into an authentic picture of the time and place. Though here and there, it's necessary to fiddle with history some, I try not to stir things too much.

For *The Guardian's Bride,* my research took me once again into the methods and madness of medieval medicine, an area where I love to muck about in stories. Besides herbs and plants, Highland medicine relied on charm stones, chants, and so on, giving me much fodder for a story. Special thanks go to my son, Josh King, M.D., toxicologist, for great information and fun discussions about how to treat (or undo) a character.

This trilogy—*Highland Secrets*—reaches a natural conclusion with the death of Edward I, who served as an archvillain in the three books. Yet the trilogy may expand, for I have threads yet to weave into the whole!

I hope you enjoyed *The Guardian's Bride.* If you read it out of order, no worries (and I hope not many spoilers)—please look for *The Scottish Bride* and *The Forest Bride* too, and I hope you will look for my other books as well. There are a lot of them by now! Please check out my website at www.susanfraserking.com. Happy reading!

Susan

About the Author

Susan King is the bestselling, award-winning author of (so far) 28 historical novels and novellas, a hefty nonfiction history, and dozens of magazine and web articles on education and the craft of writing. Her books, including mainstream historicals Lady Macbeth: A Novel and Queen Hereafter: A Novel of Margaret of Scotland, have been published by Penguin, Random House, HarperCollins, Kensington, ePublishingWorks, and Dragonblade. Praised for historical accuracy, lyrical writing, and storytelling quality, she is a USA Today bestselling author with numerous awards, nominations, and career achievement awards as well as starred reviews from Publisher's Weekly, Booklist, and Library Journal. Most of her books are set in Scotland ranging from the 11th to the 19th centuries.

Susan is a former university lecturer in art history, a private school teacher, and a founding member of one of the longest-running author blogs, "Word Wenches" (wordwenches.com). She holds a Bachelor's in studio art and English literature, a Master's in art history, and completed most of her Ph.D./ABD in medieval art history. Raised in Upstate New York, she lives in Maryland with her husband and three sons in an ever-growing family.

Website – www.susanfraserking.com